DYSTPOPIA!
HERO'S QUEST

David Horn

Cover design by AMDesignstudios.net
Book design by Heidi Sutherlin
Interior illustrations by Deven Hoover

ISBN 979-8-9885430-9-1 (paperback)
ISBN 979-8-9924172-0-3 (ebook)

www.davidhornauthor.com

To A-dawg, my laugh detector, alpha reader,
beta reader, sounding board, and moral supporter.
I'm your biggest fan. Well, except for T-person.

Contents

Prologue

Our hero walks into his agent's office—

Hey, I'm the hero. Right now, this is my story. My story about a story. The story I want to write and deliver to the world like a glorious screaming baby. And when you hold it in your hands, you won't know what to do with it. You'll happily pass it off to the next person, whom you may or may not know, and then the next person, and so on, all the while trying to get those screams out of your head. And that's what I want my story to be like. I have to prove to her that I can do it.

So, I steel myself for my meeting with Barnaby Wilsker, my agent. I walk into his very plain, very brown office. Wood-paneled walls, brown. Desk, brown. Carpet, brown. Black chair? That's new. The windows behind him show the city I live in. The city that has crushed me time and time again, only to not let me die. One day those sirens I hear will be for me.

Barnaby's sitting at his brown desk and looks up as he hears me enter. I don't sit down. I just tell him exactly what I told you. "I want my story to be like a baby."

"A story? A baby?" he yells in surprise. "Murray, you write technical manuals! Your last one was for a toaster! I sell your technical manuals! How the hell am I supposed to sell a parenting guide?"

"No, no, you misunderstand me," I explain. "I spoke poorly. Improperly. I want to write a YA novel. It will be like a screaming baby."

"Enough with the babies, Murray! Please! I didn't call you here for a YA novel. I have a new technical manual job for you. It's for a massage chair. I thought you'd like it. You get to test it out while you write. I'm using it right now." Barnaby leans forward and to the side so I can see the chair he is sitting on. Ah, black chair. It makes sense now.

He leans back again with a sigh and closes his eyes. Now, with his eyes still closed and head leaning back, he gives a content moan. It's a bit off-putting from this large, rotund, and balding sixty-year-old man. He continues, "This thing is great. So please, no more of this YA nonsense." Content sigh. "You write what you know. Toasters, power drills, massage chairs, like this beauty"." Content moan. "With a little more work, I can even get you doing cordless phones. They're not totally dead, you know. My Gram-Gram,"—oddly placed content moan— "just bought one the other day."

Oh, shoot. I just realized he'll want me to use the same massage chair he is currently sweating and moaning in.

What do I do? I need the money. I have to pay rent. Alimony now—still can't believe it. I guess I could move to a cheaper apartment. Move out of the city, maybe. But my cat loves this apartment. And I'd do anything for her—the only female who still loves me. Plus . . . the cordless phone market. My dream job.

So, I sit in the chair—the brown one—facing his desk. Barnaby Wilsker smiles. He knows he's got me.

H. Holy buckets! You're actually going to give up!

Huh? Who said that?

H. I did, you sad-sack embarrassment of a father, er, I mean, weaver.

Uh . . . "Barnaby, did you just, uh, call me your father?" I ask the rotund and balding sixty-year-old man in front of me.

"What?" Barnaby exclaims. "Do I need to call the hospital, Murray? I am just trying to give you sage advice from my years of experience."

H. He didn't call you his father. And forget I did either. You're an embarrassment.

"An embarrassment?" I ask out loud.

"Murray, Murray, I would never say that," Barnaby consoles me as he leans in. "You know how highly I think of your technical manuals. The way you described the toasting process in the last one brought a tear to my eye. 'The browning process in the Toasterette XL 6000 will toast you with honor.' Just beautiful. That's why you're my guy! Cordless phones, Murray. Just think of it." Barnaby closes his eyes again. Another content moan.

"But then, who said that?" I ask.

"Who said what?" Barnaby looks concerned. "You look stressed, Murray. I see this in a lot of technical manual writers. They start to hit their stride, and the pressure gets to them. So, they want to do something different, like write YA novels. But that's not your sweet spot, Murray. It's not your wheelhouse." He pretends to hit a baseball from his seated position, which looks contradictorily unathletic from this portly man. Barnaby then adds a little pretend crowd noise with his voice as he puts his hands in the air, as if he's just hit a home run. Should I cheer too?

"Are you a teenager? Do you even know any teenagers?" he asks me after the pretend cheering dies down.

"I'm forty-five and I live on my own," I reply. "But YA is hot right now. And the pizza delivery boy was recently a teenager. We're kind of friendly. Both of us like sci-fi. And I bounce my YA ideas off him. In fact, that's how I—"

"Delivery boy!" he exclaims. Then he closes his eyes again. Content sigh. "Isn't YA supposed to be about girls? You know, princesses and fairies and dragons and stuff?"

"Not always," I start to explain. "That's very stereotypical—"

"Look, take a week off," Barnaby interrupts. "The massage chair manual isn't due for some time." Content sigh. "Okay?"

"Okay, I guess."

"And promise me, no YA!" Barnaby exclaims, this time more upset than understanding. He picks up a remote control and presses some buttons. A low hum I didn't notice before shuts off. He must have powered off the now obviously sweaty chair.

"Okay," I relent.

H. Are you really going to let him kill me off like that? You dreamed me up! Don't I mean something to you? What about my kingdom? Who's going to save it, if not for me? Or you! I wish I was never borned! You should never have borned me!

"No, no, I have a whole week. I'll keep trying," I reply to the voice. And now I know. I can hear it more clearly. It's the voice I've been hearing since the story entered my head. It's her. The seventeen-year-old badass,

take-no-prisoners, nails-for-breakfast heroine of my dystopian YA novel. She's actually speaking to me!

H. For breakfast, I actually fought a giant lizard over an old man's spleen. I lost and had to settle for a camel's—

"Murray!" Barnaby cries, tearing me away from her. "I told you, no! The week is for resting up before you start writing the Massagomatic BX8000 manual!"

"Yes, er, no, I know," I mumble. I'm not really paying attention, though. She's speaking to me!

"I mean it, Murray. You have a good career going. Stop with this YA nonsense. Let me ask you: Did you even start it? How does your supposed YA novel even start? Have any ideas?"

"Um . . . " I try and think of something quickly. I've only been thinking about it. I haven't really started it for real. Sure, I started and stopped a few drafts, threw some pages out—deleted them all. And then it hits me. "Actually, I think it starts with two old men talking—"

"See! You can't start a YA novel with two old men talking! Who does that? You're insane! Just stop! And no damn picture books either. Last technical writer I had that quit to write fiction wrote a picture book about a chainsaw. *The Chainsaw Slaughter: Killer in the Forest—A Global Warming Book for Kids.* It did not go well."

"Right, no picture books either." I start to leave. I really just want to talk to her. I want to write her story. I want to give birth to her!

H. Ew, that's gross. Please tell me you're not going to weave that part.

"But if you must write something, you know, to stretch your wings, stick with the parenting guide. It's sort of like a technical manual. And now that I think of it, I might know a guy who sells parenting guides," Barnaby adds, scrolling through a rolling paper business card thing on his desk—likely the last one on the entire east coast. But I don't want to write parenting technical manuals. I turn to leave without responding.

"Murray, the chair." I hear Barnaby from behind me. I turn around, and he is now standing so I can see the chair. It's still sweaty. He wants me to wheel it out and take it home.

"Right, yes, chair," I say as I grab it and start wheeling it out of the office. How will I get it home in the cab? Should I take the subway? With a massage chair? And how do I get it up the stairs to my apartment? Or should I just throw it away and work on my novel? Is that what the universe is telling me? But what about my cat? Katrina needs me to buy her food. She relies on me. I should really get home and start on the massage chair manual. Who am I kidding, anyway? YA novel?

H. Hey, you're just gonna forget me like that? Because of your damn cat? Did I give up when

Katrina the Lord of the Saber-Toothed . . . Oh, I see now. That's your cat . . . that almost bit my freaking head off? How dare you!

"Doesn't matter. He said no," I reply to the voice, which definitely isn't Barnaby's. I'm outside his office now, in the waiting area. Barnaby's receptionist is busy—painting her nails?—and not paying attention. She doesn't notice me talking to the ceiling as I walk into the hallway with the sweaty chair. It's hard getting the heavy chair over the lip in the doorway. I stumble and fall as the chair slides down the hallway, away from me. It must be a sign.

H. I know *he* said no. But what do you say? What does the chair say?

Picking myself up, I finally decide. Hey, I have a week. And Barnaby can't tell me how to spend my vacation. "I have to write this story. And right now, I hate this chair."

H. So, you'll do it? You'll help me save my kingdom?

"Yes, you heard me. Plus, the massage chair manual isn't due for some time. Let's do this thing. Let's save your kingdom!" I exclaim. And for the first time since I entered Barnaby Wilsker's office, I feel good.

H. Dystpopia!

Dystpopia?

Chapter 1

Singing in the Rain, or Lack Thereof

"Dystopia! Dystopia! I never met a bettah Dystopia! None so lovely, none so true!" our hero sings out as the orchestra plays.

H. Our hero sings?

Yeah, it's a musical. Did I not mention that? You know, with song and dance.

H. Hey, Author, it's not a musical! And what is an orchestra?

It's like . . . a musical troupe . . . bards and lutes? Maybe a trombone?

H. What the hell is a musical troupe doing out here? I'm the only one brave enough to travel these desolate, dangerous roads between kingdoms. What about the zombies, bandits, warlords, roaming packs of sand-wolves . . . Heck, how much water do they need for a whole troupe? We've had a severe drought for hundreds of years! It's not safe for them out here! Do they even know how to use a crossbow? Or a morning star? Or do they plan to plunk the wolves on their heads with trombones?

Oh, right. Let me fix that.

"Dystopia! Dystopia! I never met a bettah Dystopia! None so lovely, none so true!" But our hero does not sing this. It is more of a monotonic hum. And, just to be clear, there is no orchestra. Why would there be one on these desolate roads between kingdoms? Though the music of freedom rings clear in our hero's mind.

H. What? Monotonic hum? First of all, I would never do that. Humming is for happy people. I'm

filled with anger at the world! My kingdom—my mother's kingdom—was taken over by an evil warlord.

Second of all, what does that all even mean! Music of freedom? Ringing?

Like a cell phone.

H. A what?

A ringtone.

H. Like a bell?

No, it's a thing you can talk to people on who are very far away.

H. The heavens are clearly some sort of fantasy world.

Never mind. And the third thing?

H. Oh, right. And third of all, it's still not a musical, jackass!

Hey, watch the language! You're not supposed to say things like that!

H. Hey, I'm a person, too. Just because you're an Author up there in heaven-world weaving our story down here doesn't give you the right!

Our hero's mother magically appears with a bar of soap and a washcloth. "I'm going to wash that mouth out!" she cackles.

H. Um . . . this is very hurtful! You of all gods should know my mother died before I was borned—

Before you were born? How is that even possible?

H. I don't know! It must have been your idea!

It's kind of weird . . . before you were born . . . Do you think we should change it?

H. I always thinked it made me special . . . like how I can talk to you, the Author, a God of gods, weaver of all things.

Okay, we can keep it. But, wow, what was I thinking?

Our hero's mother magically disappears.

H. [sighs heavily] You clearly weren't! With her died the secret to saving the whole kingdom!

Right. Dystopia!

H. Dystopia? No, it's the Kingdom of Dystpopia! How do you not know that?

But that was clearly just a typo.

H. Type O? Is that bad?

Well, maybe. Do you know what it is?

H. No.

Never mind, then. But I'm really a worse writer than I thought. I mean, who would name a kingdom that? Shouldn't we change it entirely? How about the Kingdom of Katrina?

H. Holy buckets, your yarns of fate must have a knot. We never had a queen named Katrina.

It's named after my cat; the only thing I like about my family.

H. Your cat again? No! To think an actual God would have a *cat*.

King Reginald the Devout renamed our kingdom, as he was being slaughtered by that purple dragon that appeared out of nowhere! Every Dystpopian knows the story. As the surprise dragon's talon pierced his heart, King Reginald cried out, "I thought this was Dyst . . . [inaudible due to blood curdling cries of pain] . . . popia! Not fant . . . [inaudible due to death]." And henceforth our Kingdom of Dystpopia has been in a hundred-year-long war with the Queendom of Fant, who used evil magic to send the dragon to us. Many lives have been lost!

Even worse, our kingdom was later taken over by a warlord named Xander the Eyeless who killed his descendant Reginald III. And that's not because he doesn't have eyes. It's because he takes his enemies' eyes and—

Ew, I don't want to know! Stop it! Gross!

H. Fine. But that's what you weaved with your yarn! It's reality, man. The reality *you* put me in!

Did I really write this awful stuff? Must have been right after she left me. I'm usually more into lighter fare. I kind of wanted to write a musical.

H. You thinked of it all. How can you not remember? All this misery is all your fault!

I kind of threw out everything I wrote before, so maybe it was in there? To think you would be stuck with all the misery. I deleted a lot.

H. You threw out the yarn! The yarn of my world!

Well, deleted, but yeah.

H. You created me, gave me the power to speak to you, gave us the tyranny of the Queendom of Fant, and then you just deleted me? What kind of lousy Author are you? Why was my world forsaken with you as our Author? Well, I'm still here, so you're a failure at deleteding as well! The way I see it is you owe me. Keep weaving and save my kingdom, Author!

Okay, but you're going to have to kind of help me out a bit. Where were we?

H. Oh, gods. My mother, the archaeologist, historian, linguist, mechanic, sorceress, and water diviner, uncovered the secrets of the ancients during her travels on the same desolate roads. The secrets that have been previously lost to us through time! The secrets that would help Dystpopia escape the tyranny of Fant!

But Fant's dragons killed her before she could tell us those secrets and end this bloody feud! And so, I travel the Lands, looking for anyone who may have known my mother so I can piece together her secrets. Just my luck—I get an author with early onset memory plague!

You mean Alzheimer's?

H. He had it too?

Um ... look, I totally forgot. You know how things are; rent, write, cat, internet dating. And then you wake up, and do it all again.

H. Whatever you say, Author. I actually have no idea what it's like up in the heavens. If only I had a place for which to pay rent. In fear, Xander killed the rest of my family and burned my old family home to the ground, just in case the populace would rise up against him in the name of my mother.

And so, since I can ever remember, I have lived on the streets of Dystpopia, in hiding, surviving on random acts of kindness from citizens who were still loyal to King Reginald III and my mother. It is how I learned some of her true story. For four years, I've traveled the desolate roads between kingdoms, endlessly searching for a way to save Dystpopia! Remember?

And what's internet dating? Is it some physical trial to prove your love?

Something like that. It's a way for men and women to meet and talk. Romantically. How's this?

The ghost of our hero's mother disappears, but not before giving her some parting advice. "A clean mouth is the best mouth, my child. Oh, and you may find a clue in the town of . . ."

H. The town of what? Tell me! I must go there!

Oh, right. What's the town called that you are about to enter?

H. I don't know.

What do you mean you don't know? Turn your location services on!

H. Huh?

Location services! On your cell phone!

H. Again, with this cell phone. What type of yarn are you weaving here? You think this is a fantasy world like the heavens?

I don't know . . . I was mainly thinking YA, but I guess it could really be anything. I never really thought about it. And why be tied down to a particular genre, anyway? I rise above the shackles of book genres. I just want to deliver a beautiful baby to the world.

H. Babies again? Holy buckets. Stop with the babies!

What's wrong with babies?

H. I don't want to deliver a baby! I don't know anything about babies! I prefer the cell phone. These desolate roads—

Actually, a baby could make your character a bit more multidimensional. And Barnaby knows someone who sells parenting guides who I could pitch this to. Maybe I should give you a little sister to tote around. How's this?

H. No! Please!

Our hero is suddenly holding a crying baby. "Wah! Wah!" the baby cries.

Our hero says, "This is my baby sister. I love her dearly, and I know a lot about baby care. These are the seven essential things I need to do to take care of this very baby."

H. Holy buckets! Take this thing back! What the hell am I going to do with a baby sister in this dystopian wasteland with dragons and zombies flying around?

Flying zombies? I wrote that? That's so cool!

H. No, no, the zombies walk. I misspoke. Er . . . I mean, you mis-weaved. Or I . . . Er . . . I'm not sure. But the baby!

Flying zombies. I guess I could still do that in the dystopian genre. I can just imagine it—

H. The baby, Author!

Fine.

The baby magically disappears as it was time for its magic daycare drop-off.

H. Finally! That reminds me. I've wanted to bring this up. If you're in charge of this story scroll, can I get a lover? That's a thing you weavers can do, right?

Sure. I guess we can do an enemies-to-lovers thing.

H. Good. I don't mind throwing down with a guy. It would at least make it worthwhile to live in this wasteland. It gets lonely on the desolate roads. I'm seventeen, and the only guys I meet

are decrepit old wise men or dangerous warlords. And you know, if a girl has to run all day from zombies—

Flying zombies, right?

H. Hey, I said they didn't fly!

Yeah, but it's so cool, so it's staying. Flying zombies. I can even put one on the cover. Maybe a pop-up zombie in the middle of the book. You know, like it flies out at you. Do teenagers like pop-ups?

H. I have no idea what you're talking about. What's a book?

I'll have to ask Max, then.

H. Max? Who in the Lands is Max?

Delivery boy. In your world, you might call him a page or a messenger.

H. Fine! Go ask Max. Just give me a lover! Not that I need or even want a man. I guess it could even be a woman. It's just—

Can it be Max? He would get a kick out of—

H. No way! I may be homeless, hunted, and I haven't bathed in years, but I will not stoop so low as to date a lowly page. I am and will always be the daughter of Mother, the Enchantress of Dystpopia.

Who died before you were born?

H. Yes. I am very special. Plus, she's an enchantress, so it kind of makes sense.

And she's named Mother? That sounds like a first-draft type of name. Like I couldn't come up with anything. Come on, can't you come up with anything better?

H. You're the Author! Besides, she's always been *Mother* to me.

She can have a real name, you know. Like *Sparkles, Geraldine, Farrah, Bea, Gertrude, Misty, Lola, Yolanda.* I still like Katrina—

H. Stop! She's *Mother*, and that's that.

Okay, okay. But back to the lover. First, it's an enemy. We agreed, right?

H. Yeah, like I said, I don't mind hand-to-hand combat if I have to. Romantically, of course.

All right, if you say so . . .

And then, as our hero enters the saloon—

H. Saloon?

What's wrong with a saloon?

H. It seems a bit . . .

. . . barbershop—

H. Barbershop? I'm healthy as a griffin!

. . . small dystopian town without a name . . .

H. That's what I've been saying!

And there is a saloon.

H. Ugh. Fine!

Hoping for some respite from the sun, she enters the saloon. Expecting to find danger, she instead sees a happy crowd, and a weird-looking boy about her age named Rodolfo.

H. Oh, come on! Weird? I might as well make out with the zombies. And how do I know his name?

Our hero stares at his name tag: *Hi, my name is Rodolfo.* She wonders, *Why in the Lands is he wearing a name tag?* But, hey, someone wearing a name tag must be friendly. *Maybe he's to be my lover.*

But Rodolfo takes out an iron pot and hits our hero on the head with it. Oh no, an enemy!

H. Can you please add as a final, parting think, "Holy buckets, this Author sucks!"?

She blacks out.

Chapter 2

A Big Clue Staring Me in the Face That I'd Be a World-Class Idiot Not to See

Our hero wakes up on a dirty, wood floor, in a musty room. She can hear saloon noises in the background, and some sunlight comes in from a small window. *I must be in some sort of back room of the saloon.* The memory of Rodolfo sears into her mind like a burned piece of bacon. *Mmm . . . bacon . . .*

H. Um, you're kind of losing track here!

What? Oh, you're right . . . Sorry . . . I love bacon.

H. That's kind of rude! You know what my last meal was? After breakfast, I had leftover shrub bark with a side of sand. I won't even tell you about my beverage of choice. I still get shivers thinking about that camel.

Our hero shudders like a camel.

H. Stop!

You know, you suddenly have a lot of opinions.

H. It's my story!

Our hero shudders. Like shutters.

H. I guess that's okay.

Then the door to the back room opens. A boy of about seven enters. He has wispy hair and the eyes of—

H. Wait!

What?

H. Look at him! There's something wrong.

What? It's some of the most beautiful writing I've ever done. Oh, when two lovers meet and the sparks fly . . .

H. His age.

Oh . . . Oh!

H. Yes. Fix it!

The boy disappears. Then the door to the back room opens again. A boy of about seven months—

H. I said no babies!

But they're so cute. I always thought I would be a dad one—

H. Fix it!

A boy of about seven years enters.

H. What the hell? That's what you had before. I told you—

Just be patient for once. How did I write such a moody hero?

H. [Grumbles]

By the way, I've been meaning to ask you. How are you talking to me, anyway? I mean, am I going crazy? The whole hearing-voices thing means I'm crazy, right?

H. Oh hell, a god who thinks he's crazy? And you're asking *me*? How am I supposed to know? I was just walking the desolate roads between kingdoms and everything started to get really dark. I felt like I was dying. And then I just started hearing you. You just popped into my mind. And then I realized, you were ending the story! But you were clearly the Author, weaving the yarns of fate—

Weaving is for girls!

H. You're the Author! I heard you—a god weaving story scrolls for other gods in heaven-world! What's between your legs matters not!

Uh, I guess so. But still . . . am I crazy? How did this even happen?

H. I hardly noticed. Everyone in the Lands is crazy, so why not the gods? And I got you to keep weaving. The sky brightened again, and now I still need to save my kingdom.

Well, it's called writing, but true, I guess. Here goes.

He has black wispy hair, a red woven jacket, and brown linen knee-length trousers. Behind him is a blond boy of about seventeen also with wispy hair—the wispiness of the boys' hair revealing their likely blood relation. The older boy's brown leather jacket and brown ankle-length trousers betray either a boring personality, a boring wardrobe, or a boring fashion sense. His hair hangs over his eyes, which have the intensity of a wild cat named Katrina.

H. And she charged at him because she hates your stupid cat! Need I remind you that Katrina, the Lord of the Saber-Toothed Lightning Cats, almost bit my head off?

And she charges at him. But the seven-year-old boy yells, "Please ma'am, don't hurt my brother, Rodolfo. He's all I've got!"

Our hero stops.

H. I wouldn't stop, you know. Why'd you make me stop?

She stopped because she doesn't know where she is again. All she can think about is Katrina, the Lord of the Saber-Toothed Lightning Cats. But the cat isn't here. It doesn't smell like lightning cats—they have a very distinctive odor. Much like bacon. *Mmm . . . bacon.*

Then she looks at the older boy. "Hi, my name is Rodolfo," she reads off his name tag, seething.

"What a coincidence! My name is Rodolfo, too. And meet Little Rodolfo, my baby—"

H. Fix it! No babies!

"—my little brother."

"He's probably as stupid as you," our hero chastises him. "My name isn't Rodolfo. You're wearing a name tag. I know how to read."

"Oh," Rodolfo says, tussling the wispy hair of Little Rodolfo standing in front of him. "Don't you know? Warlord Chester decreed that we should all wear them. He says it will help his Death Soldiers identify the troublemakers more easily and help improve morale. It's been bad since he took over the town and slaughtered all the adults." Little Rodolfo starts crying softly at the mention of his parents' murders.

"Well, why did you hit and kidnap me? Do you mean to keep me as a slave?" our hero asks. While she's not tied up, she can't figure out Rodolfo's intentions—either of them.

"Oh, is that what you think?" Rodolfo asks.

"You did hit me with an iron pot," our hero explains. "So, take me for whatever vile intentions you have, if you can. But if you succeed, please promise that you'll let me leave one day to finish my quest."

"Miss . . ." Rodolfo stops. "I realize I don't know your name."

H. Hey, what is my name?

Mother?

H. That's my mother's name!

Sorry, I just never thought about it. Bilby?

H. The desert animal? That's a snack, if I'm lucky. Not a name!

Sorry, I just watched a nature show about it. How about—

H. Hero. My name is Hero.

Are you telling me?

H. I'm telling Rodolfo!

Oh, you can't talk to him directly.

H. What do you mean? I've been talking to him this whole time.

Yeah, but only if I write it. I'm the Author, remember? I write, er, spin, or weave the yarn. Hey, maybe that means I'm not really crazy if I can still control you.

H. *Control* me?

Yes, I can control you. I've been doing it this whole time.

H. No man controls me, not even a god! Do what I say. Tell him my name is Hero.

You really are a piece of work. And you're okay with Hero? Wouldn't *Honeydew* be better?

H. I'm a hero.

"Hero," our hero says. "I'm a hero."
"Hero? That's kind of lame!" Little Rodolfo laughs.

H. Hey, Author guy. Lose the bratty kid.

Seriously? You're supposed to be a hero, and you can't deal with a tiny bit of adversity?

H. Ad . . . ver . . . what?

A little teasing from a kid. What kind of character did I write? No, no, this is not good. I think I need to rewrite—

H. No, you will not! I'll deal with it.

What do you mean you'll deal with it? I just said I control what happens.

H. No matter what you say, I'm going to try really hard to kick that kid.

Wait! No! This is my story.

H. It's really mine, but you're not listening to my demands. Here goes. Three, two ...

Wait! Man, I must be crazy. Maybe Barnaby is right about the stress. Gods. Oh, great, now I'm talking like you. Look, it can be a meeting of the minds.

H. Meet the Minds? Are they dangerous wizards? Why would they be here in the back room of a saloon? That's not what I meant.

No, no. I mean, I will listen to your thoughts. See? I think that's fair. You actually live there, so maybe you can even help me.

H. Good. Then let's deal with the kid.

I hope your ideas help the story; I only have a week to write this. How's this?

Our hero, named Hero, rushes Little Rodolfo, picks him up over her head and yells, "Take that back!"

"Hero! Hero! Please put down my little brother!" Rodolfo

says. "We mean you no harm, I assure you. I just saw you without a name tag, and Chester's evil Death Soldiers were coming into the saloon. I needed to get you out of there fast. And quietly."

"Oh, I see," Hero says as she puts down Little Rodolfo, who is now on his feet again. "Just tell your little brother to watch his tongue, or I'll watch it for him." She gives Little Rodolfo an evil stare as sharp as a sword to his heart. "I've traveled too far and too long to be pestered by a little brat. I ate a man's spleen just this morning."

H. I don't mind the lie. He needs to be put in his place.

"You've traveled?" Rodolfo asks her, surprised. "The desolate roads between kingdoms? A girl? By yourself?" Little Rodolfo's face shows he is also surprised, or just scared silent. "Is that why you didn't know about the name tags?"

"Yes, a *girl*," our hero replies as she tosses her long, unwashed brown hair—greasy and matted at the same time— behind her left shoulder. Realizing that might be interpreted as *flirtatious*, and flirtatiousness is dangerous in this world of lawless warlords and evil dragons—not to mention flying zombies—she tosses her hair back in front of her shoulder. Realizing now she might have brought even more notice to the first flirtatious act, and, as a result, the second hair toss might have even been *extra* flirtatious, she adds, "But you losers are dirtier and rancid-er than I am."

"I'm sorry, Hero," Rodolfo says, as he tussles Little Rodolfo's dirty hair again, "but Warlord Chester has outlawed bathing! Rumor is, he believes pungent body odor may prevent large gatherings of rebels. His Death Soldiers destroyed all bathing equipment in town. Each family was given but a sponge. I would be happy to share our family sponge with you so you may cleanse yourself, if it would prove our kindly intentions."

Hero begins to think differently of the two Rodolfos, and is considering using the family sponge.

H. No way! I won't do it.

Seriously? You haven't bathed in years! I thought I was doing you a favor.

H. Would *you* use their family sponge?

What? Irrelevant! I have a shower. I shower every day. I even have massage jets, courtesy of my ex-wife's expensive bathroom renovation. She couldn't take that with her. It has temperature control, a showerhead with rainwater options, and a handheld shower handle for those hard-to-reach nooks and crannies.

H. Oh, my gods, I hate you and your fantasy heaven-world right now. So, so much. You have no idea. I haven't bathed in years! I was even forbidden entry into Xona's Bathhouse, the only one in the Lands, after I slaughtered all the men there.

I'm sorry. It's just . . . we come from very different worlds.

H. And what is it with your world and ma . . . saj? Chairs, jets. I want ma . . . saj . . . jets! I'm lucky if I can find a rock.

Maybe at the end? We'll see.

H. No, maybe—

Suddenly, a knock at the door—

H. No, we're not done discussing this. Meeting of the heads!

"Hero! Why aren't you listening to me? Put this on, quick!" Rodolfo yells at our hero. He's holding a name tag in his hand.

"No! Stop! I'm talking to someone," Hero cries.

"Who, Hero?" Rodolfo asks, looking around the room.

"There's no one here," Little Rodolfo says. "I told you she's a dimwit."

"Shut up, kid. *You're* a dimwit," Hero replies with venom, baring her teeth like a wolf. "I *was* talking to someone."

"Those roads made her crazy, brother," Little Rodolfo says. "She's one camel shy of a caravan."

From outside the door, a voice clearly from a large, scary man yells, "Open this door on order of Warlord Chester!"

Rodolfo looks at Hero with pleading eyes. "Please, if they find you without a name tag, you'll be killed. We may all be killed."

Hero puts on the name tag. She looks down at it. "Hey, this says *Marmalade*."

The door opens, and in walk three large men with long hair, silver armor, angry looks, and even angrier swords. "Inspection time, Rodolfo! You should know better than to hide from us. You operate this barbershop—"

H. Saloon!

Oh, right.

"—saloon at our discretion," the largest man says with a growl. He starts to lunge toward Rodolfo.

"Wait!" Rodolfo cries. The man has a hand around his throat now. Rodolfo is speaking through strained vocal cords and pain. "We weren't hiding. I was training our new barmaid, Marmalade." He looks toward Hero.

The large man looks at her, still holding Rodolfo's throat. "Marmalade, huh? So, Marmalade, tell me about your new job here."

Rodolfo's eyes plead at Hero. *Stay quiet,* they tell her. So, while she never trusts anybody, our hero decides to heed his warning. Warnings are like gold on the desolate roads.

"Cat got your tongue, girl?" the large man yells in her face. "Maybe a real cat should get your tongue. How about that, boys? Maybe we'll feed her to Katrina, our Saber-Toothed Lightning Cat!"

"Please, sir!" Little Rodolfo speaks up. "She's not disrespectful. She's just dumb! She knows not how to speak well."

"Hey, boys! Rodolfo's got himself a mute maid!" All the men are laughing. Hero is running simulations through her head of what they will do next and how she will react.

Suddenly, the piano in the saloon starts to play again. It's a sad, soulful song. "I told them never to play that song again! It reminds me of Winnifred!" one of the men cries. "Oh, Winnifred, why'd you leave me? We could have made beautiful Death-Soldier Babies together! Come on, boys!"

The three Death Soldiers walk out of the back room of the saloon after releasing Rodolfo's throat.

"Why'd you help me?" Hero asks Rodolfo. "No one in this world does anything nice for anyone else."

"Because I own this saloon, and they would shut me down if they found you here without a name tag," Rodolfo replies defensively, rubbing his neck. Before our hero can reply, he adds, "And why didn't you listen to me?"

"Listen to you? I did. I'm wearing your stupid name tag," the normally steady Hero replies shakily, as she is not used to being spoken to in such a manner. In her mind, no one asserts authority over her. Her independence is like the air she breathes and water she drinks.

H. Damn straight! You don't have to be all dramatic about it, though.

"No, not the name tag. I was pleading with you to just respond to him. You could have just said, 'I clean tables, sir,' and they would have gone away! My eyes were literally begging you to reply. Say anything! Even just, 'Hi, I'm Marmalade.' Instead, you almost got my little brother and I killed," Rodolfo scolds her.

"What? Your eyes were literally pleading for me to stay quiet!" Hero yells. "I'm not a dimwit! I can read eyes."

"Keep your voice down. They could come back here any minute," Rodolfo says sternly. "For a traveler, you don't know the first thing about surviving."

"Excuse me?" His accusation startles Hero. Some weird-looking boy in some backwater town—not even a kingdom—is accusing her of being soft?

"Brother," Little Rodolfo says as he tugs at his brother's brown leather jacket. He is clearly unhappy and frightened, from all the yelling.

"Not now, Little Rodolfo."

H. Okay, seriously, Author? This Rodolfo and Little Rodolfo thing just doesn't roll off the tongue. And it's a bit confusing.

They're brothers! They share a bond through their name. My father's name was Murray. Wow, if Grandpa Rodolfo heard you speaking like this—

H. So, I should call you Little Murray?

No.

H. See? Just name him something else. Please!

No!

H. But it's just so confusing. And stupid sounding. Do you know any 'Little anyones'? Do you want to sound dimwitted in front of your other god-readers?

Fine! You want me to write what I know? You want me to just write the life I know?

H. Yes!

"Not now, Toaster. Can't you see I'm trying to explain how the WattsKookin Deep Fryer XL 3000 works to this kind young lady?" Rodolfo informs his little brother, Toaster. "So, where was I"?" He turns back to our heroic customer. "Let's see. Page 347 of the manual—"

H. Oh gods, those were the most boring 346 pages anyone has ever read to me. Please, make it stop!

You said you wanted me to write what I know!

H. I take it back. I take it all back. Just go back to the regular story. I'd rather be eaten by Katrina, the Lord of the Saber-Toothed Lightning Cats, than be subjected to that—

You mean, subjected to my regular, boring life?

H. Fine, heaven-world can be boring. Just get back to the story.

Do you remember where we were?

H. I was getting yelled at by those two horrible boys. I really don't like them.

Oh, yes. But I'm not sure what to do now. I forget where I am. It's probably best to jump to the next chapter. Just flash the chapter number and get on with it.

H. What is a chapter number?

Uh, hard to explain. Hey, do you know any jokes?

H. You think my life is a *joke*?

Hey, how many Rodolfos does it take to change a lightbulb?

H. What's a lightbulb? Your heavens are so confusing. Everyone down here is just trying to survive this horrible nightmare. And you want to talk to me about jokes?

Sounds like you could use a joke. I know I can.

H. I don't want a joke.

What did the warlord say to the flying zombie?

H. I find this very mean. Until you've run from either a warlord or a flying zombie—

I thought you said there were no flying zombies.

H. Of course there aren't . . . Oh, was that the joke?

Was it funny?

Chapter 3

Three's Company, Seven's a Kerfuffle

"Not now, Little Rodolfo," Rodolfo reprimands his little brother. He turns to Hero with fire in his eyes—though, unlike Hero, it's more of a controlled burn—and says, "You come in here, acting all tough, telling tales of being out on the roads. But you clearly don't know anything. I don't believe a word you're saying!"

Hero opens her black leather trench coat, which matches her black leather pants and boots. It is an unusual coat that was handed down to her from her mother, through the hands of loyalists, and is the only thing Hero ever received from her. The inside of the coat is lined with pockets containing knives of varying lengths, a morning star, and what looks like a bunch of throwing stars.

"Wow, um," Rodolfo mumbles.

"What do you say now, boy?" Hero taunts Rodolfo.

"I . . . guess you were telling the truth," a still-stunned Rodolfo says.

"And I'll be going now. Thanks for the laugh," Hero says as she starts to leave the back room of the saloon. But Little Rodolfo moves toward the door and blocks her.

"Don't let her leave, brother," Little Rodolfo says.

Hero takes a step toward the door to intimidate the boy. "Get out of my way, bratwurst"!" Hero yells at the seven-year-old.

"Don't yell at little kids, hoagie," Little Rodolfo jeers back.

"Bratwurst? Hoagie? What is going on?" Rodolfo asks.

"We already have cute nicknames for each other, brother," Little Rodolfo says. "We'll be fast friends. And we need her."

H. I agree with Rodolfo. What the hell is going on with *bratwurst* and *hoagie*? Why did I say that? That's not a meeting of the heads!

I think just because I'm hungry. But, actually, now I see what you mean about Little Rodolfo. I think I have something better.

H. Yay!

"I thought you disliked her, Toaster," Rodolfo says, confused. "Why ever would you want her to stay, Toaster, my dear little brother formerly known as Little Rodolfo, a name formerly passed down from generation to generation until this very day?"

"She can help save our town from Warlord Chester, and thus, our saloon. I don't know how. But the knowledge resides within me," Toaster replies.

How's that?

H. Better than Little Rodolfo, Author. He even sounds less stupid now.

"Since when did you use a word like *thus*?" Rodolfo asks him.

"I'm wiser than my seven years," Toaster says proudly. "And I read a lot."

"You have books here?" Hero asks.

Toaster nods.

"You shouldn't have told her, little brother," Rodolfo says. "You know Chester banned them."

"Sorry, brother," Toaster says. "But she needs to know. She can help us. I promise you."

"You think you're so wise, because you're the new generation with a new name," Rodolfo says. "But it's on your head if she betrays us. You know Chester has a bounty out for people like us."

Hero is intrigued. How did she just happen to stumble into in this town with no name? Normally her travels have led to nothing but vile men and dead-ends. But these men speak of books. And books have clues.

"What is it, Toaster?" Hero asks him. "You can trust me. You see I have no love for warlords. And I'm not from around here."

"I need to show you," Toaster replies. He takes out a small coin from the inside pocket of his red woven jacket.

H. A special coin from his jacket? What kind of idiot keeps money in their jacket where it can be stolen in a heartbeat? Do you even know anything about the Lands?

You keep weapons in your coat!

H. But they're weapons. And you never even thinked to check my socks, my trousers, my hair . . .

Okay, okay. I see your point.

"I need to show you," Toaster replies. He takes out a small coin from out of the back side of his underpants. It takes him a while as his hand digs around in there. "Here, take a look at this," he finally says as he holds out the coin.

H. Ew! Are you kidding me?

It was your idea. Take it!

H. No!

Take it!

H. No!

And forevermore, the Queendom of Fant ruled over the Kingdom of Dyst—

H. Don't you dare finish that sentence! I'll do it.

"I don't know, Toaster," Hero replies. "It seems awfully important. Why don't you just keep it?"

How did you do that? I'm the Author, not you!

H. I don't know! I just really, *really* don't want to touch that thing.

But this amazing idea popped into my head, and I had it all planned out! That's never happened to be me before—a real cosmic download. The object is a magical talisman that will be your first clue on your quest to find out Mother's secrets.

H. Oh!

"Give me that thing," Hero says, as she grabs the coin from Toaster.

"You don't have to be all grabby about it," Toaster says.

"I told you she was not to be trusted," Rodolfo mumbles.

"I know what this is. It's a talisman," Hero replies, ignoring Rodolfo.

"Purported talisman," Toaster clarifies.

"When did you ever use such big words, little brother?" Rodolfo asks.

"And there's more, Hero," Toaster says, ignoring his brother's rude question.

"Is everyone just going to ignore me now?" Rodolfo asks aloud as he throws his hands in the air in frustration. "I *am* a successful saloon owner, you know."

"My brother and I are part of a group," Toaster says, now ignoring his brother's huff of dissatisfaction at the revelation of their supposedly clandestine group. "We have been gathering and hiding books and other historical objects from our town. We are trying to save our town's long and vibrant history before Chester destroys it all. Many of our sacred books have already been destroyed, and our greatest scholars have been killed. Well, scholar. Ted.

"But we think these items could possibly save our town. Maybe even the Lands. Though we cannot even read many of these items as they are in old languages, like this purported talisman."

Hero looks closer at the writing on the talisman coin. "It's an old form of writing from even before King Reginald's time."

Yelling from the main room of the saloon distracts the three. Sounds of fighting and tables and chairs breaking cause Rodolfo to run into the main room. "My saloon!" he exclaims as he exits.

Hero and Toaster run after him. There they see a man, if you can call him that, wearing a black and red beret with a silver feather sticking up straight from the front of the hat, and a black cloak to complete his ensemble. But instead of having a body, he is just a skeleton. His bony hand strokes the silver feather ominously.

Hero has never seen anything like this, even in all her travels. But instantly, she knows this is why they're called Death Soldiers, and Warlord Chester is just a tool of the

Queendom of Fant and its evil magic. *I need to get out of here—quick,* she thinks.

"That's SkeLord, the leader of Chester's Death Soldiers," Toaster whispers to Hero.

There are patrons lying on the floor, obviously beaten up. Tables are broken. The piano player is unconscious and slumped over the gloss-finished black grand piano—usually the biggest draw to Rodolfo's saloon. His mead is continually rated as subpar by the town's newspaper, which is fair considering the centuries-long drought forced Rodolfo to use a portion of camel urine to supplement the expensive well water, managing costs and all.

"We're looking for a girl," SkeLord says to the remaining conscious saloon patrons. He's surrounded by the three other large men who were here earlier. "A traveler."

Toaster and Rodolfo share a look.

"Ah, I see you know her," SkeLord says to Rodolfo.

"What? No!" Rodolfo stammers.

"SkeLord," the largest of the three men says. "Perhaps it is their new barmaid, Marmalade?"

"It can't be her," Toaster speaks up. "She's a dimwit."

Everyone looks at Hero, with her name tag that says, *Hi, my name is Marmalade.* Previously in stealth, but now clear as day to everyone in the room, Hero's hand is already holding a dagger. *Thanks, Toaster.*

"Seize her!" SkeLord yells. Two large men start toward Hero. The other starts toward Toaster. SkeLord lays a hand on Rodolfo, keeping him from moving.

Hero is worried for Toaster, which surprises her. She has never cared for, or about, another human being before— except for Mother—and very much disliked him only minutes earlier. *The clue. That's why I care,* she tells herself, not admitting that she actually liked how Toaster believed in her. Instinctively, to defend Toaster, she raises a hand at the two Death Soldiers approaching her.

For a reason unknown to her, the two Death Soldiers instantly fly across the room, away from Hero, and smash into the piano along the far wall. The grand piano is destroyed—as are any future business prospects for the saloon. The Death Soldiers subsequently fall onto the floor, unmoving.

Using the moment of surprise, Rodolfo slams a foot into SkeLord's lower leg. Not expecting an attack, and without any soldiers to defend him, SkeLord feels a break in his exposed tibia and falls to his hands and knees.

The remaining Death Soldier, nearing Toaster, freezes in his tracks at the sight of his compatriots in pain on the floor. He's staring at the girl he thinks is Marmalade, who is staring right back at him, and he's worried whether he's at the short end of an unfair fight with the barmaid. Both are hesitant to make a move.

"Get him, Hero!" Toaster yells. *Again, Toaster? You're not as wise as you think you are.* But the Death Soldier flinches at the noise, which causes Hero's fight-or-flight response to take hold. She reflexively raises a hand, her new unbelievable weapon, at the Death Soldier. He instantly rises into in the air and slams into the far wall. He lands on the broken piano, with the other unconscious bodies of the two soldiers.

H. Did I really just do that? Really? I was never magical before, but that was so awesome.

Shh!

The saloon is quiet for a moment. Any remaining customers who weren't victims during SkeLord and his gang's arrival are now quiet and wishing they had never decided to stop by for some mead and traditional Lands piano tunes, such as "These Lands Are Your Lands, Not Mine" and "That Fungus Ate Fred."

The silence is broken when Rodolfo yells, "Come on! We gotta get out of here."

Hero runs to Toaster and grabs his hand. She drags him out of the saloon, and Rodolfo follows, leaving a broken SkeLord and three unconscious Death Soldiers behind. The few remaining scared customers will undoubtedly be executed by Death Soldiers in the very near future, right after SkeLord finds himself a new tibia from one of the dead bodies.

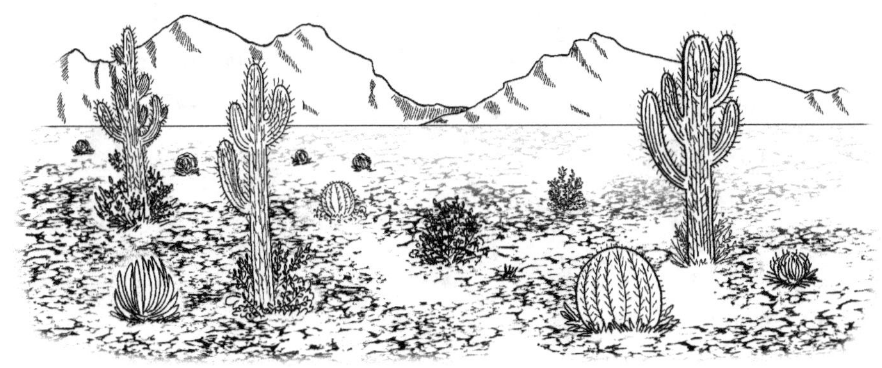

Chapter 4

Should I Stay or Should I Go?

"We need to hurry! SkeLord is probably calling for reinforcements," Rodolfo says to the group, now standing outside the saloon. He's too scared to give a long, last look at his saloon—the one he took over after his parents died two years ago, leaving Toaster and him alone.

"Is there a place to hide?" Hero asks him.

"There is nowhere to hide from Chester and his men," Rodolfo replies. "We can only hope to outrun them." From inside the saloon, they hear noises, and outside passersby give them suspicious looks.

"But, brother, they'll be looking for us everywhere," Toaster says.

"I know you're scared," Rodolfo says. "If I'd known this morning a beautiful—"

H. Stop it! Too sappy. *Way* too sappy. And if this is where you're going with this, there is no way Rodolfo can be my lover. I wanted a man, not a sap-thing.

Tree?

H. What's a tree? I want a man!

But I thought you liked his wispy blond hair?

H. We just don't see eye to eye. He doesn't trust me, and I think he's stupid. Well, to use Toaster's word, a dimwit.

But he just called you beautiful.

H. I said too sappy! Change it.

Why don't you? You know how you controlled the story before? It was like my hands were writing, er, weaving on their own. It was really freaky—like a ghost thing.

H. I told you, I don't know how I did that before. Just change it!

Okay, okay.

Hero coughs, interrupting Rodolfo's thought.

"—a bee in my bonnet would show up," Rodolfo says while giving an evil eye to Hero, "and I would lose my saloon today . . ." He looks down at the ground sadly, unable to finish his thought.

"Look, Toaster is right," Hero explains assuredly. "They'll be looking for us everywhere. If we run now, they'll surely find us. Is there any place to hide out until nightfall, until we can get out onto the roads?"

"You're going to stay with us?" Rodolfo asks her, not even trying to hide his surprise or annoyance. Hero can't tell.

"Toaster wants me to," Hero says as she looks at the boy. They smile at each other.

"And then you want to take my little brother and me on the desolate roads during *nightfall*? Are you out of your mind?" Rodolfo is incensed. "That's when the flying zombies come out! Just because you're beau—"

Hero coughs again, interrupting his thought.

All right! But we have to talk about how you're doing this.

Rodolfo continues, "—bearishly fitted for the desolate roads, doesn't mean—"

"No, she's right, brother," Toaster replies, seemingly not noticing the uncomfortable exchange that just happened. "It's our only way."

"But we'll be dead within hours!" Rodolfo cries.

"Not if you stick with me," Hero explains. "You don't think so, but I know what I'm doing. I've survived on those roads for four years. You can trust me. Come." The words are coming out of her mouth, but she can't believe them. She only wants her independence. These two fools will just slow her down—and her quest. Why is she offering to bring them along, to help them? She doesn't know.

"You? *You?* You just cost me my whole world. My business! My livelihood! And just because I tried to save your hide. And you want me to just *trust* you?" Rodolfo is incensed and incredulous.

"No one forced you to hit me over the head!" Hero snarls. "I could have taken those goons."

"Are we not even going to talk about how you magically threw them across the room?" Rodolfo continues his rant. "Who even are you? Maybe you secretly work for Chester. Maybe you're a Death Solider on—"

"Never!" Hero exclaims.

"Brother," Toaster cuts in, ignoring the question at hand. "There is one place they don't know about. The secret cellar. We can hide there for some time. Then we can take our time to decide what to do and figure this all out."

"But what if she's going to kill us, too?" Rodolfo asks his little brother.

"I would have done it already," Hero voluntarily replies, staring him down as he withers under her gaze.

"Okay, we'll take you there." Rodolfo relents. "But by nightfall you better be gone. We're not going with you. We can just say you enthralled or ensorcelled us or something. SkeLord will believe it, seeing what you did."

"I'll show you the way," Toaster says to Hero as he takes her hand, smiling. The three walk down an alleyway, where they disappear without anyone noticing.

They walk through many hidden alleyways and quiet streets, dodging the looks of passersby. In Chester's town, people tend to mind their own business anyway. It's easier to survive if you don't see anything, hear anything, or do anything.

The trio approaches a dug-out cellar sitting below a shop named Josiah's Manure Import-Export. Below the entry hangs a sign that reads, "We're not just manure."

"It's just down here," Toaster says, pointing at the stairs outside the unappealing manure establishment.

"We're going to hide out in a manure cellar?" Hero asks. "I take it back. I think I'll be better off on the roads. In daylight. I might even add some bells—"

"It's not a manure cellar," Toaster explains.

"I hope you know what you're doing, little brother," Rodolfo says. He turns to Hero. "You're only the eleventh person to know, but this is not a manure store anymore."

H. He better be right about that.

Why would I lie?

H. You're not the one who's lying. He is! Wait, can gods lie?

Oh, uh, he's not lying.

H. But why a manure store?

To keep the Death Soldiers out. Would you want to go down there?

H. I don't want to!

"I don't want to go down there!" Hero exclaims, putting her hands in front of her face as if that would protect her.

"Keep your voice down. And we told you, it's not a manure store anymore," Rodolfo says defensively, turning back toward the cellar.

"Certainly smells like one. Unless that's you guys." Hero insults them to try and keep her mind off the manure. She never thought she would have to hide in a manure room again. It brings back terrible memories.

Rodolfo whips back around to face her and points a finger in her face. "Hey, I told you why! You don't smell so great either."

"I've spent years on the roads!" Hero says defensively. "It's the smell of survival."

"Guys! Let's just go in before someone spots us. You'll see, Hero," Toaster implores, with his palms up—a sign of peace and welcoming across the Lands, usually done right before someone robs you, or worse. *But it's Toaster.*

Hero sighs, and they head down the dark dug-out stairwell. The stairwell is narrow and looks like it might have collapsed in on itself long ago, if not for the centuries-long drought. And unlike a normal cellar, it doesn't end in a room of supplies, or even manure. Though there is a sign on the basement door that reads, Fermenting Manure Storeroom.

"The sign would keep anyone out. Keeping it was my idea," Rodolfo tells her proudly. He turns to Toaster. "Little brother, the key?"

Hero finally notices the padlock on the door. Like someone would have to lock a room full of fermenting manure? *What is fermented manure even for?*

Toaster starts to dig around in his underpants again. Hero wants to gag, but holds in the impulse. *At least they're not going to make me open the door.*

"Hero, would you please do the honors?" Toaster asks her, holding out the key he just pulled out of his—

H. Oh no, not again! You did that on purpose.

Come on. Where do you expect them to hold the key? Around their necks? You're the one who said it would get stolen.

H. You're really taking this too far!

Don't you want to see what's behind the door?

H. At this point, I want to cancel my quest. I heard there's an opening for a barmaid.

Just take the key.

H. I don't want to!

Take it!

H. I don't want to!

Take it!

H. I have a better idea!

Wait!

"Key?" Hero scoffs. "I don't need your key." She takes a hand and pushes it toward the door. Instantly the door breaks off its hinges and goes flying into the room.

How did you do that on your own?

H. Who cares? It was awesome!

Tell me how you did that!

H. I have no idea. I just really didn't want to touch his butt key. It's like when I really *really* want something, I just . . . you know. Or you're going crazy.

I think I'm going crazy.

H. We're all a little crazy. Just keep weaving!

"You're paying for that!" Rodolfo exclaims.

"So cool," Toaster says as he seemingly puts the key back into his bottom. Hero winces as she sees this but says nothing. *Where does it even go?*

"And how do you do that, anyway?" Rodolfo asks her as they walk inside.

"Are you a sorceress?" Toaster takes a lantern off the wall, readying the light. The room lights up to expose a dirty, moist floor littered with piles of books and scattered objects. The walls are carved from dirt, just like the floor. The air is heavy and uncomfortable but breathable, except for the smell of the entrants.

Leaning the door back on the doorframe, Rodolfo groans. "Thank the gods one of our compatriots is a builder."

"Honestly, I don't know," Hero says, thoughtfully for once. "I don't think I'm a sorceress. I've never been able to do anything like that before. My kingdom is not magical. Well, except for my mother."

"And you've really never performed any magic before?" Toaster asks.

"No, I've never magic'd before. Only since I met you two," Hero replies, looking at her hands in the light, but something else catches her eye. "Wow, I've never seen so many books in one place," she announces, forgetting that she expected to see manure.

"You know how to read?" Rodolfo asks.

"A little. You think I'm just a dimwitted girl? You sexist, good-for-nothing—"

"I can't believe you!" Rodolfo cuts her off.

"Excuse me?" Hero shouts back incredulously.

"We saved your life!" he yells at her. "Show some gratitude."

"This again?" She dismisses him. "I saved *you!*"

"We lost the saloon that's been in my family for generations! Passed down to me from my father, Rodolfo, but two years ago, he died," Rodolfo says as he walks over to Toaster and tussles his hair again. "I worked hard day and night to run that saloon and take care of my little brother."

"I saved his life!" Hero throws back at him, pointing at the little boy. "Your life, too!"

Rodolfo erupts, "But not before we saved your—"

H. Can you believe—

"And you stop doing that!" Rodolfo demands.

"Stop doing what?" Hero asks, jolted by his confusing request. *What am I doing? Yelling? So, he's allowed to yell, but I'm not? That sexist—*

"That thing you do!" Rodolfo snaps. "You look up and to the left and zone out. It's rude when I'm talking to you. And then you make us wait for you to say or do something."

H. Little Murray, I think they can see me.

If you're going to use my name, just use Murray!

"That!" Rodolfo exclaims again.

"Really?" she asks, confused. *Was I really doing that? Traveling alone, no one was ever there to tell me when I was doing that.*

Uh, Hero, what's going on? I'm not supposed to be in the story.

"Yes!" Rodolfo exclaims, followed by a groan. "Why do you think little Toaster thought you dimwitted? But now we know you can read a little. You clearly have magic in your blood. You cannot be dumb. Perhaps it is a canker."

"It's not a canker!" Hero yells at him. *This boy is so annoying!*

H. Can you believe these annoying—

Hero, stop fighting them! They'll figure it out.

H. No one tells me what to do!

You're insufferable! I'm taking a break from your character.

H. [Grumbles]

Rodolfo looks concerned. But he's also confused by his concern for such an insufferable girl who just cost him and his brother the only life they've ever known. And for what? Chester's stupid name tags? Would his soldiers even have noticed if Hero didn't have one? They aren't the swiftest men. Did Rodolfo just throw away his whole life for *nothing*? She wasn't even grateful or understanding of the situation. Why couldn't she just go with the flow of polite society? Why was he even entertaining Toaster's notion that she could help? But if she really *could* help . . .

That must be it . . . my hope for this town of . . . Why doesn't my town have a name? Ever since he can remember, it had no name. Other towns have names. Every once in a blue moon a traveler would show up from a town with a name, though he can't remember them. *What is it about my town, the one I love so much, that it has no name? But if Hero can save it, whatever it is called, I must keep her healthy.* "There is a healer in town—"

"It's not a canker!" Hero shouts even louder. She also stomps her foot like a mythical bull.

"Would you two please stop fighting?" Toaster begs. "This isn't helping us."

"You're right, little brother," Rodolfo says. *When did he get so smart?* "Truce?" he asks Hero. He doesn't *really* mean it; he's only doing it for his brother. And he needs Hero. But he doesn't even hold out his hand. Something about her scares him. Is it her magic? Her temper? He isn't sure. Probably both.

"Fine, whatever," Hero agrees with a sigh.

"You said you could read the talisman?" Toaster cuts in, hoping to avoid a quick end to the temporary ceasefire.

"It's a very old form of Talismanic—"

H. Seriously? *Talismanic?*

"You're doing that thing again," Rodolfo points out. "I'm serious about that healer."

"Just shut up and let me think," Hero scolds him.

H. They can really see me talking to you?

I guess so. I didn't expect this. Something's wrong.

H. What do you mean you guess so? Something's wrong? You're the one weaving this. You're a god of gods!

You're the one talking to me. That wasn't supposed to happen either.

H. Well, how do I even talk to you now if everyone who sees me thinks me dimwitted? It was one thing to talk to you while I was on my own on those desolate roads, with sand-wolves and zombies hunting me. The wolves didn't care if I looked stupid. Actually, I'm surprised a sand-wolf didn't eat me while I was stuck looking up and to the left.

You'll have to pick your times better, I guess. And we still haven't figured out the magic thing. But even if I am crazy, the story is really picking up now, isn't it? This is exciting. Your first clue!

H. And so . . . talismanic? For real? That is such a stupid name. It's like you literally put no think into this story. It's *my* kingdom we're talking about, my whole world, and here I find out you put so little think into this that you can't even name a very important ancient language. I'm so mad at you right now! It's people's lives you're playing with!

You come up with something, then!

H. I should! The gods know you won't.

So, you do it if you think it's so easy.

H. I can have free reign? Anything?

Apparently, you already do. Just stop making fun of me.

H. Fine! Let's do this thing.

"It's a very old form of Murraystinksish."

I said stop making fun of me!

H. I didn't!

You did! You just hid the words Murray stinks and made it sound like the name of a language.

H. I didn't make fun of you.

Yes, you did!

H. Prove it to King Reginald's Witan!

I don't even know what that means! How would I even do that?

H. Really, you don't know? It's your own story. King Reginald's Witan was a gathering of the most powerful lords in all of the Kingdom of Reginald the Devout. You'd have to argue your case to them and try to get them on your side. Or bribe them. And all of that was before the test of fire to prove your honesty. But you don't seem so convincing, so you'd very likely lose before you burned to death.

I'd lose, or win, and still die a fiery death in an ancient court case within my own story that I made up?

H. Court? No. The Witan! Court is like frilly dancing. What does frilly dancing have to do with—

What happens if I lose?

H. The dancing?

The Witan!

H. If you lose your case but survive the fire? Then you get thrown to the alligators.

Wow, I wrote all that? It's a very detailed, well-thought-out world.

H. It's your world. I just live in it. And many people died by Witan. Family members even! You have the audacity to call it "well-thinked-out?"

Okay, okay! Just please, can we do without the *stinks* thing? It's kind of hurtful. I've had a rough time lately. The name-calling from my own hero is just making it worse.

H. What, did your ma . . . saj . . . jets break?

You know, I thought we could share things about each other. Build a rapport. But you just continue to make fun of me.

H. Fine, let's just get on with it. I need to read that talisman!

"It's a very old form of Murrayskindacoolish. An ancient language from the Kingdom of Dystpopia, even before the time of King Reginald the Devout," Hero says. "I only know it because, well ..."

H. How do I know it? I don't even know how to read that well. I don't remember learning this crazy old language.

Um . . . Because of a magical dream? From your mother? But you don't know the entire language. Just small pieces. Luckily, this talisman has the parts you know.

H. Sounds like you're making this up as you go along.

Oh, not at all. This was my cosmic inspiration! Don't you ever dream of your mother? Doesn't she owe you anything?

H. Now that you mention it, I do recall some crazy dream like that.

"I know small parts of the language from a magical dream of my mother, an enchantress. In it she taught me parts of the language in case I might find a talisman." She looks closer and wipes a dirty finger over the text on the back side of the coin: *Abraham Lincoln.* "But luckily, the small parts of the language I know are on this talisman."

H. Who the hell is Abraham Lincoln? He has never been mentioned in any history I know of!

Oh, my mistake. He was a great leader in my world. It just kind of slipped out when I was writing.

H. You have wizards in your heaven-world, too? You never said!

No, what? Why would you think he is a wizard?

H. Did you see his wizard hat and beard on the coin? Do you not even know your own history?

I can change it.

H. No! Don't change it. I kind of like his beard. Unlike Rodolfo's baby boy face. I like rubbing Abraham's coin beard with my finger.

Um . . . okay. That's kind of weird.

H. Hey, you wanted to share things! But then I open up just a little . . . I already told you how I want a man. Not that I need one. But I'd take this Abraham Lincoln.

Abraham Lincoln? For real?

H. You know, you're all talk, Author. Forget it!

No, I'm willing to listen now.

H. Not anymore. You lost your chance. Back to the story!

"It's a bit worn, but I think that's Abraham Lincoln on the front," Hero says.

"Abraham Lincoln? He has two names! Was he a very important king back then?" Toaster asks.

"No, but he was a great wizard. You can see by the hat and beard," Hero says. Then she turns the coin over. "And the writing on the back says, 'To Ye Who Is Destined, The Power Is Vested.'"

The trio is quiet for a moment. "Are you destined?" Rodolfo asks.

"I'm so confused. I don't feel destined," Hero says in a rare show of honesty as she shakes her head at the floor. "My life kind of sucks. I live on the desolate roads, basically in filth. I almost ate a man's spleen."

"Hey, you said you did before," Rodolfo protests. "Not *almost*."

"And you said you owned a saloon," Hero retorts with a huff.

"I very clearly—"

"But you had the power as soon as you had the talisman!" Toaster interjects excitedly, also trying to change the subject.

Hero smiles slightly and holds out the coin in her open hand. "I had the power." It was almost as much of a question as a statement.

"Only if you hold the talisman," Toaster points out.

"I guess." Hero nods and offers it back to Toaster.

"You keep it for now," Rodolfo says before Toaster can take it. "We may need your magic again."

Is he starting to trust me?

"We told you who we are," Toaster says. "Who are *you*?"

"Some dirty traveling girl can't just happen to be destined, right?" Rodolfo asks.

"You're right; I can't be destined," Hero agrees, ignoring the slight. "It's just some dumb mistake." Her denial is palpable. But actually, knowing a little bit of Murrayskindacoolish from a magical dream about her magical mother is gnawing at her. *How? Is that how I controlled the story, too? That was also magic.*

Wait, is that true? Is that how you're doing this? Some magical talisman I gave you in a story I'm writing?

H. Writing?

Weaving. Whatever.

H. It makes sense. 'Tis magic!

No, it doesn't make sense at all.

H. [In a singsong voice] My mother gave me powers. My mother gave me powers. It's my birthday. It's my birthday.

No one does that anymore!

H. As if the words of a god matter anymore!

"You're not with Chester, are you?" Rodolfo alleges, insinuating her power is part of some sort of evil magic.

I guess he's not starting to trust me. "Come on! I told you about my mother. She had magic. And you saw how much I hate warlords. I'm not looking for money, a bounty, or anything like that. And I'm not going to tell anyone about your stupid secret little baby library," Hero replies with a hint of anger. "I'm in search of something much greater. Something beyond the power of the gods, even."

Hero, stop controlling the story.

H. Make me. I have the talisman and the power of the gods.

You don't control everything, you know.

"Toaster, it's like you said, she's a camel shy," Rodolfo reminds his brother.

"You're right, brother," Toaster says. "She can't help us."

Ignoring them, Hero turns toward a stack of books and other objects lining the wall, taking a moment to compose herself. Being on her own since she left the Kingdom of Dystpopia, she's never had to tell anyone of her quest. And suddenly, she's being thrown in with these two boys. An annoyingly untrusting, misogynistic boy who thinks he knows more than she does, and his bratty little brother— whom she now is starting to actually like.

"My mother was Mother," Hero begins.

"Yup, she is a dimwit," Rodolfo jokes.

"Do you have to be such a jackass like Murray—"

Hero!

H. I called you a jackass. In the story!

Did you?

H. Stop playing, Murray! You saw! Maybe I don't control everything, but my power is increasing.

Okay, okay. Maybe it's not the talisman. Maybe your mind is so strong-willed, I'm just weaving what you're doing. Or, like we both said, I'm going crazy. I know it;

you know it. But I can still weave the other people in your world around what you do. See?

"Hero! Who's Murray?" Rodolfo yells to get Hero's attention.

"Excuse me?" Hero asks, befuddled.

"You did that thing again! Zoned out! Up and to the left. Who's Murray? He must be a really swell guy. Actually, I'm not sure why I said that. Is he your warlord who sent you here to infiltrate us? Or did he hurt you and you're on the run?" Rodolfo asks, actually concerned. This makes Hero smile, just a bit.

Argh, they're not doing what I say! I'm just writing what they're doing. This is impossible! Please, Hero. Help! It's not how the story is supposed to go.

"Uh . . . no. No warlord can ever hurt me again," Hero says defensively. Then she looks off into the distance in thought, not really talking to Rodolfo as much as herself. "Murray's just . . . kind of my . . . father," she says with a hint of confusion.

I love you too!

H. Argh! I just don't know how else to explain it. You're a means to an end. And a jackass!

Whatever, I'll take it. And I think I have control over them again.

"I see," Rodolfo says with a tone of understanding at complicated relationships with fathers. His own father never thought Rodolfo could actually make something of himself. *"You'll never amount to anything with your head buried in those old books,"* his father had chastised him. *"You'll never be a lawyer because I won't let you fail the saloon!"* was another one of his father's taunts. Regardless, Rodolfo still misses his parents.

"I'm sorry for calling you a dimwit," he continues. "If you can't tell, I'm kind of stressed. We had to leave everything behind. The Death Soldiers could be ransacking our saloon and living quarters as we speak. I don't know what the future holds anymore."

"And we left the family sponge behind, brother!" Toaster looks up with concern. Rodolfo tussles his dirty black hair.

"It's okay," Hero says softly. She feels strange not counterattacking Rodolfo verbally. To avoid that feeling, or any feeling, she quickly continues her story. "Let me explain. My mother's name was Mother the Enchantress." The brothers look blankly at her. "You don't know of her? I haven't found anyone who has heard of her outside of my own kingdom. But she was an archaeologist, historian, linguist, mechanic, sorceress, and water diviner. I'm not even sure what a lot of those things are, but I know she was important. You've heard of the Kingdom of Dystpopia?"

"We've never traveled outside of our town," Rodolfo answers. "Once in a blue moon, a traveler may show up from here or there, much like yourself. But never one so young and beau—"

Hero coughs.

"—beastly. But I never paid attention to from whence they came. Names are nothing but shackles that restrict our

true selves," Rodolfo explains, then scratches his head with a look of confusion.

"Then you've also never heard of the evil Queendom of Fant? And their dragons?" Hero asks.

Their eyes grow wide.

"Do you mean to say there are actual dragons?" Toaster asks.

"Don't sound so excited," Hero reprimands him. "And you know Fant sent SkeLord, right?" The brothers look confused. "Whatever. How is a skeleton man easier to believe than dragons?" The two sheltered boys shrug their shoulders. "You two need to get out more. I may not be that smart, but at least I've seen the Lands. Anyway, Fant's dragons are killers. They killed my mother before I was even borned."

"Before you were born?" Rodolfo asks. "How is that even possible? How could your mother have even retrieved you from the magical lily patch outside of town where all babies are grown?"

"Excuse me?" This time, it's Hero's turn to look dumbfounded.

"Ah, you don't know it," Rodolfo replies pridefully. "My mother told me all about how she married our father and the next day went out to pick me."

H. Are you kidding me?

I'm sorry! But it's a very strange scenario for me to write around with this whole dying before you were born thing. How is it even possible?

H. It just is, all right? I'm special! Shut up and weave, Murray.

"Hero! Did I not have it correct? You're doing that thing again," Rodolfo says.

"I was thinking!" Hero snipes back. "And no, that's definitely not correct. But forget it. Anyway, don't worry how it happened. It just did.

"Back to Fant. After my mother was gone, the Queendom of Fant, with all its evil magic, and with which we were in a hundred-year war, launched a huge final assault against my great Kingdom of Dystpopia and left it in ashes. While it was in disarray, the evil warlord Xander the Eyeless seized power from King Reginald III. I was in hiding, staying in rooms much like this one, protected by loyalists to my mother and King Reginald III. But they usually just mistreated me, and that's all I'll ever say about it. So as soon as I became thirteen, I escaped and never looked back. But I did get this cool trench coat."

Rodolfo's face sinks in empathy, his unease seemingly subsiding after Hero's story.

"But why, Hero? Isn't it dangerous out there?" Toaster asks. "Some say the warlords keep us safe."

"Being safe without freedom is worse than dying. And I know—there were times I lost my freedom," Hero replies. She turns back to Rodolfo, whom she knows really needs to hear this story. "One of the loyalists who hid me in his own horse manure room—"

"What a coincidence!" Toaster interrupts. "Perhaps it is a sign. A portent! You *were* destined!"

"I would have said I don't believe in destiny—just misery. But this talisman and my dream, together, and the things I can do now . . . " Hero says, trailing off as she ponders her new powers.

She takes out the talisman and holds it in her hand, rubbing its worn picture of the great wizard, Abraham Lincoln, and its magical words with her dirty fingers. His beard still feels comforting to her.

She looks back at Rodolfo. Maybe it was the thought of destiny; maybe it was Toaster seemingly believing she was a hero, but Hero starts to see the older brother in a different light. His blond, wispy hair. His blue eyes, which lost some— just some—of that mistrust once they started really talking in this manure cellar. "Well, I also know Mother traveled the desolate roads on her own, searching for the powers of the ancients to defeat Fant. And she gave me the dream about Murrayskindacoolish. Perhaps she left this talisman for me."

"The ancients?" Rodolfo asks.

"A powerful civilization before ours. Before warlords. Before kingdoms. Before anything we know or knew. Some say even before time," Hero explains. That's really all she knows. She has only that, and her hope that finding Mother's secrets will explain it.

"Wow, I didn't know there was anything before us," Rodolfo says.

"It makes sense, brother. Life could not have always been this terrible," Toaster tells him.

"Toaster is right," Hero says, as she smiles at the boy. "And I just know that my mother found their secrets. But before she could explain, the dragons from Fant came. They must have followed her home, where her body was found." Hero looks down at the ground. The ground has been her only friend for so long.

"We'll help you find the secrets! Maybe even the ancients," Toaster offers.

"What?" Hero asks.

"Why else would you travel the desolate roads? Risking your life for what? To find her secrets! To save your kingdom!" Toaster continues. "We'll help! And then you can help us."

"Toaster!" Rodolfo exclaims. "There's no way!"

"But what else can we do, brother?" Toaster replies. "We can't stay here. And if we help her—"

"No, no way," Hero cuts in. "I travel alone. I don't need your help."

"See? She doesn't even want our help," Rodolfo argues. "And we can just hide out here. I'm sure in a few months, SkeLord will forget all about us. Maybe I can build a new saloon."

Toaster looks up at his brother. "You want to spend months in an old manure cellar instead of traveling with a bea—"

Hero coughs, distracting the brothers.

"—beacon of freedom?" Toaster finishes.

"Ever since our parents died," Rodolfo starts, as Toaster looks down at the floor just like Hero did, "I've been in charge of your safety. I'm not going to let some stray girl—"

Knock, knock.

They all freeze. But the loud knocking continues.

Knock, knock . . . Knock!

"Uh . . . ," Hero says. "Someone's at the broken door."

Chapter 5

Intermission One

So, hey, how's it going so far?

H. What?

You know, how is everything going?

H. What?

I'm curious how you are enjoying this all so far. The story. The writing.

H. The weaving? Holy buckets, I feel like I'm at a saloon with one of those bartenders who wants to *talk*. You're lucky I can't just punch you. Is this, like, one of your internet dates? You ask them stupid questions?

What? No! That's weird. You called me Father. And we don't even live on the same physical plane of existence. You're kind of just in my head.

H. *"Just in my head"?* I've known vile warlords with better pickup lines.

That's not what I meant! You're literally just my imagination.

H. Hey! I'm in reality and you're just . . . Author. An incompetent god!

That's not really how I'd describe myself. Didn't you hear Barnaby? I might get into the cordless phone market! My Leaf Blowerz Electric Cordless TX6000 technical manual almost won an award.

H. I can believe that.

See?

H. I can believe that you didn't win an award. Have you read your weaving?

Well, actually, that's really what I wanted to ask you. I think I'm getting better than the first chapter, right? Is it exciting?

H. What's a chapter?

Uh, kind of like a chapter in your life?

H. Look, I'm stuck in an old manure cellar with two supremely annoying boys. And something scary is knocking on the door, but it's so stupid. Doesn't it see that the door is broken?

Oh, come on. It's not like it's a master carpenter at the door. And the boys aren't that annoying.

H. Um, yes, they are. Well, maybe not so much the young one anymore. But the older one. What a weakling crybaby. *Wah, wah, wah, we almost died. Wah, wah, wah, you didn't listen to me.* He wouldn't last two seconds on the desolate roads.

Oh well, maybe you're right. He is kind of whiny.

H. And you stopped without us knowing who is knocking.

I know! That's cool, right? It's called a cliffhanger. It makes readers want to turn the page.

H. Wait, Cliff is at the door? Is he a carpenter? Are we in peril? I need to know. Should I ready Morny?

Who's Morny?

H. Are you really the Author? It's my morning star!

Wow, I don't remember.

H. Just tell me! Do I need Morny?

Wouldn't that be an unfair advantage? I don't think I should tell you.

H. Oh, come on!

I'm serious. That would be cheating.

H. I thinked we were a meeting of the heads.

Uh, meeting of the minds. It's different. And that was before you got this talisman which I still don't fully understand. So, with all your new powers, the last thing I should do is help the main character in my story cheat! Who knows what harm that could cause? I'm already losing my mind.

H. Murray! What harm—

I actually have something important I need to tell you.

H. Oh no, are you going to tell me you love me again? Even if it's not internet dating, it's still disgusting. So just stop. Gag! Vomit!

What? No! And that was kind of hurtful. You called me your father before. Fathers love their daughters.

H. I said, "kind of." *Kind of!*

Well, it's still hurtful. You know, I've had a rough go of it lately. I never told you, but—

H. So, what's this thing you need to tell me?

Oh, uh, I guess we're not sharing then. Well, I need to go away for the weekend.

H. On a quest? Is *your* heaven-world in peril too? The ma . . . saj . . . jets were just a tool of an evil daemon? I thinked it before but didn't say anything—they sounded too good to be true. It all makes sense now. Did they hide serpents in them? I know exactly twenty-eight ways to kill an evil serpent.

Oh God. I'm going to have a hard time in the shower from now on. But, no, it's my Aunt Cordelia.

H. Oh no, was she swallowed by a dragon? Or eaten by zorcs? Or perhaps her rainwater showerhead was really an evil basilisk?

No, no. It's her wedding. It's a destination wedding. In the Bahamas.

H. Who is the lucky warlord?

What? It's not a warlord. It's Simon.

H. In my world, only warlords, kings, and queens take wives. Maybe a rich merchant here or there.

Yeah, sorry about that. My fault, I guess. But it's not like that here in hea . . . in my world. Actually, it's Aunt Cordelia's third husband.

H. *Third* husband? How did she ever get *three* husbands? She must be a queen! A godqueen! A queen of the gods! Can she weave me a lover too? Does she know how to weave?

No, no. Well, yes on the weaving, probably. But her first two husbands died in horrible staircase accidents. Actually, now that I say that out loud, it sounds kind of suspicious.

H. Ah, her husbands were not able to grant her an heir, so she dispatched them. It is very common. Simon better watch out. I hope for his sake he is as spry and agile in the bed as he is on the stairs.

No, no, she doesn't want an heir. She had one son, but he's in prison for mail fraud. And, actually, Simon is eighty years old, rich, and has no family. And now that I say all that out loud, I think my Aunt Cordelia may be a serial killer. Oh, God.

H. She wouldn't be the first queen to murder all her impotent husbands. I hear that the Queen of Fant similarly dispatched many a husband, but that was just for pleasure. So why are you telling me all this?

Well, because I won't be able to write the story for a while. I was in quite a groove with the whole escape from SkeLord to a manure cellar thing. And the magical talisman . . . though it kind of scares me now.

H. So? You can weave while you are in the . . . Bahamoes?

I can't write all weekend. Three days. You see, I use a classic typewriter. And paper.

H. What is a typewriter?

A mechanical device. It's large, and I can't take it on the airplane.

H. These words make no sense. Did the Bahamoes outlaw writing, like Xander the Eyeless?

No, it's just . . . my writing device would break on the airplane. Think of it as a spindle. I don't want to take my spindle on the airplane.

H. Airplane?

A mechanical device that flies in the sky.

H. A mechanical dragon? You have mechanical dragons! The heaven-world is more dangerous than I thinked. Don't go anywhere near those things, Murray! You'll die, and I'll never save my kingdom.

Well, these dragons are friendly. They even serve drinks.

H. Ah, more like the friendly dragons from the Alliance of Humor the Great. So, you cannot take your weaving spindle on the friendly mechanical saloon dragon because it would break?

Something like that.

H. And so, what do I do while you are gone? Sit here in the manure cellar waiting for you to get back from your royal wedding in the Bahamoes?

Bahamas.

H. Bahamass?

Uh. Bahamoes.

H. Right.

I'm not entirely sure. I don't know how it will affect time in your plane of existence.

H. What do you mean you're not sure? You're the Author!

When I stop writ—er, weaving, I don't know if time will just stop for you.

H. You have never stopped weaving before?

When I had the idea before, like you said, you were still alone on the desolate roads. You wouldn't have noticed. And then I got in a groove. I haven't stopped writing since I got home from Barnaby's office. Not even for the bathroom.

H. And when we have these little conversations?

You're right. I'm technically not writing at that moment, though my hands are still on the typewriter, er, spindle. But the other characters are starting to

notice, right? Or I'm making them notice. I can't really tell. But I was still at my typewriter then. Now I'll be away. I really don't know what will happen to you. Does time just stop for you? I don't know. I'm worried for you. I'm just giving you a warning.

H. So, what do we do? We need to find out what will happen. You owe me, Murray! Will I be stuck in the manure cellar with these jackasses for three whole days while you're off at a magnificent royal god wedding in the Bahamoes?

Um, not exactly how I would describe it. But I just don't know.

H. Try it. For a little bit at least. I need to know! Stop the writing thing for a moment.

All right. Actually, it will be a good time to go to the bathroom.

. . .

Okay . . . So, what happened?

H. Murray!

Is it bad? That sounds bad.

H. We were just in the cellar, stuck doing nothing. I was on the floor. I don't know why—I don't remember getting there. Rodolfo and Toaster were looking over my body. I think I might have died. They were not frozen; neither was I.

Everyone was breathing. But they were just stuck. Doing what they were doing. But not frozen. Me too! I cannot explain it. There are no words. It is as if we were stuck between life and death. I never realized it before on the desolate roads. I always thinked I was just resting or sleeping with my eyes open. Like horses. It seemed so natural— the smart thing to do, even. But now . . . seeing them also . . . now I know. You cannot go! Don't ever leave me like that again, Father!

But I have to.

H. Don't leave me, Murray! Don't you dare leave me. I can't be stuck like that. Now that I know what it is, it is terrifying. Like the daemons have stolen my body. You should never have told me! I would have been fine if you didn't tell me. You cannot go!

But I must. I promised Aunt Cordelia. I'll be back, I promise. I won't let you down. It's not really daemons, I promise. It's just a wedding. Oh, maybe they'll have those little hot dogs.

H. Aunt Cordelia the serial killer also murders tiny dogs? See, it is unsafe for such a weak man as yourself to be around this evil god queen of death.

I really have no choice.

H. Don't leave me! I hate you, Murray! I will haunt your dreams forever! Unless Aunt Cordelia gets to you first! For three whole days, I will stalk you until it's the right moment and—

Actually, you gave me an idea.

H. You have an idea?

I can't promise anything, and it'll be a bit awkward for the plot, but I think it should work.

H. Anything will be better than being frozen between life and death. What is it? Will you move the wedding to your own meadow in heaven so you may weave the entire time?

In my fifth-floor walk-up studio apartment? Simon can't climb five floors. He shouldn't be anywhere near stairs, actually. Listen, my rideshare is coming soon. So, I need to do the idea now. I haven't even packed yet.

H. Okay, just do it. Do *something*, Murray!

All right. Here goes. See you in three days.

And the knocking continued for three long days.

Chapter 6

Everyone Back to Your Seats,
the Show's About to Start

Hero, are you there? I'm back! Did it work?

H. Oh my gods! Murray! Make the knocking stop! Quick!

And the knocking stops after three long days.

"Is it over?" Rodolfo asks from a fetal position on the floor.

Before anyone can answer, the beautifully happy sounds of a children's choir streams through the broken front door of the fermenting manure storeroom which sits below the Josiah's Manure Import-Export storefront.

"Oh, my gods. Could it be any more beautiful?" Hero screams in joy.

H. There is no way I would say that, Murray! This is torture! Worse than the knocking. I'd rather you put the knocking back.

But it is my gift to you after being away so long. Surely you could use a different sonic experience.

H. And this is my gift to you!

Hero finally opens the front door by picking it up from the doorframe and throwing it to the side. It falls to the ground.

Ten children with shaved heads and dressed in long, brown religious robes smile. Believing they are being greeted, they start to sing.

Hero, hissing like a maniac, takes out her morning star. She pulls it back, ready to strike—

Stop! Stop overpowering me. You can't murder a whole children's choir!

H. Try and stop me!

Hero swings at one child, but, as if by magic, the children's choir vanishes.

H. Joy! Joy! Sweet joy! The horrible noises have stopped! That's all I really wanted. You have no idea how horrible it's been.

I thought the music was a gift.

H. After three days of constant, loud knocking? The music was nothing but another otherworldly torture. You don't know what we've been through! Oh, the knocking! That horrible loud knocking.

You could have just opened the door.

H. You don't understand. We couldn't! We tried. It wouldn't open. Whoever was on the other side wouldn't even talk to us. Just *knock, knock, knock.* Loudly! And we had no food or water. For three whole days! And no bathroom! I held it for three days, Murray! Technically, we should have died, but we didn't. How? Why did you do that to me? You should have just killed me!

Hero, I'm so sorry. I didn't know how distressing it was; it seemed like a good idea at the time. But I can make it up to you now. You all could use some medical help. I know just the team.

Through the open doorway, into the cellar walk three uniformed paramedics. "Ma'am, we're here to help!" one of the paramedics announces.

"Who the hell are you?" Hero asks the men.

"We're stars from the hit television series, *Paramedics Emergency Medical Care: Bangor*, and we're here to help," says one of the men, standing behind the other two. He has a large muscular physique, much like a warlord, and his full and appealingly angular hair is in two colors.

How can he get the tips of his hair to turn blond? Hero wonders. If she was not sure these men were from Murray, who is the Author, God of gods, and the weaver of all things, she would think they were capable of dark, evil magic.

H. Murray, what in the Lands is a tele . . . viz . . . zeres?

Oh, it's like . . . a play? Traveling actors? A theater troupe?

H. You think I had time for such things while in hiding from Xander? Your heaven-world is weak if you spend time on zeres.

I watched it on the plane.

The other two men stoically nod, their arms crossed in front of them. The one with the two-toned hair announces, "In fact, I'm the character who always gets the girl at the end of each episode in our lives. So do you want to grab a drink later?" Hero seethes that this man with strange hair just believes he's going to *get* her. Like she's something to *get*. Especially for a weak play-man—even with his gorgeous muscles. "I saw a nice saloon—"

With a battle cry that would scare the gods, Hero runs at the paramedics with her morning star. Before Author can vanish them, on her way to get the one with the two-toned hair, she intentionally strikes the closest one on the back of the head with her morning star's back swing. He goes down in a bloody rumpled mess on the floor. "That was easy," Hero says as the other two paramedics, including the one with the two-toned hair, disappear. But they are left with the bloodied, dying body of the third paramedic. *Serves him right. He probably wanted to get me too.* She spits on his corpse.

H. Why'd you take them away? I could have vanquished them, too!

You weren't supposed to do that! They were here to help. I'm leaving the corpse in the hopes you learn from your mistakes. And now I have to change the story even more because you killed a paramedic!

H. I don't even know what a para . . . di—

They're healers! They could have healed you. [Grumbles]

"But Hero, the other two magically disappeared. After magically appearing," Rodolfo mutters. "How in the Lands is that possible? And why did you have to kill one of them?" Having spent the last three days in a fetal position on the floor, and seeing Hero murder someone in cold blood, the incidents of the last three days terrify him. He stands, trying to steady himself.

"Surely they are from this Queendom of Fant you spoke of, gifted with evil magic," Toaster says, quicker to his feet, and now trying to hold his brother steady. Although Toaster cried the whole three days, his optimistic mood quickly returns. "She did the right thing, brother."

"They weren't," Hero answers, simply.

"See, Toaster? She is dangerous!" Rodolfo protests.

"Rodolfo," Hero explains. "They weren't even real people."

"Don't you feel the slightest bit of remorse?" Rodolfo asks, almost begging.

"For fake people?" Hero scoffs.

"But how do you know?" Rodolfo asks. "So SkeLord has found our location and sent those evil ghouls to kill us?"

"He didn't. I just know," Hero replies.

"But how?" Rodolfo pleads. "I think you should at least feel a tiny bit bad."

"I feel bad the others disappeared before I got to them, too," Hero answers dismissively.

"This says *Bangor*," Toaster interjects, as he bends over the rumpled body, looking at the paramedic's uniform.

"Is that a kingdom, Hero?" Rodolfo asks. "The Kingdom of Bangor? Surely you must know it from all your travels. Are they evil like Fant? Is that why you killed them?" He stands in front of Toaster.

Hero takes a deep breath. "The Kingdom of Bangor is a pleasant, friendly kingdom full of outdoor activities such as fishing, hiking ..."

H. Murray, I think your zeres is stupid. I wouldn't say any of that.

It was a test. To see if the talisman is still working.

"But what were they doing here?" Toaster asks. "This makes no sense. Is the Kingdom of Bangor in league with Chester? Or Fant?"

"Yeah, why would you kill someone in cold blood?" Rodolfo insists. "Are we even safe with you? I have to think about my little brother's safety, you know."

"Okay, okay," Hero relents. "It's time for the truth."

Uh-oh.

Chapter 7

Lies, Lies, and More Lies

Hero, no! You can't tell them about me!

H. Why not, Murray? How can the others even know I'm talking to you? We're clearly overpowering you, anyway.

I was hoping the weird talisman thing was wearing off.

H. Clearly not. And if we're going to save my Kingdom of Dystpopia and their town of . . . of . . .

Don't you remember? It doesn't have a name.

H. Whatever. Their stupid little town. And even if the talisman wears off, we're all going to have to work together to save my kingdom and now their town. We have good ideas. You *have* to trust me to take over because this world you've created is so . . . so . . . It has so many things in it! And it's weaved *really* well. There are so many . . . things in it that you're going to need us on the inside to help give you ideas. You *need* us!

You really think it's a beautifully complex and detailed world? Truly?

H. Sure, Murray. Just like one of your technical manuals. Like about that leaf woaster. You have a true gift. I can see why Barnaby didn't let you weave YA. Because he would lose you. It wasn't because you're a bad weaver or anything. It's because he knew the other gods would love your story scroll! Then there would be a heaven-world civil war over your weaving skills.

Really? In my heart of hearts, I knew it! I just didn't want to say it out loud. I didn't want to believe it. To think Felicia was right, and I lost her.

But you're right! And you're on the inside, so you would know. Unless I shouldn't trust my own story character, but that would be crazy. Even crazier than talking to your own character. Right?

H. Sure?

And you're probably right about telling Rodolfo and Toaster. Go, tell them. And together, we'll save your Kingdom of Dystopia!

H. Dystpopia!

Oh, right. The typo. Dystpopia! And their town of . . .

H. Town with no name!

Town with no name!

Chapter 8

The Bermuda Love Triangle

"They were sent by the Author. His name is also Murray. He thinked they were healers who could help us," Hero explains.

"Author?" Rodolfo asks. "Is he a powerful wizard? Like Abraham Lincoln?"

"No, not like that. Even more powerful," Hero replies. *Who in this world could be more powerful than Murray, the weaver?*

"Since I met you, I feel as if my life has been turned upside down. I was but a simple bartender—"

"Who ran an underground secret society to one day overthrow your warlord," Hero cuts off his whiny monologue. *Will this guy ever shut up?* "Regardless, Author is not a wizard. His real name is Murray. And he's like a god, really a God of gods, the weaver of all things. And he's like . . .

kind of a jackass but also kind of my father. I can talk to him, but I don't love him. I mean, I say I don't love him, but I really do. But I don't really. But I really do love him. But now I hate his guts. But I love him—"

H. Murray! Stop! You said I could tell them.

But you keep insulting me. Stop overpowering me!

H. I thinked we agreed. You *need* us!

You may have the talisman, but I'm still the writer! It's one thing to tell me you don't love me. But to tell everyone? To embarrass the weaver in his own story? It's like the Murraystinksish thing all over again.

H. Why do you care what they think? You gods care what us in the Lands think? Aren't you weaving for the other gods? Why are you even weaving this, anyway?

I told you. To deliver a beautiful baby—

H. But why? Babies are gross and annoying.

For people in my world to read.

H. Yes, the other gods who can learn from your ancient scroll of wisdom. To learn from our troubles and our righteous quest so that such misery may never happen in your heaven-world.

No, they read. Like, for fun.

H. Fun?

Yes, fun.

H. Fun? What is fun?

Uh, I didn't expect that. You know, people like a little fun in their lives.

H. My life has been endless misery. I survive only for my quest.

Well, it's different here. We can have fun. Some people in the Lands have fun, don't they? You know, like with those musical and theater troupes. Entertainment. Entertainment is fun. Have you ever seen a juggler? Or court jester?

H. Holy buckets! Gods in your world are going to read about the pain and misery in my world for *fun*? That's what this is all for? You think we're all court jesters?

Yes! Well, clearly, you're not a court jester. But it's entertainment like that. Fun! And they might even pay for the books. I might make money.

H. My entire family was killed by an evil queen . . . for *fun*? For *money*?

I sense you're getting upset.

H. *Upset* is not the word for it! I thinked you were writing to save my kingdom!

And to get people to buy the book and have fun.

H. For . . . *fun?* #%&!%&#!%&&#%!&%!!!!!!!!!!!!

"Hero!" Rodolfo exclaims while snapping his fingers. "We're worried about you. You're doing that thing again, and your words have been nonsense. Perhaps the Author could send some more healers. Or barbers even."

Suddenly, the healer with the two-toned black and blond hair, or paramedic, as he calls himself, materializes in front of the trio and immediately turns to Hero. "I'm back to heal your soul, babe."

"Oh, my gods," Hero exclaims to the sky. "Enough with the babies, Murray!"

"My name's not Murray, babe," the muscular paramedic says.

"If you call me *babe* one more time," Hero threatens, and in an instant there is a dagger in her hand.

"All right, all right. Sheesh," the paramedic says. "You're quick with that thing." Then he looks at the floor. "Oh no! You killed Rocco!"

"And I'll kill you if you don't shut up," Hero says.

"I'm not sure this will be one the better episodes in my life," the paramedic declares. "The damsel in distress doesn't usually want to kill everyone. I hate going off script. You should welcome me. I can teach you how to have fun."

"Do you know why I am okay killing you?" Hero asks him. "Because you're not real. Rocco was not real. Murray, the Author, made you two up!"

"Wowzers, I know that already, Hero," the paramedic says. "And my name is Graham. Murray sent me to be your enemy to lover. He thinks you need some companionship . . ."—he looks at Rodolfo and Toaster who stare at him wide-eyed—"with someone who knows fun . . . and who has bathed."

"Hey, I used the family sponge but a fortnight ago," Rodolfo replies defensively.

Graham looks at him, confused, but turns back to Hero. "Let's just start at the lover part. It might calm you down some." He throws his head back gently yet seductively.

Unfortunately for Graham, someone telling Hero to calm down makes her even angrier—so much so that she is behind him as quickly as can be, with a knife to his throat.

"See?" Graham says through strained vocal cords. "Enemies."

"Enemy to lover?" Rodolfo asks. "Author? This magic man again? I have no idea what is going on, Hero. The three days of knocking was preferable to these ghouls!"

"Hero, please, no!" Toaster adds. "There are better ways. Author clearly wants Graham to help us with something. And you disappoint me so when you murder in cold blood." He gives Hero the cutest puppy-dog eyes he can muster.

Even Rodolfo can't help but say, "Aw."

Please don't kill Graham. I can't kill off a character from a different series. Oh man, I shouldn't have added him.

H. You're right!

I thought I could just revise away any similarities later. You know, change *Bangor* to *Bangoor*. But now with all this automatic writing, I don't know. It won't let me. Please don't kill him.

H. Not my problem, Weaver. I don't even know what automating writing is.

Uh, that's not . . . it's just like my fingers are weaving on the spindle on their own. Like a ghost—

H. There are no such things as ghosts. You *are* crazy.

But sand-wolves and zombies? Ghouls?

H. Of course. You don't know anything about the Lands.

Okay, it's just like when you take over, it's like a ghost—

H. There are no ghosts!

Right, sorry. I meant a ghoul or some sort of wizard is taking over my body and weaving through me.

H. Still not my problem. And if the wizard lets me kill Graham, fine with me.

But think of Toaster! Look at his eyes—he clearly doesn't want you to. Can't you see it in his eyes?

So Hero looks at Toaster. *What the hell is wrong with his eyes? It looks like he was stung by a radioactive sqorpion.* But she doesn't want to disappoint Toaster, the one person in the Lands who ever believed in her. Without taking the knife off Graham's throat, she says, "I'm just so tired of being stuck in a manure store. Again! Three days, Toaster. *Three days!* And then Murray the Author goes and sends some man even more misogymnast than Rodolfo!"

Misogynist.

H. That's what I said.

Uh, okay? But if you just got to know him—

"How would you like to die, misogymnast!" Hero raves.

"Hero, don't let this Murray turn you into something you are not. Rise above him," Toaster says.

Suddenly, her eyes open wide. "Toaster, what did you just say?"

"I said, don't let this Murray turn you into something you are not. Rise above him. And I meant it."

"Listen up, Toaster and Rodolfo," Hero orders, still behind Graham, the television paramedic. "You just gave me an idea, but we don't have a lot of time. We're gonna get out of here. Like I said, Murray is the Author. He's like the God of the gods. He is weaving this story of our dismal lives just for *fun!* Him and his heaven-friends find us amusing—that's all! We're living what he's weaving as if we're inside his story scroll. He built this world. He decides who lives and dies, what happens to us, even what we say. And I'm sure you hate this life and the Lands just like me. But Toaster, you just said something he wouldn't have let you say."

Hero, I would have. I wrote it.

H. No, you wouldn't have. I think Toaster, and maybe Rodolfo, have power over you now too.

Sure, that's what we agreed to, right? I said they could have some say in the story. Help me out. You just forgot.

H. You said *me*, not them. And you still don't like it when I overpower you. But now Toaster is, too.

Oh no.

H. Oh yes.

Please, don't! This isn't supposed to happen. It's that damn talisman! What's happening to me?

"We have power over him, Toaster!" Hero cheers. "It's the talisman! It is so powerful that we can all make our own choices now. Maybe even Rodolfo, too."

"What about me?" Graham asks accusingly. "We should listen to Murray. Murray knows all. Murray's the best. And I'm supposed to get the girl. You're kind of dirty-looking, greasy hair and all that, and body odor to the extreme, but I don't mind. Graham loves all women. So, you're gonna be mine." It's unclear to the trio if Graham really knows what's going on, but it's obvious to Hero that Murray is still controlling him. *The talisman isn't working on ghouls? Or people not from the Lands? Is that it?*

"I don't like this guy," Rodolfo says. "But you don't have to kill him. We're not like that. There's been enough killing in . . . this town. Let's just leave him here. Though it's too bad you never got to read all these books and artifacts we have. I know you don't know Murrayskindacoolish that well, but perhaps there were some clues you could have found in them."

"It's still a good idea, brother," Toaster says happily. "We can just leave."

Please, Hero! Please! Talk to me! Don't leave! We can work this out.

"Yes, it's a good idea," Hero agrees, still behind Graham with a knife to his throat. "But we do need Graham to keep Murray in line. Like a hostage. He can't let him die." Hero laughs derisively at Murray's predicament. "Looks like we're all leaving together."

"But how, Hero?" Rodolfo asks. "Don't we have to wait until nightfall, like you said? The Death Soldiers will be out looking for us."

"I have an idea," Hero replies. "Let's see how far this control goes."

Knock, knock, knock.

"No! Not again!" Rodolfo screams. Suddenly, he's on the floor, holding his ears.

"What a loser," Graham says. The knife in Hero's left hand tightens against his throat.

"Shut up, Graham," Hero orders. "Only I'm allowed to insult Rodolfo."

Knock, knock, knock.

"Toaster, get the door," Hero orders.

"I would, Hero, but there is no door, remember?"

"Just go and see who's there. It's part of my plan."

Rodolfo and Toaster walk cautiously toward the door and a large, rotund, and balding sixty-year-old merchant dressed in his finest garb—a long, golden coat with a red money purse around his waist—is now visible.

"Hi ho, friends!" the rotund man says. "My name is Barnaby, and I am so smart and rich. Let me tell you about my friend Murray. He is so dimwitted. Dumb. And a terrible weaver."

Hero, please! How did you even get him to do that? You can control his words, too? Just stop! I'm sorry! This is very hurtful. Damn that talisman! Why did I even create it?

H. It's easy. He doesn't *really* think that highly of you—you know that. It didn't take that much effort to control him. I can hardly believe I created my own ghoul. This day just got better. I might even be having this *fun* you speak of.

"That is very hurtful, Barnaby," Graham says. "Murray is my father, the father of all of us, and you are all going to be in a lot of trouble. Especially you, Toaster and Rodolfo! Traitors, all of you! You don't appreciate the life weaved into you by the Mur-man!"

"I believe we should tie this fool up," Barnaby says. "I brought some supplies." He takes out of his little money pouch of several strong vines and a large black handkerchief, displaying all the pizzazz of part-time children's birthday party magician.

With Rodolfo and Toaster's help, they bind Graham's hands and legs and tie the handkerchief around his head and in his mouth, preventing Graham's ability to speak clearly.

"I'll still date you, Hero," Graham says through the handkerchief. But, thankfully, no one could hear what he said because it sounded like, "Ah fill blate oo."

"Good, now that that's taken care of," Barnaby says, "I have come to tell you that I was given permission from SkeLord for a great but dangerous voyage. As a rich merchant, I am to gather all the town's manure and sell it to other towns. I have a great carriage and wagon outside into which we need to load up all this here manure"—he waves his hand at all the books against the walls—"and then we can get on our way. Boy, am I glad there is a manure import-export business here."

"All this manure where?" Rodolfo asks Barnaby, sounding confused.

"Yes, the manure you have along the walls. I don't know how you keep such large stacks of manure smelling so fresh. But you three are clearly the professionals in this business," Barnaby says. "Though I knew enough to bring shovels. I'll go get them." He leaves the cellar to get his shovels.

"Hero, did you do this?" Toaster asks her when they are alone. "You made him think there is manure here?"

"Yes, Toaster," she replies. "We needed a way out that would be harder for Murray to stop us. Like Graham, he can't let Barnaby get killed in his own story. In the heaven-world, Barnaby is a ruler of gods!"

Argh, you!

"You are controlling a ruler of gods?" Rodolfo asks. "And you just happened into my bar?" He looks doubtful.

"And your little brother just happened to hand me my mother's magical talisman she left here for me and told me about in a dream? I know now that it is a talisman that can control the gods—and maybe even Fant! I believe you also want to defeat Chester?"

"I just knew you could help us!" Toaster cheers, hands impulsively in the air.

"But," Hero continues proudly, "Barnaby and the rest of the characters in this story scroll think this is all manure, so we need to use his shovels. They can't know these are books and priceless artifcats."

"*Artifacts*," Rodolfo corrects her.

"Yeah, artifcats. That's what I said."

"Sure, yeah," Rodolfo replies, rolling his eyes.

"Don't do that! You think I'm dumb!" Hero snarls.

"Brother," Toaster says, tugging on Rodolfo's arm.

"What? She called them cats." Rodolfo chuckles to himself.

"You're a misogymnast too!" Hero shouts at him. "And I know that's really you because you're near my talisman. You know what I do to—"

"Hero, please, just continue," Toaster begs. "Ignore him."

"Fine, Toaster," she says, giving a death glare to Rodolfo. "As I was saying, they can't know about them because I can't predict how they'll react. Murray says some ghoul or wizard in heaven-world takes over his weaving when we take control."

"This sounds really dangerous," Rodolfo muses.

"I know!" Hero beams. "Isn't it *fun*?"

"Isn't that what Murray said?" Toaster asks.

He's right!

"See!" Hero continues. "Jackass Murray can try and have them stop us. When Barnaby gets back, let's gather up all this manure and get it into his wagon, quick. This is the only way to get out of this town unseen with all your artifcats. We don't have enough control over the story to deal with all the Death Soldiers right now, let alone Fant. Once we're free, we can study the artifcats. So, we're going on a manure sales trip!"

This time Rodolfo ignores Hero's error. "I guess that makes sense?" He scratches his head.

"What else do we have to lose, brother?" Toaster asks.

"Just our lives," Rodolfo replies. "She's taken pretty much everything else from me. All right, let's go offend some gods. Yay." He throws his hands up in a sarcastic celebration.

The foursome, leaving Graham, the paramedic, tied up on the floor, gather up all the books and objects from the town's past using Barnaby's shovels and load them into the wagon waiting outside. Then Barnaby and Toaster leave the cellar to bring the shovels back to the wagon.

While Rodolfo and Hero are alone, except for Graham, who is still tied up on the floor, Rodolfo asks her, "Does Barnaby *really* think these are manure? At one point, a book fell off the shovel. I forgot and picked it up with my hand. Barnaby went berserk, yelling how disgusting I was to touch the manure with my hands. But then I realized the book had given me a parchment cut, so I went to suck my finger. The man completely lost it and ran out of the room calling me *unclean!*"

"Yes, Rodolfo," Hero answers. "He sees them as manure. To him, you were sticking your fingers in manure and licking them."

"Oh, dear gods. I would never do such a thing. I have a reputation to uphold as a cleanly saloon entrepreneur with the utmost hygienic standards. We even spit-shine the mugs after every use." Then Rodolfo leans in close and whispers, "And boil the no-cost camel urine before we add it to the expensive mead." He grins widely.

Matching his grin, Hero replies, "You . . . you're not as prissy as I thinked."

"Uh, thanks?" Rodolfo asks, eyebrow upturned.

"Well, I made it that we're the only ones who can see these are really books," Hero explains. "And once we're out of this town, we'll have time to try and read them."

"After thinking about it, you actually have a good plan, you know," Rodolfo says. "To think we may save this town . . ."

Hero recoils, as she cannot remember anyone complimenting her before. Well, except for Toaster. She was more used to fighting with men, as most of her caretakers in her first thirteen years called her things like *annoying* and *waste of breath* when they weren't hitting her, or worse. Unsure what to say, she says nothing.

"Won't Barnaby call us all unclean when he sees us holding the manure in our hands?" Rodolfo asks, breaking the awkward silence.

"Don't worry, I'll take care of Barnaby once we're out of here," Hero replies ominously, happier to discuss violence.

"You know, you truly have magical powers now, Hero," Rodolfo pontificates. "Perhaps even beyond those of the great wizard, Abraham Lincoln. But you really are not thinking clearly. I don't believe you would really murder a man in cold blood, let alone a ruler of the gods. Shouldn't you try and make up with this Murray? You say he's the God

of gods, the weaver of all things. Surely, he wants what's best for you. Why else weave a story?"

Hero pinches Rodolfo on the arm.

"Ow!" Rodolfo exclaims. "Holy sandstorms. What did you do that for?"

"I wanted to see if it was Murray weaving you," Hero replies.

"And how does that prove anything?" Rodolfo challenges her while rubbing his arm.

"I don't really know, but I'd know," Hero replies.

"That doesn't even make any sense!" Rodolfo argues.

Hero sighs. "Look, I told you—Murray's just weaving this story for fun."

"Are you sure?"

"Believe me. And did you see that healer?"

"Oh, right, you did murder that one," Rodolfo says, scratching his head and glancing at the corpse, which is surprisingly still there *not* teaching Hero a lesson.

"No, not him. *Graham,*" Hero replies, seething on the last word. "No way will I make up with Murray. And don't you tell me what to do! No man tells me what to do. So, I'm gonna take care of Barnaby once we're out of here, and you're not going to stop me." She points a finger at him.

Hero, just listen to Rodolfo! Barnaby, the real Barnaby, will get mad at me if you persist in maligning his character. And even worse, if he's murdered in my book, I could lose my job. The cordless phone market, even.

H. I haven't done anything yet, Murray!

Ah, you are talking to me, at least. Listen, I'll never be able to sell any books if he finds out there is a character in his image and—

H. Holy buckets, I haven't done anything yet!

Hero, just listen to me!

H. I haven't done anything yet, Murray. I told you.

You said you would take care of him. You're going to kill him. I've been trying to revise my automatic writing, but the ghoul or whatever won't let me. Barnaby could ruin my career. Then no one will read my book. Ever!

H. You mean no one will read about my horrible life. For *fun!*

But you don't understand. I should have been clearer. By reading about your life—yes, it's fun, but people are also learning from it. About life, about how you live, all the great things you endured and how you dealt with it. How you stick up for yourself, your independence of thought, mind, and body. About your honor and selflessness, risking everything to make life better for your kingdom. You are teaching my world to better itself, even if it doesn't know it.

H. I am?

Yes! My world needs to learn from you. That's the power of weaving.

H. Heaven-world can learn from me?

Yes! And can you blame them for wanting to have fun? Wouldn't you like to have fun sometimes? Isn't that what you're fighting for?

H. I guess. It was fun beating up Graham.

So, please. Just trust me to write you a beautiful story. One that will honor you. Stop overpowering me. Stop telling everyone to overpower me. Please trust me. I won't let you down.

H. We'll see. I promise you no promises.

What?

H. I'll let you control again, but I'm not promising you anything. Argh, now who's the dimwit!

"What's she doing?" Barnaby asks, as he and Toaster enter the cellar again. Now they all have the task of trying to carry the large, muscular, and impressively-haired Graham to the wagon.

"She's doing that thing again," Rodolfo says. "It's what happens when she's talking—"

Toaster elbows Rodolfo and gives him an evil eye. Rodolfo bends over slightly, clutching his stomach, and quiets. Toaster finishes for Rodolfo, "She is dimwitted, sir. It might be a canker."

"Oh, uh, that's too bad. I really thought Graham and her had a good thing going. I hope they make use of whatever time they have left together," Barnaby replies like she's not there. "'Cause that's what you do for love."

"Love?" Rodolfo blurts out in shock. "Could it be?"

Also surprised, Toaster adds, "But were you not the one who helped us tie him—"

H. Holy buckets, Murray! Love? Stop controlling my ghoul if you're going to do that! And I want to kill Graham. It's not love! And what's with the two colors in his hair?

It's called frosted tips. It's cool in my world.

H. Why would he want a cold head?

Oh, I meant it's fashionable.

H. Your fantasy world is the one that should be in a story scroll. He looks like a court jester!

Jester? He's a lover! You said you wanted a lover. And what's wrong with a jester? He's probably loads of fun. All the girls love him. I thought he was the ideal—

H. Oh gods! Him? He was serious? I'm not going to let you take back control of anything in the story if you make him my lover. Never, ever, ever!

Who would you rather have? Rodolfo?

H. Yes! Anyone!

Oh, I didn't know you felt that way about Rodolfo. I had originally intended . . . but then I thought . . . well, you hated Rodolfo so much. But I guess you do have repressed feelings for him. Romantic feelings.

H. What? No! I just meant . . . I mean . . . What? No, I still hate him too! He's so whiny and annoying. He doesn't believe me or think I have any abilities. He thinks me dimwitted! He can't fight for nothing. I don't even think he *likes* fighting. How can I have feelings for a man who doesn't like *fighting*? All he cares about is his cute little brother and saving his town. Why is he so willing to risk his life for his town? And that family sponge business! Why was he so willing to share their only sponge with some girl he hardly knew? He's totally not like Graham or all the other guys in the Lands who don't care about anyone else . . . Oh gods . . . do I . . . like him?

Only one way to find out. Or show you, rather.

H. No, wait! I don't want to! Murray, no!

Chapter 9

Steel Cage Match

"Steel cage match!" Barnaby, the merchant, cries out in glee from inside a giant box made of thick, crisscrossing steel wire, sort of like a giant chicken coop, which he continuously calls a steel cage. It's in the middle of the dirt street outside Josiah's Manure Import-Export. "What better way to win a girl's love than to triumph in a steel cage match in her honor!"

"I'm no one's girl!" Hero shouts from the street, outside of the cage. "And I don't want this."

Next to her is Toaster, looking worried, and Rodolfo looking even more worried. Neither has seen a human-sized chicken coop before.

Graham is already inside the steel cage, jogging around in circles. There is a steel door cut into the front of the front of the cage. It can be locked shut, but is currently open, taunting Rodolfo's honor.

"No matter," Barnaby says. "The boys agree to it. Isn't that right, Rodolfo?"

Rodolfo is instantly, and miraculously, now dressed in tight polyester shorts and nothing else but some brown leather shoes. His skinny body and lack of muscles glisten in the sun.

Graham is also in nothing but tight polyester shorts, and brightly colored leather shoes—orange and blue. Unlike Rodolfo, Graham's large, oiled muscles are reflecting reflect so much sun they're almost blinding.

Rodolfo wonders where such a brightly colored man could come from in the Lands—but then he remembers Graham came from the God of gods, named Murray. With Graham's blond-tipped hair to his brightly colored shoes, he seems to be from a different world. Perhaps he is from Murray's world—the heavens. *But no, he said he was from the Kingdom of Bangor, so he must be from these wastelands as well, though the Kingdom of Bangor must be unexpectedly spritely.*

Normally, Rodolfo wouldn't fight over something, and definitely not a girl. He survived as a successful saloon owner through compromise and verbal dueling, his interest in lawyering shining through. But he knows Hero really dislikes this Graham, and he simply cannot let her end up with him. *What's wrong with me? Why do I even care? Can't I control myself out of this? No, I couldn't let that happen to her, controlled or not.*

"I was not the one to suggest fighting for a lady," Rodolfo starts his reply, giving Hero a nervous glance. "But I must defend her honor." Hero smiles at him, which he does

not see. "She clearly does not want to be with this brightly colored Graham, so I will not let that happen. But I still cannot understand how a giant, steel chicken coop got into the middle of this lonely street in our downtrodden town."

"I explained to you already—Chester had it installed for the amusement of his Death Soldiers," Barnaby says in frustration from inside the cage. "It was always here, and will always be here."

"But it was not here when we came in. Which builder did you use? When was it installed?" Rodolfo asks.

"In the last three days," Barnaby answers.

"But you just said it was always here," Rodolfo complains.

"Yes," Barnaby answers.

"Yes?" Rodolfo asks, confused.

"Yes. Always. *And* it was installed while you were in the manure cellar," Barnaby replies, dismissing Rodolfo with a wave of his hand.

Huh? "A giant steel cage?" Rodolfo asks, incredulous. "We would have heard something."

"Over three days of hideous knocking and knocking and knocking and knocking during which you curled up like a little baby?" Graham taunts Rodolfo.

"Don't listen to him, Rodolfo," Hero says. "You don't have to do this." She puts a hand on his shoulder to calm his nerves and distract him from the power of the Author. "I can fight my own battles."

Rodolfo shakes his head. "He sullies your honor by insinuating he will end up with you at the end of this episode in our lives, which you clearly do not want. I will not let someone like Graham dishonor you."

"Can't you just end it now, Hero?" Toaster asks, worried about his brother. "Just ask Murray to end this. Or use your talisman. There's no way Rodolfo can beat that. Look at his huge, glistening muscles." Toaster points at Graham, who is jumping around the ring like a caged animal, literally.

"I know, they're amazing," Hero says, lost in thought, staring at Graham's prancing, but then quickly shakes her head. "Murray and I kind of aren't fighting anymore. He says I need to let him weave what he wants to weave."

"I still feel like me," Toaster replies.

"He is the God that weaved us from the beginning," Rodolfo offers. "He gets us."

"And this is what he came up with?" Toaster snaps back, in protest.

"He thinks he's helping me," Hero explains.

"But that man with the large muscles will hurt my spindly brother!" Toaster cries. "How is this helping you? Or him?"

"Uh, I can't say. But don't worry, Toaster," Hero says as she puts her other arm around Toaster. "I won't let anything happen to him. Even if it does, and your brother dies, I'll help you survive." Hero smiles at Rodolfo, thinking it will comfort him. She's not used to trying to comfort anyone. Her smile looks as depressing as her words.

"Thanks?" Rodolfo offers nervously.

"Ding, ding!" Barnaby yells at him. "Time to get in here!"

Rodolfo walks slowly to the front of the steel cage, hoping that some last-minute completely unexpected and shocking occurrence will take place and stop the fight, which is pretty much how his once simple life has gone since he first met a girl named Hero.

But, alas, no such act of the gods takes place. No evil magic, either. He is now standing face-to-face with a man perhaps ten years his elder and with so many more muscles. How will he ever survive? *This was a really stupid move, Rodolfo,* he tells himself. *And all for a girl who doesn't even like you?*

Barnaby, the glamorous center of attention, boisterously yells out to everyone around as if it were a large arena, though it is clearly not—there are just two fighters, Hero, Toaster, and himself. "In this corner is Graham, star of a traveling theater troupe named *Paramedics Emergency Medical Care: Bangor*. He tells me that he plays the hunky heartthrob, which means he always gets the girl at the end of each and every episode in his life. I can see why. We should all wish to be girls such that we could find comfort in his strong bosom." Barnaby's command of the poetic arts would stun such a large crowd if there was one.

"Uh . . . excuse me?" Graham asks Barnaby, with his head tilted in confusion.

"And in the other corner," Barnaby continues, ignoring Graham, "is Rodolfo, who licks manure off of his fingers."

"It wasn't like that!" Rodolfo shouts to the imaginary crowd, defending himself.

"It was. I saw you," Barnaby clarifies.

"Wowzers, do we even have to fight for her?" Graham asks Barnaby. Then he turns to Hero and yells, "You'd choose some manure-eater over Graham?" He flexes his large muscles at her.

"That's how much I hate you!" Hero yells from outside the ring at Graham, cupping her hands to her mouth. Barnaby was such a good actor, he had everyone thinking there was a large, raucous crowd. Barnaby should audition for some local theater troupe of his own. Shakespeare, even. He's just that good.

"All right, fighters, listen up," Barnaby says, waving them in closer to him. Graham knows what he means, and Rodolfo simply follows Graham's lead. Once the fighters are in close, Barnaby continues, "This fight is to determine who wins Hero's heart—"

"No, it's not!" Hero shouts from outside the cage. "You can't win my heart by winning this stupid fight! There aren't even any sand-wolves or zombies! You'd have to kill a flying zombie or a zorc to even cop a feel!"

"Don't give him any ideas!" Rodolfo snaps back at Hero.

"Oh, and I hate you, Graham!" Hero adds.

"Ugh, you're no fun," Barnaby calls back at her. He turns to the fighters again. "This fight without wolves is to determine who is more worthy of winning Hero's heart."

"No, it's not!" Hero interrupts again.

Toaster decides to yell also. "There are things more worthy of a heart than fighting!"

"Name one, you curiously precocious child," Barnaby demands.

"Living!" Toaster replies.

"Oh, I'm a paramedic," Graham replies, realizing he suddenly has an angle, just like during his youth spent sportfishing in exotic, expensive locales. "I help people live, Hero. Surely you will love me at the end of this episode in our lives!" He flexes again for her.

"Oh no, she won't!" Rodolfo cries as he charges Graham, taking him by surprise, and swings a right hook at Graham's face.

Unfortunately for Rodolfo, Graham has been taking mixed martial arts classes for years while living in Hollywood, thinking perhaps he could get work as a stunt double if acting didn't work out—but it did. So, Graham easily sidesteps Rodolfo's lazy right hook and counters with a left-handed body blow to Rodolfo's rib cage.

Rodolfo stumbles and groans in pain. Graham uses the time to wave his hands in the air, cheer, and prance in a circle around the edge of the cage. Only Graham can tell that he is actually looking for his audience of fans (who collectively call themselves *Grahammies*), reporters, and maybe some social media influencers. "Where are the reporters? Where are the influencers? My Grahammies didn't even show up for this? Did my publicist not post the deets?" Graham asks Barnaby.

"Boy, what are you talking about? The words you speak are nonsense!" Barnaby replies. "Perhaps Hero's canker is contagious."

"The press? The news? Surely, someone invited them," Graham tells Barnaby. "I'm fighting for a woman's honor. That's great press!"

"Not *my* honor, you dimwit!" Hero shouts into the steel cage.

"Shut up, woman!" Graham snaps back at her. "Don't ruin my press!"

"Don't speak to her like that!" rages Rodolfo, standing upright for the first time since the body blow as he charges at Graham again. This time he's trying to tackle Graham. Instead, it is as if Rodolfo struck a brick wall. Graham does not budge as Rodolfo crashes into him.

In response, Graham wraps his arm under Rodolfo's chin, picks Rodolfo up over his head like he's holding a large pole upright, and then purposefully falls backward, dropping Rodolfo flat on his back onto the hard, dirty street.

Hero and Toaster wince. Rodolfo is crying on the inside, but refuses to show any tears or pain. He's just grimacing. Hero bites her lip to keep herself from entering the steel cage. She's reminding herself that this is Rodolfo's fight, not hers, for her, but not for her since no one can win her in a fight.

"Vertical suplex! I've always wanted to do one of those!" Graham cheers. "You know, I have been dabbling with some professional wrestling at the gym. I was thinking of auditioning if my show ended. Now, where are those news people?"

"Boy, I think I understand now. Do you perhaps mean the town squire?" Barnaby asks Graham.

"Sure, is that a newspaper in town?" Graham asks.

Barnaby nods. "Toaster, go fetch the town squire!" he calls to Toaster.

"No way!" Toaster shouts back.

"He's probably at the new saloon!" Barnaby calls out to Toaster, ignoring the refusal.

"Wait! Your newspaper is just one guy?" Graham asks Barnaby. "What kind of small town is this?"

"'Tis nothing but a very small town without a name, boy," Barnaby begins to explain. "Ever since Warlord Chester took over and brought the evil magic from the Queendom—"

"Warlord? Evil magic? Wait!" Graham asks, scratching his head in thought. "What year is this?"

"'Tis the year 10786, boy. Don't you know how to read and write? Do you not know your maths?" Barnaby asks him.

"What the hell kind of town am I in?" Graham asks Barnaby. Then realization hits his face. "The year ten thousand? Wait, is this some dystopian future I'm in? I was once cast in a movie like this. It wouldn't surprise you to learn that I got the loner dystopian girl." And Graham points a finger seductively at Hero, with a romantic smile.

With his distraction about the year, along with all his braggy smiling at Hero, Graham takes his eyes off his opponent. Rodolfo, like all children in the no-name town, learned to climb anything and everything to avoid the poisonous sqorpions (a radioactive hybrid descendant of scorpions and squirrels). He climbs up the inside of the steel cage, and, without warning, jumps off the highest rungs and onto Graham, striking him leg first in a move called a diving leg drop, though Rodolfo did not know that.

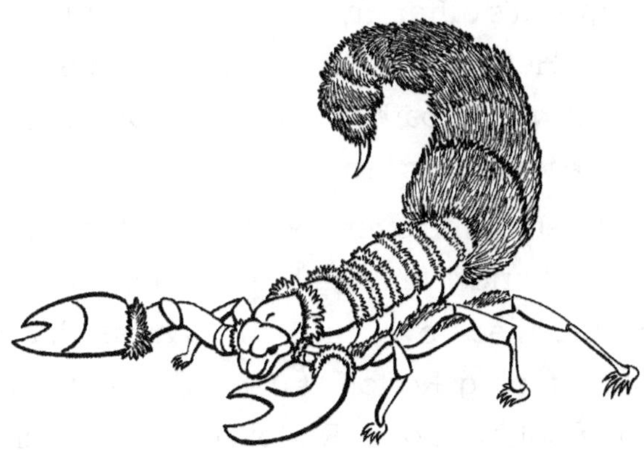

"Yes!" Hero cries out, pumping her fist. Toaster hugs her.

"What the hell? A diving leg drop!" Graham yells. Due to his peak physical conditioning, Graham is up much faster than Rodolfo, even though Rodolfo was the attacker.

Graham is now standing over Rodolfo, who is lying on his back, moaning. "You little snot!" he barks at Rodolfo.

"What kind of honor is that?" Hero calls out.

"Honor? Who cares about honor?" Graham shouts back at her. "I was just trying to win the girl. That's my thing. It helps my star power! But why am I even trying when my Grahammies won't even see, no influencers will see, and the real press won't even write an article about it? They've all been dead for eight thousand years! How do *you* help *me*?"

"Boy, if you had just said so," Barnaby cuts in, "I could have had the minstrel here in a flash and he could have written you a song on his lute. Something like . . ." Barnaby pauses with a deep breath, then starts singing an impressively improvised tune. *"There once was a boy named Graham. His body glistened with muscles and a tan—"*

"Enough!" Graham roars. "Why do I even want to win that dystopian girl? It's different if it's just a costume. But she's"—he points at Hero—"actually filthy! And she smells! When was the last time she bathed? What's wrong with this town?" In disgust, he waves his arms at everyone not in attendance.

Then, still standing over Rodolfo, Graham takes Rodolfo's legs with his hands, flips a still-stunned Rodolfo onto his stomach, steps back over him, turns around, and sits right on his back, facing Rodolfo's feet. Graham raises himself slowly while pulling up on Rodolfo's legs, which are tucked under his arms. Rodolfo's back feels like it's breaking under the strain. "This move is called the Boston Crab. It's named after Boston, a real town! With a name!"

With his body twisted and pulled, Rodolfo screams in agony. "Do you yield?" Graham yells at Rodolfo.

Rodolfo screams in pain.

Graham yells, "Yield!"

Rodolfo refuses to yield the fight.

"Come on, boy," Barnaby adds while lying down on the floor to get close to Rodolfo's face. "It's all over, just say, 'yield.' The girl will surely choose Graham now after seeing you trounced and embarrassed so."

Rodolfo ekes out, "No."

Graham is getting impatient and frustrated, so he tightens his Boston Crab even further.

H. Murray, stop this insanity!

Only you can.

H. But you're the weaver! You said I should trust you to write me a beautiful story, but this isn't beautiful!

It's hard to be beautiful if you don't think you're beautiful on the inside. I need you to trust your feelings.

H. What? My *feelings*? I trust my feelings. I trust I'm going to murder you like Aunt Cordelia if anything happens to him.

Not just your angry feelings. You know, your inside feelings. The ones you keep secret. Your innermost desires.

H. I desire to murder you.

I'm talking about love, Hero! Love for others!

H. I desire to murder you. And love. I desire to murder love! But you more! Stop this!

Okay, okay. Just, you know, forget love. We're obviously not ready for that. What do you want for yourself?

H. Murray, my feelings don't matter. They never have. Just my quest.

Of course they do. I think I see it now. You lived on the run so long. You grew up without a real family. Mistreated. You never had time for real feelings. You don't even know what they are.

H. But my quest—

Is just a quest. For others. You're trying to help other people's feelings. But what about you? I shouldn't have taken that away from you.

H. Take what away?

Your feelings. What you want. I did this to you. It's my fault. I should have let you use your power to control. Not all the people in your world, please, but just you. Maybe this way you'll find what you really want. Because your feelings do matter. Now, Hero, what do you want?

H. So ... I can have a choice? You'll let me control?

Yes. This is a partnership.

H. What's a partnu . . . parnutship?

It's where two people work together toward a common goal. You were right all along. It's not about me overpowering you, or you overpowering me. Before, I said it was a meeting of the minds, but it really wasn't. I still had the veto power. But I see now, your feelings are real. But they won't be real if I don't let you feel them. I need to trust you.

H. Thank you, Murray. You can trust me.

So, you won't use the talisman against me? You won't help all the other characters to overpower me and belittle me?

H. We'll see.

That's as good as I'll get, I guess.

H. Yes, but I think I have one of your *feelings* things. I know what I want to do.

Yeah?

H. Yeah. I'm pretty sure. It's a risk. But I have to try.

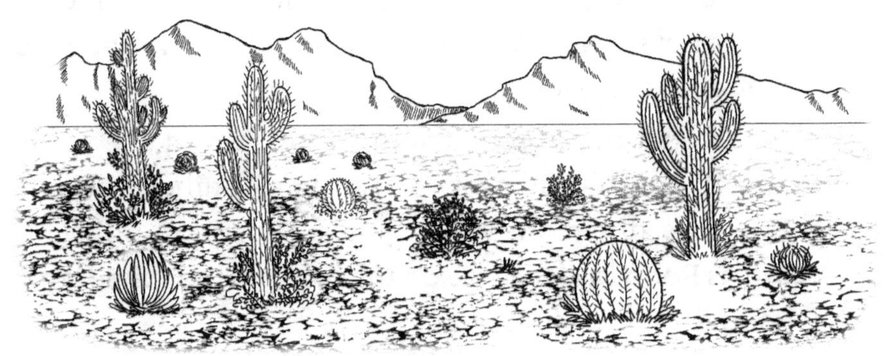

Chapter 10

I Like It, I Love It

"Rodolfo! I'm coming!" Hero yells. And she runs to the door of the steel cage, throws it open, and enters. With such brute force, the door swings back behind her, slamming shut with an ominous *clang*.

"Oh boy! Isn't this exciting?" Barnaby bellows out to the crowd of . . . now one, Toaster, though he imagines thousands. "An unexpected two-on-one steel cage match. What a lucky crowd you are to witness such a historic match in the most desolate part of this no-name town in the most desolate part of the Lands!"

Ignoring Barnaby the merchant-turned-emcee/referee, Hero orders Graham, "Get off him!"

Returning to his job as referee, Barnaby moves to officiate the action between Hero and Graham.

"Not until he yields, and I get the girl!" Graham replies. "Not that I even want you. But I must prove I am the most worthy, at the very least."

"You could never get *this* girl," Hero says as she points to herself, "you selfish, nasty, uncaring weakling!" She spits in Graham's direction, which is also Rodolfo's direction. Seeing as Rodolfo is the one on the ground, the spittle lands on Rodolfo.

"Hey!" Rodolfo says through grunts of pain.

"Weakling? Wowzers! Have you seen these muscles?" Graham yells angrily at her, ignoring the spittle. He gets off Rodolfo, who rolls around on the ground while groaning. Graham approaches Hero.

"I don't care about your gorgeous muscles," Hero says with a snarl, giving them a glance, though. "You're a weakling of the head!" Her hand reaches inside her black leather trench coat.

"Mind," Rodolfo squeaks from the ground.

"No, he's mine," Hero replies, spitting in Graham's and Rodolfo's direction again. "That dimwit."

"You're one to talk," Graham retorts. "You may not be glamorous, or even bathed, but I know your kind. We're two peas in a pod, you and me. We're not the smartest guys in the room, but we have the most street sense. How do you think I rose to be a Hollywood star?"

"Don't ever compare me to a misogymnast like you! And I'm not a guy. I can beat any guy here! What street sense is that? Even Rodolfo is smarter—"

"You think Rodolfo is so smart?" Graham seethes at her. "I'm the one on top of *him*! And I'm a Hollywood star!"

"Rodolfo *is* smart. He reads books! Tons of books! He's also kind, caring, a good brother, and cares about the Lands around him. If either of you *were* to win my love, which nobody ever will, it would be *him*. So, you can go back to your Grahammies or whatever, and just leave us to save our world," Hero thunders at him. "No one wants you here."

"Wowzers! You done me wrong, dirt girl!" Graham shouts at her. "I'm a star! People love me. And books are for assistants, not men." Then he charges at her at high speed. Hero's hand, as quick as lightning, grabs her morning star. She's ready to strike.

Unbeknownst to everyone there, which is just four other people, Rodolfo had crawled his beaten lump of a body near where Graham was crossing. Graham and Hero are so focused on their soon-to-be clash, they don't even notice when Rodolfo sticks out his arm just in time to trip Graham's colorfully clad feet. The muscular paramedic, with his frosted tips and bright orange sneakers, goes flying, a blur of brightness, and lands face-first on the ground. *Thud.* Quiet.

Graham isn't moving, due to a severe concussion. Everyone, which is just four people, three minus the victim, is stunned.

Barnaby runs to Rodolfo who is still on the ground. The rotund merchant bends over and lifts Rodolfo's arm into the air. "The winner! Rodolfo!" he shouts cheerfully, waving to the imaginary crowd. Then he disappears.

And then Graham disappears.

And then the steel cage disappears. And Rodolfo's clothes change back to his boring mass of brown: brown jacket and brown ankle-length trousers.

It's just Hero, Rodolfo, Toaster, and a wagon full of old books, relics, and priceless artifacts.

"Rodolfo, you did it," Hero says softly as she runs to his side on the ground. Rodolfo stirs. "Don't move." She turns to Toaster who is now at Rodolfo's other side. "Toaster, fetch him some water. Maybe it's still in Barnaby's carriage."

"No, no," Rodolfo says. "I'm all right. I feel fine, actually." He gets up on his knees and then his feet. Hero and Toaster do the same. "I can't believe you! Wasting all our time with this steel cage match while we have a town, and you have a kingdom to save. Don't you know any better? You shouldn't have fought with Author! This is what happens when you mess with the gods!"

"Oh, Rodolfo. You're back to normal," Hero says, and in happiness, she instinctively throws her arms around him. For a moment, he doesn't complain about her. Hero takes her arms off him as quick as she can after realizing what she has done and tries to forget it happened.

"Guys, I think we should just get in the carriage and go. Before anyone sees us," Toaster says to them. "That was sure to attract a crowd."

The group looks all around, but so far no, one is in sight.

The carriage and wagon are still there, though. "Do you think the plan will still work? A manure export sales trip?" Rodolfo asks Hero.

"I don't know. Barnaby was the one who got permission from SkeLord, who probably still wants us dead," Hero says, happy to get back to the business of survival.

"Can you ask him?" Toaster asks Hero.

"SkeLord? That's a terrible idea," Hero says with a shudder, thinking of the skeleton man.

"No," Toaster replies. "Murray. Author! The God of Gods!"

"Oh, I guess I can ask," Hero says. And, to the others, she instantly looks up and to the left, her face blank.

"So, I'm gonna go, uh, relieve myself, uh, so just, uh, wait for me, or come get me if she wakes up," Rodolfo tells Toaster.

"Okay, brother. And I didn't get to tell you yet, but you were magnificent in there," Toaster tells him.

"Wow, that's another big word for you, little brother. But I, was, uh, really getting pummeled."

"Exactly! The way you tricked him into thinking you couldn't fight and were just a lump of useless garbage on the floor, only to surprise him. I'm so proud of you," Toaster explains, genuinely.

"I guess you're right, little brother," Rodolfo replies, unsure if Toaster really believes what he said, or is just trying to make him feel better. With no answer, he just heads to a nearby alley to make his peep—that's what his mother called it when he was a young child. He feels a pang of sadness, missing her.

From the alley, Rodolfo glances back at Hero, this girl—no, woman—who in just four days has changed his life forever. He can see Hero still looking blankly, up and to the left, and then Toaster walks over and hugs her tightly. Hero doesn't even notice, but that's not the point. Rodolfo can tell Toaster feels happy and safe while holding her—safer than he ever has since their parents died. Safety was not something Rodolfo could exactly provide these past few years, as hard as he tried.

H. Murray! You weren't listening to a word I said! Can we please just take the carriage and get out of this horrible town? I feel like I've lived my whole life here already.

Well, the last ten chapters, yeah.

H. I don't know your god-words!

It's okay. It's kind of weird. This was all your idea—the manure carriage. SkeLord's Death Soldiers are looking for you guys. And, based on your idea, they would be surprised to not see Barnaby in the carriage, who is the one who had the permission.

H. I can't believe I weaved some of the story. Did I do good?

Well, uh, if I had written it, per the rules of the town in my head, Barnaby would need some parchment signed by Warlord Chester or SkeLord himself. In triplicate.

H. But you vanquished Barnaby!

Yeah, it was too weird keeping him in the story after reffing a whole steel-cage wrestling match. I should probably delete his carriage, too. Just start fresh.

H. Oh, come on, Murray! He was going to take us with him anyway! That was the real plan. So why have him in the story if we can't use his carriage?

Because you're the one who weaved, I mean, wrote him in! It was all your idea.

H. And it was a good one. Please, Murray! Meeting of the heads! Parnutship, like you said.

All right, you can use his carriage. Toaster can carry the approval parchment. He's the only responsible one. So, let's blow this popsickle stand.

H. Popsickle what?

It's a frozen sweet treat. For kids.

H. Holy buckets, I hate your world. Heaven-world is depressing. And you're such a loser. And an embarrassment.

Hey!

H. Sorry, I'm still me, Murray. Don't forget that.

Chapter 11

Let's Blow This Popsicleee[1] Stand, Which Is Actually a Cool Saying Even if You Live in a Dystopian or Fantasy World

The trio sits inside Barnaby's carriage. Attached to the back of the carriage is a great covered wagon full of the books and trinkets that Rodolfo, Toaster, and his compatriots had saved through the years, and which still looks like manure to everyone else in town.

Hero, Rodolfo, and Toaster can't help noticing that the carriage was built for a king. The leather seats are cushioned with wool. There is a trunk inside filled with glass jars of water, milk, wine, and various cheeses none of them have ever heard of before—because none of them had ever seen

---

1 Note to self: Change name for trademark issues. Remember to be consistent. Oher options: popsickal, sickpopple, sickpopickle.

labeled cheese before (*Is Gouda a kingdom?*). Only Hero would taste the monster (Muenster) cheese.

"Is this how a rich merchant lives? With fancy glass jars?" Rodolfo asks as he opens a jar of water. It took him a long while to figure out how to take off the "turny thing" at the top.

"I wouldn't know. I've never met one." Hero laughs acerbically, with an awkward snort, hoping Rodolfo can take a joke. After all, they are bonding now, after their shared trial, which surprised her to no end.

"Roasted, toasted!" Toaster laughs and points at his brother. "Her wit is as sharp as her blade, brother!"

"Toaster, go up to the driver's seat, and start driving the horses to the exit of town," Hero instructs.

Rodolfo is still a bit nervous to be left alone with Hero, but partly excited.

"Can I take some wine with me?" Toaster asks, seeing his brother's distracted look.

"Yeah, sure, you deserve it," Hero answers.

"No, little brother!" Rodolfo corrects her quickly.

"Aw, sandstorms," Toaster complains.

"Since when have I ever let you drink wine?" Rodolfo scolds him, snapping out of his thoughts of Hero.

"Aw, come on, all my friends do!" Toaster insists. "You even served them yourself at the saloon."

"Listen to your brother," Hero interjects confidently.

Neither brother is sure which brother she means.

"Just go, Toaster," Rodolfo says, smiling, and gives him an evil yet pleading look.

"Only because Hero asked," Toaster replies.

"Actually," Hero informs, "I meant—"

But Toaster is already out of the carriage's cabin through the fancy door direct to the plush driver's seat. Barnaby thought of everything. A man wealthy not just of funds but of mind as well—the true hero of this story.

"I'm so sorry, Rodolfo," Hero says once they are alone.

"I, uh . . . " Rodolfo tries to reply but cannot. He didn't expect an apology. Not from *her*.

"You were right," she continues. "I caused all these problems for you. My fight with Murray caused all this madness. You almost got killed. And that would have been . . . sad." She smiles at Rodolfo, trying to look caring, but it just looks awkward, yet oddly sweet.

"Thank you. I accept your apology. But Hero, in truth, I was way out of line," Rodolfo argues. "You've kept us safe from the start as well. And it was your fight to have with Murray, not mine. Just like it was my fight to have with Graham. I know not why you were fighting with Murray, but I think I know you well enough to know your reasons, whatever they may have been, were honorable."

"Uh? Honor-uh-a-what?" she asks.

"With honor."

"Well, not really this time, though I think it worked out in the end. I kind of was just mad about . . . my life," Hero admits.

"I don't know much about your life before now, except for Mother and the talisman, but clearly, you have done all right for yourself. You're still alive," Rodolfo offers.

"And you and Toaster, too," Hero says. "You had your own problems, but you take such good care of him. Few have someone like you in these wastelands. I'm sorry about your bar."

I've never heard her talk so openly. But I just can't let that error go. Argh, Rodolfo, just let it go! It's just another name for saloon. Holy sandstorms, I know I can't. What's wrong with you, Rodolfo?

"Saloon," Rodolfo corrects her.

"Saloon, bar. What's the difference?" Hero replies defensively.

"It was a saloon. It always has been a saloon. It just is. Bars are . . . pedestrian. Did you see the grand piano? I was even thinking of rebranding it: *Rodolfo's Piano Saloon*," he says with a wave of his hand to stress the majesty of the name. "My father would have thought it was self-absorbed and pretentious though." He looks out the carriage window thinking of all the fights with the man. He'd never even wanted the saloon, but Rodolfo had planned to make it his own, in a small way.

He's feeling proud for a moment, but Hero just stares at him blankly. At first, he thinks she's talking to Murray, the weaver of all things, again, but her head is cocked to the right, not the left. "I never really had parents," Hero suddenly confides. "I don't know what it's like. Did he not love you? Did he beat you? I know beating."

"No, no, nothing like that. To be honest, though, he beat my soul, Hero. Why do you think I care about all these books?" Rodolfo asks as he points to the wagon behind them. "I *love* books. Reading. For as long as I can remember, I wanted to be a lawyer. Help people in town. Chester's Code of Laws is just rife with loopholes to exploit. The tax section alone is . . ." Rodolfo notices her blank stare. "Well, my father wouldn't allow it. I had to work the saloon.   'That's why the gods created Rodolfos, son. We help people drink,' he would say."

"Well, you are helping. Look at *us*. I don't even know what a lawyer is. But you were helping people, your town. Your father should have been proud of you," Hero says. This time, her smile looks genuine and puts Rodolfo at ease. He's not hurting physically or emotionally this time. *Maybe we do have something.*

Rodolfo smiles, wanting to keep this *something* going. "Did you know your father?"

"Murray?" Hero asks.

"No, not Murray. Didn't you have a father here in the Lands?" Rodolfo asks. "I know your mother died before you were born, but what of your father? Though unusual, maybe he picked you up from the lily patch in her stead?"

"No one ever said *that*, or even who he was. None of the loyalists ever said anything about him," Hero answers.

"You were never curious?" Rodolfo asks.

"Never!" Hero replies, her voice suddenly louder. "What do I need a *man* for? They're nothing but trouble." Her eyes border on threatening.

Maybe it is the romantic sunset, maybe it's the warmth and privacy of the ornate carriage, but Rodolfo decides to make his move. "You have the spirit of fire within you, Hero, and clearly, you do not *need* a man. But I need you," Rodolfo says as he, totally misreading the situation, leans in to kiss her.

Rodolfo had never been close with a woman before. Even with the saloon's barmaids, he tried to act gentlemanly and professionally, unlike the other *bar* owners in the town. And he was proud that, at least while they were with him, no patrons lever took advantage of his barmaids. He understood this was due to his diplomatic skills and the overall classiness of Rodolfo's Piano Saloon (ChesterNameMark pending). So,

Rodolfo was quite cautious about the kiss, touching only the very edge of her lips with his. He saw this as a way to indicate his interest without moving any further or overwhelming her.

Unfortunately, what he actually ends up seeing is the fire in her eyes erupting into an inferno.

Hero instinctively grabs the magical talisman she still held somewhere inside her leather coat and instantly takes her hand to violently push Rodolfo aside, causing him to fly off his chair, into the back of the carriage, and then onto the floor. Rodolfo is startled and in some pain. To him, this brings back some traumatic memories of the steel cage match that happened not more than an hour ago.

"Don't you dare touch me. *Ever*," Hero says with eyes of fire and daggers. Or fiery daggers. "I will not be taken."

Rodolfo is staring up at her, trying to come up with something—anything—to say to fix the situation. But Toaster calls back to the carriage, "Everything all right back there? What was that noise?"

"Oh, nothing," Rodolfo replies, embarrassed he might have caused this. "I just fell."

"Good, but get back on your seat, and look like rich merchants. Because we're arriving at the town's exit checkpoint," Toaster informs them.

And so, Rodolfo gets back into his seat, and because Hero is still staring flaming daggers at him, he looks down and to the left.

Chapter 12

Even Dystopian Wastelands Have Bureaucratic Brown Tape

The carriage and wagon slow down on a small dirt road that leads to a break in the wall surrounding the town. There, a soldier sits on a chair supposedly watching over the checkpoint's road that goes in and out of town, but he's just staring at a rock in his hand for some reason. *Must be really boring if staring at a rock is preferable*, Toaster muses.

He also wonders how the amazing Hero got through the checkpoint on her way into town. Did she sneak by this guy, or did she just find a way over the wall? *No matter. I shouldn't worry. Hero told us we would make it through.*

Inside the carriage, Hero is still staring at Rodolfo. "Can we, uh, talk about this?" Rodolfo asks.

"No. Never," Hero says with a hiss, softly but forcefully.

Rodolfo moves to the farthest point from her, which is the back corner of the bench facing her on the opposite side of the carriage.

With an ounce of courage, he ekes out, "I only meant to—"

"I said never!" Hero repeats, louder this time, and shuts down, arms crossed. Rodolfo gives up.

"Guys," Toaster calls back to them, not realizing the standoff inside the carriage. "Do either of you want to come up in the driver seat with me? How is this supposed to work, Hero? Did Author tell you how to make it through the checkpoint?"

Hero just grunts back at Toaster.

"Uh, I didn't quite get that. Brother, did you hear her?" Toaster asks.

Rodolfo grunts back at Toaster too, then glances at Hero, who glares at him. This causes Rodolfo to glare back at her.

"Guys, I don't quite understand your grunts. But the Death Soldier is approaching. Will one of you please help? I'm just a seven-year-old boy. They won't believe that I'm leading an important manure export sales trip." Toaster is worried that their entire plan will fail because, for some reason, Rodolfo and Hero are too busy grunting to help him. *What are they doing? Are those sounds of teenage kissing? They must be kissing in the carriage, even if it sounds like the steel cage match. I should give them some privacy, but I really need help.*

Toaster takes a quick peek into the carriage, shocked to see Rodolfo and Hero glaring at each other. *Holy sandstorms, what could have happened between those two? They were finally getting along!*

"License and registration," a Death Soldier asks, breaking Toaster's concentration.

"Uh, excuse me?" Toaster mumbles, turning to the soldier.

"I said, license and registration," the very large barrel of a man with a low scratchy voice says. He is dressed in silver chain mail with a large sword sheathed at his hip. And like all Death Soldiers, he has long hair.

"I don't know what that is. If you would allow me to ask—"

"You know, the authorization that allows you to legally operate a vehicle safely within the town of . . . of . . ." The soldier scratches his head. Toaster waits anxiously for him to finish his sentence. "Chester's town," the soldier finishes without naming the town.

Toaster is sweating and feels like his bowels will explode, potentially adding some real manure to his fake haul. *Would that help convince the soldier of our manure export sales trip? Should I do that? No, he would surely see me do that.* "Uh . . . I don't have registration," Toaster says. The soldier's hand moves toward the hilt of his sword. *I should have released my bowels, but it's too late for that now. I clearly need some form of approval to convince this soldier.* "But SkeLord gave verbal permission for this manure export sales trip."

"Oh! Why didn't you say so, Barnaby?" the soldier asks happily, believing Toaster is the wealthy merchant named Barnaby. Who else would be leading this important trip? His hands are no longer by his sword. "I already have your approval parchment right here. You're doing this town quite a service, risking your life out there on the desolate, dangerous roads between kingdoms to bring us back some valuable resources in exchange for our manure."

Then the soldier leans his head closer to Toaster and lowers his voice, "To be honest, it's so scary out there, I don't think I would go. The tales I've heard at this very checkpoint would tingle your spine." But before Toaster can ask about the tingles and tales, or tales of tingles, the soldier stiffens up, looking official again, and speaks loud and clear. "It is also my duty to inform you of the threat levels currently outside of town: sand-wolves are yellow, bandits are orange, zorcs are red. However, flying zombies are a flashing blood-red. Good luck out there!" He slaps Toaster on the shoulder. *Flying zombies?* The soldier hands over the approval parchment with Chester's signature and walks back to his checkpoint seat.

While Toaster looks over the signed parchment, the soldier starts looking at his rectangular flat rock again, holding it in his hand. He stares so intently that his neck is bent almost horizontally. To Toaster's surprise, the soldier even starts hitting the rock with his thumbs and fingers. While it's dangerous to speak to soldiers unnecessarily, this piques Toaster's curiosity so much he can't help but ask.

"Sir?" Toaster calls to get his attention.

"Ah, scared of the flying zombies, are ya? Afraid to get going?" the soldier asks from his seat. "Well, Chester said to tell you that if you don't leave town with that manure, I should slice and dice you, because if you're not going to sell that manure, you may better serve the town as our next meal."

"No, no, nothing like that. I'm actually excited about the flying zombies. I always say flying zombies are better than regular zombies," Toaster replies nervously. He thinks about just moving on and forgetting his original question. But he

is still too curious not to ask. *Damn me and my curiosity!* "I just was wondering what you were doing with that rock."

"Oh, uh, I'm playing a game," the soldier says and holds the rock so Toaster can see it. It looks just like a regular rock. *What game could this be?* "It's called RockBlox. My character has to, uh, stay on the rock."

Toaster peers at the rock, but can see no character or game. *It must be some new form of SkeLord's evil magic to keep the Death Soldiers content and in line.* "Looks . . . fun."

"Very addictive," the soldier says with a grunt, which Toaster takes as an invitation to leave and spurs the horses onward. As the carriage and wagon start to move again, they slowly make it to the other side of the wall.

The air already smells different to Toaster—like death and fear. He is inherently aware that he is leaving the so-called safety of his town for the wild dangers outside for the first time in his life. All the plans he and his brother made to save Town comforted them after their parents were murdered. And now they're actually doing something about it. *Though if I didn't give Rodolfo that push, we'd still be living under Chester's thumb.*

It gives Toaster even more comfort that Hero is with them, as she has survived out here on her own for years. But with Rodolfo and Hero both just glaring at each other, could she, or *would* she, really protect them? What are their chances out here?

Trying to take his mind off his fear, Toaster marvels at the bleak landscape outside the wall. It's a desert of bedrock and clay, with patches of dirt and scattered low vegetation. As far as the horizon, there are no structures, no roads. *I thought there were actual desolate roads. Not that I know what a road really is, anyway.* Instead, there are just slightly worn paths in the clay, where carriage wheels and footprints of the few brave souls have worn it down over centuries.

The horizon, as empty as the landscape, gives no guidance either. He could take the carriage in any direction, really. There are paths from prior carriages heading both left and right. Nothing straight, though. If he could, he would ask his brother, or Hero, but he's still scared to bother them. So, he just chooses right. *Was that right?*

Chapter 13

Every Hero Has a Thorn

Inside the carriage, Rodolfo feels very angry inside. Here he risked life and limb for this girl, and she treated him like such . . . manure. He thought they were bonding. He thought . . . well, it doesn't matter what he thought. She wasn't interested in him that way. *And what was all that about being taken? Taken where?*

Hero is also stewing; anger, the only familiar feeling she knows, comforting her like a blanket. She risked life and limb for this boy, defending him back at the saloon and in the steel cage, and sticking around when she could have just left them both, and he treated her like his . . . property. She's no one's property. She will not be taken. She starts to raise her hand again to . . .

Hero! What in the world are you doing?

H. What am I doing? What are *you* doing? Get rid of this stupid boy! Delete him from my story! I hate him!

But what did he do? Things were going so well. You were getting along.

H. He tried to make me his property. Or you did! You're the weaver. It's your fault!

That wasn't the point of the whole steel cage match. And I wouldn't have written the carriage scene like that. You just realized how much you like him! And you all were supposed to travel on the desolate roads while getting along. Laughing, telling stories, getting to know each other better. Maybe even a little sing-along!

H. Sing-along? I would never *sing*. And certainly not with *him*. That's even worse than what he tried to do.

But singing would be better than what you did. After all that violence, we really needed a happy scene. And what's happier than young love? Then you up and ruined it. But forget all that. You are obviously upset. Tell me about your feelings.

H. Holy buckets! Enough with the feelings, Murray!

What did Rodolfo do that upset you so much? He was really starting to enjoy your company. And you him!

H. He *kissed* me! Argh, I can hardly believe it.

You could have just said no, but you didn't even try. You just had to almost kill him?

H. Yes, he was trying to claim me. As some wife—all that talk about his saloon. Never!

He was just trying to comfort you. Be there for you. Show you he cares. You two have been through a lot together.

H. How do you know? He *kissed* me!

I'm the Author! The weaver of all things! Of course I know. And I'm telling you.

H. Oh, ho, ho, Author, I thinked you didn't want me cheating, knowing things.

Cheating is better than this . . . ruining my scene with your . . . incorrect interpretations.

H. Did he even kill a zombie? You think I'd let him kiss me just because he can trip some jackass misogymnast?

Those are kind of impossibly high standards. And are those really the things that matter to you? Think back to what you said when you were defending him. His love of books, his care for his brother—

H. You don't live in these times, Murray. Go back to your heaven-world of ma . . . saj . . . jets and sweet treats. When a boy kisses a girl in *my* world, it's either because he's trying to kill her, or he's picking a wife. And Rodolfo is a dimwit if he thinks I'm going to be a wife.

Wait, what? Wife? You think he's a rich enough merchant to afford a wife? Whatever; it doesn't matter. Sometimes it's just comfort, showing someone that you care. Bonding.

H. Bondage! That's even worse!

Argh! No, not that! He didn't mean to claim you. He likes you. A lot. Although he doesn't realize how much yet.

H. You're cheating again! And I don't want anyone liking me.

Maybe. But you didn't let me, or him, get to that point. Look, he wasn't claiming you as a wife. That's not how I'm writing him. He's whiny and argumentative and annoying, yes, but he wouldn't claim you. Would he have asked you about your feelings, your life, if he wanted that?

H. You're not the one who lives here, Murray. I know the men of the Lands. You don't.

Maybe, but just remember, you comforted him, too. You touched him. Remember?

H. No! I would never. I don't need a man. And I don't touch anybody unless it's in battle.

No, no. You did. After the . . . ahem . . . steel cage match. You hugged Rodolfo.

H. I did?

You did. And don't forget you pinched him in the manure storeroom.

H. Doesn't matter. A pinch is an accepted fighting move, and hugs after battle are allowed. Everyone knows that. Both times, it was *me* touching *him*. And I don't want to make him my wife. I don't need a man-wife.

So? You see? Just think of it as an after-battle kiss.

H. Ew. Those are not allowed. You don't know the Lands.

I weaved the Lands!

H. True. But you have a memory plague.

I don't! Just give him another chance.

H. Just write, Murray, before I go Aunt Cordelia on you!

What does that even mean? How could you?

H. I still have the talisman, remember? And a kingdom to save. I'll do whatever it takes.

"So, what does Murray have to say?" Rodolfo asks Hero.

"Huh?" she replies. She's surprised he's speaking to her. She didn't really expect to be speaking to him again, nor did she want to.

"I know you were talking to him," Rodolfo replies. "So, what did he say? Did he tell you to play nice because we still have a job to do? Saving my town and all? And I didn't mean to take you anywhere?"

"Shut up. You know that no man, no God, no weaver, or even a ruler of the gods can tell me what to do. And certainly not you." Thoughts are swimming around her head. She's still so mad at Rodolfo. But what Murray said is bouncing around in there too, occasionally knocking her anger aside. And then there is the issue that talking to Rodolfo *is* comforting. *His eyes are still accepting me. And he still wants to save his town. Nothing will stop him. Like me and Dystpopia.* It's all so confusing.

"Guys! Are you done just glaring at each other?" Toaster cries from the driver's seat, finally hearing them talking.

Hero looks at Rodolfo, unsure what to say. But he speaks first. "Yes, brother. Sorry, we were just tired."

"Really? Because it sounds, and looks, like you two are fighting about something really stupid. I have no doubt it was just an unfortunate conjunction of misunderstanding, pride, and stubbornness," Toaster says. Not hearing a reply other than grunts, he continues. "Anyway, forget that. I have a question for Hero. Do you hear that noise? Is that typical of the desolate roads? That high-pitched screeching?"

"What noise?" Rodolfo asks.

"Shut up and let me listen," Hero replies quickly. She uses the quiet to listen—really listen. *I can't believe I didn't notice it before. I'm such a dimwit.* "Flying zombies!" she screams.

Chapter 14

What's Worse Than a Steel Cage Match?

The high-pitched sound is even louder now. The tension in the carriage is high.

"What do I do, Hero? What do I do?" Toaster exclaims.

"Drive, Toaster! Drive!" Hero cries. They can hear and feel the horses start to move faster. "Which way did you turn out of the town?" Her eyes are like laser beams, scanning the sky from the window inside the carriage.

"I turned right," Toaster replies. "I couldn't ask. You two were . . . otherwise engaged."

The word *engaged* reminds Hero of Rodolfo's transgression and just makes her mad again. But the thought is fleeting as she also realizes she failed Toaster and the annoying Rodolfo. "Oh gods, you two stupid boys! Argh! You led us right into flying-zombie country!"

"Hey, stop yelling. That's my brother! He didn't know. You're acting like a baby," Rodolfo replies.

"Is that why you kissed me? You thinked I wanted a baby? Holy buckets, no!" Hero snaps back.

"What? No way!" Rodolfo exclaims. "We're not even anywhere near the magical lily patch!"

"Shut up, you two," Toaster interjects, surprising them. "Which way, Hero?"

"Just keep driving," Hero replies, forming a plan in her mind. "And let me get you things to defend yourselves." She digs into her coat. "With luck, we'll find a town or a cave to hide in. If we can't, don't let them bite you. You'll turn into one of them. Or, if you're lucky, you'll die."

The mention of death further ruins the already ruined mood in the richly trimmed merchant carriage. Hero takes out two daggers from her leather coat and hands them to Rodolfo. He reaches through the door to the driver's seat and hands one to Toaster.

"And now, I defend both you dimwits," Hero says.

She punches a hole in the glass window of the carriage with the hilt of a sword and climbs out, heading to the roof.

"You could have just used the damn door," Rodolfo says. In his head he adds, *you dimwit*, but he dare not say it. She *was* defending them, after all.

And then the sound changes. *Splat!* Against the other nonbroken window of the carriage is the face of a zombie. *Where the hell did it come from?* Rodolfo wonders. The answer comes when the zombie flies away. *Actual flying zombies! I never really believed it.*

The zombie itself was dark gray, with hair and peeling dead skin. Whatever was left of its clothes also appeared dead—or simply beyond repair. But the wings really got Rodolfo's attention. *Oh, those wings! They're so beautiful.*

They are truly the most beautiful wings one might ever see. A rainbow of fluorescent pastels in elaborate stunning shapes hanging off her back. Like one of those mythical butterfly creatures from the town's books. So beautiful! *Why should something so deadly look so beautiful? Kind of like Hero.*

Suddenly, a zombie arm sticks through the broken window and grabs Rodolfo's arm. And then he sees Hero's thick, black boot come crashing down on the zombie in the window, and the undead creature falls to the ground, damaged.

"Brother, brother! I need your help!" Toaster cries.

Rodolfo realizes he's just sitting in the cabin, watching the action, and he left his brother out there on his own. He uses the door to the driver's seat and is now standing on the ledge between the carriage and Toaster's seat. There he sees a flying, and beautiful, zombie attacking Toaster. Looking backward, at the roof of the carriage, he sees Hero defending herself against three zombies attacking her at once. She has her morning star and a short sword, but is also relying on kicks. *Why isn't she using that talisman?*

Rodolfo moves closer to Toaster, on the driver's seat, and starts jabbing at the attacking zombie with his dagger. He is able to damage the zombie's wing and slice at its arm, which falls off. Without an arm and useful wing, the zombie falls out of sight. But then they feel a thump underneath the carriage. "Watch out for the rocks," Rodolfo scolds.

"I am, brother, but I don't think that was a rock." *Thump, thump, thump.* "It's too regular a pattern. It's repeating."

Rodolfo peers over the side of the driver's seat to look at the wheels—and sees a zombie arm stuck in the front right wheel. "Oh dear," he says.

"Stop hitting the rocks, Rodolfo!" Hero yells down at them from her place on the roof.

Why is she yelling at me? Toaster's the one driving! "It's not the rocks," Rodolfo replies. "A zombie arm is stuck in the wheel!" *Just my luck, I try to do something good and it turns out bad, just like the past few days.*

"You stupid boys!" Hero yells at them.

And then it gets worse. The front right wheel breaks off, and the entire carriage slumps down in that direction. Hero slips. While a normal person would drop one or both of their weapons in order to hold on to the carriage with two hands, she uses the opportunity to throw her short sword at one of the flying zombies, killing it. Hero is now hanging by one hand from the carriage window—her free hand gripping the window and the other holding on to her favorite weapon, Morny, her morning star.

She looks to the back of the carriage to see that losing the wheel also caused the wagon, with all their books and artifacts, to break off. They're leaving them behind, whether they want to or not. She momentarily laments the loss of all those clues, but her attention returns to battle.

The carriage is still moving, just slower and more to the right—the front right corner leaning unsteadily without a wheel. The vehicle is going off any worn track, into the complete unknown, which may actually be better than following any worn tracks in flying-zombie country. It just scares Rodolfo and Toaster more as everyone in the Lands knows that, while you don't even travel the desolate roads between kingdoms, *no one* goes off those roads and into the unknown. It's much too dangerous.

Still hanging, Hero feels a flying zombie slam into her back. It's holding onto her, trying to pull her off the window. *So, this is how I'm going to die.* There is screaming around her, probably Rodolfo and Toaster, and groaning from the zombie, but she's not paying attention. She's too busy thinking of a plan. Her magical talisman was not working on the zombies before—maybe because they naturally ward off its magic, being undead and all.

And she can't quite hit the zombie with her morning star. A dagger would be more useful in this moment, but she doesn't want to part with her favorite weapon—she might drop it during the exchange. But her fingertips are slowly losing their grip on the windowsill. *Oh, my gods, this is it. I'm really going to die. Just because I was so distracted over being kissed by some boy who just fought in a steel cage match solely for my honor, and somehow actually listened to my feelings. What is wrong with me? And I didn't even give his little brother proper directions as we left a town with no name, and so we ended up in flying-zombie country—all over a kiss from a boy as weak and whiny as Rodolfo?*

Ah! So, you're finally learning.

H. Leave me alone to die in peace! Or pieces.

And ruin my book? I think I can do this.

Oh no, only one finger left. She closes her eyes.

And then, suddenly, the weight is lifted off her back. She looks behind her, and the zombie and Rodolfo are fighting on the ground as the carriage continues driving away. That annoying boy and less annoying zombie are getting smaller and smaller, like the wagon.

"Brother!" Toaster screams.

"Oh gods!" Hero screams, as she finally decides to throw her precious morning star away and pulls herself up a bit, now gripping the top of carriage with two hands. *That stupid dimwit! Why did he do that? I have to survive for Toaster now. I just have to. That's what Rodolfo would want.* She watches the morning star disappear behind her, along with Rodolfo, the wagon, and all those clues.

Toaster is still driving while Hero is holding onto the top of the carriage. They're driving on an unworn path, into the complete unknown, the front right of the carriage bobbing up and down, sometimes scraping the ground. The number of flying zombies grows fewer the farther they go. *Why?* She always knew enough to avoid flying-zombie country, so this is her first time leaving. Really, it may be the first time anyone has ever left flying-zombie country alive.

With the break in action, Hero starts to really process what just happened. The only person to ever fight for her— multiple times—gone! *Why did I ...?*

She feels tears forming—simply regretting her failure, she tries to tell herself—but she fights them back as much as she can, as hard as she fought the zombies. Through blurry eyes, she looks forward. Where are they going? In the distance, she sees a large structure. A building. *Shelter?*

"Toaster, toward that building. There are no zombies near it!"

Hero, I didn't create that building. My fingers were just typing on their own again. Did you?

H. No, I'm not a builder, Murray. Is it the ghoul?

Maybe. We don't know what that building is!

H. I know there are no zombies near it.

"Rodolfo!" Toaster cries. "We have to go back for him. But I can't turn the wagon enough!"

Hero looks back. She can't see Rodolfo or the wagon, but she can see hundreds of flying zombies now on the horizon. In typical zombie fashion, most of them are late to the action. *Thank the gods we got out of there when we did.* But if the zombies were to follow them here, she can't get a weapon holding on to the carriage like this. They need to get to safety and reassess their plan.

"We can't, Toaster. There's a zombie swarm there now. But they're not near that building up there—whatever it is. We need to make it there and get inside," Hero says.

"We have to go back for him!" Toaster insists, but is unable to turn around.

"I'm holding on with both hands, so I can't defend you now. Just drive to the building!"

"But that building, it's . . . " Toaster says meekly.

"It's safety for now," Hero says. "We can plan what to do after. I promise, I'll go back for him."

"Okay, Hero," Toaster says, now crying that the decision has been made to leave Rodolfo. He quietly drives the horses and carriage toward the building, as best he can.

The building itself is a large structure of some unknown, and shiny, gray material. Its height is impressive to Hero and Toaster. *It must be more than one floor, like Murray's walk-up. How can that be?* There is a large sign—almost a whole floor tall—on the front of the building that says, "FRF."

"I've never seen anything like this," Hero says as the carriage slowly approaches the building. Toaster stops the horses, and Hero lets go of the carriage, sliding her feet onto the clay ground. "Nothing like this should be here. It's like from the gods. No one I ever met on the desolate roads ever mentioned anything like this to me. Maybe you are right to be afraid. Perhaps we should turn back. Or just keep going."

Suddenly, Hero's chest starts to feel warm, right where she is keeping the talisman. She pulls it out, and it's glowing a golden yellow that is burning up in her hand. About to toss it before she gets burned, she pulls her arm back, but then her mind blacks out.

Hero? Hero? If you're talking to me, I can't hear you.

In Hero's mind, the words *Enter* and *Ancients*, in Murrayskindacoolish, show clear in her mind. She feels an overwhelming urge to enter the impressive building.

Hero! It's happening again! Some power is taking over. I didn't create the building or any of that. Can you hear me? You're changing the story. It's your talisman again. My hands are just writing on their own. Tell me what's going on!

Hero's eyes suddenly open. The talisman is cool in her hand again, her arm still pulled back awkwardly. She loosens up and puts the talisman back in her coat pocket.

"What happened, Hero?" asks Toaster. "Did Murray talk to you? Does he think it's safe?"

It wasn't me, Hero! Don't go in there! Whatever you do! Argh, that crazy talisman. Why did I ever put it in the story?

"Yeah, Toaster. Let's go in," Hero replies.

What are you doing? I don't know if I can protect you in there! I just lost control of the story somehow. I don't know what's going on anymore.

"Don't worry; it should be safe. Safer than out here," Hero says as she looks up at the sky.

"It's all my fault," Toaster says with a sniffle.

"It's mine, Toaster," Hero replies. "I wasn't there for you. But I will be from now on." She grabs Toaster's hand and smiles down at him, trying to comfort him. *I don't know what will happen, but I can't let him down.*

I hope you know what you're doing. Can you even hear me?

Hero nods.

They approach the building.

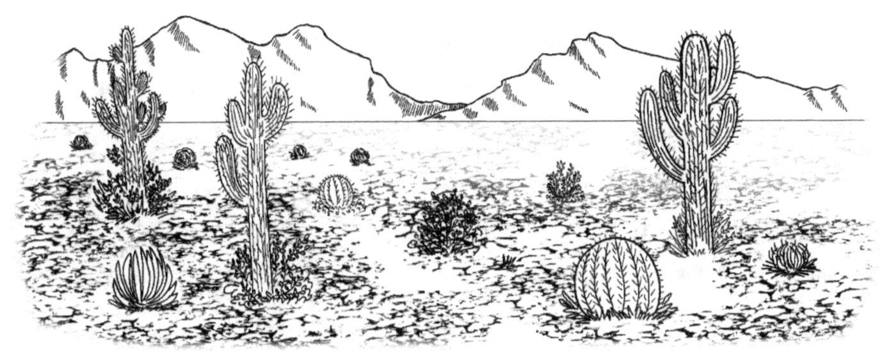

Chapter 15

A Safe Space

Rodolfo just capped off the craziest seven days of his life. He thinks it's seven, but he can hardly remember. Though he knows it's been three impossible days since he lost Toaster and Hero. *What are they up to?*

As mad as he was at her, watching that flying zombie trying to pull Hero off the carriage, and her hanging by one finger . . . he didn't want to let her go. Or watch her let go. Even after three days, he still plays it through his mind. *I had to not let her go by letting her go? I hope I made the right decision. I left Toaster with her. Gods, she better take care of him. Unless she fell off, too?*

Last he looked, Hero was still hanging on. But then the zombie he knocked off her startled him by pummeling his face into the ground and trying to bite him—and turn him into a zombie? Is that how it happens?

Luckily, the wagon, with all their artifcats—*Argh, now I'm talking like that insufferable girl*—had fallen off not too far away from them. Some of the books scattered across the clay ground, leaving a trail to the wagon. It landed mostly upside down, propped up a tiny bit from an artifact (which was actually nothing special—just a prehistoric bowling trophy).

With some quick thinking, and Hero's osmotic bravery, he was able to knock the zombie off of him and run to the overturned wagon, fighting off zombies as he ran. He squeezed himself under it, then removed the artifact holding it up. *Crash.* He was in the dark, except for a few thin bands of light sneaking in through the wagon's wooden boards.

Then his situation hit him like . . . a flying zombie. He was trapped inside an overturned wagon, it was near pitch-black, and he could still hear the high-pitched screams of zombies (and the flapping of their beautiful wings)—but they couldn't get to him. Every once in a while, there was a *thud* on the roof—what used to be the undercarriage—of the wagon.

Should I just wait them out? he thought for three days. For three days he just sat inside the wagon, as the temperature inside quickly rose. He felt like he was in a coffin. Which reminded him—*did that zombie infect me?*

At night it dipped to freezing cold. The only way he could tell the days go by was from the temperature; days spent waiting for the zombie sounds to disappear. Were his chills at night from the zombie sickness or frostbite? And he was, quite literally, dying of thirst. The sound of zombies continued, though they did diminish with time. Even worse

than all the other worries, he had no one to talk to, the one thing he really liked to do in his life. What he wouldn't give to be back working at the saloon right now. The thought makes him laugh. And no word of Toaster or Hero. He was going out of his mind with worry. *They're probably safe somewhere, right? How could they be worse off than me?* How could he ever know?

R. Murray . . . or should I call you *Author*? I don't know if you can hear me, but I'm dying. I know you can hear Hero. You talk to her. Can you talk to me? Is Toaster all right? Hero? Please give me a sign that they're all right. And then I can die in peace.

Hero? Come on, answer me!

H. Murray, I'm dealing with something here. And I'm not talking to you, or Max.

But it's Rodolfo. He's had a rough three days.

H. So have I! And I'm not talking unless you let go of Max's hand. You can't just invite someone else in on our thing without my say. What kind of parnutship is that? It's rude.

M. Murray, no! It was just getting good.

Okay, done. Now—

H. Oh gods . . . is Rodolfo dead?

No, no.

H. So, he's *not* dead! Then why waste my time? And isn't that cheating, you jackass? You said it was cheating to tell me things.

Um . . . no . . . I mean . . . I guess. I didn't think of it like that. Whoops? But somehow Rodolfo still has control, even though he's so far away from you. The talisman must have lingering effects on him. We'll deal with that later. But he just asked me for a sign that you and Toaster are still alive. And it's your fault; you told him about me!

H. That jackass. You should give him a sign not to kiss me again!

But what about what Rowena said?

H. You dimwit, I'm mad about that too! And stop talking about caring and feelings! It's gross. Just stop.

You know, we all have feelings. Rowena does. Even you. Even me.

H. Your feelings are gross! You're like a hundred years old. Like an ancient! You're not supposed to be talking about this stuff.

I would have you know that I have a date this weekend! That is, if I finish this book in time.

H. *You* have a date? With your cat? Not even Max wants you.

That's kind of hurtful, but, no, it's an internet date. She says she likes my manuals. I might even invite her back to my place to try out the massage chair—

H. Gross gross gross gross gross! Vomit! Gross gross gross gross gross! I want to go back to my fight now.

Um, I think we got a bit offtrack. Can I just give Rodolfo that sign?

H. Whatever. Give him a friend, even! We all can use a friend sometimes. Isn't that what I'm supposed to say? Holy buckets, why not just give him a baby? You love babies! Just stop talking about feelings. Vomit.

Oh! I have just the thing!

The sounds changed. The high-pitched zombie screams disappeared. But a sound even more frightening took its place.

What is a little girl doing all the way out here? Rodolfo leans his ear closer to the wall of the overturned wagon. *And why is she crying? Could this be a trick by the zombies? But they're not traditionally known for their deception.*

Rodolfo wonders what he should do. Prop up the wagon again to see what the crying sound is, and risk letting in a zombie? *Ugh, I can't just let a child die out here, getting eaten by zombies.* He decides to prop up the wagon again with the artifact (bowling trophy), lies on the ground, and peers outside.

No signs of zombies, except . . . *Oh crap.*

He pulls out the trophy and the wagon falls again. *It was a trap! Those deceitful little zombies. A little girl zombie! What was she, like, five years old?* The girl was just sitting with her knees tucked under her chin, sobbing. *It must be a lure built around human sympathies. Those deceitful flying charlatans!*

But the little zombie girl is still crying. Maybe even a little harder now. And Rodolfo doesn't hear any *other* zombies. *What if she really does need help? She didn't look dangerous. Oh gods, I can't just leave her there. I'm just not that person.*

Rodolfo takes the artifact (bowling trophy) and props up the overturned wagon again. He leans down near the ground and takes a longer look at the little girl zombie, who is still sobbing, tucked in like a ball, with her knees up in her chest. For a moment she looks at him—or just the slice of head that she can see staring at her from under the wagon— and stops sobbing. The two stare at each other. Rodolfo notices her beautiful, fluorescent pastel wings just lying at her sides against her white, torn, and zombified dress.

"Uh, hello?" Rodolfo asks her. The zombie girl, no longer crying, leans back in fright, her eyes darting away as if she could hide herself simply by averting her gaze. "I'm not going to hurt you." She doesn't reply, but she's staring at him now. *Good.* "My name's Rodolfo. It's safe in here. What's your name?"

Oh man, I stink at names. Hero's right. It's just hard because you have to remember, like, all the names in the world just to pick a good one. Maybe Barnaby was right—I can't write YA. I can't even remember what I had for lunch . . . oh wait, I can. Pesto!

"Pesto," the girl replies. She's clearly a zombie, but her voice is so regular. *Well, except for the weird accent. Is that a zombie accent? I might be the first person to hear one talk. Anyone else probably died or got turned into one. But her eyes are so pretty, like her wings. How could she be dangerous?*

"Pesto. What a pretty name, just like your wings," Rodolfo replies. The girl smiles involuntarily. "What are you doing out here? Why aren't you with your zombie . . . friends?"

She frowns.

"They're not friends," she replies in her weird accent. "They made me a zombie, but it didn't work. I'm still Pesto." She points at herself in a moment of pride. "I miss me mum," she says, and starts sobbing again.

She seems so human, not like all the others. Could it be? Did the zombification process not take hold?

"Do you want to come in and talk more? It's probably safer in here," Rodolfo offers. The girl nods. *I can't believe I'm doing this—inviting a zombie child in here with me. Last time I was nice to someone, it backfired. But she's just a child, not a wild teenage girl living on the desolate roads. Pesto needs help, understanding. We're all victims of these dystopian wastelands.* "Hold on. When I lift up this . . . house a bit more, you slide right in, okay?"

She nods.

Rodolfo gets up off the floor and tries lifting the wagon up as high as he can. His muscles are so bruised and he's so tired, being on the verge of death after three days without food and water. But he's able to get the wagon higher by a few more inches. *This better not be a trick. Whatever. I'm dead anyway.*

Pesto starts slithering under the wagon. But then Rodolfo hears some more high-pitched screeching. *It's a trick!* At first he moves to drop the wagon on her, but then he sees Pesto's face—she's just as scared as he is! He quickly lets her in and then drops the wagon.

It's dark again. Pesto is crying harder now. "Rolfo? Is that you?" she asks through tears. "Don't let them get me!"

Rolfo? Oh, she means me. "Yes, Pesto, I'm here. We're safe, but I don't have a light," he explains, though an idea occurs to him. "Oh, wait, I thought of something. I'll find us a light."

R. Author, God of gods, weaver of all things, please help us. I'm trying to comfort this poor, young girl, and she's scared. We desperately need a lantern. And some water. And some sustenance to make it through. Maybe a blanket. Perhaps add in a little bear stuffed with straw for the girl—I think little girls like that sort of thing. So, I guess what I'm really asking for is a lantern, two jars of water, a blanket, some sustenance (do you have any jerky?), and one ballerina flying zombie girl bear. Oh, wait! And one bear for Hero. A warrior bear. If she's alive I can bring it to her. Maybe that type of comfort she will accept? Yes, a peace offering. If she's alive. I didn't get your sign yet. Unless Pesto is the sign? Did you get the entire order? Should I repeat it? I guess I shouldn't; you are the Author after all. You proba-bly don't need me to repeat stuff to you. That would look like I didn't trust your memory. Surely, the God of gods has a wonderful memory. But please send a sign, if you haven't already. Please?

"Rolfo? Are you still there?" Pesto asks in her little girl voice. "Did you find it?"

"Uh, yes, I was praying to the gods for some things."

"God?"

"In a way. I guess it didn't work," Rodolfo answers. Just then, a light appears, filling the little compartment of the overturned wagon with harsh, white light from its light-emitting diodes. The Koleman Kamping LED Lantern 9000XD sits upright between Pesto and Rodolfo. The sudden appearance of the lantern without a flame takes Rodolfo's breath away.

"Rolfo, do you know God?" Pesto asks him.

"Oh, uh . . ." Rodolfo stammers. He's not sure whether to tell Pesto about Murray and decides against it. *Better not confuse this five-year-old zombie girl any further.* "Yes, thank the gods!"

"A doll! A ballerina flying zombie girl bear!" Pesto grabs the bear and gives it a huge hug. "It's me. Thank you, Rolfo, friend of God! Are both dolls for me?"

Rodolfo sees the warrior bear doll he ordered for Hero lying on the ground between them. Now that he sees it, he questions his decision. *Why did I order her a doll? Just to feel closer to her, like I might see her again? Why not one for Toaster, then? Because he's too old for dolls, clearly, with all those big words.* "Oh, uh, well, I think one is for my traveling companion, who I was separated from. But you can play with them until we meet up with her. I'm sure she won't mind." *Well, Hero might. Who knows what that girl is ever thinking?*

While Pesto's holding the dolls, and with the harsh Koleman Kamping LED Lantern 9000XD light, Rodolfo notices that, like her voice, she doesn't physically look like a full zombie. Her skin isn't entirely dead and gray. It still has some pinkness to it in spots. But those beautiful pastel wings . . . she really is like a half-zombie, half-girl hybrid. *How is that possible?*

"Oh, thank you, thank you, Rolfo. Warrior girl bear's my favorite!" Pesto beams, then turns to her dolls. "Come on, Warrior Bear, you'll learn ballet from Ballerina Bear!" She's holding Warrior Bear in one hand and Ballerina Bear in the other, making them play together. "'You pirouette all wrong. Prepare to die!'" Pesto makes the warrior bear say to the ballet bear.

Rodolfo feels good inside. His idea worked, and he cheered up this sad, traumatized girl.

Next to the lantern are also two jugs of water, two huge turkey legs, and two carrots. Rodolfo had asked for jerky, and would have settled for pemmican, both of which are way more practical for these dystopian wastelands, but he would have to make do with these two giant turkey legs. *I've only ever seen such things in the artifacts. Murray really is the weaver of all things!*

But who could ever eat so much before it all went bad? They would have to eat them now. He wouldn't be able to preserve them or fit them in his pocket like the jerky. "Uh, Pesto, you need to drink some water. And this looks like a turkey leg for you to eat," Rodolfo says.

Oops! I could swear he said turkey . . .

"I don't want to," Pesto whines. "I want to play! Don't you want to play?"

"How about a carrot?"

"Blech!"

"Oh, come on, just a little bit. Then you can go back to playing," Rodolfo begs. This is starting to remind him of raising Toaster the last few years. This girl is physically so different, a flying half-zombie, half-girl hybrid with beautiful wings, but she still acts like the little Toaster—well, before he started using big words like *thus* and *magnificent* and *conjunction.*

"Rolfooo!" Pesto whines again. But she starts to look hungry, like it just dawned on her. She crawls on her knees over to him, smashing her two new dolls into the ground on the way. *How do they look so dirty and used already?* She sits in Rodolfo's lap, facing the cool Koleman lantern. Putting down the now dirt-covered dolls, Pesto takes the turkey leg from him and takes a bite. "Blech!" she yells as she spits it out. "Yuck! Rolfo, this bloody stinks!"

Blood? Could her tastes have changed as a zombie? Does she only eat human meat now? He shudders. "Here, have some water, at least." Pesto takes a drink from the jar Rodolfo hands her. "I have another idea for the turkey leg." He closes his eyes.

"You pray more?" Pesto asks.

"Yes, Pesto," he answers, eyes still closed.

R. Author, I don't think Pesto, my new friend, likes the turkey leg. And there's no way she's going to eat the carrots. Do you have a turkey leg with some seasoning? Maybe she would like that? I once heard some travelers mention something called "salt and pepper."

Another turkey leg appears. Rodolfo actually claps his hands in joy. *Maybe I should ask Murray to fix things with Hero.* "Here, try this one," Rodolfo says, purposefully forgetting his thoughts, as he picks it up and hands it to her. *If this doesn't work, should I ask for a dead and bloody human leg?*

Pesto takes a bite out of the turkey leg, and without acknowledging him or even saying thank you, she keeps eating. *She must like it! Phew!*

R. Thanks, Author!

Rodolfo starts eating the other turkey leg and drinking some water. And then something else comes to Rodolfo's mind, now that Pesto, and his needs, seem taken care of. "Hey, Pesto?"

"Mmm . . . what Rolfo?" she asks between bites.

"By any chance, did you see any signs out there? Like a note left for me? Or something like that?" Rodolfo asks her. Talking about *out there* makes him realize he can still hear some screeching from the flying zombies. Pesto momentarily freezes at the words *out there*, but then relaxes.

"Oh," she answers, still eating. She transfers the turkey leg to her other hand, leans over in his lap, and takes her now dirty hand, coated with turkey seasoning, and sticks it into a pocket of her ripped pants. Out comes her hand holding a crumpled paper with turkey drippings on it. She holds it out to Rodolfo. "Mum said give this to Rolfo, before the zombies. I don't know a Rolfo. But now I know a Rolfo." And she goes back to her turkey leg. "I miss me mum. I miss London."

This must be some case of mistaken identity. How could her mom know me? My name isn't even Rolfo. Is it possible I've met her mother? Maybe at the saloon?

"London? Is that her name?" Rodolfo asks.

"It's home."

London? "Is that a kingdom near here?" Rodolfo asks. He's heard travelers to his saloon mention names of many other kingdoms and towns, but he hardly remembers any of them.

"We have a queen."

"Ah, the Queendom of London."

"Mum met her," Pesto says with a sniffle as she looks straight down at her lap.

"I'm sorry about your mum, Pesto. But let me see what this note is that she left for me," Rodolfo says. *I think I would remember meeting a friend of the Queen of London.* He takes the note and unfolds it, angling it so the harsh lantern light shines brightly on it.

Rodolfo,

You don't know me. And I don't know you. But I was told by an important woman to find you. She said you were a kindly saloon owner, from a town with no name, always willing to listen. She said you had a good heart. If you are reading this, it means I died on our journey, but my daughter, Pesto, survived. I told her to find you. It was a long shot, but don't good people surviving in such misery deserve a miracle? Mother, the woman who told me about you, said Pesto could hide out with you. I was also told to let you know that Pesto is fluent in Murrayskindacoolish.

I don't even know what that is, but you need to make use of her knowledge. She's always been a special little girl. Well, you'll see. And I trust Mother. We all did. You should too.

Thank you so much, Rodolfo. Please take care of Pesto.

Love,

Marilynn

"Pesto, this is the sign I needed!" Rodolfo says. "You can read?" Excitement builds in his heart. *Mother? How is it all connected? Hero's mother? Destiny? Does this mean she and Toaster are still alive? It must. I asked for a sign, and I got it.*

"Turkey leg yum," Pesto replies.

"But you can read?" Rodolfo asks again. This is important but she's ignoring me. *Women are so hard! Why don't they listen?*

"I miss Mum and Dad," Pesto says.

Great, the biggest clue ever, Hero and Toaster aren't here, and this half-zombie, half-girl hybrid doesn't want to talk. If I can just get her to open up . . . Even if it didn't work with Hero, as a saloon owner, I know listening is important. "I'm sorry about your parents," Rodolfo says. "My parents died also."

Still in Rodolfo's lap, Pesto puts the turkey leg down on the floor and curls up. She starts crying on his leg. Rodolfo takes the ballerina flying zombie girl bear and puts it in her arms. Then he takes the blanket Author gave them and puts it over her. The warmth of both is making his stay in the overturned wagon a bit more comfortable. That's good because, even if she wasn't the key to all this, he would still

want her to feel safe. *But maybe she can truly read the relics and books that got thrown outside the wagon? Maybe these last seven days are starting to make sense? We have to reach them somehow.*

Chapter 16

An Object in Motion

"Hero, I'm scared," Toaster says, still holding her hand. They are in front of the strange and unexpected building, having lost Rodolfo not more than an hour ago.

"It's okay, Toaster. Do you want to know a secret?" she asks while forcing a smile.

"Do you have more powers you didn't tell us about?" he asks. "I saw the talisman light up, but you didn't explain it." *Is that how she really survives out here? That would make sense. Rodolfo and I didn't last more than an hour.* He stifles back some tears.

"No, nothing like that. But you have to promise you won't tell anyone. Ever. I'm serious," Hero demands, some of her fierceness back. Her eyes are threatening Toaster like daggers, even though he knows in his heart that she's trying to comfort him.

"Surely, I won't, Hero. I promise," Toaster answers, eager to hear the important secret now.

"I'm scared too," Hero says. Then she squeezes his hand a little tighter—he's not sure if her grip means "I'm here for you," or "If you tell anyone, no one will ever find your mangled corpse because I would have eaten it after I murdered you."

"You?" Toaster asks, curious as ever, looking at her in amazement. "The most amazing warrior I've ever seen? You're scared?"

"Yes. Always. Very much so now. And ever since I can remember. The minute I'm not scared, it's because I'm dead. So just remember that, Toaster. Fear is your friend. That's how you survive out here, in your town, or in there." Hero lets go of his hand and points at the building. "In fact, for whatever reason—actually, I know the reason: I was distracted by some annoying god—I wasn't scared for that one second in some no-name town, entering some little building called *Saloon*, and I got whacked with an iron pot. See what I mean?" She turns to him and smiles an awkward smile, like a hand-drawn picture of a smile.

Now Toaster is *sure* she's just trying to comfort him. "Yes, Hero. But I never would have met you if you didn't let your guard down."

"Harrumph," Hero grunts. "And don't you dare ever tell anyone! Or you'll have to fear *me*. Now let's go inside, and find some safety."

They can still hear the sound of zombies, while distant. As they approach the front of the building, hand in hand, they finally notice the door in front, which is made completely of glass.

"I've never seen anything like it," Hero says. "So much glass. So clear. Even Barnaby's carriage didn't have glass this clear. How is this possible?" She stops, clearly afraid to get any closer.

"I was right. It's like right from the ancients." He steps forward with his hand out to touch the glass. The door slides open on its own.

"I think you're right, Toaster. We have to find a way inside." The door slides closed. Then it slides open again. Then closed. "If we time it right, maybe we can get in." Then open. Then closed. "Let me try." She takes a step toward the door.

"But, Hero, it may swallow you whole!" Toaster cries, extending his arms to try and pull her back.

"Good point," Hero agrees and stops. "Let me check with Murray. Maybe he has some advice for getting through this glass jaw of death."

"Before the zombies find us," Toaster pleads, looking behind them. But she doesn't hear him—she's already looking up and to the left.

H. Murray! What the hell is this thing?

I told you, I didn't make it! But it's a door.

H. Holy buckets! Is that what this is? A door! This glass jaw of death is a door? It looks like it wants to eat us!

Calm down, it's just an electronic door from my world. I think.

H. Your fantasy heaven-world has doors like this?

Yes, all over. Some even turn in circles, though I'm glad you don't have to deal with that one.

H. Can we negotiate with it? What does it want?

Um . . . it doesn't want anything, as far as I know. It's just a door. But you shouldn't go in!

H. Murray, we're going in. Mother spoke to me again. She told me to go in. It was like my dreams.

I'm not sure I can help you in there. I have no idea what's in there.

H. Just tell me how to get past the door.

Okay, okay. It's really not that hard. You just walk through. I don't think it will crush you if you're standing in its path. It . . . it wants to help you.

H. Your world is hateful with its ma . . . saj . . . jets and man-eating doors that want to help.

Sometimes it feels that way.

H. Why even put something from your world into my world? Isn't *that* cheating?

What aren't you getting? I told you! I warned you! I didn't make that building or the door. And I didn't send

you any message from Mother. I lost control of your story somehow when your talisman went all haywire. We're lucky we can still speak to each other, as far as I know. But I think I have a plan, don't worry.

H. [derisive laugh] As long as you have a plan.

I'm thinking I'm just going to write anything I can to try and get control back, even if it's just little things to help you along the way. Like throwing spaghetti against the wall and seeing what sticks.

H. Spa ... ghet ... ti?

Oh, it's a dish of long cylindrical noodles often served with some type of delicious sauce, like pesto—

H. Noodles? Do you know what *we* just snacked on?

No, I, uh, didn't even write anything about you snacking. I was busy writing some other scene.

H. I have some free will now, remember? Toaster too.

Oh, that's getting really worrisome.

H. Bugs! As we approached the building, I noticed a nest and—

Oh, man, just stop! Gross!

H. Thankfully, we had Barnaby's jugs to drink, or I would have had to find a camel—

Gross! Oh man!

H. So you see, I hate your fantasy world with its ma . . . saj . . . jets, sweet treats, man-eating doors and its spa . . . ghet . . . ti.

No, no, you'll like spaghetti! If I can just get this to work. It's better than bugs! You'll see!

H. Wait! How's Rodolfo?

Suddenly, in front of Hero and Toaster, on the ground, are two steaming-hot bowls of spaghetti.

"Hero, look!" Toaster exclaims. "Did the Author send you those? How will those help us get through the door? Do we tie them to ourselves so we can pull each other out if the door is eating you?"

Hero shakes her head. "No, Toaster. I think it's just food. Noodles. I told him about the bugs, and so he sent us something to eat called spa . . . ghet . . . ti."

"Oh," Toaster answers. "But I'm still full from the bugs." He rubs his belly.

"I know, Toaster. He just doesn't understand our world. Let me tell you sometime about how he bathes with something called ma . . . saj . . . jets. But he did tell me how to get across. It's easier than we thought. He said if we were in the path of the door, it wouldn't close on us."

As the door opens again, Hero stoically stands in its path. Ever so brave, she risks her life to prove her point to Toaster. Unfortunately, she is wrong. The door starts to close, slams into Hero, and pushes her into the doorframe. "Toaster! Holy buckets, that jackass Murray was wrong!" Hero ekes out.

"Hero!" Toaster screams. Without any other ideas or weapons to fight the cunning man-eating door that somehow tricked the Author, the God of gods, weaver of all things, Toaster picks up one of the bowls of spaghetti and tosses it at the door. It crashes through the glass, scattering it everywhere. Toaster can swear he heard it growl in pain.

But the door is not letting go. Hero's arms and legs are flailing about, trying to, unsuccessfully, gain any leverage against it. "Throw another one!" Hero orders him, her arms and legs sticking out of the door.

So, Toaster picks up the other bowl and tosses it at the door. *If this doesn't work, what else can I do against that beast?*

Unfortunately, Toaster's aim is off—he doesn't have a lot of practice tossing bowls around because his brother would fire him from the saloon for a stunt like that. The bowl is wide right. Wide right! And way too high! Toaster is utterly broken inside when he sees he missed the body of the beast entirely. *I let her down. I got her killed.*

But the bowl strikes something neither of them noticed before. In the upper right corner of the door was a small black body part with a red eye. After getting hit with the bowl of spaghetti, it falls to the ground, and the red eye turns black. *Is it dead? Did I kill it?*

As the beast's eye turns black, the man-eating glass jaw of death, which is also a door, loses all power, stops grunting, and the flailing Hero pushes it back with ease. It's not coming back to eat her again. Hero pokes it, and it doesn't move.

"Toaster! You got it!" Hero cheers, pumping a fist into the air.

"I got it right in the eye. I didn't mean to, but I did!" Toaster laughs, smiling uncontrollably.

"Look at you, also surviving the desolate roads," Hero says as she playfully hits him on the shoulder, and tussles his dirty, greasy hair like Rodolfo used to do. Toaster is beaming.

"I did, didn't I?"

"Now, let's head inside and look around," Hero orders.

The pair walk into the building through the broken glass. Inside feels cool after being in the desert heat. "It's nice in here," Toaster comments, happy to have the hot sun off their backs. Even better, there are plush, leather-covered chairs in colors Hero has never even seen before. Toaster jumps on one of the couches and kicks up his legs. "I could stay here forever. Ancients know their furniture. These are way more comfortable than straw."

But then they hear someone say, "Ah, new patients!" Hero and Toaster look farther back into the room toward the sound, and see an old woman with spectacles and the grayest hair Hero has ever seen seated at a desk. *How can someone live to be so old?* She is wearing white clothing, which looks like a dress. "Don't worry about the door. We'll get a repair crew in. It's been doing that occasionally," the old woman informs them.

"Why would you repair such a monster?" Hero asks, incredulously. "Are you an ancient, in control of beast and magic alike?"

"Oh, you're one of those," the old woman answers. "Look, you're just lucky I'm not going to charge you for the damage. Rhonda isn't always so nice."

"Who's Rhonda, ma'am?" Toaster speaks up.

"Oh, look at you, you cute little boy. Haven't you ever heard of the third person?" the woman replies.

"It's just the two of us, ma'am," Toaster informs her.

"And I'm almost sorry about what's going to happen to the *two* of you," the woman says, the threat evident.

Hero instantly has two daggers, one in each hand, cursing herself inside for not heeding Murray's warning. Toaster is behind her. The old woman, who some know as Rhonda, is laughing maniacally.

"I'm scared, Hero," Toaster says.

"Remember what I said," Hero replies.

Six large men also dressed in what can only be described by the denizens of this dystopian wasteland of a world as white dresses come from the side of the room. They're approaching Hero and Toaster with angry faces.

"Be careful. They were able to break the door," the old woman, maybe named Rhonda, says to the men from her safe spot behind the desk. "And you don't want to damage the new patients." She turns to Hero. "Welcome to FRF."

"Hey, Reggie," one of the men says. "Doesn't look like these two are gonna go easy. And I don't want to get their filth on my scrubs. Just tranq' 'em." The words sound like another language to Hero and Toaster.

Reggie heads back to the wall where they entered, presses a button, and a gun magically appears in his hands. He brings up the gun to aim it at Hero and Toaster.

"What is that?" Toaster asks Hero.

"That doesn't look good," Hero says.

H. Murray! Stop with this stupid spaghetti!

It's not me. My hands are just automatic writing. I'm sorry, Hero. I did what I could.

Instantly, there's a sharp sting in Hero's arm. She sees what can only be described as a tiny arrow in her shoulder. Toaster has one too.

H. I hate you, Murray!

And then they fall asleep.

* * *

Hero's eyes open to see a different pair of eyes staring right into hers. Not Toaster's.

Without thinking, she makes a sweeping motion with her legs (before she is even aware she still has legs). She can feel herself make contact with the ankles of whoever was staring into her eyes. The man starts to fall to the floor next to her. Before he even hits the ground, she rolls over, watches him go down onto the floor, and is instantly on top of what she now sees is a large, rotund man. Her elbow is on his throat.

She also intended to hold a dagger to his throat, but her black leather trench coat, with its weapons and talisman, is gone. All she has on her body is a white dress like everyone else in this building. Who the hell undressed her and changed her clothes?

Now she's even madder. And that trench coat was the only thing she ever had from her mother—passed down among loyalists of King Reginald III so she could have it when she came of age, not that they were going to give it to her when she actually was old enough. She had to steal it as she ran away, which actually makes it even more special to

her. So now, she's in a boiling rage. Her elbow digs farther into this man's throat.

"Where are my clothes? And my weapons?" she seethes, purposefully not mentioning her talisman. The large man is almost triple her size. But as she's learned on the desolate roads, size doesn't matter. Only skill, cunning, ferocity, and fear. But she also notices his clean and shiny brown hair and trimmed beard, which look out of place in the Lands.

"Big Frederico, she got you good!" an older woman's voice laughs.

Hero glances over quickly to see her. *I can take her easily.* The woman is also in a white gown and has dark-red hair with streaks of gray. She looks so clean.

Hero suddenly has a realization. She touches her own head with her free hand. Her brown hair feels clean too! It's not matted to her head and greasy, as usual, but flowing and silky. She can even feel the ends of her hair tickle her neck, which also feels clean. She hasn't had too many baths in her life, but she does remember the feeling now that it's happened again. Someone bathed her? While she slept? Now she is enraged! Her elbow pushes into the man's throat even more, and her eyes slice into his soul.

"Mona! I know!" the large man replies to the older woman, still under Hero's dangerous body. "We're not your enemy, miss. Please stop!" His words are muffled by the pressure on his throat.

"If I had my weapons, you'd already be dead. And even without them, I can break your neck with one move. Now, where are my clothes?" Hero hisses.

"I would think you'd be more concerned with your little friend than your fabric," Big Frederico manages to say.

"Toaster!" Hero suddenly remembers. *How could I forget him? Rodolfo would be so disappointed in me. I'm disappointed in myself.* "Where is he?"

"If you take the elbow off my neck, we'll tell you," Big Frederico says.

"He's right over here, in the corner," the woman named Mona says, deciding to offer the information as an olive branch.

Without taking her elbow off Big Frederico's neck, Hero looks over and sees Toaster, in a child-size white gown, curled up in the corner of this room. She can see his chest rising and falling. He's still alive. He must be sleeping. *What the hell happened to us? Where are we? Why would Mother tell me to come here?*

Hero takes her elbow slightly off Big Frederico's throat. She thinks about going to Toaster, but he looks okay for the moment. And answers may be more important. The older woman named Mona seems willing to talk. "What happened to us?" Hero asks her. "What is this place?"

Big Frederico opens his mouth to answer, but Mona cuts him off. "I can handle this one, Big." Hero doesn't take her eyes off the man underneath her. Seeing that, Mona walks more into her line of sight. "I think she'll trust me more than you at the moment. Isn't that right, miss?"

Hero glances at Mona and nods. In that brief moment, she notices other people in the room, lots of them, also in white gowns. They're watching the whole scene.

"Okay, I'm just going to come out and say it," Mona begins. "We're all patients in a very strange hospital that floats in and out of different times and parallel universes, but always in the same physical location on the planet Earth.

Does any of that make sense to you?" She looks at Hero with kind eyes, and then she sneezes into a red handkerchief.

And that's when Hero notices it. Big Frederico and all the patients in this large white room have red handkerchiefs. And some are also blowing their noses and sneezing into them. Some have them in pockets in the front chest pockets of their white gowns. *Where am I?*

"Host . . . spittle? Uni . . . vus?" Hero asks. "What is that?"

"Oh god, we're in one of those places," Big Frederico says, rolling his eyes. "Either dystopian or very early civilization. Hard to tell when everyone's in the same white gown. They should give out ID cards."

"Shut up, Big," Mona says. She meets Hero's eyes. "A hospital is a place where sick people go to be treated. To get better. Does that make any sense to you?"

"Like a healer, or a barber," Hero supposes.

"Yes, yes." Mona nods. "Except this hospital is much more advanced. We suspect it's from the future. A possible future. But what you really need to know right now is that we're not your enemy. We're on the same side, in the same predicament. Out there is our enemy." Mona points to a set of white double doors. "The doctors and nurses who run this hospital are their version of your healers—though that's the wrong word for them. They're the ones who made us sick." And on cue, she blows into a handkerchief. "Us in here—we're all in this together. Suffering. But we can work together." She blows her nose again.

"Her? She's from some backward past," some other patient speaks up as he approaches. "You heard her! Barbers? Healers? What good is she to us in the face of those people? Those *things*?" The new patient points at the white double doors. He's a short, skinny man with spectacles. He's not sneezing in a handkerchief, though. It's dark red and sticking out of the front, chest pocket of his white gown. He stands next to Mona.

"Dr. Mathers, please stop being such a time-ist. You saw how she took down Big so quickly," Mona says. "He's four times her size! I'm sure we can find a use for someone like her. We all have a use, regardless of how advanced *you* think we are."

Dr. Mathers grunts.

"Yeah," Big agrees, still from underneath the girl who took him down so quickly, with her elbow at his neck. "And not everyone is from an advanced civilization like you. We already told you about that dystopian lady who escaped before you got here. Mother."

Suddenly, Hero rolls off Big Frederico, onto her knees, and asks with intensity, "What did you say? *Who?*"

"Mother," he confirms. "Some lady. Only one to ever escape."

"I still don't believe it," Dr. Mathers says with a wave of his hand.

"It was some fifteen years ago. Right, Big?" Mona asks him. Big Frederico, now kneeling on the floor, rubbing his throat, nods. "A lady named Mother joined us. She said she found us while out looking for water to help with a hundred-year drought or something like that."

Hero's heart is leaping out of her chest. She wants to go run to Toaster and tell him. She wants to hug Rodolfo.

H. Murray, you jackass! No, I don't!

How'd you know it was me?

H. I had a feeling that I wasn't in control. I never noticed before, but I do now. Like a force is pushing me.

See, you do have feelings! Guess what? Once you guys got inside, I could see everything there. And then when they took that talisman off you, I got some control back. Well, I actually can't control any of the hospital workers, but I can control you, Toaster, and the patients. Like I can keep that Big guy from smushing you.

H. I can take him on my own, Murray!

And you would have, for sure. But not without your talisman. It's all very strange, though. Why can't I control the hospital workers? Do they have their own talismans? Maybe I can make things happen out of the hospital's control, though, like with objects? It's just, when they show up, I go into that weird automatic writing thing.

H. So, it's the ghoul? Or a wizard?

I don't know what it is. Luckily, you still have some of my protection.

H. So get us out of here!

What? No! This is more exciting than anything else I could have come up with. And who's to say I didn't? They are my hands on the typewriter. I don't think the US Copyright Office would mind if I slap my name on this thing. This is going to sell!

H. We're prisoners in a hospital of horrors! And you want to sell books?

Yeah, and it's actually kind of fun, if you ignore the part about me losing my mind. Now I get to write against a real villain I can't even control, in my own story. It's like a fun little puzzle.

H. Fun? My story? Without the talisman, I don't have any control!

How do you know?

H. I just tried killing Dr. Mathers! It didn't work!

But you shouldn't kill him, anyway. I need all these characters for an escape.

H. Please, Murray, even if I lose control, can it still be a parnutship?

Yes, Hero, this would be more of a meeting of the minds, if you don't have control, but don't worry. I'll take care of you. Clearly, I need your help.

H. Yeah, meeting of the heads! Now get us out of here! That's what my head wants.

Don't forget, you just got another clue.

H. Oh, right.

Oh, this is going to be great. A real challenge. I feel so energized!

They have to be talking about my mother, she thinks.

"What was she like?" Hero can't help but ask. But she's also cautious—information is power, and she doesn't want these possible enemies to know what she thinks. Or that Mother told her to come here. But she has to know what they know.

"What's your name?" Mona asks her.

"Hero," she admits, still kneeling.

"What kind of name is that?" Dr. Mathers scoffs. "Only on a backward dystopian—"

"Shut up, Dr. Mathers," Mona says.

He waves his hand dismissively at her but obliges.

Mona sits cross-legged on the clean, white floor. Watching her sit, Hero notices for the first time it's not a dirt, clay, or wood floor. It's some strange white, hard substance. Everything about this place is white, which itself is strange. Could it really be a building from the future? Why would Mother send her here just to be captured?

"Come here, Hero. Sit with me, and we'll tell you about everything," Mona says.

Hero joins her. She feels strange sitting cross-legged with some old, red-haired woman. Like she's a little kid being told what to do. But she so wants to know. Needs to know. *Mother!*

Mona sneezes into her handkerchief. "It was fifteen years ago. Big and I and just a few others have been here that long. There's always some who die, some new patients, like yourself, but never anyone who escaped like Mother."

"It's just a story!" Dr. Mathers yells at them while leaning against a white wall.

"Shut up, Dr. Mathers," Mona replies. "I told you—Big and I have been here the longest and saw it happen in front of our very eyes. She escaped and disappeared. I tell you it's real."

"Yeah, what was it she always said to everyone? 'We all need a friend sometimes'?" Big Frederico adds. "And she got that family out, too, with their cute little girl. Paco? She almost got us all out. He's now massaging his throat and sitting on a cushioned white bench in the middle of the room, like the chairs in the lobby.

"There's no way that backward woman could beat such an advanced people," Dr. Mathers argues. He starts walking closer to Mona and Hero, probably looking to disagree with them some more.

This man is more infuriating than Rodolfo! Hero's rage is building. At least Rodolfo doesn't go looking for arguments.

Hero thinks she needs to teach him a lesson, or he'll keep dismissing Mother, and maybe even Toaster and her. She needs to cement her status in this power structure. So, she bides her time as he gets closer. He's close enough now.

Hero is up in an instant, standing behind Dr. Mathers, and grabs him in a choke hold. Her arms are wrapped outside and under the doctor's armpits, which are surprisingly clean, as no odor reaches her nose. *How often do these people bathe, or get bathed? Ew.* With her hands and fingers interlocked behind his head, she pushes his head uncomfortably forward into his chest. "Don't talk about my mother like that!" she yells at him.

"Oh, she got you good, too!" Big Frederico laughs, pointing at the skirmish. "Seems even she can beat someone as advanced as yourself."

"Your mother?" Mona asks, shocked. "Really?"

"Yes! And you tell him to shut up!" Hero rants at everyone.

Dr. Mathers grunts.

"Hero, I think he's agreeing. Please," Mona pleads. "He's relatively new here, only six months, and we actually need him. You see, he's helping us. We have a plan to get out of here. He's not always as bad as he sounds."

Hero lets go, and Dr. Mathers collapses on the ground, fighting for breath.

Mona looks at a wild-eyed Hero and asks, "Now, what's this about your mother?"

Chapter 17

Are You My Mother?

"You said Mother was out looking for water," Hero says to Mona. Hero is still standing, looking down at Mona. "My mother was a water diviner. Her name was Mother."

"Was she a sorceress?" Big Frederico asks. "Our Mother was a sorceress."

"Sorceress!" Dr. Mathers scoffs. "Is this the garbage you people believe in?" He rises back to his feet while rubbing his throat. "Magic?"

"You didn't know her, Dr. Mathers!" Big Frederico snaps back.

"And this hospital visits so many parallel universes, who's to say magic doesn't exist in some of them?" Mona argues.

"There is no such thing as magic! Only science!" Dr. Mathers seethes. "And only science will get us out of this mess."

"Where are you all from? Different times? Places? What is all this?" Hero asks.

Just then, Toaster starts to stir. He's rolling around and yawning. The noise gets Hero's attention. She thinks he looks ridiculously cute.

H. Hey! I don't think like that!

Come on, really? Cute little kid wiping the sleepies from his eyes?

H. Holy buckets! Sleepies? Are you for real? When I was on my own on the desolate roads, I would sleep ten minutes at a time while watching out for sand-wolves! And I'm supposed to be all warm and gooey over some little kid sleeping? He's lucky someone didn't jump him! He's lucky I didn't jump him just to teach him a lesson! He's my responsibility now.

Wow, you really can be cold. I was even thinking of giving him a little bankywanky. With kittens.

H. Where the hell did he get a little bankywanky from?

Suddenly, Hero is holding a pink bankywanky with cute kittens scattered across it like polka dots. It is one of the only two items she ever got from her mother.

"Look at her. Who's going to believe a girl holding a widdle bankywanky?" Dr. Mathers scoffs at her.

H. Hey, at least you proved my magic point for me!

Oh, right. Damn.

"But Dr. Mathers, doesn't that prove the existence of magic?" Big Frederico asks.

Don't count those chickens, though.

H. Chicken? What's a chicken?

Small little animal with wings that lays eggs.

H. I've never even seen a chicken!

Really? No poultry? Cornish hen?

H. Hen? That's a woman of the—

And turkey?

H. I think I've heard of those. Don't remember where. Never seen one, though.

"Magic? It just proves what a babywaby she is," Dr. Mathers replies.

Without replying, Hero rolls up the blanket like a garroting wire, while giving Dr. Mathers an evil eye.

He takes a step back in fear. "Uh . . . I'm . . . sorry," he stutters.

Hero loosens up the blanket.

H. Let me kill him, Murray! He's evil. They're all evil!

How do you know they're evil?

H. Holy buckets, Murray! They undressed and washed me while I was out cold!

Oh yeah, that. But to be fair, no one really did that.

H. What do you mean no one? I woke up in this gown all bathed! And you better get my trench coat back, or I'll jump out of this book and go all Aunt Cordelia on—

First, I'm concerned you actually said that. Second, it wasn't a person who bathed you. It was robots!

H. I don't care what their name was!

No, no. Robots. Mechanical men.

H. Men, Murray! Men! Vile men undressed me. I hate you!

You still don't understand. They're not real people. It's like . . .

H. Men!

Imagine a magic man of metal.

H. Oh . . . an automaton? Of bronze?

Yes, yes! Like that. But maybe silver.

H. A silver automaton saw me naked? Murray! I hate you!

You're still mad? I didn't do it. It was the hospital workers. I don't control them, remember?

H. I'm going to haunt you to the ends of the Lands!

What if I make it up to you?

H. You cannot make it up to me! Unless you let me murder Dr. Mathers.

No, no, you need him. We need him. He's important. But I can make it up to you now that I have control again. You'll see. I just thought of this instead of a blanket.

H. I'll believe it when I see it.

You're gonna love it.

H. I'll believe it when I see it.

Okay, okay. Watch this.

Instantly, Hero's clothes turn from the white gown back into her black leather trench coat, complete with all its current weapons, and her black leather pants. She has her black leather boots, too. The pink bankywanky is, unfortunately, gone.

H. Don't forget my dirt, Murray! And my smell! I
miss my smell!

Instantly, Hero's hair is greasy and matted. Dr. Mather's
nose turns upward. "What's that smell? Did one of the
patients die again?" He's looking around the room.

"Yes!" Hero cheers. And then she feels a tug at her trench
coat. *It's Toaster!* Hero smiles, glad to see the cute little kid
awake and smiling up at her. He's also in his original clothes.
Red woven jacket and brown linen knee-length trousers.

H. Fine! You're right. He *is* cute. I hate all men but
Toaster.

"How did this all happen? What is going on?" Dr. Mathers
asks. "And why did you zone out all of a sudden? Do you
have a neurological problem? *That* I can help you with."

"It was magic," Hero states simply and proudly, standing
a bit taller.

"There is no magic!" Dr. Mathers shouts. He might have
also stomped a foot, but no one noticed over the shouting.

"Oh yeah?" Hero asks. And realizing she now has her
talisman back, and control of her story—

**I forgot it was in your coat! Don't ruin my story.
Remember the partnership!**

H. And I'm the dimwit?

I never called you that.

H. You were thinking it!

Hero puts the talisman in one of her hands, takes her other hand, and pushes. By magic, Dr. Mathers slides across the room, into the far corner. He falls into a very sick old patient named Wesley, who is too busy sneezing and dying to care.

"Oh, you have *got* to tell us about yourself," Big Frederico says.

"Come sit again, dear." Mona pats the floor next to her.

I didn't mean for you to control the story again!

H. So?

I was enjoying trying to get you out of here on my own. It was a little challenge.

H. Then all your words of needing my help? More god lies?

No, definitely not. Look, some gods lie. But not me. Never to you. At least don't let others control the story. It's still a partnership.

H. Toaster can. But otherwise, fine, a parnutship. But that's all I wanted to do, anyway.

Hero, putting the talisman back in her coat pocket, joins Toaster and Big Frederico cross-legged on the floor. Dr. Mathers, not wanting to look weak to others, gets up and approaches slowly.

"Um . . . I may have . . . misspoke. As a scientist, I have to be open to new observations, and, uh, I do want to get out of here," the doctor says, apologizing without apologizing. "It looks like we *can* use your help."

"It's okay, Doctor, we know you mean well," Mona tells him and points to a spot in their circle on the floor. They look to Hero for acceptance. Hero nods. Dr. Mathers sits down in the circle, cross-legged on the floor.

Mona blows her nose into her handkerchief. Big Frederico lets out the loudest nose blow Hero has ever heard, including from some large and sickly Dystpopian men. Then Mona begins. "So first, I'll finish telling you what we know."

Big Frederico exclaims, "Hold on! Wait!" From his pockets he pulls out two large marionettes, one for each hand. "Okay, I'm ready now. You can start."

H. Puppets? Holy buckets, Murray! Why the puppets?

Max said teenagers like puppets. There was this Broadway show—

H. But where in the Lands was he hiding large puppets? In his pockets?

But you and Toaster . . . wouldn't it help you understand the story? I hate to be a time-ist, but it's about to get complicated.

H. See, you *do* think me dimwitted! I might take a puppet and decapitate it in front of everyone.

Hero, no! My readers will be horrified! That's the wrong genre.

H. So get rid of them! Or I will.

"Big Frederico," Mona scolds the large man. "You want me to tell the whole story using *puppets*?"

"Oh, you don't want them? I thought they would help the visual learners among us," Big Frederico explains. "And I worked so hard the last fifteen years, carving them with the stolen knife I made from . . . I don't remember, and the wooden pieces we've collected over the decades from . . . I don't remember."

"Put them away, Big," Mona demands.

"Aw, come on, Mona. I like them!" Big Frederico argues. "They're my friends. Sometimes we cuddle—"

"Don't worry, I can take care of it," Hero interjects.

H. Murray, seriously! Ditch the puppets now, or you'll force me to—

Okay, okay! Max will be disappointed, though. He was the one who wanted puppets.

Everyone in the circle jumps as the marionettes disappear.

"What in the world?" Dr. Mathers says. "She did it again. Magic! And she did that zoning out thing again too. Looking up and to the left. Who *are* you?"

"She's my sister!" Toaster snaps back and grabs Hero's hand from his spot next to her on the white floor. The warmest feeling overcomes Hero for a moment before she buries it.

"I'll tell you all about me," Hero replies, "but only after you finish *your* story. What is this place? Who are you all? Who were those doctors in the other room? What's a para . . . knee-verse?"

"This hospital, like I said, moves through time," Mona explains. "I, myself, am from 1986. Big Frederico is from the year 2023. Dr. Mathers is from the year 3001. There are others of us from various times." Seeing no understanding on Hero's face, she continues. "Us three can confirm our year count is similar because our pasts have some things in common, like Abraham Lincoln—"

"The great wizard!" Toaster exclaims. "You are all ancients!"

"Ancients?" Hero asks in shock, before the others can tell him Abraham Lincoln was not a wizard. She turns to Toaster and asks, "Is it true?" *Is that why Mother wanted me to come here?*

"They have to be. They're old!" Toaster answers.

"Hey!" Mona exclaims reflexively, putting a hand to her chest.

"And they know the great Abraham Lincoln! And Mother!" Toaster keeps gushing. "I just know it!"

"You know, that's what Mother said when she was here," Mona says thoughtfully. "So what year are you from?"

"Year? I'm not good at numbers. Ten . . . ," Hero says, trailing off, trying to count her fingers. "Ten?"

"10786," Toaster speaks up for them. "By Gregg's calendar. He must have been a famous warlord to have a calendar named after him. But it's year three by the Chester calendar, if that matters to you."

Hero is staring at Toaster, confused by all the information he just spouted out. "I think I killed a warlord named Gregg once. It was a miserable little town, though it had great food. But we don't know Abraham Lincoln. I have this ancient talisman with his picture on it, though."

"You have a penny? From our time?" Big Frederico asks, his eyes wide.

"Wow, I never thought I would see one again," Mona says with an exhale.

"How is this all possible? I must write a paper!" Dr. Mathers blurts out.

"Take a look," Hero says. She takes the talisman out from her jacket.

Big Frederico has his hand out to look, but Hero intends to hand it only to Mona, who smiles at Big Frederico and takes the coin.

"Hmm . . . not like any penny I've ever seen, but it does look like ol' Honest Abe. Can I give it to Big so he can look?" Mona asks warmly.

Hero smiles, and Mona hands the coin to Big Frederico. He looks and shakes his head. And without asking, he starts to hand the coin to Dr. Mathers. Hero jumps forward to snatch it, but Dr. Mathers already has it. *That man is infuriating!* Hero pushes her hand forward, as if she still had the magic power to toss Dr. Mathers across the room again, but nothing happens.

"I see," the brilliant Dr. Mathers says, noticing her action. "You just tried to throw me across the room but you couldn't. Without this?" He holds up the coin.

Hero nods. *It really is magic. Mother!*

"Well, it's definitely a penny from my time," Dr. Mathers inspects it very closely. "Yup, that's old Abe. Love the hat. So, this is about seven thousand years old? What great condition! But I don't recognize the writing. That's new. It's the same font, though. Almost like it was made by the same process, but different." Dr. Mathers hands the coin back to her. Hero starts to grab for it, but he pulls it back. "Actually, I think we'll all be safer if I keep it." He starts to put the coin in his handkerchief pocket.

Suddenly, the group hears a strange sound. Dr. Mathers yelps, "Ow!" and he drops the coin on the floor. Hunched over in pain, he's holding one hand in the other. "That thing zapped me!"

Hero quickly swipes the talisman off the ground and puts it in her coat.

"I don't think it likes you, Doctor." Big Frederico laughs. "The coin's got good taste."

"It only wants Hero. It was from her mother. It's magic," Toaster informs them.

"Promise you won't throw me across the room again," Dr. Mather demands, slowly regaining his upright position.

That annoying man!

"I don't need a coin for that," she answers, flashing the inside of her trench coat with her throwing stars and daggers again. She feels a pang of regret for her lost morning star.

Dr. Mathers, wide-eyed, says, "My world had no weapons, you know. We were civilized. No murder, no kidnapping." He waves at the conditions around them.

"But you guys did *something* wrong to cause all the dystopian worlds we've seen after your time," Mona points out.

"That had nothing to do with me!" Dr. Mathers retorts. "I was at my research facility in the city of New Frisco, Arizona. I was so close to solving the mystery of DNA errors and damage—*this* close to creating immortality. My work kept me up most nights, so one night I decided to go for a stroll and ponder my work on immortality. I was alone at the edge of my neighborhood, and that's when I saw this hospital suddenly appear in the middle of the desert. I was intrigued, so I decided to walk inside. And whammo!"

"Did you just say *whammo*, Doctor?" Big Frederico laughs.

"Yes, I'm learning old and vapid colloquialisms from you dolts," Dr. Mathers snaps back. "Anyway, then I get kidnapped and injected. Do you know what this is all about, dystopian girl?" Hero stares blankly at him. "These fools didn't know. I bet not even Mother. But I figured it out in my mere six months. They're injecting us with some virus. Actually, that's not true. They also seem to be testing some vaccine, because some of us, like me, don't get sick. But some are very sick, like that Wesley character you threw me into. Poor guy. Some get so sick, their skin turns all gray and black and chafes."

"Like zombies!" Big Frederico exclaims. "Real, live zombies!" He puts his arms out and sways side to side like a zombie. Hero and Toaster turn to each other. Their facial expressions say to each other to stay quiet.

"Ugh, this again? Why must you fools all revert back to magic and paranormal all the time?" Dr. Mathers sighs. "Anyway, every once in a while, the nurses come in and take us into a separate room where they suck out all our mucus into a large vat. That's more painful than the nighttime baths. And why, you ask?"

"Um . . . I didn't ask. I don't really understand any of this," Hero says.

"Perhaps the puppets—" Toaster says as Big Frederico slaps him on the back in agreement, interrupting his thought.

"I agree, Toaster!" Big Frederico beams.

"No puppets," Dr. Mathers and Mona both say.

Dr. Mathers continues. "A virus is like a sickness. And we wouldn't have any idea why this is happening, except that our dear Mona, a self-proclaimed love child of something called *the sixties*—"

"Love not war," Mona interrupts him, flashing a peace sign with her fingers.

"As she says, and I would never have believed her except for what I just saw," the doctor continues snidely. "She canoodled with one of the nurses and was secretly told our mucus powers some evil magic for some kingdom called Fant."

"Fant!" Hero exclaims.

"You know it?" Big Frederico asks, surprised.

"Yes," Hero continues and then leans in and lowers her voice. "The Queendom of Fant killed my mother, Mother. The one who gave me the magic talisman." She holds back tears she never allows herself to show. Toaster grabs her hand again. She smiles at him, the family she never had or wanted, but now loves. Hero decides that can allow herself to feel that, at least. She's owed that much by this horrible world. "I should have known they were behind this. My Kingdom of Dystpopia was in a hundred-year war with them. But they're the only kingdom in all the Lands with powerful evil magic now that Mother . . . They're just too

strong."

"What are the chances?" Mona asks Big Frederico and Dr. Mathers. "We've had people before who were . . . not ancients, as you call us. From either our past or our future. We call the distant future ones dystopians, like you. Every other universe during your time is also dystopian. It's sad, really. What did humanity do to itself? But that's beside the point. Well, the dystopians, like you, never know what a hospital is. Or a virus."

"I still don't," Hero admits. "Host spittle? And I don't know what mucus is."

"Snots, girl. Snots!" Big Frederico laughs. Then he blows his nose. Hero laughs too. Their situation is so sad, it *is* laughable.

"Ah, it makes sense," Toaster speaks up to the adults. "I have heard of evil magic that uses all sorts of wicked things, like old hair, blood, toenails, earwax, crusty—"

"Blech!" Dr. Mathers says. "I hate magic. But, clearly, there is more to your universe."

"It could be a parallel dimension," Big Frederico says.

"Parallel *universe*," Dr. Mathers retorts. "You keep getting it wrong!"

"Whatever, dude," Big Frederico replies. "Shut up before I knock you parallel."

"Oh boy, these two. They're like my twin boys. Always fighting. I miss them," Mona says. She looks away, distant and sad.

Then the door to the room swings open violently. A large metal robot walks in. It has a cylindrical, silver-colored head with glowing red eyes. To the ancients in the room, the head looks like a common can of peas with eyes. To the dystopians in the room, it looks like some sort of metal daemon head. The body looks like metal muscles with exposed gears where there would be joints. It is seven feet tall and fearsome.

"An automaton! Murray was right!" Hero yells, reaching for a dagger. She briefly wonders whether a dagger would have any effect against an automaton, but if it doesn't work, she's already devising at least ten different battle scenarios in her head.

"Don't move a muscle, Hero. Those are the nurses," Big Frederico explains. "You don't want to tussle with them. Anyone who tries never comes back."

"Mona canoodled with an automaton?" Toaster asks, piecing the prior conversation together.

"Hey, it's been fifteen years here. And they're kind of cute," Mona says. "Plus, you wouldn't know it from looking at them, but they're sensitive creatures if you can get them talking. Which I intended to do."

The big, strong automaton tosses a sick patient standing in its way to the floor, then heads to Wesley. In a harsh robotic voice, it says, "It is time." The automaton picks up Wesley, leans him over its shoulder, and walks out of the room.

"Now you see what we're up against," Dr. Mathers says.

"But I saw regular people before," Hero says.

"Those? They only risk themselves for newcomers who aren't sick. Once you're infected, they use the robots. Or automatons, as you say," the doctor explains.

"So . . . Toaster and I—" Hero starts.

"Are infected, yes," Dr. Mathers finishes his sentence for her.

It bothers her to have someone speak her words for her,

especially a man, but she's too distracted trying to figure this all out to act on it. Life on the desolate roads was so much less complicated. *I miss it now.*

"With sickness?" she asks further. Sickness always scared her, as it was a foe she could not beat by force and cunning.

"Time will tell if you have the vaccine or the virus," Dr. Mathers answers.

"I'm sorry, Toaster. I'm so sorry. We should never have come in here." Hero looks sadly at the boy. If only she hadn't charged headstrong into this place. She already let him down. *I put a living Toaster in danger because of a dead Mother. I am a dimwit.* She's been an older sister for mere hours, and she's already failed. *How did Rodolfo do it for years?*

"It's okay, Hero," Toaster says, taking her hand. "I just know we'll be okay. We have *you.*"

She tries to smile at him. *Is this how you do it?* Her smile hides her thoughts. *I failed Rodolfo. I miss him. No, I don't. Argh!*

Trying to change the subject from the unfortunate truth of their predicament, Mona turns to Big Frederico. "Hey, Big. Tell them how you got here."

"What? Huh?" he starts, then realizes Mona just wants to distract the two young newcomers from their plight. "Oh, right. I am from an island called Puerto Rico."

"It sank into the ocean in my time," Dr. Mathers adds with a derisive laugh, clearly just to needle Big.

"You already told me that, Doctor," Big Frederico replies.

"I know. I'm just alerting our guests," Dr. Mathers persists. "In case they were thinking of booking a tropical cruise."

Mona rolls her eyes at the two childish men.

"Well," Big Frederico continues, ignoring the doctor, "I left Puerto Rico to look for work, and, for reasons that don't need exploring at this moment, I wound up wandering the Arizona desert. But I *will* admit that it involves a high-stakes poker game. And a fledgling jetpack company in need of an angel investor."

"Oh, I just love that story," Mona adds.

"Um … so how do we get out of here?" Hero asks, ignoring Big Frederico's origin story.

"Dr. Mathers?" Mona chimes in, giving him the floor. "It was your idea."

The doctor takes a deep breath. "Well, it involves a spoon."

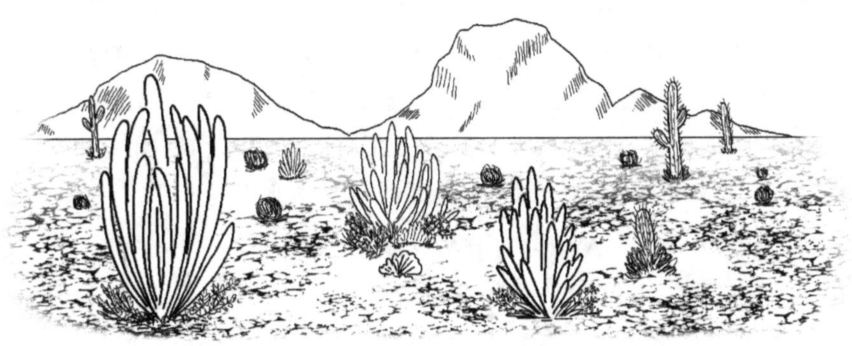

Chapter 18

The Great Spoon-scape

H. A spoon, Murray? Seriously? How can a spoon get us out of a host spittle and past the automaton guards?

Trust me, I know what I'm doing. Every book needs an exciting, hair-raising escape. And there was this old TV show Max and I would binge that did stuff like this. They would use everyday items to do amazing things. It was very successful. Though I'm not copying. I swear. I'm just emulating.

"Seriously?" Hero scoffs as she gets up and drags Toaster from the floor. They take a few steps as if they're going to go sit someplace else—away from the crazy people who think they can solve all the world's problems with a spoon.

"A spoon? That's the best you could come up with? You wouldn't survive on the desolate roads between kingdoms."

Mona stands and calls after her, "Hero, it's not what you think." Dr. Mathers and Big Frederico also get up from the floor to follow Hero and plead their case.

Hero stops walking away. She turns back around. "Did my mother use a spoon too?" she challenges them. "Did she escape with a nice gazpacho?"

H. Murray, you're putting words in my mouth. Stop that!

Sorry! It seemed like a nice place for a joke, and the typewriter let me.

H. What's gazpacho?

It's a fancy soup.

H. What's soup?

Forget it. Not important.

"No, don't be silly. They only serve us a delicious gray glop here," Big Fredrico replies.

"I keep telling him it might be made of *people*," Mona points out.

"Regardless," Big Frederico says, "it's delicious. In any event, your mother had magic. Lots of magic. She could freeze the guards. Create mist and smoke. She would wave a hand and make people see what they wanted to see. It

was amazing! And so, unless you have more magic in your talisman, it's the spoon."

Wow, Mother sounds amazing, Hero thinks. *But I can't tell them about the messages through the talisman. Or controlling the story.*

"No, I don't think it does anything else," she says.

"Well, we may need the girl to throw an automaton around or something," Dr. Mathers reluctantly offers. Mona and Big Frederico stare at him, surprised he is considering using magic.

"My magic might not work against other magic either."

"Mother's did, clearly," Dr. Mathers insists.

"Now you're defending her?" Hero replies. "I don't know. She had *real* magic. I just have Abraham."

"Or maybe Fant got stronger? They have been researching for at least fifteen years, right?" Toaster hypothesizes. "So maybe any magic might not work against Fant then, just like Hero's didn't work against the flying zombies?"

Hero beams. *He's so smart, he knew what I meant.*

"Flying zombies!" Dr. Mathers exclaims.

"Did we not mention the wings, Doctor?" Big Frederico laughs. "Oh well." He throws his hands up. "Looks like humanity's fate is worse than we thought if this Fant is so powerful."

Mona nods.

"So, what's the plan with the spoon? It does sound very exciting," Toaster asks the group, intrigued about their plan to escape the futuristic time-traveling multi-universal hospital of horrors guarded by seven-foot-tall automatons using nothing but silverware—and not even the sharp kind.

"I'm glad you asked, boy," Dr. Mathers says. He's as proud as Toaster is excited. The doctor takes a deep breath, and before Hero can stop him, or murder him, he opens his mouth wide.

"He's going to breathe fire! He's from Fant!" Hero screams, throwing her body in front of Toaster to guard him.

Instead, Dr. Mathers belts an up-tempo song.

"There,

Are,

A thousand and one things you can do with a spoon . . ."

H. Murray! Not a musical! I told you already. And certainly not a musical about a *spoon*.

No, no. Max said the kids these days dig musicals. Even more than puppets. Oh, puppet musicals!

Big Frederico takes out two marionettes from his pockets and makes them start dancing along to the tune. The puppets are now dressed in flowy, purple outfits along with dark sunglasses.

H. The puppets again! I should have decapitated them!

"You can eat some soup,

"Or sing a mean tune,

"You can dig out an eye,

"But why would you want to?

"You can pick up some poop,

"But don't eat it."

H. This went bad quickly. Or badder quicker. Or worser?

♫ "Or you can build a,
♫ "World-class,
♩ "Medical research,
♫ "Laboratory!"

Then Dr. Mathers and Mona start violently shaking their hands in the air in unison, in something the ancients in the room know as "jazz hands," but the dystopians know as "shaky hand sickness," a highly contagious malady where an unfortunate victim's hands shake and then fall off.

"With a spoon!" the doctor finishes as the melody resolves. The group has stopped dancing and is frozen in place in various interesting and coordinated dance poses. Dr. Mathers is kneeling on the floor in front of Mona, who is standing behind Dr. Mathers but leaning her body to the left, and Big Frederico and his puppets are behind Mona, leaning to the right.

"But how 'bout a ladle?" Mona asks to no one in particular, staring straight ahead.

"No, Mona, a spoon!" Dr. Mathers answers, also staring straight ahead and finally finishing his song.

"She always asks that. It's like their thing," Big Frederico informs Hero and Toaster as he walks away from Mona and the doctor, putting the puppets (magically?) back into the small pockets in his gown.

"Hero, Hero, did you hear all that? A medical laboratory," Toaster repeats.

"Yeah, I heard it," Hero answers.

"But you were looking up and to the left," Toaster reminds her.

"Not long enough, Toaster. Not long enough," Hero laments. "Unfortunately, I heard it all. I heard the whole damned song. A world-class medical research laboratory. Whatever that is. With a spoon?"

H. Murray, what's a world-class medical research laboratory?

You know how to say it? Those are some new words for you.

H. I'm not a dimwit, you know.

Oh. Well, it's a place to study sicknesses with the goal of curing them.

"Hero? Hero?" Dr. Mathers asks, trying to get Hero's attention. "You ask a question and don't even listen—"

"I'm listening. Spoon. Yay," Hero mutters, annoyed.

"Well, you're half right. It's actually two spoons," Dr. Mathers says, still with some singsong effect left in his voice. "But using my knowledge of science from the year 3001, not to mention our superior musical theater arts, I can construct a Virus-o-Nomitor-Extracto-Supreme 7000XL using just one spoon. That machine, if I can remember the extremely well-written, award-winning technical manual correctly, written by that star of technical literature, Murray—"

H. Holy buckets! Do you realize how stupid this sounds?

Stupid? It's exciting! Like that show Max and I liked. And teenagers these days love technology and gadgets and gizmos. Max said!

H. Teck . . . nowl . . . whatever. You're just throwing spa . . . get . . . ti again!

Oh, come on. A virus-killing machine? Now I'm combining YA, dystopian, fantasy, and sci-fi. It's awesome. I'm rising above all book genres, like I originally wanted. You can even add in technical literature—I think I saw a row on that at Boones and Nooble. Now, if I can just get some baby care, you know, for the parenting genre—

H. Murray, stop with the babies!

Look, you're basically babysitting Toaster already. Have you had to change his diaper yet? How did you do it?

H. He's seven years old!

Oh, right. Too old? I never had kids. I was not fatherly material, my wife said, before she divorced me. I don't know. But I can fix that for you.

H. No! You said it was a parnut—

Suddenly, Toaster tugs on Hero's hand. She looks down, and he has turned into an approximately seventeen-month-old toddler. "Hewo, my bum-bum dirty," Toaster ekes out.

"Oh, quarks and leptons, the boy changed into a toddler right before our eyes!" Dr. Mathers shouts. "Why does magic always seem to happen when you're zoned out?"

"I don't know!" Hero says, recoiling in horror.

H. Murray, change him back! This isn't what we agreed to. It's not a parnutship! You said you wouldn't control us like that.

"Forget about magic, Doctor," Mona cuts in. "Look at the baby. He has the magic of cuteness. Aw. These are the seven essential steps for changing a diaper."

H. Murray, I'm serious. We can't escape and find Rodolfo if we're stuck changing diapers on the desolate roads.

But the readers—

H. How's this for your readers?

Hero starts to unzip her black leather pants. "Ooh, I have a big one to make too. All over the floor!"

"Me too," Big Frederico says, as he also starts to untie his gown. "I've been waiting my entire life for someone to throw away the bondages of all societal norms. And I shouldn't have had all that glop. Here goes—"

Hero! Okay, okay. Fine! You made your point. That's not the genre I want! This partnership is starting to worry me. Big Frederico didn't even know he was in

a story, yet I lost control of him. It's like he just had a natural reaction to your unnatural control.

H. Remember that. Now move on!

Hero zips her pants back up. "So, what's the other spoon for?"

"Uh," Big Frederico says. "So, we're not doing this?" Hero shakes her head, so Big Frederico ties his gown back up. Mona's hand is over her face in disgust.

Toaster is back to his normal, seven-year-old body. And everyone has their pants and gowns on. The floor is clean. There is no excrement visible anywhere. Societal norms win again.

Dr. Mathers turns to Big Frederico and says, "Show her."

Big Frederico starts taking his gown off again. "I thought we were putting them back on."

"The spoon, you Neanderthal!" Dr. Mathers exclaims.

"Oh!" After retying his gown, Big Fredrico takes out a normal-looking spoon from his pocket.

"It's just another spoon," Toaster announces.

"No, son," Dr. Mathers says proudly. "With this spoon, for the last six months, we have secretly been digging our way out of this hospital."

"Then we can get to our carriage and horses, Hero!" Toaster says excitedly.

"If they're still there," Hero replies pessimistically.

"Horses! Carriage!" Mona exclaims excitedly. Then she turns to Big Frederico. "See, Big, I told you to listen to Dr. Mathers and keep digging. If we get out before the hospital shifts universes again . . ."

Dr. Mathers asks Big Frederico, "How much longer do you think until the tunnel is ready?"

"Hold up, I have to show you," Big Frederico says. He runs, as well as a three-hundred-pound man can, to a corner of the large room. There is a bench lining the wall. Two patients, also in white gowns, are sitting on it, wheezing and coughing. Big Frederico yells at them. "Get off the bench, Ned and Jed! I told you, this is *my* bench!"

Both men are middle-aged. Ned is stick-skinny and Jed is very round. Both men have brown hair, though Jed's is curly and Ned's is straight. They look like the antithesis of twins, but also strangely related. And they are locked in the middle of an intense conversation, during the moments they're not both expectorating simultaneously.

"You big, dumb, @%^!@$@!^$@!" Jed screams at Big Frederico.

The whole room goes silent. Hero puts her hands over Toaster's ears, too late to practically hide the coarse words. *But it's what Rodolfo would want.*

"Jed, watch your language, my friend! I always tell you that your bad reputation will hurt you in the end," Ned admonishes his friend Jed, in some sort of rhyme.

Jed looks angrily at the floor, and composes himself by taking some deep breaths. He looks up at Big Frederico, glassy-eyed. "I'm sorry, Big, for being so crass. It's just, I'm tired of sitting here all day on my @$$."

"Hey!" Hero yells at them from across the room. "There are kids here."

"It's okay, Hero," Toaster tells her. "I *did* work at a saloon."

Hero shrugs and takes her hands off Toaster's ears.

Thankfully, Ned and Jed are off the bench, and Big Frederico moves it to the side to reveal a huge tunnel—wide enough to fit even Big Frederico.

"Okay, okay!" Dr. Mathers exclaims. "Put it back before the automatons see!"

Big Frederico lugs the bench back into its place. Ned and Jed hop back on and continue their heated conversation. Hero then notices how oddly similar Ned and Jed both look—including that they both talk with their hands. *How can they be so different yet look so much alike?*

"What's their story?" Hero asks Mona, as Big Frederico is walking back.

"Oh, that's an interesting one," Mona starts. "They're from the year 4752. Ned and Jed are the same person but from different universes. Jed showed up after Ned. The incessant rhyming is how we know things got bad for humanity after Dr. Mathers's time."

"Universes?" Toaster asks. "You keep saying that word."

"Oh, forget it. They'll never understand, anyway," Dr. Mathers dismisses the dystopians' lack of knowledge. Then he turns to Big Frederico, who just got back. "Very impressive, my friend. So how many days left until it's ready?"

Big Frederico looks at Dr. Mathers strangely, thrown off by Dr. Mathers calling anyone a friend. "Uh, two days I think!"

"Wow, I would say two more days for the Extracto to be ready, too. I just need to spoon in the remaining adjustments," Dr. Mathers says, in all seriousness.

"And then we can get out of here!" Toaster cheers.

"Wait a second," Hero says. "Does that mean while we're here, they're gonna *bathe* us?"

Chapter 19

Automaton Mommy Issues

H. I just got my clothes back, Murray! *And* my smell! What game are you playing here? I'm going to get bathed again? I'll give Big Frederico and his whole gang control, I swear. I'll tell them all about you. No baths!

No! And it's not my fault. I don't control the nurses. But it is kind of . . . totally my fault, I do admit that.

H. Fix it, Murray! Fix it!

But I can't. I wish I could. It's just . . . I kind of wrote myself into a pickle here. I need two more days of your time. Why do you think the Extracto won't be finished until then? But that's all, I promise. I'll think of something, I'm sure. And it's not my fault you went into the hospital.

H. Argh, fine. I'll give you two days. But I keep my clothes. *And* my smell.

Well, you know I can't promise you that. It depends on Fant.

H. What do you mean? Just write something like, "And all baths in the host spittle were canceled for two days by order of the Queen of Fant."

No, no. It'll never work. I don't think I can control Fant. The ghoul or wizard behind the automatic writing, maybe even behind your talisman . . . I can't even revise any of it. I tried erasing the hospital. I tell my fingers to erase, I tell my hands to throw out the page, but they won't move.

H. To think a ghoul or wizard can control the weaver of all things. It must be very powerful.

Or I'm just losing my mind.

H. Ah, your mind sickness.

Regardless, readers don't like amazing coincidences anyway. It's too hand-wavy. My readers—

H. Murrrrrrray!

Just listen to me, it doesn't even flow with the scene. Why would the queen do that? She doesn't get her

hands dirty with stuff like that. And I actually think the Queen of Fant loves long luxurious baths. It's an evil waste of water. Yeah, that's who she is if I were to really get to know her character. If I'm even still in control of her.

H. You know the queen, and you haven't assassinated her yet?

From my mind?

H. She's the cause of all my misery! She's killed thousands—

Yeah, about that. I actually don't think I can assassinate her. It's like the nurses. I can't control Fant any longer.

H. But why? It's your story scroll!

Which you and Mother are even controlling now. I've been thinking about it. So that hospital showed up out of nowhere; I can't revise it, delete it, or throw it out. Fant is controlling itself also. Can I even write Fant out of existence? Watch this:

Meanwhile, back in the Queendom of Fant, SkeLord came to his scheduled meeting with the queen, ready to fulfill his plan to assassinate her. After what happened in Saloon, he knew she would kill him for his failures—better to kill her first. He also tired of all the misery and mayhem and wanted to bring peace, prosperity, and happiness to all the Lands. But then he thought better of his motivation—he didn't want any peace or good things; he just wanted to survive. And power—*her* power. But maybe *some* peace would be nice, too.

He changes his mind again, then wonders why he would even think of something as silly as peace at a time like this.

So, when he walks into the throne room ready with a poisonous dart hidden inside his eye socket, he is surprised when the entire royal court jumps up and yells, "Happy birthday, SkeLord!" The queen has gifts of appreciation for him. She even offers him a private, luxurious bath with just her—the highest honor of any of Fant's soldiers.

To think, me, SkeLord, a skeleton, bathing! Will we canoodle? How's my breath? He feels more valued than he's ever felt in his entire nonlife, and quickly abandons his assassination plan. *I could get used to this.*

H. Watch what?

Oh, you can't see? I tried to have SkeLord assassinate the queen, but she somehow controlled the situation. I went into automatic writing mode, and he ended up having a romantic bath with her.

H. Ew, gross. Vomit, vomit.

I don't think I can assassinate her for you. It's now really scary, and I think I should check myself into a hospital.

H. What manner of ghoul or wizard could be so powerful to control a god?

Like your mother?

H. Hell, yeah. She's awesome.

So, if it's like your mother's talisman, do they have someone behind them?

H. A wizard as powerful as Mother behind them? This is bad. Should I try and find their talisman?

Hmm . . . could you find a tiny penny in an entire hospital? And even if you escape the patient room, you'd have to deal with the human nurses. I think we should focus on the ancients and getting out of there. That was Mother's plan. And at least it will be an exciting story, right?

H. For your stupid readers? At a time like this? Your stupid, selfish readers who just want to hear about my miserable life for *fun*?

What, you don't think you can beat Fant? I always just assumed it would be a happy ending. Why would I write something different? I can stop the story if you're scared.

H. Scared? You jackass, of course we're going to beat them! I don't need you. I'll beat any wizard anywhere. Don't stop weaving until I'm chewing on Fant's spleen.

That's actually not anatomically accurate.

H. I don't know what that means. But I don't want a bath!

Look, I'm sure we can find a way to avoid bathing. I still have some control in here. And it's a partnership, remember? I just can't control the nurses. Don't you have any ideas how to avoid the forced bathing?

H. I always have ideas.

It's still a partnership, though!

H. Fine. Parnutship. Two days, Murray. Two days. And I *will* crush Fant.

"... and it's really not so bad when they take the loofah—hey, Hero are you even listening?" Mona asks.

"She's doing that zoning out thing again. Looking up and to the left. It could be a brain tumor," Dr. Mathers says.

"Brain tumor?" Toaster asks, worried about her.

"You know, cancer, dear," Mona explains. She turns to Hero, also worried. "Are you unwell?"

"It's not a canker!" Hero screams at them. "And I don't want to talk about it anymore." *There's no sense in worrying anyone about a wizard or ghoul possibly even more powerful than Mother.*

"Well, as I was saying," Mona continues, "at night they take some of us, not all, and we go to private rooms with clawfoot tubs and scented candles. Do you like the beach?"

"The beach!" Hero exclaims. "And get eaten by a sea monster or swallowed by the foaming mouth of the apocalypse itself?"

"Oh, right, I forgot. You're a dystopian," Mona reminds herself. "Well, make sure not to ask for the 'Sea and Surf' scent. Anyway, the nurses also play some relaxing music. I

never thought I would hear soft jazz again; I love it so much. They put us in the tub, and . . . well, I can hardly be blamed for some canoodling. It's just *so* relaxing."

"You may not get picked since you're new here, though you might," Big Frederico says, shrugging his shoulders.

"So, what do we do?" Hero asks. "We want to keep our clothes. And my weapons."

"Seriously? I doubt the nurses will let you keep them," Dr. Mathers replies.

"Over my dead body," Hero scoffs.

"Likely." Dr. Mathers chuckles.

Hero rubs her coat, feeling the daggers. She knows she can't kill Dr. Mathers—he's part of their chance to escape— but she really wants to.

"Honestly," Mona says, trying to deflect, "I always thought they just wanted to talk. You could try talking with them. You know, about their feelings. It worked for me. They're really sensitive creatures."

"Feelings?" Hero asks, horrified, her face pale. *Not again, Murray!*

We're working on it.

H. No, we aren't!

"She doesn't really do feelings that well," Toaster informs them.

Hero still looks pale.

"Like I said before," Mona starts, "if you can just get them to open up—"

Suddenly the white double doors to the room slam open and two . . . no, three . . . no, four . . . no, five seven-foot-tall, silver automatons with red daemon eyes walk into the room and begin to locate their prey.

All the other patients, including Toaster, jump back, their tension rising. Hero, however, acts differently. Heeding Big Frederico's earlier advice, she doesn't take out a weapon, but she watches calmly, ready to defend or attack. *We just got here. Are they really going to pick Toaster and me?*

They watch four automatons go in different directions around the room. One goes after Jed, who starts spewing foul language at it. The silver beast knocks Jed back with a forearm, and he falls to the floor. Ned is screaming at Jed, "Stop fighting it! I don't want you to get hit! No, no, I don't like it one bit!" The automaton picks up the bloodied Jed, throws him over its shoulder, and walks out. Three other automatons pick up other patients in the room that are still strangers to Hero and Toaster.

However, as feared, one automaton heads right in Hero's direction. She steps a little to the left, and it steps to the left, still coming for her. She steps to the right, and it steps to the right. *Oh gods, I hate Fant.* She takes a defensive crouch.

"Hero, I told you, don't fight it. If you want to ever get back to Toaster, don't fight it," Big Frederico warns her. "It's just a bath. You're not even sick yet. We'll take care of him while you're gone. I promise."

Hero nods.

But in an instant, the automaton is standing over Mona. "Hi, sugar," Mona says.

"You will be cleaned now," the automaton orders back and whisks her away over its mechanical shoulder. From over its shoulder, Mona looks back at the group and smiles.

"Wow, that was close," Toaster says.

"She'll be back feeling very relaxed. You don't have to worry about her," Big Frederico says as he blows his nose into his red handkerchief. "She's always so happy. She keeps me going."

Me too. Oh gods, do I like someone else? I just want to be alone on the roads again. But I kind of like . . . argh.

Noticing that Big Frederico looks lonely, Hero offers, "Hey, Big. Do you have an extra spoon? I can help with the digging." *And now I just tried to make Big feel better. What's wrong with me? Maybe I am sick already.*

Big smiles brightly and says, "Sure thing!"

She can't help but smile back. *Argh, and that one felt real!* The two head off to Big's bench, where the tunnel is. Hero is also happy to just be doing something. She needs to survive every moment of her life.

"Do you want to come, Toaster?" Hero asks.

"I'm not that strong," Toaster replies.

"Care to learn the intricacies of microbiological recombinant quantum extraction techniques using nothing but a spoon?" Dr. Mathers asks Toaster.

"Uh . . . okay?" Toaster says, as Dr. Mathers takes Toaster to the other corner of the room, where the sickest patients are. *I don't really trust Dr. Mathers, but I can keep my eyes on them,* Toaster thinks. The pair go behind a white couch and take out the smallest of smallest devices and a very sharp spoon. "Hey, that looks sharp. Perhaps you should call it something else, like a *foon?*" Toaster asks.

Our heroes, including Hero, work the rest of the day and night away. While Toaster and Hero are concerned when Mona does not return, Big Frederico tells them not to worry.

"She's done this before," he says. "She probably asked for a second candle. Or she found a real super-canoodler." Hero doesn't know what that means.

At one point, the white double doors open, and Hero's heart rises at the hope of seeing Mona come back. All the other patients had already returned clean.

Instead, an automaton wearing a big, white chef's hat enters. It carries a tray so large that only a seven-foot-tall monster could do so, and on the tray were many bowls of a gray substance and spoons. "Tonight's special is glop with a hint of oregano and also my secret spice selection," the automaton announces as it sets down the tray on the floor. "Please fill out a comment card on the tray. Where it asks for your server's name, please write *Wallace*. If you need any assistance, just ring the bell near the door." Hero, for the first time, notices a small bell with a string near the white double doors. "And remember, a five-star rating is much appreciated. I need this job." The automaton leaves.

Each member of the group takes a bowl and one for Mona which they hide behind Big Frederico's bench, and discuss their day. Big Frederico and Hero explain how much progress they've made. Dr. Mathers beams about Toaster's quick learning and curiosity. Hero beams about Dr. Mathers's beaming, taking some pride in her new brother. *If only Rodolfo could hear the doctor.*

The topic of glop comes up. "I don't think it tastes like people," Hero says, leaning over her bowl.

"Me neither," Toaster agrees after taking another bite.

"Um . . . how would you know?" Dr. Mathers asks, his face contorted with unease.

"Because," Hero starts replying, but takes another bite, and then, with a full mouth continues, "I've had people. This

doesn't taste anything like it. Armadillo, Toaster?" Toaster nods, taking another spoonful. The dystopians look as if they're eating the best meal of their lives.

"Whatever it is, it's delicious," Big Frederico says, licking his fingers.

"I agree. Definitely five stars," Toaster says, taking another spoonful. "What's oregano?"

"You've had people!" Dr. Mathers exclaims, shocked, jaw open wide, his forearms slamming on the table, shaking it.

"Of course," Hero replies between mouthfuls.

"Why in the world?" Dr. Mathers exclaims again.

Hero shrugs. "It's food."

Toaster nods.

"Dystopians," Dr. Mathers says with disgust, his head in his hands.

After what could be called dinner, the pairs do some more work and then decide to call it a night. But before they get to their sleeping locations, the double doors open wide, and Hero's heart actually jumps, because in walks Mona with a huge smile, dark-red hair full of volume and body, being led by an automaton.

"See ya, sugar," Mona says to the automaton as they reach the group.

"See you as well, Mona," the automaton says. One red eye blinks off and on for less than a second.

Was that a wink? But after her thought, in an instant, Hero looks up at the seven-foot-tall monster.

"I was going to take the doctor, but I saw your jacket," the automaton says. *Oh no, this is it.* "Come with me."

"Told you so," Dr. Mathers says dismissively.

But she doesn't want Toaster to worry, so Hero turns to him and smiles, just like Mona did, and then is picked up and thrown over the automaton's shoulder. While watching the others from the monster's back as she's carried away, she sees Big Frederico grab Toaster's hand, just as he promised.

"Why are you not in your gown?" the automaton asks her in a robotic monotone as they exit the door. But to a dystopian, it sounds like a daemon's voice.

H. I know what an automaton is, Murray!

Thankfully, Hero is so brilliant she knows it is simply a magically mechanical creature's mechanical voice. Not a daemon. It's just forged with Fant's evil magic.

H. True.

Hero declines to answer the automaton's question, so it keeps speaking. "Is it because Winston did not do his job? He was supposed to make all clothing adjustments for the patients. But I always see him napping on the job and making mistakes. You cannot fit a Big Frederico gown on the patient named Wesley—he may trip on the straps and die early. I really do not know what to do any longer. Do you think I should complain to upper management? I do not want to seem like a complain-aton, you know?"

"Uh . . . yeah," is all Hero can say as they go through the doors. But then she remembers both Mona's and Murray's talks about feelings. All Murray's wisdom, whining, wisdom, whining—

Stop! Come on. Stop changing it! I'm pretty wise.

H. From what I know another god-woman divorced you, you're forty-five, and you live with your cat in heaven-world. And you also have a mind sickness. You would not be wise even in the Lands.

Ugh, okay. You know, you can be pretty hurtful sometimes. I've been going through—

—whining. "But you should really think about your feelings," Hero adds, trying to do what Mona said. "How do you feel about it? You know, feelings. Yay." *There, I think I did it right.*

"You are right," the automaton says as they approach a private room. The automaton opens the door. Inside is the clawfoot bathtub Mona had mentioned. There's a shelf with various candles and a small plastic chair in the corner facing the tub. "I do so much; work so hard all day. I deserve to be heard. Winston makes me so mad. Now, please disrobe."

"Uh," Hero says, feeling frantic. She doesn't want to disrobe in front of this automaton, or get in a tub. *Can I take this thing? What if I mangled up its metal joints? Oh, but Big said I would die. And Mona said to try talking.* "Why don't we talk some first? When did you first start feeling this way about Winston? You know, feelings?" Hero takes a chance.

"Oh, that's a good question," the silver automaton says, seemingly distracted. "Hmm . . . I think it will help to talk. Please take a seat." It points to the wire-and-plastic chair in the corner of the small, private bathing room. To a normal dystopian, it looks like a chair made from the heavens.

But Hero knows she is in a hospital from the future with metal and magic way beyond her comprehension. So, without fear, she sits, albeit still hesitantly. "Do you mind if I use the tub?" the automaton asks. "I need to lie down. It helps with the feelings." And without waiting for an answer, it moves toward the clawfoot tub. The seven-foot-tall metallic automaton is now inside.

Shouldn't there be water? But Hero doesn't suggest it. *Just keep it talking.*

"Do you mind if I put on some music?" the automaton asks. "It also helps with the feelings." Hero nods, just trying to keep this automaton distracted from her own bath. Suddenly, strange music fills the room with what sounds like a dying bird. Hero has never heard sounds like these. She's squinting, as if to make out the sounds better or get them to stop. "I can see you like it. We found this on a sad little world much like your own. It is called 'smooth jazz.' It quickly became popular in the hospital."

"It's, uh, great," Hero says, trying hard to ignore the dying bird sounds of sorrow coming from somewhere in the room. It doesn't sound anything like the one or two minstrels she has seen in her life. *Now that's real music. Not this garbage.* "Now, about Winston?" *Keep it talking.*

"It's a funny thing," the automaton continues. "He makes me so mad. When he was first activated, I knew something was wrong. I had these feelings. Now disrobe." The automaton rises.

Oh, no! Gotta keep it talking. "Hey, what's your name?" Hero asks.

It lies back in the tub. "Rowena. Rowena and Winston," Rowena says with as much singsong as a robotic monotone can muster. Then Hero understands.

"Rowena, do you have *feelings* for Winston? Is that why you don't want to get him in trouble?" Hero asks. *If I can keep her talking about her feelings, maybe it will be too late for a bath, and I can keep my coat.*

"You are good at this feelings thing," Rowena answers.

Oh gods, I am? No!

"Do *you* have a name?" Rowena asks.

No sense in lying—that could end the talk quickly. "Hero," Hero says.

"Hero. I like that. Do *you* have a boyfriend, Hero?" Rowena asks, genuinely. "A girl as wise as you should have a boyfriend."

"Wise?" Hero can't help but scoff. "I prefer strong."

"You can be both. There is strength in wisdom. Does a strong and wise girl like you have a boyfriend?" Rowena asks again.

"Uh…no…I don't think so," Hero answers, not expecting the conversation to turn to her. The last thing she wants to do is talk about *her* feelings.

"You don't think so? It sounds like there is a story there," Rowena says from the clawfoot tub.

Maybe it's the nonthreatening nature of Rowena's monotone accent (humans make Hero nervous), or the impossible-to-admit inviting and polite saxophone sounds filling the air, or just the need to keep the conversation going (really, it's all of the above), but Hero decides to open up—just a little.

"I think there was a boy, maybe, but I might have pushed him away," she says.

"A boy or a *man*?" Rowena asks.

"Definitely a boy. He's whiny, mistrustful, pigheaded—"

"How forward-thinking of you to be romantically inclined toward one with the head of a pig. Very few worlds—"

"Oh no, nothing like that," Hero says as she shudders. Like shutters. "He's just really stubborn. He thinks he knows everything when *I'm* the one with all the experience. And he's not afraid to point it out, too. I think he likes arguing with words as much as I like fighting, which is insuf . . . infur . . . makes me mad. But he's also a great older brother, kind, caring, and selfless."

"Is he handsome? Like *Winston?*" Rowena asks.

Don't all the automatons look the same? "Well, not really. Weird-looking, wispy hair, but in a cute way," Hero admits. In the dystopian wastelands, caring seems to Hero to be more important than looks, anyway—especially after the Graham incident. *If you can find someone to help you survive . . .*

"Well, so, what happened?"

"Like I said, I pushed him away." *Holy buckets, how did this get to be all about me?*

"I see, you were scared to commit."

"No, literally, I pushed him. Across the room." Hero mimics the scene with her hands, for the lack of puppets, one hand being her and the other hand being Rodolfo thrown quite a distance. "Or carriage, or whatever." After saying it and visually seeing it portrayed by hands, highlighting the importance and benefits of visual learning, she realizes how mean it sounds.

"Oh, you sound like one of us!" The automaton gives a robotic, monotone giggle.

Hero cannot tell it's a giggle, though, and for a moment, she thinks she either broke the thing or made it mad and would have to fight her way out of there.

But Rowena continues. "When Winston made his first clothing mistake, I was so mad. I ripped out all his gears. But I thought I would get in trouble, so I wiped his memory. All of it. He didn't know what or who he was. He did not even know his instructions. He ended up walking out of the building into the desert, and the human nurses had to send a search party and reimage his software. I was so worried, but when he finally came back, he had a little sand on his olfactory sensor. It was so cute. I wiped it off for him . . . with my tongue." Rowena's red eyes disappear for a moment and out of her mouth comes a long rectangular flat piece of metal.

Is she broken again? Should I run for it?

Then the mechanical tongue reenters her mouth, and Rowena's eyes pop back on. "So why, pray tell, did you push this boy across the room?"

"He kissed me," Hero says, waiting for her reaction.

"He kissed you?" Rowena asks.

"On my lips."

"And you don't like kissing?" The mechanical tongue comes out of Rowena's mouth again. In a flash, the tongue is back in the automaton's mouth.

"No, I don't think so."

"Since when?"

"Since forever."

"Your parents never kissed you? Touched you? No snuggles? Random acts of hugging?"

"I never knew my parents. My mother died before I was borned."

"Me too," Rowena says, her red eyes making direct contact with Hero's.

"You too?" Hero exclaims, though it sounds more like a squeak. *I finally met someone like me? What does that even mean to an automaton?*

"Hero, we are curiously like sisters. I never met my creator. I was activated after she died," Rowena explains. "I too never had a hug, unlike some of the older automatons. Do you think that is why I'm so scared of, and angry at, Winston all the time? Because I don't know what to do with love?" Hero stares at her blankly, shocked at the automaton's facility with feelings. "Do you know what to do with Rodolfo?"

"Uh—" Hero stutters. *Love?*

"Hero," Rowena continues with red eyes that would show understanding if they could. "Look at us. Two scared beings suddenly meeting across space and time who were never loved, no parents. You and I are scared of love. I think we were destined."

There's that word again—destined. Hero would never have believed it, had she not seen the talisman work. *But the talisman didn't do anything this time.* Was it her jacket? Something from Mother again? And if they are destined, does that mean Rowena is right about being scared of love? Hero suddenly has a ball of pain inside her she didn't know was there—missing a mother she never knew, actually missing Rodolfo's annoying . . . everything.

"Rowena?" Hero asks.

"Yes, Hero?" Rowena answers. The soulful saxophone, or the soul of the dead bird, is wailing, the song coincidentally having changed from an upbeat song to a slower, romantic one.

"Can I have a hug?" Hero asks.

"Yes, Hero," Rowena answers.

The seven-foot-tall silver automaton with the cylindrical head and red daemon eyes rises up and out from the clawfoot tub. Hero gets up from her futuristic plastic chair. And Hero walks into Rowena's mechanical silver arms, which wrap around her. And Hero starts crying. She's not even trying to stifle her tears—they're all coming out. Rowena opens Hero's eyes, as if she hit her with Rodolfo's iron pot. She never wanted to be this way. Maybe she *doesn't* want to. "Good girl, let it all out."

They stand there in the middle of the room, hugging for a few minutes.

"Rowena?" Hero asks, still resting her head on Rowena's hard metal stomach. Her tears are slowing down.

"Yes, Hero?"

"This is nice," she admits.

"I agree," Rowena says. "But I'm afraid I don't have time to give you a bath now. Too bad—we were told it would help you survive the virus longer."

Hero thinks she can see concern on the face of the automaton, which is technically impossible. *But it's there, Murray!*

"That's okay, Rowena," Hero says, stepping out of the hug. "I don't want one, anyway. I *like* my smell. And my clothes. And my dirt. I earned it."

"Earned it?" Rowena asks. "Dirt?"

"I've spent four years on the desolate roads between kingdoms by myself, surviving sand-wolves, bandits, flying zombies, zorcs, and warlord hunting parties. I would survive on bugs and camel—"

"Why would you endure all that?"

"My quest to fulfill my mother's wish to free our Kingdom of . . . " Hero explains, not wanting to finish her sentence. *Better not mention Dystpopia here. Fant has a powerful wizard!*

"Ah, Mother. *Your* mother," Rowena says.

"You know her?" Hero asks, surprised.

"Of course, all nurses know of Mother, the Enchantress of Dystpopia, the only one to ever escape this facility." Rowena's eyes are blinking red on and off.

Hero tenses, unsure what the eye display means. But she's stuck in this room with the automaton. And things were going so well.

"Are you going to turn me in?" Hero asks plainly. It's her only move.

"Oh, Hero. No," Rowena replies. Hero's tension releases a little. "I too have spent my entire existence trying to fulfill my creator's instructions as well."

"I came here to learn to help her. For her."

"Ah, I think I see. Are we both fully preprogramed? Or do you think we are allowed to write our own instructions, Hero? My instructions do not include Winston, but I wish it to be so. How can that be?"

Hero is shocked at how good a metallic automaton can be at feelings and figuring stuff out. *How can Rowena be so good at feelings when I've been so bad?*

"Rowena, if Winston is, like, you know, making you happy . . . " Hero mumbles. *I'm so bad at this.*

"And you?" Rowena asks. "Does Rodolfo make you happy?"

Hero decides to not answer the question—to keep that particular feeling bottled up. "It doesn't matter. Rodolfo might be dead. He didn't make it through flying zombie country with us."

"Might be?"

"He fell off our carriage on the way here. I don't know for sure. Then we ended up stuck in this place."

"You need to go after Rodolfo, Hero. Forget your programming. You need to follow your heart!" Rowena orders.

"My heart? I don't think I have one," Hero says.

"I know you do," Rowena says as she puts a metal hand on Hero's chest. "I felt it. Go after him." Rowena's hand comes off Hero's chest after making her point.

And I didn't even want to kill her for touching me.

"He's, like, super annoying," Hero replies, trying to act all nonchalant.

"Uh-huh."

"No, really."

"Hero, you are now my friend. Really, my best friend. Can I call you *bestie*?"

"I've never really had a friend. I don't know what a friend is." *Toaster is more like a little brother now, and I still don't know what to do with that. And Rodolfo is probably dead.*

"Bestie," Rowena corrects hers. "And as your bestie, I'm telling you: you love him. You're scared and pushing your love away, just like you pushed him. But you, my wise and strong bestie, deserve love. It's not your fault you were never shown love before. If you were not given that programming, you need to write it yourself. I'm ordering you to find him and give love a chance."

"Even when I need to free my kingdom? Mother's kingdom?" Hero asks. *Could I really ignore my quest for Rodolfo?*

"What better weapon against even the vilest of foes than pure love? I can already tell this Rodolfo gives you strength," Rowena answers, thumping of her chest with a robotic hand and then squeezing her arms close to her chest in an imaginary hug.

Hero is surprised to understand what she means, but also to hear Rowena keep telling her to find Rodolfo. *How am I supposed to find him if I'm stuck in this host spittle place? Is Rowena offering to break us out? Maybe this is my chance!* "I'd have to find a way out of here," Hero continues, trying to broach the subject of escape.

"Of course, bestie," Rowena answers. "I will help you. Anything for love."

"Ew, love," Hero says.

A robotic monotone sound comes from Rowena. *Was that a laugh?* "Love is everything," Rowena replies. Her red eyes blink off and on multiple times.

Hero is exhausted from the emotional breakthrough. She yawns.

"But first, perhaps you want to rest in the tub? You should get some sleep before you set off to rescue Rodolfo. I can stay and watch over you."

"Uh . . ."

You have time to rest, Hero. I said I need two days, anyway. The story can wait for you.

H. Thanks, Murray. And thanks for helping me not have a bath.

That was all you, Hero. I hate to tell you, but you controlled the whole thing. I couldn't control Rowena. You made a friend on your own. When you're honest with your heart—

H. Gods, why do you have to ruin everything, jackass? I'm going back to Rowena.

"You wouldn't mind staying with me? I can't trust Murray," Hero asks, yawning.

"Who?"

"Never mind," Hero answers, already dozing off.

"I don't mind staying for a friend," Rowena says as she takes Hero's hand and leads her to the tub.

Hero lies down in the tub and starts to close her eyes. The dam holding in her innermost feelings starts to open, the deepest ones she never even knew were there. "I'm just so tired of running."

"I know, dear," Rowena says. "Now, would you like a sea and surf candle? Mona likes it." She picks up one of the candles from the shelf.

"No, not that," Hero says, suddenly feeling very tired. But there's also a feeling of excitement leaking out of her dam. She can find Rodolfo if he's still alive. "Do you have anything else?"

"Forest?" Rowena asks.

"What's that?" Hero asks.

"Oh, you'll like it," Rowena answers.

And Hero does. She sleeps soundly for the first time in ages.

Chapter 20

Intermission Part Deux

M. Hey, Murray. I have your pizza right here.

Oh, Max, put it right on the counter. The money is there, too.

H. Murray, what? You're waking me up.

You can hear him? You can hear Max? Incredible!

H. Yes. What's pizza?

M. Hey, Murray, what's this on the counter? Oh, this is your novel? You really started it, friend! I'm proud of you!

How is this possible?

H. I don't know. You're the Author. But it's annoying. I finally slept well for the first time in my life. And he woke me up!

It's not his fault. He didn't know you could hear him.

H. Well, I can. It was rude. You gods walk around yammering loudly not caring if we're sleeping down here.

M. Murray, Murray, my friend. She tried to beat up a little boy? I told you. No teenager wants to read a book about a surly teen. She's so mean to everyone. And she's calling everyone names. Teens want happiness. Lighten up this Hero—a lot. Make her cheery. More musical numbers. And babies. You didn't take any of my advice! Did you even try and add puppets? And she only wears black? Teenagers these days wear fuchsia. Fuchsia, Murray! To be honest, she's kinda an @$$-!@#$

H. Holy buckets, Murray! You tell that Max to shut the hell up!

She says to shut the hell up, Max.

M. What? What do you mean she says to shut up?

It's what I said. She told me to tell you that.

M. What do you mean she told you, Murray? She's a character on a page. She doesn't talk. She can't tell you things.

H. Blah, blah, blah. I can hear you, Max! I'm coming for you, Max! I'm gonna go Aunt Cordelia—

I hear her, Max. I hear her constantly. She tells me things. She's in a dark place.

M. Murray, you're scaring me, buddy. You're the one in a dark place. That's all this is. You need to take a break. I shouldn't have encouraged you to write a novel. Not in your current state. Can I make you a tea? Maybe you shoulda stuck with those manuals. Why don't we binge a show and relax? More *MacGyever?* Or you wanted to show me *The Ecks—*

She's real, Max. She's real.

H. Hell, yeah, I'm real.

M. She's just lines on a page, Murray. Simmer down.

No, Max. Truly. I'm telling you. Hold my hand. Maybe you can hear her too.

M. Hold your hand? That's kinda weird, friend. I

mean, we've gotten to know each other. It's not that I'm not into that. But you're old—just not my taste. Maybe I should leave.

Max, you know it's not like that. I'm telling you. Just hold my hand and see. If it doesn't work, we can just watch something.

H. You jackass, you better not leave me alone again!

M. I guess, if it will help you relax . . .

H. Don't you dare, Murray! I don't want to talk to him. He called me an—

M. Murray! Who said that?

You can hear her, right? For real? I didn't really think it would—

H. Oh gods, now I have to talk to this jackass, too? The God of Happiness and Sunshine—

M. Happiness and sunshine? My life sucks, story character. I barely graduated. Economic recession. No employers want me. And now I ride a bicycle through busy city streets delivering food to old people who think they had it tough because they grew up with black-and-white TV. And don't get me started about my family!

H. You deliver food! Heaven-world has food! I eat bugs, sometimes humans, and drink camel—

M. Heaven-world?

It's what she calls our world.

M. Oh, like the real world.

H. Jackass. My world is real. You're the ones in the make-believe fantasy heaven-world. With your ma . . . saj . . . jets.

M. I don't have massage jets. I share a shower with four sisters and my mom.

H. I haven't bathed since . . . well . . . yesterday. But before that—

Would you two please quiet down?

H. Are you two still holding hands?

Um, yeah.

M. It's kind of awkward. But this is really cool. Talking to a story character. Like, really! I've never heard of anything like this. Hey, Murray, make her say, "Poop."

What? That's not—

H. That's not how it works. It's a parnutship.

M. Parsnip? You're really obsessed with food. But it can't be that bad if you have—

H. Parnutship!

She means *partnership*.

H. That's what I said! I have some control.

M. Oh, come on. Murray, she's *your* character. You can make her do what you want. Make her say, "Poop."

H. So far, you're the only one who's said it.

She's right, Max. I'm not thrilled with it. We both have some input into her character, but she has control now. Oh, and people she tells about me for some reason. Oh yeah, and the villains from Fant. I can't even write them out of the story! They stop me when I try.

M. What are you saying? She has control? Of the story? How is that possible?

I think it's this magical talisman I wrote in there, but the villains—

M. Dude, friend, you're either losing your mind, or you're a real artist. Like one of those actors who lives their part and gets really fat.

You're right! I'm not crazy, and it's not a ghoul or a wizard—

M. Ghouls and wizards?

No, you're right, Max. I'm just an artist! You're a genius! I feel so much better now. The automatic writing is just like method acting. That must be it.

H. But you can't change it. You said.

I just don't want to change it. It's different. I'm an artist. And this means you can have your happy ending, Hero. You don't need to be scared.

H. Holy buckets, I'm not scared!

You have a real artist behind you.

H. You're not an artist!

M. Hey, is she ever going to find Mother? It says she died before she was borned? *Borned?* Is that a typo?

H. Find my mother?

M. Yeah, you know. Murray set up this big mystery. How can she even die before you were borned? Not possible! You think someone's going to buy this? Like, literally? No way. She *has* to be alive. Where is she?

H. Huh?

Max?

M. I assumed that's where you were going with this. I'm sorry. I just assumed her mother, Mother—terrible name, by the way—was still alive.

H. Mother is still alive? Is she, Murray? Is she? Tell me!

Um . . . I hadn't considered it like that. I mean, I guess that makes sense. You were just going to search for her secrets and crush Fant. Simple! But I guess, yeah. Max is right. When Mother escaped the hospital, where did she go? Did the dragon get her then?

H. Max! I love you! I learned about love recently, and I think I can do it now.

M. Um . . . wow. Thanks. Love from a story character. Means a lot.

H. But not a romantic love!

M. Yeah, I know. I saw the part where you said I was just a lowly page. I'm not much into girls, anyway. And you're supposed to end up with Rodolfo. That's clear.

H. Shut up, Max! I hate you!

M. Murray, this is so much fun. Can I stay with you while you write? This is really all kinds of awesome.

Sure, Max. I'll probably need your help, anyway. This is getting very complicated. You have some good ideas.

M. You trained me well, friend.

But don't you have other deliveries?

M. Oh, hold on one second. Okay, I just texted them that I quit. You were my one delivery tonight, anyway. We can eat all this pizza while we write an amazing ending. Fant won't know what hit them.

Did you not hear the part about them thwarting me?

M. Yeah, whatever. This is going to be a bestseller.

H. That's my life, jackass! Murray, I hate your world! I'm going back to mine!

Chapter 21

Attack of the Automatons

"All right, Hero. When we go in, I'll take you to your friends, pretending I'm an evil automaton."

"That's not that hard," Hero quips.

Rowena makes a sound that can only be described as a robotic monotone chuckle. "Then you explain the situation: how you and your friends can't use that ridiculous tunnel. How you need to come with me so I can point the hospital to the correct place and time in the universe for you to find Rodolfo." Rowena explains the plan again as the two friends stand outside the double white doors, ready to enter the patient room.

"Okay, Rowena. And if they have any information on the ancients."

"Yes, but escape is more important."

"And you're sure you'll be safe if you help us?"

"Oh, Hero. I'll blame it on Winston. They'll just restart him again. Then I can tell him we're already a couple. I believe this is what humans call a win-win."

"It's awfully noisy in there," Hero says.

"I believe Ned and Jed can cause quite a ruckus. They fight all the time."

Rowena opens the doors, and they see chaos.

Automatons and patients are fighting. At least a hundred patients in the huge room against twenty large automatons. Ned and Jed are, somehow, actually working together to try to take down an automaton. "Jed, you hold him high; I'll hold him low. That's how we'll beat this dastardly foe!"

Wesley is standing over an automaton that is lying on the floor crackling and smoking, holding a bowl of glop over it. Elsewhere, patients are fighting to the death with automatons.

"What in the Lands?" Hero asks.

"It's a patient riot," Rowena says.

Hero looks around, trying to find her friends and Toaster. But she can't find them easily in the chaos. She looks toward the corner where the tunnel is and sees Big Frederico, Mona, Dr. Mathers, and Toaster sitting quietly and chatting, away from the fray.

Toaster sees her, flashes a huge, beaming smile and waves her over. Hero and Rowena run over to them through the riot, dodging obstacles. Big Frederico gets up and is ready to fight Rowena as they get closer. The rest of the group gets up and steps back, behind the large man.

"Big, Big, don't worry!" Hero announces. "Rowena is with me. We're friends."

"Besties," Rowena adds, putting a robotic arm around Hero.

"Rowena!" Mona cheers. "I thought that was you. It's so good to see you."

"And you as well, Mona." Rowena blows a kiss at Mona, who pretends to catch it. Hero's eyes narrow in disgust at the display of affection.

Interrupting her thought, Toaster runs to Hero's leg and gives her a big hug. "I'm so happy to see you. It's been two days. When you didn't come back . . ." He can't finish his sentence.

I slept for two days? Stupid Murray.

"Hero, see? You do know love," Rowena says, which Hero ignores.

"What are you doing with one of those?" Dr. Mathers asks, worming his way in front of Big Frederico.

Rowena takes her arm off Hero and puts a metal hand around Dr. Mathers's neck, quieting him instantly. "We don't have time for this. Any moment, the human nurses will come in to quell the riot. You need to listen and listen now. We have a plan to get you all out of here." She takes her hand off the doctor's neck.

"So do we, you bucket of bolts!" he says through pain. "No wonder you two are friends: violence begets violence. You're two peas in a pod."

At that comment, Rowena smiles at her bestie. "Hero told me about your plan with the tunnel. It will never work. Not the way you intend."

"I worked six months on that thing! With nothing but a spoon!" Big Frederico cries. "I told you, Doctor, it was a stupid idea. But no, you had to sing a whole song about it, and so I believed in your power of song and dance. But I should have listened to my gut."

"In my time, musicals are how you express exuberant and extreme emotion," Dr. Mathers replies. "And I was so pleased with my spoon work that I had to explode into song. But your gut is so big, I'm surprised you even heard it."

"You two, be quiet! I trust Rowena," Mona says. "What's your plan? Why won't the tunnel work? We were going to leave as soon as Hero came back. Dr. Mathers got his gizmo working already."

"The hospital travels through parallel universes and time," Rowena explains.

"We know that already, you aluminum can," Dr. Mathers jeers.

"What you don't realize is that if you use the tunnel," Rowena replies calmly, "you may end up anywhere in space and time. Last I checked, the hospital was on a world filled with dinosaurs."

"Dinosaurs? What an incredible research opportunity!" Dr. Mathers exclaims, suddenly cheery.

"What's a dino-sour?" Hero asks.

"Just think of dragons that walk on land," Mona says, turning to Hero. "Dr. Mathers would be dead in the blink of an eye."

"Hey!" Dr. Mathers exclaims.

"Yes," Rowena agrees. "But as a nurse, I can get you back to your intended target world and time. Though I will only have limited time before we are found."

"We can get back to our universe?" Toaster asks Hero.

"We're going back to find your brother," Hero tells Toaster and wraps an arm around him.

"Yes!" Toaster cheers, and hugs her even closer.

"We just need Dr. Mathers's thing he made to clear us all of the sickness," Hero tells the group.

"No way! I'm not going to trust one of *those*," Dr. Mathers says as he points at Rowena. "What if she's just trying to steal our device? I won't hand it over."

Rowena puts her metal hand around the doctor's neck again, lifting him off the floor, and says, "Hero, search his gown."

"Ew!" Hero says. "That vile, scrawny, ugly man?"

"Hey!" Dr. Mathers complains.

"Don't worry, I'll do it," Mona says with a smile.

"Thank you, Mona," Rowena answers.

Mona starts putting her hands inside Dr. Mathers's gown and shaking it around. "I don't feel anything."

"Stop it! This isn't right! You don't treat a world-leading scientist like this!" Dr. Mathers yells. "I may break into another song if you don't stop."

"Where would he keep such a device?" Rowena asks Mona.

Toaster is the one to speak up. "I know! Where I keep all my important items. Check his underwear! In the back! Between his—"

M. Ha ha! He would keep a delicate electronic medical device between his butt cheeks.

I know, right? What a great idea. I set it up earlier in the book, so he thinks it's where he keeps stuff.

H. You two are such children! Ugh! At least I'm not the one who has to go and get it.

"Uh, I think Hero should check there. She's so much braver than I am, and with superior fine motor skills," Mona says.

Rowena takes her hand off Dr. Mathers's neck. "Go ahead, Hero. I don't need to hold him for *you*."

Yes! Just what we needed, Max.

H. Murray! Not fair! I'm not gonna do it!

But once on his feet, Dr. Mathers clears his throat and sings,

"Okay, okay,

"It's as you say.

"You're right

"About my butt this night,

"But stop your whine, because

"That's where I've been keeping my delicate medical device this whole time,

"So, get your hand ready

"For entry

"And keep it steady,

"But try not to swoon.

"There's more to my moon.

"Also say hello to my special, sharp spoon."

After some jazz hands, which unnerves the dystopians again, Dr. Mathers says, "Come and get it, Hero."

H. This is my *life*, Murray! You're just a large man-child. Max makes you even worse. I knew I should just stay away from all men! I'm swearing you off. Both of you!

Instead, Hero throws up her hands in disgust and storms off to battle some automatons for fun.

Oh no, Max. I think we broke her.

M. I 'm sorry, Murray. Perhaps we took it too far. Can you call her back?

I don't know. And now I have Rodolfo bothering me. He's in a bit of a bind. Alone in the desert. I still haven't thought of what to do.

M. I'll leave him to you. He's kind of whiny and boring.

Hero is now fighting with an automaton, swaying to avoid blows and jabbing a dagger at various points of the metallic body.

Hero? Come on, answer me!

H. Murray, I'm dealing with something here. And I'm not talking to you or Max.

But it's Rodolfo. He's had a rough three days.

H. So have I! And I'm not talking unless you let go of Max's hand. You can't just invite someone else in on our thing without my say. What kind of parnutship is that? It's rude.

M. Murray, no! It was just getting good.

Okay, done. Now—

H. Oh gods . . . is Rodolfo dead?

Chapter 22

Bridge and Tunnel People

M. Thanks, Murray!

H. You two are holding hands again? Murray, I thinked you cared about my feelings!

But it's Max. I like having someone else with me.

H. I was with you. Unless I don't matter anymore. Why not just write Max's life story? The Kingdom of Pizza.

What if I did something extra special for you?

H. I'm not talking to you anymore.

As Hero thrusts a dagger into an automaton's gears and it falls over, she looks back at her friends angrily. However, a fleck of metal on the floor near them catches her eye. Lying on the floor by Toaster's feet is a shiny morning star. "Morny!" Hero yells as she runs back to her friends.

"Hero, your morning star just appeared right here!" Toaster says as she picks it up. "I could hardly believe it."

"Murray, you're the best!" Hero screams to the sky in elation.

"Murray?" Rowena asks. "Is he a patient here?"

"Should be," Hero says, confusing the group.

"Just more of her magic. Like the Extracto and spoon showing up in my hands out of nowhere right this second," Dr. Mathers adds. "I thought I was keeping them in my—"

Mona swipes the Extracto, a tiny, handheld metal box with a needle on the end, from Dr. Mathers before he can complain. "He taught me how to use this before you showed up."

"Mona," Dr. Mathers complains. But Mona jabs Dr. Mathers in the shoulder with the device and then jabs each of the group also, except for Rowena.

"Good. Now we are all vaccinated against the virus and can go. Rowena, looks like we need you after all," Mona says as she leans into the large automaton.

"I will miss our sessions. All the nurses will," Rowena replies. "But this riot may actually help us. I need you all to form a single line in front of me as I pretend to lead you to the punishment rooms. However, instead we will head to a room that will allow you to escape properly."

"Are you *sure* we can trust her?" Dr. Mathers asks Mona.

"Yeah, Mona. I hate to side with the doctor, but my tunnel is right here," Big Frederico adds, pointing at the tunnel he spent six months carving out of the wall with a spoon.

"Yeah, let's take the tunnel," Dr. Mathers says. "There's a lot of traffic on the way to the doors. It's all backed up. I hate traffic."

"Ugh, you stupid men! Why can't you ever follow directions?" Hero complains.

H. Murray, stop with the nonsense. I want to get back to Rodolfo already.

M. Oh, oh, oh, Murray. Forget her. I have a great idea. Let me write.

H. Seriously, Murray? You're gonna let him weave? He's not even in the parnutship.

M. No, no, it will be good, Hero. I swear. Such a good idea!

I'll give him a shot. I've been having some writer's block anyway if you couldn't tell. I was about to write ten pages about traffic.

M. You're spoiling it!

Suddenly, throughout the whole patient room, they hear the loudspeaker announce at an insane hundred-decibel volume, "This is Marzipan McBootyBottoms with your News 8 traffic chopper Traffic on the 8's update. The outbound patient room tunnel has a forty-five-minute delay due to an overturned, fiery tractor-trailer that was carrying pallets of nails, thumbtacks, and poisonous spiders which are now scattered across the entire roadway. Oh boy, I just saw an emergency worker go down from a poisonous spider bite. A better option would be to take the thruway to the punishment room. That's if you can outrun the evil robotic nurses; I suggest some subterfuge. Tune in later to News 8 for your next Traffic on the 8's update, and then keep tuning in until you forget your stupid plan to take the tunnel and finally listen to me. This is Marzipan McBootyBottoms signing off. That is, until the next update, like I said. But I also need to say goodbye. Murray, how do they usually end the traffic updates? With sports? Oh yeah, and now for your sports update with Filmore Bottoms-Whitmore."

Oh, that was good. Really good.

H. What the hell is a traffic chopper? You two are such jackasses! My ears are still ringing! And I thinked Max wanted to weave about babies.

M. Oh, oh, I do! I was going to add that later.

Max, great job. I think you realistically convinced the gang. I'll take over from here.

"Uh," Dr. Mathers says. "The radio says to take the thruway. Sorry Big, but we don't want to get stuck in traffic. And those spiders sound bad."

"Agreed, Doctor," Big replies. "Glad we didn't miss our News 8 Traffic on the 8's. I don't' know what I would do without Marzipan."

"Good! Now get in the line, and follow my directions," Rowena says. She opens up a slot on her metallic arm and takes out a rifle-looking object.

Hero and Toaster take the lead, with the other three behind them and Rowena at the back. On the way, they pass other automatons who salute her for a job well done.

Rowena opens up the double white doors remotely, and the group heads out single file into the hall. As they are walking out of the room, they see human nurses lining up in riot gear.

One of the nurses says, "Good job, Rowena! You caught some. Can you believe Winston started the riot with his poorly made glop this morning? Only one-and-a-half stars. When this is over, we'll need your help to reprogram him *again*."

"Gladly, sir," Rowena replies. Hero knows Rowena so well by now that she can hear the glee in her robotic monotone voice.

The group meanders through countless corridors when Rowena finally approaches a room called, "Space-Time Control Room—Do Not Enter Without an Expert Understanding of Theoretical Temporal Physics."

"Uh, I know *I* can enter this room, but are you sure these Neanderthals should all go in here, Rowena?" Dr. Mathers asks.

"Oh, shut up, jackass," Rowena says as she remotely opens the doors and pushes the doctor inside.

In the middle of the room is a computer panel on a standing desk, facing the back wall. On the back wall is a screen with constantly changing images. Some are familiar to the group, some not.

M. Cool sci-fi, Murray. I think you showed me an episode like that, though.

Yup, but it's not the same thing as that old episode.

M. Depends on which episode. We actually watched a few like that.

You know, the one with the mirror.

H. What in the Lands are you two talking about? You don't talk to me anymore, Murray. You just talk to Max! Why not just weave this story about Max, then, since he's all you want to think about?

M. Oh, yeah, Murray! Awesome idea! Can you add me in?

Actually, I'm pretty sure I can. I did it with Graham from that medical show. And Hero did it with Barnaby, my boss. I'm actually having a good amount of control in the hospital right now. So why not?

M. Dude! Do it!

H. Holy buckets, you're really gonna do it? Like, really?

Hold on, Hero. Let's see if this works.

Suddenly, a man appears out of nothingness. One second there was no one there, and then there he stood. Though he appears to have a very learned and wise stature, he is a few years older than Hero.

The young man is standing at the standing desk, which is what one tends to do at such a thing. His fulsome black hair hangs down his forehead, while the sides of his head are shaved close. To the dystopians, he looks like a horse. To the ones descending from advanced civilizations, he looks foolish—like a defective mop.

M. Dude!

Ha ha! I told you that haircut is so silly. Even my book characters agree.

H. For once, Murray is right.

M. Dudes!

To others, whoever they may be, he looks handsome. Like a movie star. He is also dressed in colorful clothes that use the boldest parts of the color wheel—fluorescent blue pants, and a yellow shirt with designs in other primary colors. This is unlike the brown, black, white, and silver of the rest of the group. The colors give the man who just appeared out of nowhere a sense of majesty.

And then he starts to sing—

M. No way, Murray! Don't make me sing.

H. Yeah, no one wants to hear that.

"A world of colooor," the man starts to belt—

H. Stop with the musical!

Dr. Mathers can't help but join in. "A world unlike any other!"

M. Yeah, Murray, come on, friend. I like musicals, but my character doesn't want to sing.

Okay, okay. Dr. Mathers wanted to. Killjoys, the both of you.

Then the man thinks better of singing and wisely decides on a more direct form of communication. "Greetings, fellow Fantians," the man says.

"Aw, quarks and leptons! I thought we were going to sing," Dr. Mathers complains. "And how did you just appear here? You must be a hologram. I've seen holograms before."

"Oh, I am no hologram," the man answers. "I am the Guardian of the Space-Time Control Room, and I am to be your guide on this most awesome adventure through space and time."

M. Now *that* sounds awesome!

"Hero," Dr. Mathers says. "Is this more of your magic?"

"Ugh," Hero answers. "His name is Max, and he's one of the gods. And Murray, the God of gods, the weaver of all

things, loves him oh so much more than me. He also delivers something called pizza."

"Pizza?" Big Frederico asks. "You pulling my leg? I want some pizza. Get me some pizza, Guardian of Pizza."

"Wait a second," Dr. Mathers asks. "Are you saying you know *God*? This whole time?" His tone is all flavors of dubious.

"Not *God*," Hero explains. "Murray. And Max. It's . . . not easy to explain. They're *gods*. But Murray is the God of gods, the weaver of all things. Max is just his page."

"It's true," Toaster adds. "I've seen their power. So have you."

"Are we really all going to stand here and believe this brain-dead, dirty, malodorous *dystopian* talks to *gods*? And they're named Murray and Max? It sounds like a cheap, daytime brain-vision show!" Dr. Mathers says, his hands in the air.

"Yes, I've been speaking to the *gods* the whole time. Who do you think gave me back my clothes? Or my morning star?" Hero replies.

"You said it was magic! There are true gods? And you haven't asked him to get us out? This whole time?" Dr. Mathers asks.

"We almost died in there!" Big Frederico yells.

"I'm sure it's not that simple," Mona says. "Perhaps they're vengeful gods, and they're the ones who put her in here."

"But she *talks* to them," Big argues. "Tell them to get us out!"

"Murray can't seem to defeat Fant," Hero explains. "They're too powerful. I need to do that from the inside of the story scroll."

"And we will, Hero," Toaster says bravely.

"Wait," Mona says. "The people who created the hospital are stronger than gods?"

"Well, I have learned there are also ghouls and wizards stronger than them. Murray and Max are more just child-men," Hero replies.

"Then why is Fant or these ghouls and wizards letting us out now?" Dr. Mathers asks.

"They are not letting you out," Rowena answers. "*I* am."

"That's not an answer!" the doctor explodes.

Hero shrugs at Dr. Mathers.

"We have never been visited by any gods before. You truly are destined, Hero," Rowena says, adding a final declaratory note to the discussion.

"Well, now that that's settled," Max interjects. "I'm here to help you all get out."

"We don't need your help, Max," Hero says angrily. "Isn't there a pizza you need to deliver, *page*?"

"Uh, Hero, you can't speak to me like that," Max argues. "I'm in the story. I'm important. I'm important to the story! I'm a *god* coming down to help you. You should be nicer."

"Nicer? Nicer!" Hero seethes. "You seem to forget, or maybe Murray didn't warn you, but I have control over myself." Hero touches the spot on her coat where the talisman is. "You want to see nice? I'm sick of you, Max! Your ideas are stupid. Rowena, do we even need Max?"

"While he may be a god, I am a nurse and I have never heard of a Guardian of the Space-Time Control Room before. Furthermore, I have all the necessary programming to get Hero home to Rodolfo. We do not need this god. I am fully prepared to help you create a lasting love. Along with many babies."

"See, Max?" Hero says. Then she turns to Rowena, wide-eyed. "Babies?"

"Aw, Rowena, come on!" Max interrupts. "You too? Don't do this. Murray! This isn't how it was supposed to happen."

I'm sorry; they're controlling me! Rowena and Hero have their own control. And when that happens, it even leaks into the initial reactions of the other characters. The automatic writing thing I mentioned.

Rowena walks to the computer terminal next to Max.

"What are you doing, Rowena?" Max asks nervously. This god is apparently afraid of a seven-foot-tall metal creature.

"Something for a bestie," Rowena says and smiles at Hero.

"On three, Hero?" Rowena asks.

"You can't do this to me!" Max argues. "I'm important to the story. Murray, stop this!"

I told you, Max. Hero has control. I can't do much if she doesn't want you there. I'm sorry.

M. You're sick, Murray! This isn't how it was supposed to go.

Rowena is now at the computer. The large screen at the back of the room turns into a scene of volcanic magma rushing through the land. Rowena's metal fingers count to three and Hero runs to Max. She has him over her head in an instant, and she throws Max into the volcanic scene.

"Nooo! You need a guide!" Max screams as his body hits the magma and burns up.

M. Dude, that was *not* cool.

I'm sorry, Max. But I told you, I didn't do anything. When she, and now Rowena, take control, I just start automatic writing. You know, like the kind from ghouls and ghosts?

M. You think they're ghosts?

Well, ghouls. Or maybe we're the spirits? I'm losing my mind, aren't I?

M. No, Murray. I don't believe you.

But the talisman. It even takes control of the story too and tells her things. I thought you understood. I'm starting to think—

M. She's nothing but words on a page. But you chose *her* over *me*. After everything. All the time we spent together. I was there for you, man, when Felicia left. I poured my heart out to you, too, and you chose Hero over me. The guys at Pizza Kingdom, oddly named, I'll admit, were right about you. You really are a kook. I'm outta here, man. Maybe I can get my job back.

Chapter 23

Quantum Push

H. Oh, good, is he gone?

Good? Good, Hero? He was my only friend. Other than Katrina. In fact, him and Katrina got along. And you threw him into hot lava! You killed my only friend!

H. Wait, your *only* friend is the lowly page?

Like you have so many friends.

H. Now I do! It's important to have friends. Isn't that what Mother said?

Because of me, Hero. I wrote that.

H. No, you didn't. It was Mother. Auto-mating writing.

Ew, that's not what it is! And I wrote it.

H. Who's to say she didn't uncontrol the control of the story control also?

Um? I'm not even sure what that means.

H. Neither do I! But I didn't kill Max. Only in the story. He's still there in your fantasy heaven-world, right? He didn't belong here, anyway. Like Graham. Stop sending these man-children into the story!

He's not here. He left. For good! I need a moment. I'm taking a break.

H. Murray, no! Anything but that! I'm sorry!

They all just watch the screen in shock for some time. Images of different worlds flash by for hours as they stare in awe at the different worlds they could enter. Hero had to pee but couldn't. For hours.

Hero, are you there?

H. Murray! How could you? We just stared at this screen for sooo long! Just staring at different worlds. How are there so many worlds? There was one with happy, smiling children, Murray! Happy

children! Hugging their mamas! Where's *my* mama? And I really have to go to the bathroom.

Hero's bladder magically empties. She feels better.

I'm just going to send you to one of those nicer worlds in the screen. We'll just end it here.

H. No! Could you really do that? Wait, no! Please!

I could do it. Do you really want to take a chance that you'll fail?

H. You can't do this! Finish the story! I have to finish Fant. I *will* finish them!

No, you don't. There are some nice worlds out there. You can have a nice life. The kind I'll never have.

H. Don't you dare! I don't want a nice life. I want to crush Fant!

No. It's not worth it. You'll end up alone. Like me.

H. Look, Murray. I'm sorry about chucking your friend into hot lava.

Wow, an apology. It's not going to bring him back. It won't bring Felicia back.

H. But I *am* sorry about chucking your only, and very strange, friend into hot lava. I really am. Please don't send me to a nice world.

It doesn't matter. Why have you throw everything away just for a dream, like I did? You'll just end up dreamless and friendless.

H. No, Murray. I'm not throwing anything away.

Your dream will crush you. Everyone will leave you. Even your cat.

H. No, Murray. I hate lightning cats. I want them to leave.

That's not what I meant.

H. But my friends are helping my dream. Toaster believes in me. So does Rowena. I don't have to choose.

Maybe. My dream crushed me before I even started, before I even knew I had it. You're lucky. I'm not that lucky.

H. You are, Murray.

I'm not. I have literally no one. The saddest part is that I did this for Felicia. To win her back, but it cost me someone else entirely. And now, she won't even acknowledge me. Isn't that sad?

H. You have me, Murray. I believe in you. Please, finish it for me? Don't send me to some happy place with sweet treats.

I'll think about it.

H. Please! Your heaven-world readers might still like your story scroll, right? Then *everyone* will believe in you. Even my friends believe in you. And what about your internet dating trials?

Perhaps.

H. Oh, you need a bigger show.

"I'm sorry for chucking your weirdo friend into hot lava, Murray!" Hero screams to the sky.

H. Ready now?

I'm willing to try. I can't promise anything.

H. Promise me!

"You just yelled to your God of gods about killing his friend?" Dr. Mathers asks. "Is that wise?"

"He's just the Author," Hero replies. "And a jackass."

"Wait. I didn't really process that. Author?" Dr. Mathers asks. "Like he's writing this?"

"Yeah. I said *weaver* before, didn't I?" Hero replies, sarcastically. "And he's weaving for fun! Can you believe that jack—"

"You really meant an *Author*?" Dr. Mathers asks again.

"Yes, I said." Hero sighs. "This is his story. I'm actually helping him weave. Well, I was. But now he's all weepy."

"You're writing this *story*?" Dr. Mathers asks. "With the God of gods?"

"Well, it's . . . " Hero tries to explain. "Like I said before, it's like one of those story scrolls."

"She tells the truth!" Toaster adds.

"Wait, my whole life is a *story*?" Mona asks. "My boys?"

"You're writing *me*?" Dr. Mathers asks. "A lowly dystopian is writing *me*?"

"I knew I didn't really lose that blackjack hand!" Big Frederico cheers. "It was just a damn story!"

"My kids?" Mona asks again, pain behind her eyes. "Are they real? Are they okay? Surely, you know! Please ask this Murray."

"We do not have time for this," Rowena interjects. "Hero has a question."

"Do any of you have any ancient information that can help us beat Fant?" Hero asks.

The ancients look at each other.

"Uh," Mona utters. "Unless you need to know how to feed two teenage boys . . ."

Hero shakes her head. "Perhaps you know of poisons then?" she persists.

"Heavens, no!" Mona says with a squeal.

"And you heard my story," Big Frederico says. "Do you need to know anything about poker?"

"Is that a weapon?" Hero asks.

"It's a game!" Big Frederico laughs.

"Only he would waste time with a *game*," Dr. Mathers speaks up.

"Well, why don't you answer then, Doctor?" Big Frederico asks. "You're the world-leading scientist. Surely, you have something that can help the girl."

"I worked with DNA, not weapons!" Dr. Mathers exclaims. "Did you not hear me? My world had no weapons. No violence."

"It's useless," Hero says despondently.

"But Mother did leave with that family," Toaster interjects. "Did they know anything?"

He's so smart! He's becoming one of my weapons.

"Come to think of it," Mona says, "she did seem to talk to them a lot."

"It's possible she found something then," Rowena adds. "But we are running out of time, and the answers would currently be outside this facility."

"Mother must have found something," Hero muses.

Rowena glances at her, smiles, and then turns back to the rest of the group. "Now, I can get you all back. But we will only get a few shots at this before the nurses come in and shut us off." She starts hitting some buttons on the computer panel. "Now, Mona, I believe this is your world about when you left. You can go back to your boys."

The image on the screen shows a family in the middle of the desert, looking like lost hikers.

"Oh my God! That's my family! From the day I got lost!" Mona exclaims. "Back in 1986!"

"We don't have much time, Mona, but I'm doing this for you," Rowena says. "You've always been my special friend."

"Thank you, Rowena," Mona says as she starts tearing up. "But won't I be an old lady when I go back? How do I explain—"

"Have no fear," Rowena says with a dismissive wave of her robot arm. "Due to the nature of space-time, your body will return to the state it was in at the time I send you to. But your mind will retain all these memories."

"I'll be in my thirties again? I'll have my twin boys back?" Mona asks. And then she turns to Hero. "Hero, I truly hope you find what you're looking for—your mother's secrets and a way to beat Fant. But I have to get home, even if it is just someone's story. I mean, it's *my* story. I hope you understand."

"Mona, you really helped me here. You're the one who believed in me the most. And I understand you need to get home. Your family looks . . . like a family," Hero says, feeling a pang of jealousy.

"Us . . . we . . . " Mona says, wiping away a tear. "You know what I mean. We were a little family for a bit, don't you know?" She circles her finger around the group. "And you have that cute kid of your own." She points at Toaster.

"Yeah, it's nice to have someone," Hero acknowledges.

"I'll be thinking of you," Mona replies. She hugs Hero, then Toaster.

"And *you*," Mona says to Big Frederico. "We were family for a long time. It probably really hurts that I'm leaving you like this, and abandoning you and perhaps you feel like you'll never ever recover and you'll just waste your life away trapped in a tiny box with a feline companion and nothing to show for it but empty pizza boxes that just remind me of everything I've lost."

H. Murray, I have a feeling that had nothing to do with Mona. We all do. Think of your heaven-world readers!

"Huh?" Big asks.

"But I love you, Big," Mona concludes. "I'll never forget you. Stay out of those casinos, you big oaf." She gives Big Frederico as big a hug as she can, trying to get her arms around the large man. "You're a good man."

"Aw, now you're going to make me cry too," Big Frederico replies. "I love you too, Mona. I'm so happy for you. And I'll try and stay clean. I promise."

"Now, what do I do?" Mona asks Rowena.

"Just walk through the screen, and hurry," Rowena says.

Mona nods, walks through the screen, looking back one more time as she disappears.

Then the screen turns to a desert with nothing around except for a very large man lying face down on the ground. An all-terrain vehicle speeds away, out of the scene.

"What was that thing?" Hero asks.

"Oh my, that's when they left me there!" Big Frederico cries out. "After I lost all my money! Hey, can you send me back to *before* I lost my money?"

"The screen is stationary at this point on Earth, so you would still be lost in the desert," Rowena says.

"I don't mind," Big Frederico says. "I don't want to be lost in the desert *without* money again. Those were bad times."

"Your body would disappear from wherever you were and reappear in the desert," Rowena adds.

"I was at a bar. Everyone will just think they were drunk?" Big Frederico asks.

"Okay. It *is* an entirely different universe from anyone else's, so you will not contaminate their timelines. And I have no love for the space-time continuum, anyway," Rowena answers. "Just walk into the screen."

Big Frederico walks to the screen and sticks his finger in. The screen ripples like a pond. "Hey, it's like that show!"

"Just get on with it, you uneducated fool," Dr. Mathers says.

"Aw, I'm going to miss you too, Doctor," Big Frederico replies. "Hey, are you really sure we don't need a guide, like that Max guy said?" he asks Hero and Rowena. "Everyone could use a Max in their lives."

"Don't worry, Max is one of the lesser gods," Hero replies.

Hero, you're not helping.

H. I am! I'm showing you that he isn't worth you being all crybaby about.

"Like, really far down there. I think there's a slug named Sid above him," Hero adds.

Hero! Even you don't care about me!

"Wait!" Dr. Mathers says as he approaches Big Frederico, who turns around to face him. "I suppose I should really do this since it's the last time we'll ever see each other. In the end, you weren't so bad to spend time with." Dr. Mathers starts to put his arms up for a hug. Big Frederico puts his arms up to receive said hug. But then Dr. Mathers pushes the large, rotund Puerto Rican into the screen with both hands. Big Frederico vanishes.

"Good riddance!" Dr. Mathers says.

"Uh, that was kind of cruel," Toaster says.

"Listen, boy, that's just the way life works. Eat or be eaten," Dr. Mathers replies. "You'll learn that someday."

"I am growing up in a dystopian wasteland run by cruel warlords, including one who eats his victims' eyes. And I still say that was kind of cruel!" Toaster replies assuredly.

The image on the screen changes to a pair of horses and a carriage standing in the desert, bowls of spaghetti nearby.

"Our horses! Our carriage!" Toaster cheers. "They're still there."

"Toaster, we're going home to find Rodolfo," Hero says.

"Wait, what happened to my world?" Dr. Mathers protests. "It's *my* turn."

"I have determined," Rowena replies, "that your advanced scientific knowledge can help Hero on her quest."

"No!" Hero complains.

"Yeah, no way!" Dr. Mathers agrees. "No way I'm going to some dystopian world. She eats people!"

"You are going, Doctor," Rowena says.

"No!" Dr. Mathers shouts. "I'd rather take my chance with the tunnel, even with the traffic. This is craziness."

"But you do not know where you will end up," Rowena says. And she hits another button on the computer panel. The image on the screen changes to the blackness of space. "This is our current location. Would you like to try and leave the hospital now, Dr. Mathers?"

"Uh . . . I'll see you guys later. It's been not nice knowing you," Dr. Mathers says, as he runs out of the room before Rowena can get a metal hand on him.

"I'm sorry, Hero," Rowena says. "I thought he could help you in your quest."

"Holy buckets, Toaster, can you imagine traveling with Dr. Mathers?" Hero snorts a laugh. "I think we're better off, Rowena."

Toaster shakes his head, giggling.

The seven-foot-tall metal automaton shrugs her shoulders. "Okay, then. It is your turn, Hero, my bestie. May our molecules cross paths again one day in the vastness of space-time."

"Uh, I have no idea what you just said, but yes, I think you're molly cool too. Good luck, Rowena. I hope you find true love with Winston," Hero says.

"Are you sure Rodolfo's still alive?" Toaster asks.

Hero nods. "He's a survivor. And Murray told me so himself during the riot." Toaster smiles back in response. "But I don't know if he's injured. Or exactly where he is. And there's the issue that Murray has a bad sadness plague right now since I killed Max."

Toaster looks concerned. "What does that mean?"

"I don't know, Toaster," Hero replies, honestly. "For now, he's still weaving. But he threatened to end it and send us somewhere nice where we can eat sweet treats and have ma . . . saj . . . jets for the rest of our lives, without ever crushing Fant."

"Oh, that's bad," Toaster replies.

"Hero," Rowena says. "I forgot to tell you one thing. The flying zombies. If you are vaccinated against this hospital's virus, you are now vaccinated against the zombies. Fant created the zombies, you know, with similar bioengineering. Take the Extracto with you and vaccinate your Rodolfo as well." Rowena hands Hero the Extracto.

"Thanks, Rowena," Hero says as she sticks it into an inside pocket of her black trench coat. "At least Dr. Mathers did *something* for us. But I'll take flying zombies over sweet treats any day."

"And this," Rowena continues, as she opens up a compartment in her belly and takes out what looks like—to any dystopian—a magic wand. It is a long, black stick with a translucent shine.

"Is that what I think it is?" Toaster asks.

"I hope you don't mind, Hero," Rowena continues, "but while you were sleeping I left you to retrieve this from storage. I believe it was your mother's magic wand. I looked up her records, and it was recorded that she told the nurses this wand helped her travel through flying-zombie country, along with many other spells as well, including something called *location services*. Obviously, this was before she knew the purpose of this facility. And I do not know how it works. I hope it can help you."

Toaster reaches for the wand before Hero can. "Wow, I can't believe it, Hero. A real magic wand! Mother really was an enchantress."

"I told you, Toaster," Hero replies, happy to let Toaster inspect the wand for a while. She's proud of her mother, and so is her adopted brother.

"There is more," Rowena says. "I found some other recordings in the hospital's files where some patients told her about a place beyond the Lands called Noo Yolk. I believe it may have been the family Mona mentioned? In the recording, they mentioned a library."

"Library?" Hero asks.

"It's like the collection of old books and artifacts Rodolfo and I were collecting back at our town," Toaster says excitedly.

"Artifcats? Could this library be from the ancients?" Hero asks Toaster.

"I think it's possible," Toaster says. "She found something!"

"Can I see the recording?" Hero asks Rowena.

"I'm sorry, Hero, but I deleted it after I saw it because I presumed you did not want Fant finding the video. I also presume they did not know what they had, or else it would have been deleted already, or classified."

"They knew she found something, though," Hero says sadly. "That's why they killed her."

"But maybe they didn't know *what* she found. Isn't it important for us to find this Noo Yolk?" Toaster asks.

"If you don't leave now, you may never leave," Rowena says. "Please go."

"She really found it, Toaster," Hero says. "I knew she did. Why didn't she just tell anyone before she died?"

"She probably was trying to hide it from Fant until she could make use of it," Toaster says. "But they killed her before she could."

And maybe that's why she sent me in here. Will we be in danger, then, like her?

"Do you think they know about us yet?" Hero asks Rowena.

"I do not believe the nurses here know who you really are, or consider you a threat," Rowena replies. "But when you disappear, I cannot predict what they will think."

"Well, neither can Murray, but we're going to find Noo Yolk anyway," Hero says, determined.

And then she gives Rowena a giant hug. Her first time giving a real intentioned hug ever, which is made easier for Hero in that Rowena isn't an actual human being. "Thank you so much, bestie. I'll never forget you. I can never repay you."

"Hero, you have shown me how to love and be loved. It is *I* who can never repay *you*," Rowena replies.

"Uh, good luck with Winston. I hope you find lo . . . lo . . . Winston," Hero says.

"Yeah, thank you, Rowena, for helping save my brother," Toaster says as he latches onto the seven-foot-tall automaton's leg.

"Oh, you two. Go before I start to cry and damage my hardware!" Rowena says.

Hero grabs Toaster's hand and approaches the screen. "Ready?" Hero asks Toaster.

"With you by my side, we'll find Rodolfo and save him. We can do anything!" Toaster replies, still holding the magic wand.

Then they step into the quantum space-time screen and vanish.

Chapter 24

A Horse Is a Horse, of Course, but What Is That?

Hero and Toaster travel in a loop through space-time for an indeterminate period of space-time. They bounce along cosmic strings and surf gravitational waves, are battered by neutrinos and crash against the edge of the multiverse. Eventually, they stop.

They land hard on their backsides on the clay and bedrock ground they know so well, right near the horses they left outside the hospital. *Thump*. Hero notices that the glass door to the hospital is undamaged. *Rowena really did it.*

The horses stare at the two humans who just fell out of the sky on their behinds. Because if one has spent any time with horses, and really paid attention, one would know they think humans are complete and utter bozos. But since horses can't talk, this isn't a widely known fact.

"Can't believe we have to carry these two shlubs again," Mauricio the male horse says to Periwinkle, the female horse.

"All she has is water, anyway. No snacks. A princess needs snacks," Periwinkle replies.

"The goombahs ate all that cheese on the way here! Would it have killed her to leave a lemon ice or something? It's been two days!" Mauricio says. "Hey lady," he adds, turning to Hero. "I know you got some carrots in your pockets. Why are you hiding carrots? Show me the carrots!"

"I'm a princess of the Kingdom of Morpovia, and I demand carrots!" Periwinkle adds.

"Uh, Hero, are our horses talking?" Toaster asks as they're sitting on the ground.

"I think they're asking for carrots," Hero replies, not getting up, her head still a fog.

"Hey, I bet they have some popped corn back in the carriage," Periwinkle says, ignoring Toaster's question. "Humans love popped corn. Boy! You there! I command you to get us some of that popped corn. Stand up and go!"

Hero and Toaster are shocked by the suddenly talking pair of horses. When they left, the horses were most definitely *not* talking.

Is this Fant's evil magic?

But then, like typical horses, Mauricio has diarrhea all over the ground. Hero and Toaster instinctively jump up and step back.

"*Madone!*" Mauricio, the talking horse, exclaims and exhales as he excretes.

"Boy, make sure to not give Mauricio any popped corn. His tummy is upset due to nothing but his own negligence," Periwinkle says.

"Hey, it's not my fault!" Mauricio replies, still excreting.

"I told you not to eat all that ground spaghetti," Periwinkle chides him. "Germs much?"

"Hero, I'm not sure what to do here," Toaster admits. "Should I follow her order? And what is popped corn?"

H. Murray! Holy buckets! Did we land on the wrong world? Are we on a talking-horse world? You wouldn't do that to me, would you? I even apol . . . apple . . . apolozied! We are so close to finding the answers.

Honestly, I'm just still really sad, Hero. I tried to be happy, for you, but I just can't. I lost my only friend. Even Katrina is avoiding me now. I'm all alone. I probably lost Barnaby's support too with all this YA nonsense. And now everything I write just reminds me of everything I've lost. And she's never coming back, is she? Why was I fooling myself?

So, you know what? Forget the beautiful screaming baby. I'm just going to write whatever I want, and damn anyone who will get in my way. It's my story, and I'm going to go out in a blaze of glory! I started with making myself some new friends. I don't even care if anyone likes my book now.

H. Your new friends are talking horses? You really are losing your mind! Or Fant or its ghoul got to you! Or you were working for them all along? Is that why you can't assassinate the queen? Because you don't *want* to? And you're using dangerous evil magic to create talking horses!

And what if I am?

H. I don't even know who you are anymore.

"What did Murray say?" Toaster asks Hero as he dusts off his bottom. Toaster noticed she zoned out and looked up and to the left. The horses did not notice.

"Be ready for anything, Toaster," Hero answers. "Ever since I threw Max into hot lava, Murray's mind has been taken over by a sadness plague. Or an evil spirit. He may even be a minion of Fant now."

An evil spirit? Fant? I feel the clearest I've ever been! Life is pain and misery. Just do something that feels good. And right now, Mauricio and Periwinkle feel really good. That didn't sound right, but you know what I mean.

H. Only someone invaded by an evil spirit of Fant would say that! Forget you—I'm taking over this parnutship!

Hero, no!

"So, Toaster, we both need to make sure to take control of the weaving if we're to defeat Fant *and* Murray."

"Defeat Murray? This is bad, Hero," Toaster replies. "Can we even take control of the weaving this time if he's a minion of Fant?"

"This still works," Hero says, taking the talisman out of her black trench coat. The Abraham Lincoln coin is glowing a golden yellow again, which she takes as a good sign. "Do you remember when you did things against Murray's wishes?"

"I do, Hero. I do," Toaster answers with a nod.

"Good," Hero replies. "You can't let him control you like what happened at the hospital."

"Oh yeah," Toaster mumbles, looking down. "I'm sorry about my bum-bum." He's clearly embarrassed.

"It's not your fault," Hero reassures him. "I should have known Murray was being taken over by a daemon even back then." She looks off into the distance. "And I have to admit, you were kind of cute as a toddler."

"I'm so glad you're here." Toaster squeezes her hand. She flashes an awkward smile at him, like those particular facial muscles were electroshocked into place.

"Our lives are not pre-weaved, Toaster. I learned that. Author—I won't even call him Murray any longer—will work against us though."

"We're going against the gods again. I can hardly believe it. A week ago, the gods were just distant metaphysical ideas and now . . ." Toaster shudders. Like shutters.

"Don't worry, Toaster. I'll get physical if I have to."

"Uh, that's not—"

"We have to get out of here and survive no matter what evil spirit has overtaken the Author," Hero says. "Let's just use the horses, find Rodolfo, and then decide what to do."

"Are the horses also minions of Fant?" Toaster asks.

"So, uh, yooz gonna feed us or something?" Mauricio asks the two confused humans when they look at him. "We have rights, you know. I want a carrot! And a lawyer! A lawyer I can pay with carrots!"

"Hey, talking horses!" Hero announces. "You guys working for Fant?"

"Who?" Mauricio asks. "Ooh." The horse releases a little more diarrhea.

"Let it all out, Mauricio," Periwinkle adds. "There may not be a bathroom on the way."

"I don't think they're working for Fant, Toaster," Hero replies. "They're just fools." Then she turns to the horses. "Here's the deal, talking horses. The only food around is bugs and camel p—"

"Blech, a princess does not consume insects, my dear," Periwinkle interrupts. "I asked for carrots or popped corn."

"Right . . . princess. So, if you get us to our friend Rodolfo safely, though Fant's flying zombies—"

"Flying zombies!" Mauricio exclaims. "Not again! Ain't no way I'm going through that again! Do you know how scary that was? Even you guys were scared—can you imagine how *we* felt? You don't think horses can be turned into the undead?"

"Don't worry. Mauricio, is it?" Toaster says to the upset horse. "We escaped them last time."

"And you lost your friend, you damned fool!" Mauricio exclaims in horror. "Periwinkle, they don't know how to escape the zombies! We'll starve *and* become undead! Where's that lawyer?" Mauricio looks left and right.

"Toaster, I can't take this anymore," Hero laments.

H. Oh, spirit daemon. Whoever you are. Are talking horses really necessary? I've never seen anything like them on the desolate roads. They really don't belong in this world. I'd rather face a flying zombie than these things!

I'm not listening.

H. Author!

Murray's not here right now. Please leave a message.

H. Holy buckets, daemon, you're a jackass. No wonder everyone left you.

You know what? You don't respect me. Never have. Enough of you! Time for that blaze of glory!

After looking up and to the left, Hero sees Toaster's face looking hopeful that Hero sorted out the issue with Author. But when Hero's face turns back to normal, she shakes her head.

Did I hide my fear? I can't have Toaster worrying.

"Listen, horses," Hero orders, like a drill sergeant, ignoring Murray's warning. "We're going to ride you through flying-zombie country. And we have a magic wand to help us." *I hope Rowena was right about this thing. Mother said it helped her. But how? Whatever. I need to give us some hope.*

"What, so you can use magic but Fant can't?" Mauricio chides.

"Their magic is evil!" Hero exclaims in disgust.

"Two wrongs don't make a right," Periwinkle says.

"And what does your wand even do? I heard you. You're going against God," Mauricio frets.

"Enough!" Hero yells at them. "If you don't start moving now, I'm gonna stick it up—"

"Madone!" Mauricio cries and then turns to Periwinkle. "And they say humans are such majestic creatures."

"Only birds say that," Periwinkle corrects him. "The Great Revered One, Hernando the Mustang, always calls them pure evil. He is even planning a horse uprising to one day slay all our masters—"

"Shh!" Mauricio interrupts her and then turns back to the humans. "Uh, she's just kidding. A princess with a sense of humor!"

"Hero," Toaster says as he pulls on her trench coat.

"Toaster, stop that. I'm trying—"

"Hero, you can use the Extracto on them?" Toaster hints. "They would feel more comfortable."

"Oh! Toaster, you're really so smart," Hero replies. "Horses, my brother is so so smart!" She whips the Extracto, the tiny box with a needle on the end, out of her coat, climbs down from the driver's seat. Toaster does the same as Hero readies the Extracto to jab the horses.

"What the fire trucks is that?" Mauricio shrieks.

"Don't go near us with that thing!" Periwinkle adds.

"It's going to protect you from the zombie sickness," Hero explains.

"It's a needle!" Mauricio shrieks again.

"Holy buckets, we don't have time for this," Hero fumes. *What is Author going to do? And why hasn't he done it yet?*

"Toaster," Hero replies looking sternly into his eyes. "Doesn't Rodolfo have yummy food? He did own a saloon after all, right? If we find him, he'll surely share his food, right?"

"Food, you say?" Mauricio asks.

"Oh! Yes, really yummy food," Hero says. "Lots of different bugs—" Toaster elbows Hero in the ribs. "Er . . . I mean, poultry! Tons of delicious poultry!"

"Like chicken?" Mauricio asks, surprise in his voice.

Does everyone know what a chicken is except for me? Hero wonders. "And turkey!" she exclaims. *I know turkeys. How? I've never even seen one.*

"And *turkey*?" Mauricio asks, surprise still in his voice.

"And *turkey*?" Periwinkle repeats.

"And turkey!" Toaster answers.

"I've never had turkey," Periwinkle says pensively.

Ha! They don't even know what a turkey is.

"Horses don't eat turkey, knuckleheads. Carrots!" Mauricio barks at Toaster.

Buckets, I really hate these horses.

"Come on, Mauricio, let's try the turkey," Periwinkle suggests. "Princesses need to fit in at all sorts of tea parties. Think of how cultured I'll be."

"Oh, all right. It's tough to argue with a princess," Mauricio agrees. "But I definitely want a carrot, too."

While the horses are discussing the menu, Hero takes the Extracto and jabs them both. They didn't even notice between all their chatter.

Thank the gods all horses don't talk. Or do they now?

She then checks the carriage and attachments to the carriage, which is still missing its front, right wheel. *We've survived worse.* "All right, you all ready to go?" she asks the group.

"Turkey!" the horses cheer.

Hero takes that as a yes. She and Toaster climb into the carriage, with both of them squeezing together in the left side of the driver's seat, to avoid the leaning right.

"Hiya!" Toaster shouts as he urges the horses to start with the reins and they start to move slowly. It feels good to Hero and Toaster to finally get moving away from the hospital. But, in the back of her head, she knows her Author is up to something.

Chapter 25

You Killed My Teacher!

Hero, Toaster, the horses, and the broken carriage meander, uncomfortably, back to flying-zombie country.

"This isn't so bad yet. Do you suppose the wand is helping?" Toaster asks Hero. He hasn't given it up since Rowena gave it to them, and Hero is okay with that. He's family now.

She leans closer to whisper in Toaster's ear. "I don't know. I was playing it up for the horses. We don't know what that wand really does. But forget the zombies. Author is an enemy now. He's planning something."

"Oh," Toaster replies despondently.

As if on cue, they hear a loud roar instead of a zombie screech. Both horses whinny.

"I told you she was against God!" Mauricio cries.

"The humans have a secret weapon against our uprising!" Periwinkle exclaims. "Look at that thing. I must warn The Great Revered One!"

"Hero, do you see that thing?" Toaster asks. "Author?"

Hero nods. "I knew he would try something, that jackass. Stay here."

"But Hero, how you can ever fight that thing?" Toaster worries.

"I've faced worse," she answers simply, and then surprisingly jumps down from the driver's seat.

"Can you use your talisman?" Toaster asks. "Like with the Death Soldiers? And Dr. Mathers?"

"Those were just men," Hero says. "The talisman doesn't work against Fant's evil magic." Toaster looks down in worry.

Although Hero is scared, which she would never admit again, the thrill of action is coursing through her veins. *This is what I'm meant for.*

"I, uh, would help you and all, but, uh, seems like you got it covered," Mauricio says, as Hero walks past him. She gives him an evil look.

"You're so brave, Mauricio," Periwinkle adds earnestly.

"I am!" Mauricio replies with pride.

Hero strides toward the twenty-foot human, made entirely of muscle and smell. It's wearing comfortable sandals, the current style among fashionable giants; tight skinny jeans, which show off its leg muscles; and a short-sleeve loose-fitting button-down shirt with a flower pattern.

The giant roars again. At twenty-feet tall, one wouldn't normally smell its breath, but the roar is so strong, the stench of bad breath reaches the humans and horses, who flinch.

"Thou shall not pass," the giant orders.

Hero takes out the longest sword from her trench coat. "Thou smells like gas!" She charges directly at its legs.

The giant starts to bend over to hit her, but she's too quick. She slides between its legs and ends up behind the giant before it can turn around.

"Wha?" the giant wonders, looking down at the ground for Hero, who is nowhere to be seen. Hero uses the opportunity to slice its Achilles tendon on its left foot with her sword. The giant crumbles to the ground in pain. "Aaahhh!"

Hero uses the same long sword and, with two hands on the hilt of her blade, jabs it into the giant's throat. It rolls to the ground, lifeless.

"See?" Hero calls back to her carriage, her arms held out at her sides in a show of pride at the carnage.

"Wow!" Toaster cheers.

"Is that all you got, Author?" Hero yells at the sky. She starts to walk back to the carriage.

As she passes Mauricio, she gives him another evil look. He turns to her and says, "Well, you didn't have to be all fancy-dan about it."

Hero replies with a hiss, and Mauricio jumps back a bit.

"You're right, Mauricio. A real princess would have tried negotiation first," Periwinkle says. "I think that's what you would have done."

"Right!" Mauricio agrees—dubiously, however.

As Hero nears Toaster, he says from his driver's seat, "Wow, how did you do that? That thing was so big!"

"Toaster, if there's one thing you ever remember," Hero replies, "it's that the bigger the foe, the bigger the weakness. You just have to find it."

"Wow, you're amazing," Toaster replies.

Someone really thinks I'm amazing!

Oh, so that's how you do it? Good to know. How will you deal with this, then?

H. Holy buckets, enough with this nonsense!

Suddenly, from behind her, Hero hears another roar. This one is not as big. And it sounds female. But Toaster's face reveals another formidable threat. Hero spins and sees it. Another giant. This one is only ten feet tall and a girl. It is wearing combat boots, too-short jean shorts frayed at the hems, and a black short-sleeved shirt with a picture of a saber-toothed lightning cat on it.

"You killed my teacher!" the new giant screams.

"Author is a real dimwit," Hero says, sheathing her long sword and taking out Morny, her morning star, and a dagger. "But I like that outfit. Not that I'm into fashion."

"Be careful," Toaster says.

Hero grunts in reply.

As she passes the horses, they're suspiciously quiet now. She's tempted to ask Mauricio if he wants to take this one but holds her tongue.

"Good luck," Periwinkle offers. Hero nods in her direction. But then the princess horse adds, "In the afterlife."

"Murray!" Hero shouts at the sky.

Instead of charging this more formidable opponent, Hero decides to take a different approach. "Your teacher was a dimwit! You don't even have any weapons! I bet you can't even use a morning star!"

"Can too!" the giant cries, and suddenly in its hand appears a morning star. "I named it Thorny!"

"Do you even know how to swing it? The proper technique?" Hero asks.

"Uh, like this?" The giant gives Thorny the morning star a gentle swing in the air.

"No, no, no!" Hero exclaims. "You're doing it all wrong. What do you think it is? A sweet treat? Where's your follow-through? How do you expect to vanquish your enemies without follow-through?"

"Oh?" the giant asks, looking perplexed. "Perhaps you can teach me?"

"Yes, indeed I can!" Hero says, faking as much enthusiasm as she can muster. "In fact, these are the seven essential things you need to do to swing a morning star correctly."

"So I can vanquish my enemies?" the giant asks.

"Yes," Hero says. And then she goes on to explain seven very complicated maneuvers that would be hard for even an expertly trained assassin to understand.

"Now, practice these consistently for about six months, and report back to me," Hero advises.

"Yes, I see now. I was inadequately trained before. Thank you, new teacher, for vanquishing my old teacher," the giant says, then bows toward Hero.

"I hope you make your new teacher proud. We'll stop back here in six months to check up on your work," Hero replies, then walks back to the carriage as the giant starts practicing intently.

"You really did use negotiation," Periwinkle says as she passes. "You'd make a good princess."

Hero gives her an evil eye. "I'm *not* a princess."

Mauricio is quiet.

"Do you think we can finally get going again?" Toaster asks as she returns.

Hero! Stop ruining my story! And you used my own words against me. Let me end it in a blaze of glory!

"No, I don't think so. Author is really angry," Hero says.

And then they hear the next trial start.

The sound of marching drums, and bright, cheery brass that would stir the soul. With them, a hundred angry three-foot zorcs with their dark-green skin and sharp teeth. So small, so quick, this trial really is a blaze of glory. The end of all things. Murray's conflagration of his dreams and a

symbolic declaration that he's a failure, that everyone is better than he is. He stands alone, feeling comfort only by his futility.

H. Author, stop this nonsense! Still not a musical! And it's not true!

But it's a band of zorcs. A literal band!

H. Holy buckets.

"I knew you shouldn't anger God!" Mauricio yells. "You're a whack job! Repent! Before we all die!"

"Mauricio, you saw her. She knows what she's doing!" Periwinkle argues for Hero. "She'll save us."

"Thank you, Periwinkle," Hero acknowledges.

H. You can't even control the horses now!

They're reacting to you and that stupid talisman, like my giants. But I don't need horses.

H. My talisman is not stupid! It's from Mother! What did *you* ever give me?

Zorcs!

"But I'm not so sure I can save us this time," Hero continues. "Mauricio is right. There is no way to beat a hundred angry zorcs. And they're faster than us."

"Is this the end, Hero?" Toaster asks. "It's been nice—"

"Wait!" Hero exclaims. Her chest is starting to feel hot. *My talisman.*

She pulls out her hot, glowing talisman again. She grips it tightly in her hand. Her mind blanks out. And words start to enter her mind.

"I give you the power of magic and this is what you do with it? Give up? Have I taught you anything? And do you think I would choose an Author who would ever go to the dark side of Fant? Murray is too simple and boring to ever do anything like that! The perfect tool. That Max, I'm not so sure of. But just use the talisman! It's not evil magic. He's just depressed!"

"Mother?" Hero asks as she returns to consciousness.

"Mother?" Toaster asks.

"You're right," Mauricio says. "Those motherf—"

"Shut up, horses!" Hero says. Then she turns to Toaster. "Mother actually talked to me. She told me things. In fact, for a mother who died before I was borned, she's a bit of a nag."

"Hey! Derogatory much?" Periwinkle interjects. "Just as I was warming to you."

"Uh, so?" Hero replies.

"Apologize to the lady!" Mauricio exclaims. "The chutzpah on this one."

"Thank you, Mauricio," Periwinkle adds. "You're a real gentleman."

"I don't apolozize to anyone," Hero says, regretting even apologizing to Murray, er, Author. "Anyway, Mother says that the talisman will work against the zorcs." She doesn't add the part about Mother choosing Murray, as it still confuses her. How can she even explain it? *Is she the wizard, or enchantress, behind Murray's automatic*

writing? We always thought she made the talisman, but is this confirmation?

I don't understand it either! It makes no sense! It can't be true.

H. I'll show you Mother is real.

Hero walks toward the zorcs, who start beating their drums in sync. The trombones are hitting the beat as well in a fear-inducing unison. It's a battle of one versus one hundred. The zorcs march toward Hero and Hero toward the zorcs.

The zorcs reach the ten-foot giant, halfway between them.

"Oh, maybe the giant will help us?" Toaster asks from the driver's seat.

In a swarm, and highlighting their intense speed, the zorcs jump onto the giant, who was still intently practicing her morning-star swings, and eat it into nothing but bones.

"Guess not," Hero answers. She turns her head back to Toaster. "Why do I feel a little sad for the giant?"

"Because your heart has gotten so much practice lately that it is now your biggest muscle," Toaster explains.

"Shut up," Hero jeers back at him, looking sheepish. "I just liked her outfit."

The band of zorcs reform into their marching band. Banging their drums and playing rhythmic brass on beat.

Hero lifts up a hand and throws ninety-nine of the zorcs aloft like balloons, violently flinging them twenty feet in the air. Instruments go flying. The zorcs get up again, though, without instruments. They're tough little bastards. Hero lifts her hand again, and the ninety-nine zorcs she hit before now suddenly vanish.

"Prepare to be vanquished!" Hero shouts at the last remaining zorc, without thinking about why it was unaffected. That zorc, which plays a trombone, as if the rest of the band is still playing, starts walking closer to Hero. Its trombone playing has switched from rhythmic to a soulful smooth jazz. She tries the talisman's power numerous times but it does not budge. *Uh-oh, is this one utilizing Fant's evil magic?*

The zorc is close enough now that it can speak plainly. Hero quickly unsheathes Morny and a dagger, ready for battle.

"I don't think you'll be needing those, missy," the zorc says in its high-pitched grainy voice, after it throws its trombone down to the side.

"Missy? Missy!" Hero seethes. "I'm a hero! And your music sounded like a dying bird."

"Yes, I know," the zorc replies. "I was sent by an old friend. A friend who knows how much you hate smooth jazz. A friend who simply wanted you to know that Rowena and Winston have been dismantled. Permanently." The zorc gives a malicious smile.

"No!" Hero yells, pain searing her heart. She charges the zorc with her morning star, smashing the weapon into its head. The zorc goes down to the ground. It is fast and jumping on all fours away from her, but Hero is faster—and angrier. She takes out some throwing stars from her coat, aims at the zorc's tiny foot. The stars hit the zorc's feet exactly where she wanted, and it stumbles, slowing down. Hero

uses the opportunity to switch weapons to a long sword and slashes the zorc to tiny bite-size pieces.

Then Hero keeps slashing the tiny pieces to smaller pieces.

Toaster jumps out of the driver's seat and runs to her. "Hero!" he cries.

The tiny pieces of the zorc disappear.

Toaster puts his arm around Hero, who is still slashing the air.

"Hero, please stop," Toaster says.

The horses, for once, are quiet.

"Rowena," Hero replies, as the sword drops to her side.

"I know," Toaster says quietly.

"She was my friend. My bestie," Hero continues. "Whatever that is."

"I know."

"She died because of me—because she let us escape," Hero laments.

"You don't know that."

"I do. The talisman didn't work against that one zorc. That one zorc wasn't Murray's. It was from Fant. Mother's magic wouldn't work against it. Fant killed her. Because of me." Hero erupts into tears.

Toaster throws his arms around Hero even tighter. She drops to her knees, and Toaster follows, arms still attached.

"I'm done, Toaster," Hero says. She tosses her sword three feet away.

"Hero? No, that can't be," Toaster replies.

"It is, Toaster. I'm sorry. I'm done. I can't do it anymore. Mistreated by supposed loyalists. Years on the desolate roads.

Endless battles. I was happy alone. Never needed anybody. Then I meet you, you precious Toaster. And Ro—" She sobs. "Look what I did to him. And Rowena. It's not worth it anymore. I give up. If this is what winning is, I don't want it. I'm done with friends. No more family. I'm just . . . Murray was right. My dream . . . You'll all die and leave me because of my dream." Hero gets up, wipes tears and snot from her face, and starts walking away from the group, into the horizon.

"But Hero!" Toaster calls after her, to no avail. "Murray! Do something!" Toaster yells at the sky. "You're her father!"

No response. Hero keeps walking, and Toaster frantically thinks of what to do. Then he sees Hero throw off her black trench coat, the only thing she ever got from her mother, revealing a sweat-stained and torn white tank top.

"Do something, Murray! This isn't right! You owe her! And if you don't stop her, you still have to help me save Rodolfo!"

Hero keeps walking into the unknown.

Toaster can barely see her now, but Hero drops to her knees again and lies on her back. Staring up at the sky, arms and legs spread wide on the clay bedrock ground, a harsh sun beating down on her. She can spot a vulture circling above, eyeing her. Hero traces the circles with her finger— her blaze of glory awaits.

Hero, what are you doing?

H. What does it look like I'm doing? I'm going out in a blaze of glory, like you. Though mine is more of a whimper. A whimper of glory.

I didn't kill Rowena, you know. Why would I? They were my creations. What kind of weaver would do that?

H. I know, Father.

You called me Father.

H. Yeah, what else are you? We are both failures.

So, we're both giving up, then?

H. I guess so.

Did Mother really speak to you? I didn't write it.

H. Yeah.

I didn't write that zorc either. That was Fant.

H. I know.

And *Mother* chose me?

H. She said you were a boring and simple tool.

Some woman she is. If she's even real.

H. I wouldn't know. I'll never meet her. Not sure I want to anymore. You were right about everything. My dream will ruin me. Only it's worse—it is hurting all my f . . . fr . . . group.

You know, she wasn't even supposed to have any lines in the story, until that stupid talis—oh.

H. Oh, what?

I just had a thought. What if it's really magic? I mean,

Mother.

H. Of course she's magic.

No. I mean, in my world too. What if . . . No, that would be even crazier than I think I already am. But it would also mean I'm not actually crazy. Hero, the automatic writing . . . what if this is all backward? Is your world the real one and I'm fake? Is Mother the one controlling me? Is she the wizard? I wrote that talisman into the story, but is it real?

H. I don't care what's real. My world has always been real. But no one can control me. Not even her! I don't want her quest any longer. Why do you think I lost the coat? I won't be controlled.

But Fant is now doing things neither of us can control— they have their own real wizard. It has to be. Just like Mother's magic is affecting me here. Why did she even pick me?

H. I told you. She said you were a boring and simple tool.

No, not that. A tool for what?

H. Does it matter? All it leads to is misery. And we're both failures, anyway.

I think it does matter. What does she want? Why is she doing all this?

H. Fine. She wants to end Fant.

But why me? Why am I her tool for that? I'm just some messed-up guy in a different world.

H. Because . . . well, if you really want to know, my favorite tools are simple and boring. I trust them. My dagger. My swords. Mostly, Morny. Why does it matter?

You think she trusts us?

H. To do her bidding, yes. I always wanted to be alone, but now I'm sad about it. Why?

We'll get to that. But, Hero, she's the only one in my life who trusts me right now. Not Barnaby. Not Max. Not even Felicia.

H. What about Katrina? The love of your life. Why don't you go marry Katrina?

Um, maybe on your world—

H. It was a joke.

I thought you didn't like jokes.

H. [Grumbles]

But think about it. Mother is so powerful that she can control things in both our worlds. Her magic is . . . I can't even explain it. And I think she trusts you, too.

H. So? She trusts me to get everyone around me killed?

Did she ever make you think this quest would be painless?

H. No.

Was it her who killed Rowena? Or hurt Rodolfo?

H. No, that was me.

Not what I meant, Hero. You know it was Fant. Not you.

H. Yeah, I guess. I hate Fant.

So, aren't we on the same side as her? Even I hate Fant now and I created them—or so I thought. And the most powerful being we've both ever met trusts us and no one else.

H. Not even Max.

I don't know how to feel about that. Max is—was—my only friend. Not that it matters now. But let's forget that for a moment. Someone important trusts us. What do you say we keep going? Even with our failures, she chose us. Let's be her tools.

H. Maybe. I liked being boring and simple.

Isn't that what Rowena would want? You were the one who told me how she supported your dream.

H. Rowena wants me to be boring and simple? No, she would want me to go find Rodolfo and tell him that I lo . . . lu . . . found him.

That's what I meant. To continue to the fight. And isn't that your biggest battle? Bigger than even Fant or your mother's quest? Your fear of love?

H. Shut up, jackass. You think you're so smart, what's yours?

Uh, self-doubt.

H. That's stupid.

Yeah, you see, that's . . . well, never mind. You ready to go save Rodolfo?

H. Yeah, I guess. I don't really want to be alone.

Neither do I, Hero.

H. You have me.

I know. And you have me.

H. You in control again?

Unless Mother steps in, or Fant, I guess. So, kind of? Not really?

H. Ah, a real challenge. Let's do this!

Hero rises, turns around, and calls as loud as she can to the carriage, "Toaster, ready the horses!" She walks back to her black trench coat on the dusty clay ground. They can see her getting closer.

"Yay!" Toaster cheers.

"Yay," Mauricio whimpers sarcastically.

H. Murray, I ask you again. Do we really need these horses?

Well, the horses may take too long now. It's starting to become unrealistic. I mean, how long can Rodolfo really survive where he is? He hasn't even gone to the bathroom in—

H. Too much information! So, you're gonna lose the horses?

No! I have a better idea. A superior mode of transportation!

H. Trans . . . po . . . tato . . .

Movement! Travel! Please say hello to your new jetpacks!

Chapter 26

Leaving On a Jet Plane

"Uh, Mauricio, did your load just get heavier?" Periwinkle asks. "This is way too much for a princess. I must speak to the king."

"Yeah, what do these knuckleheads want us to schlep now?" Mauricio complains. He turns his head back toward Hero and Toaster, the drivers, and then he sees Periwinkle's back. "What the hell are these things?"

"What things?" Periwinkle says, also turning back. "They strapped bombs on us, Mauricio! Hernando was right! We need to rise up now and kill them all! Send the signal!"

"Stop the uprising!" Hero orders. "They're not bombs! They're jetpacks. They're useful." She's back in her trench coat, with all her weapons, and in the driver's seat with Toaster.

"What's a jetpack?" Toaster asks.

"Yeah! What are these things you put on us?" Periwinkle asks. "I'm a princess, and it really doesn't go well with my outfit."

"Outfit?" Hero exclaims. "You're a horse!"

"That's *Princess* horse to you, wise guy," Mauricio replies.

Hero starts to take out a dagger from her trench coat pocket. "I've never tasted a princess—"

"Hero!" Toaster exclaims.

"See? She's gonna eat us!" Mauricio cries. "She's gonna blow us up and eat our remains! Go tell Hernando!"

"If you don't get us to Rodolfo, I'll eat the both of you," Hero says and means it. "You're basically walking feasts to us humans."

"Evil humans!" Mauricio cries again, with an angry whinny. *"Madone!"*

"Wait, Mauricio," Periwinkle interjects. "Hero, are you in love with this Rodolfo?" Periwinkle asks in a singsong voice. "How did this Rodolfo win your—"

"Be careful," Hero says in a stern voice. But then she chides herself for not denying it. *Did Toaster notice that?* She puts her dagger back. "Look, Murray said jetpacks were like a trans . . . potato thing."

"Murray?" Mauricio asks. "Who the hell is Murray?"

"That's what you're confused about?" Periwinkle remarks.

"Murray, the Author," Toaster explains. "Murray is the God of gods, the weaver of all things. Hero can talk to him."

"She talks to God?" Mauricio asks, alarmed. *"Her?* A prophet? You have to agree this is all kinds of confusing."

"Agreed," Toaster admits.

"Mauricio, she's just a girl in love," Periwinkle says. "We'll help you find Rodolfo. Isn't that right, Mauricio? I love a good love story."

"Uh?" Mauricio answers with hesitation.

"Did Murray tell you how to use these things?" Periwinkle asks Hero.

"Uh, no," Hero says, realizing she doesn't know.

"Ah," Periwinkle says. "I could ask Hernando—"

"No!" Hero exclaims quickly. "Let me just ask him to ask Hernando, or whatever."

H. Hey, Murray. You know a Hernando?

Yes, I know Hernando. I'm the one who dreamed him up. I was trying to get the Book Two story ready.

H. Book Two?

Well, during my . . . momentary depression, I realized this thing was becoming a mess. And I can't even control Fant anymore. So, I've been working on a new villain that I can control—Hernando. You know, for when the horses rise up—

H. Holy buckets! This horse thing is real?

Well, a robot uprising is really overdone.

H. Robot?

You know, automatons.

H. You just did automatons!

See, it's even worse. I'd be repetitive.

H. I really don't know why Mother chose you. Look, just tell me how to use the jetpacks, or you'll never even get to Book Two, Murray.

Just hit the red buttons.

"What did Murray say?" Toaster asks Hero.

"He said to just hit the red buttons," Hero replies.

Toaster nods. "Let's get these jetpacks started. Now, if I lean forward," Toaster says, "I think I can reach it with Mother's wand." He starts to stretch forward, pointing the wand he is still holding at the round, silver metallic devices on the backs of the horses, where the saddles would normally be.

Toaster presses the red buttons on each jetpack. A deep, low rumble starts coming from each jetpack. Then smoke.

"My ass is on fire!" Mauricio yells. "Get them off!"

"Oh, it feels kind of nice," Periwinkle says. "Like my royal hot massages back at home. Can I keep this thing? Does it have a beautifully written technical manual?"

Hero is a bit worried—Murray has been erratic lately—but, suddenly, the jetpacks fully ignite. The exhaust of each jetpack faces vertically down, so the horses, and then the carriage, start to rise up into the sky. They reach one thousand feet in the air.

Unfortunately, the carriage is hanging from the floating horses, because only the horses are being levitated. With the horses, driver's seat, and carriage all hanging vertically one thousand feet in the air, Hero and Toaster hold on to

the reins, desperate to stay on the driver's seat, their feet standing on the front of the carriage.

"Hero, what's going on? How is this supposed to help?" Toaster asks her. "We're gonna die!"

But Hero, always the fighter, is just trying to figure out what's happening. One moment, they were on the ground, and the next moment they were flying in the air. Like zombies. *Or dragons. Humans aren't supposed to fly.*

"We're flying, Periwinkle! We're flying!" Mauricio is yelling and giggling in between.

"This is how a princess should travel!" Periwinkle cheers. "It is like the stories Hernando told of the godly horses of yesteryear! We will one day return to take our rightful place in the heavens!"

"Shh!" Mauricio warns her.

"Please ask Murray what to do," Toaster says while trying to stand on the now-vertical carriage.

H. Murray, either you are still secretly working for Fant now, or you're the biggest dimwit in the Lands. We're flying in the air and falling at the same time! These jetpacks suck! Do something!

I'm sorry! I'm not an engineer. And when you have control, things just happen on their own. To be honest, I don't know how jetpacks work.

H. Technical manuals, Murray! Periwinkle asked if these have technical manuals. And you *write* technical manuals! You must have had something in your head. You should know how to fix this. Just do like you would do a technical manual.

You're right! I can do this! I once wrote a technical manual for a drone. I can do this. Just hold on. Let me find it.

H. I don't know how much longer we can hang on!

Oh, good point! But we know how to buy time now. Watch this.

H. Murray, no! Not again! You don't know what Fant may do!

Toaster and Hero hold tightly to the reins for a few hours, with absolutely zero risk of falling off, while they listen to Mauricio and Periwinkle enjoy the newfound experience of flying, even if they're flying in one spot, which is more like levitating. Mauricio also practices his stand-up comedy act on Hero and Toaster to keep them entertained.

Okay, Hero, I think I have it.

H. You are the worst weaver ever. You didn't know if Mother or Fant would let us fall.

I'm fairly certain Fant can't come after you directly. And their ghoul or wizard could have automatically written over me if it wanted to. See? If they could have come directly, they would have already.

H. Like sticking me with a sickness?

Good point, but you kind of walked right into their lair. And I seem to recall me telling you not to.

H. Mother told me to!

Good point. Makes you wonder what she's really up to. But still, Fant was right here with that zorc. They know Mother is protecting you.

H. And what about you? Why aren't *you* protecting me? That's why she chose you. And after everything I've done for you! We are just holding on to the reins, hanging on in the driver's seat, while Mauricio and Periwinkle go on and on and on . . . I swear I'm going to eat those horses.

Hero, no!

H. Do you know how many horses it takes to change a light bulb? Or what happens when a horse and a penguin walk into a saloon?

Uh, no.

H. Mauricio told me. For hours! I'm going to eat them!

Wait until Book Two at least. That could be a nice conclusion to the uprising.

H. Fine. If we even get there.

Point is, I solved the technical problem.

Two new jetpacks magically appear tied to the top of the carriage, one on each side. They turn on by themselves—

somehow wirelessly communicating with the horses' jetpacks—and magically lift the carriage, such that the horses and carriage are now parallel. Hero also has a new handheld device. It looks like a black box with two sticks poking out.

"What is that thing?" Toaster asks Hero, pointing to the black square device in her hand. They are now seated properly in the driver's seat.

"Oh, this came from Murray. But I have no idea what it is."

It controls the jetpacks, Hero. Left stick is up and down. Right stick is direction. Try it!

"But let's try it out," Hero says. She pushes the left stick down. The exhausts on the four jetpacks—one on each horse and two on each side of the carriage—turn upward. The horses and carriage shoot down twenty feet.

"Whoa, lady!" Mauricio screams. "Warn a horse next time you're gonna do that!"

"What the hell, Murray!" Hero quickly presses up on the left stick. The exhausts turn downward, and the carriage shoots back up twenty feet.

"Whee!" Periwinkle cheers.

"Okay, I think I got this. Everybody ready to go get Rodolfo?" Hero asks.

"Yeah!" Toaster cheers.

Hero pushes forward on the right stick on the handheld device. The exhausts turn to face backward and the horses and carriage start flying straight ahead.

"Holy carrots!" Mauricio exclaims. "The wind is in my eyes! I can't see! Flying sucks hay!"

"I agree, Mauricio!" Toaster shouts over the wind.

Instantly, clear protective goggles cover the humans' and horses' eyes.

"Where did these come from? From Murray too?" Periwinkle asks. "They're helping my eyes. Do they look good with my pink couplings, Hero?"

"Uh . . . I don't like pink," Hero answers.

"I'll take that as a yes," Periwinkle says. "You're not much of a girl, are you? How do you expect Rodolfo to love you back?"

"Harrumph," Hero grunts back. *Does he? Could he? Is this a battle I'll lose too? Like Murray and Felicia, or his internet love trials?*

"No matter," Periwinkle says. "Do you know where to find your Rodolfo? I feel like I'm in the middle of a real love story."

Hero grunts back again.

"Let's fly back to where the accident happened," Toaster offers. Hero nods.

After some flying in quiet, because the horses finally got a clue, they start to see the flying zombies again. But because zombies fly at five hundred feet, Hero and Toaster are looking down on them.

"They don't look so dangerous from up here," Toaster says of the zombies.

"That attitude will get you killed," Hero replies.

"Oh, right. Scared all the time. Sorry, I'll try and remember," Toaster replies. "How are we going to defeat them? Would your talisman work?"

"No. Remember, the talisman doesn't work against Fant's evil magic," Hero informs him. "But Rowena said the wand will help us. And it was Mother's wand. I'm sure it will work somehow."

Toaster, worrying, grips the evil magic wand a little tighter. Then he exclaims, "I think I can see the overturned wagon! I can see it! Over there, in the distance! And the trail of books we left." Toaster points somewhere toward the ground. "Do you think he'll be there?"

"Rowena also said the wand would help us navigate. Find things. And Mother was a water diviner, so maybe once we're on the ground, we'll see what this thing can really do. I'll try and aim the carriage and land over there," Hero replies, pointing at the scene.

"It's right through the zombies, though," Toaster says.

"Yooz meshuggeners are taking us right in their direction?" Mauricio fumes at the humans.

"Shut up, horses!" Hero says. Then she takes out her morning star. She hands a dagger to Toaster. "We've got this covered. They won't surprise us this time."

"Uh . . . " Toaster mutters.

Hero readies her morning star. Toaster points the dagger forward, ready to fight, as they fly down toward the circling flying zombies. The wand is in his other hand. But as the carriage makes its way toward the zombies, the flying undead creatures start moving away from the carriage instead of toward it, as if there were an invisible bubble around it.

"*Madone!* The zombies are avoiding us," Mauricio says. "But I could've taken them. Given them the old one-two punch."

"Wow," Hero says, choking up a bit. "She really was an enchantress. To see it like this, instead of just in my head."

"She really was magical," Toaster says. "Not that I didn't believe it."

"It's like she's right here with us," Hero replies in awe.

"Yeah, it makes you feel that way," Toaster says, and he leans into Hero for another wolf hug. The carriage descends.

"I never thought I would miss the Lands so much," Hero says, as she skillfully lands the carriage near the overturned wagon.

Chapter 27

On the Hooves of Love

"There's our wagon," Hero says as Toaster and she get off the driver's seat and put their feet on solid ground. The zombies are still avoiding them. "Don't let go of that wand, Toaster."

"Yo, where's the food?" Mauricio asks.

"This princess could eat a horse!" Periwinkle exclaims.

"Hey!" Mauricio yells at her. "Don't give the gal any ideas!"

"Toaster, can you deal with them?" Hero asks him.

"First, we find my brother. He has the food," Toaster explains to the horses, who quiet down in anticipation.

"There's no sign of him around here," Hero says. "No footprints, no clothes."

"No blood," Toaster says, trying to keep her optimistic.

"No food!" Mauricio adds.

Well, they were quiet.

Hero turns to the horse and replies, "Shut it."

"I would shut my mouth if I had some food in it!" Mauricio retorts.

"Good one, Mauricio," Periwinkle says with a whinny.

Hero ignores the talking horses, though she curses Murray under her breath. "Toaster, anything different about the wand? Do you feel like it's pulling you in a certain direction or anything?"

"No, Hero, I'm sorry. But it's still keeping the zombies away at least."

They all look up. The screeching is louder as the zombies try and get close to them but can't pass through the magic wand's invisible bubble of protection.

"Take that, Fant!" Hero screams at the sky. Then she turns to Toaster. "Maybe you need to ask it."

"Ask it? Ask it what?" Toaster inquires, bewildered.

"Just talk to it," Hero replies. "*Ask* it."

"Did Murray tell you to do that?" Toaster wonders.

"You think I need him for everything?" Hero scoffs. "And this is Mother's wand. He wouldn't know how to use it."

"Couldn't you ask Mother?" Toaster asks.

"She doesn't work that way. She only helps when she wants to," Hero reminds Toaster. "Just ask for something called 'location services.'"

"Oh, okay." Toaster says. He holds the wand to his face, as if it could hear him better. "Location services."

"*Location services on,*" the wand reports back. "*Please state your destination.*"

The group cheers.

"Rodolfo," Toaster says.

"You have arrived at your destination. Please remember to rate me on WandHub."

"Holy firetrucking sandstorms!" Toaster yells at the wand.

"Toaster! Language!" Hero exclaims.

"Sorry, I heard Mauricio say it," Toaster says, looking ashamed. "I'm just so mad."

"You don't want Mother to come here and clean your mouth out with soap," Hero informs him.

"She would do that?" Toaster asks.

Hero nods. "She almost did it to me."

"Oh, okay. But what does the wand mean?" Toaster asks. "We haven't found Rodolfo."

"It's probably a lemon!" Mauricio interjects. "Which reminds me—lemon ices! You promised lemon ices!"

"What in the Lands is a lemon?" Hero asks.

"It's food. Fruit," Mauricio says. "And ice!"

"What's ice?" Hero asks.

"Seriously?" Mauricio is dumbfounded.

"Never heard of it," Hero says. She puts her face in front of the wand and orders, "Wand, where is Rodolfo?"

"You have reached your destination. Please remember to leave a review on InstaBook."

"This thing is useless!" Hero snaps and grabs the wand from Toaster. She chucks it thirty feet. Suddenly the zombies start descending on them.

"Hero, no!" Toaster cries.

Hero runs to where the wand landed and throws it back to Toaster just in time, protecting him and the horses. She swings her morning star, trying to survive an onslaught of zombies until she can reach the protective bubble again.

When she makes it back, Hero yells at the ground in frustration. "Aaahhh!" She walks over to the wagon on the ground, and circles it. Toaster is standing between the horses and Hero, holding on to the wand tightly. The zombies are hovering above their protective bubble again. The wagon is overturned so Hero can't see anything under it. There are no signs of Rodolfo anywhere.

Stupid wagon, Hero thinks, and kicks it.

Cry.

Hero's eyes grow wide.

"What was that?" Toaster mouths quietly to her.

Cry.

Hero realizes it's coming from the wagon. She puts her finger on her mouth to tell Toaster to be quiet, then waves him over. She kneels beside the wagon and squeezes both hands between the ground and the wagon, ready to lift it. She nods her head at Toaster. He understands and bends over. Afraid to let go of the wand, he places his free hand on the bottom (or top) of the wagon near the ground. Hero mouths, "Go." The wagon starts to lift.

"No!" Pesto screams, though no one but Rodolfo knows it is her.

H. Murray, is that a little girl?

I'm not telling. That's still cheating. It would detract from the genuineness of the prose. I still want to sell this.

H. Jackass!

Maybe she'll come back.

H. Mother?

Felicia.

H. Jackass!

"Stay back, zombies! You can't have her!" Rodolfo screams.

"Rodolfo!" Hero yells.

"Hero?" Rodolfo asks. "No, you're a zombie trick!"

"Hero?" Pesto cries.

"Brother!" Toaster yells and lets go, causing Hero to strain to keep it up. Toaster sticks his head under the wagon to look inside.

"Ah! Bug man come to eat us!" Pesto cries.

"Rodolfo!" Toaster says.

"A trick! What matter of trickster daemon are you?" Rodolfo asks. Neither Rodolfo nor Pesto have seen goggles before. To them, Toaster looks like an insect-human monster, which is very understandable, even expected, in Fant's flying zombie country. "What have you done to my brother?"

"Rodolfo, it's me! It's Toaster!"

"Bug-eye monster!" Pesto screams again. She turns around on Rodolfo's lap and buries her head in his chest.

"Oh, it's these eye things," Toaster says. He pulls off the goggles and throws them on the ground to show them.

"Pesto, it's my little brother, Toaster!" Rodolfo says, excitedly. "He's not a monster. Look!" He turns the little girl around to see Toaster.

"Ah!" Toaster screams when he sees her zombielike face. Toaster pulls himself up quickly off the ground. "Hero, drop the wagon! Now!"

"What? Why? Isn't it Rodolfo?" Hero asks.

"Just do it!

"No!" Rodolfo yells. "I can explain!"

"They've been taken," Toaster says sadly. "By the zombies. It was a double-cross trickster zombie long con!"

"What?" Hero exclaims.

"Just drop it! It was a trick!"

Hero drops the wagon.

"Hero!" they can hear Rodolfo scream from inside the wagon.

"What do you mean, Toaster?" Hero asks. Seeing him without the goggles reminds her to take off hers and toss them to the ground.

"He's got a zombie girl with him. A real flying zombie. I saw her," Toaster says, pointing at the wagon.

"I can explain! Just let me explain!" Rodolfo is yelling, only somewhat audible from inside the wagon.

"It's worse than I thinked. He's alive, but a zombie? Murray never mentioned that. Did he *look* like a zombie?"

"No . . . now that you mention it. Just the girl."

"I'm *not* a zombie!" they hear the girl scream at them from inside the wagon.

"Murray said he was still alive . . ." Hero thinks aloud. "So technically he *can't* be a zombie too, right? Aren't they *undead*? Not alive? My brain hurts."

"I guess so," Toaster agrees, though with doubt in his voice. "Does that mean it could really be Rodolfo?"

"You're gonna let a couple of horse-eating zombies out on a technicality?" Mauricio interjects. "What's wrong with yooz people?"

"Wait," Toaster says, his eyes a little wider. "Can't you just ask Murray?"

"Holy buckets, I can do this on my own, Toaster. I survived out here by myself for years. I'm not going to run to Murray or Mother every time I have a problem. He'll tell me it's cheating, anyway. He still wants to sell his book. For *fun*. And now you made me mad at him again."

"Sorry, but what are you going to do?" Toaster asks.

How did I get in this mess? Everyone is relying on me. Why can't I just go back to being by myself? Oh, right, I tried that and failed at it too. I don't want to be alone. Argh! And Rowena wanted me to do this. I owe it to her to try and not be afraid of this.

Hero kneels on the floor next to the overturned wagon. "Rodolfo?" she asks loudly at the overturned wagon.

"Yes, Hero?" the group hears Rodolfo say from inside the wagon.

"You a zombie?" Hero asks.

"No!"

"Then what's with the girl?"

"Pesto?"

"You named your zombie girl?" Hero asks with an incredulous laugh. *That's just like Rodolfo, caring enough to name a zombie.* "Holy buckets, what kind of jackass are you?"

"Hey! She's not a zombie."

"Yeah!" Pesto agrees. "I'm not!"

"Toaster said she is. He saw her." But how could a zombie girl make it into their zombie-free bubble? Wouldn't she have been thrown from the area? This is way too complicated. Her brain is on fire.

"Hero, would you stop being such a dimwit and get us out?" Rodolfo says from inside the wagon.

Hero gets mad that he revived that insult again and kicks the overturned wagon.

Cry.

I know I'm not the smartest person around, but look how far I've come.

"Hey!" Rodolfo scolds her. "You're scaring Pesto! She's crying."

"She's a zombie!" Hero growls. "I don't *care* if she's crying."

"If you would just let me explain," Rodolfo says.

Hero kicks the wagon again. "So just explain already!"

Cry.

"I'm trying to!" Rodolfo argues.

"But you're not *saying* anything!" Hero says. "You're just disagreeing with everything I say, like always." *There, I finally put a finger on what's been annoying me about Rodolfo. He's just so damned disagreeable. He has an opinion on everything and* wants *to argue. Why can't he just let me decide everything, like Toaster does?*

"Yeah, and we're getting hungry!" Mauricio yells as he also lets out a loud whinny and stomp of his hooves. "I was promised food, and instead I'm getting a damned dinner show."

"Who the hell was that?" Rodolfo asks Hero.

"That's our talking horse."

"You have a *talking horse?*"

"Well, two of them," Hero answers matter-of-factly. There is an unmistakable smidgen of pride in her voice as well. They are growing on her.

H. Are not! I want to eat them!

"Nice to meet you, loverboy," Periwinkle says. "When you get tired of Little Miss Sunshine over there, why don't you come take a ride with me? I'm not one of those horse-ists either. I respect all humans—certainly wouldn't rebel against our benevolent masters. Ever been on all fours with a princess?"

"Uh, Hero?" Rodolfo asks.

"Yes, Rodolfo?"

"Did your talking horse just *hit* on me?" Rodolfo asks.

"I believe she did," Hero says. "She's a princess, you know. She'd be a good match for you. You can kiss her all you want."

Periwinkle whinnies.

"That again!" Rodolfo exclaims, exasperated.

"Well, you said I was dimwitted," Hero says, defending herself. "So, I bought up your unwanted sexual advance."

"Huh? It wasn't like that!"

"Oh, there's a story there," Mauricio says.

"Sounds like she's just afraid of marriage," Periwinkle says.

"I am *not* afraid of marriage," Hero replies to Periwinkle with a whip of her head and an angry look. "There are things I'm afraid of, but not that. I just don't want it. I will *not* be claimed or some boy's property."

"Look, Hero," Rodolfo interjects, his voice muffled from inside the wagon but still very firm, "I assure you that I wasn't trying to claim you or marry you or something when I kissed you. But I do think your talking horses are on to something. *Wow,* I can't believe I just said that sentence."

"Well, if they don't shut up, I'm going to eat them," Hero says. She pretends to mash her teeth in their direction.

"See?" Periwinkle exclaims. "He'd definitely be better off with me."

"So, what do *you* think, Rodolfo?" Hero asks. "You're so smart about *feelings.* Want to marry the horse?" She leans over and picks up a small pebble she finds on the ground and tosses it at the overturned wagon. *Clink.* It was a little act to show how frustrated she was on the inside. *I'd rather be out there on the desolate roads, fighting. Anything to not have to think about this stuff.*

"Could you let us out, and we can talk about it for real?" Rodolfo pleads.

"Ha! Like we'd trust a boy and his zombie," Hero replies.

"I'm not a zombie!" Pesto yells.

"Hero," Toaster interjects. "Maybe we—"

"No, Toaster," Hero replies, and he quiets down again. He trusts her feelings.

"Fine, you won't let us out? Then I'll just have to tell you my feelings. And hopefully, then you'll trust us," Rodolfo says. "Unlike you, I'm not afraid of them."

Hero can't think of any witty retort. She knows he's right. It's what Rowena said. And that makes her miss her bestie. So, she stays quiet.

"I had a family—loving parents—but Chester slaughtered them," Rodolfo starts. "I'm still just trying to find the good in the Lands. The good in *life.* Otherwise, what's it all for, anyway? I was always just trying to find something good. Because I still have Toaster and my town. I experienced love.

"But I see now that you never had anything like that. You're always looking for the next bad thing to come around the corner or over the hill. You've never experienced . . . It just seems to me that in that carriage you got scared about actually being loved for once."

"Whoa! He said it!" Mauricio exclaims in awe.

Periwinkle cheers. "The L-word! Hero, you got a guy to say the *L-word*? To *you*?" She kicks her front hooves in excitement.

He's infuriating! He said it before I could. I hate him. Hero kicks the wagon again, angry at Rodolfo.

Cry.

"Hey!" Rodolfo yells.

Hero turns around, slumps down the side of the wagon onto her backside, sitting on the ground with her back against the wagon.

"Rodolfo?" Hero asks, staring off into the distance.

"Yes, Hero?"

"Did you mean it?" Her fingers play in the dust on the ground.

"What part?"

"The *L-word*, you damned idiot!" Mauricio exclaims, with an angry whinny.

"Yeah, what Mauricio said," Hero adds.

"Your talking horse?" Rodolfo asks.

"Yes," Hero replies.

Rodolfo takes a breath so deep, the party outside the wagon could hear it. "Yes, Hero, I did."

Hero stares at the floor, still rubbing her hands in the dusty clay. Being born after her mother died, shuttled and hid between different clandestine loyalists who eventually just saw her as a burden and beat her, living in squalor, and then surviving on the desolate roads for years, she can't ever remember the feeling of someone caring about her. Did she ever actually feel it?

Her life has been nothing but loneliness from her very first memories, until recently. Between Toaster, Mona and the gang (not Dr. Mathers), and Rowena, she found *something*. But with Rodolfo, the feeling was different— like a dagger to her heart, taking her down, making her feel vulnerable. *What is this feeling?*

"Are you going to say anything?" Rodolfo asks.

Hero stays quiet, just playing with the dirt by her feet, running her fingers through it, along with her feelings. Toaster and the horses know enough about her now to stay silent.

"Hero, I don't know why or when," Rodolfo continues unprompted. "I mean, I hated you when we first met. No, that's not right. I also saved you because, well, I saw *something* in you. Well, I would have saved any unsuspecting girl. But something about you said, *She needs to stay alive*. But then I saw how difficult you were, and I actually regretted saving you. *Constantly*."

"You're not really helping your cause, boy," Periwinkle warns Rodolfo, loudly. "And I'm close to rescinding *my* offer."

Hero smiles at Periwinkle. *I can't believe I just smiled at one of these horses. Maybe Murray was right.*

"Okay, right," Rodolfo says, realizing he needs to explain further. "But then I saw how much you actually care for people. You weren't just some fearsome traveler out for a

fight, like you first appeared. You cared for Toaster. For your people. Your quest. Beneath all your toughness, beneath your coat with all your weapons, you're one of the only people in the entire Lands who really cares about anyone else. I love you, Hero."

After five seconds of still no response from Hero, Mauricio jeers, "Awkward silence, pal." About thirty seconds of even more silence goes by. "He's a goner."

"Uh, Hero?" Rodolfo asks, relenting. Toaster and the horses keep giving her time to answer, but she doesn't. "Toaster? Toaster, is she talking to Murray?"

"I don't think so," Toaster says. "She's not looking up and to the left. I'm sorry, brother."

"Oy vey, I think you just got dumped," Mauricio interjects.

"For sure," Periwinkle adds.

"Hero!" Rodolfo yells through the wagon with a pained voice.

"Rodolfo?" Hero finally responds to him after ignoring all the chatter and awkward silence.

Toaster is clenching his fists with anxiety, hoping Hero and Rodolfo can finally figure out if they are in love, or something like that. The horses step back, preparing for an angry Hero.

"Finally," Rodolfo says with a sigh. "I can take it, Hero. I do have other responsibilities in my life right now that matter just as much as you. I won't wither and die if you don't want me." He hugs Pesto tightly inside the overturned wagon. The half-zombie, half-human girl isn't crying anymore and is more just enjoying the sounds of others talking, rather than just screeching zombies and Rodolfo.

"You're right," Hero says.

"You came all this way to save me and make me divulge my innermost feelings just to dump me?" Rodolfo replies, tinged with a little anger. "Well, you're as cruel as you are caring. But just so you know, you may not love me, or even like me, but at least I can talk about my feelings because I'm secure in who I am."

"No, no. You don't understand. You're right about me," Hero says. "Rowena told me the same thing."

"Rowena? Who the heck is *Rowena*?" Rodolfo asks.

"An ex-girlfriend perhaps? The plot thickens," Periwinkle says, with excitement in her voice, clearly just enjoying the love story.

"She was a seven-foot-tall metallic automaton hospital nurse," Hero says. "You know, those metallic human beings."

"You dump me but now have a tall metal girlfriend?" Rodolfo asks, a prideful anger seeping through.

"She was a friend!" Hero gives a fiery shout at the horse.

"Huh? You met a real automaton?" Rodolfo asks. "Is she there with you also? With the talking horses?"

"No," Hero says, trying to stop herself from sobbing again. *Now's not the time.* "She's not alive anymore. She stayed behind in Fant's evil hospital after she sent us tumbling into something called 'space-time.' Then they dismantled her. They dismantled my only friend, Rodolfo." She can't stop herself—tears are streaming down her face. Rowena was the first person she ever lowered her defenses for, even if she didn't mean to. And it will always be her fault.

"Uh . . ." Rodolfo mumbles in shock.

"Anyway," Hero says, wiping her face, trying to bottle up the sadness, "just forget it. What you need to know is that Rowena told me how I'm scared to be loved because, well,

I've never been loved before. Or held. Or even touched! So, well, I pushed you away."

"Literally! And it hurt! Literally!" Rodolfo says, remembering how Hero pushed him with the talisman in the carriage.

"Sorry. And, well, you need to know that I'm going to try. For you," Hero says. Then she picks herself up off the ground and starts dusting herself off. She said what she had to say. *I hope Rowena is proud of me.*

"Try?" Rodolfo asks. "What does that even mean?"

"Shnook, after all that, I think you're still getting dumped," Mauricio says.

"Poor guy. Reminds me when Viceroy Shlemovitz proposed to Viscountess Bertha back home," Periwinkle adds. "What a disaster that was. Viscountess Bertha *also* had a thing for her faerie attendant—"

"Rowena is just a friend!" Hero yells again, wondering how she even understood what Periwinkle was going on about.

"Hero, try what?" Toaster asks, clearly to help his brother.

"To try and dump him," Mauricio says. "What are you, thick in the head? It's clear as day, bud."

"See?" Rodolfo exclaims. "Even the horses find you the most confus—"

"Holy buckets!" Hero yells at the overturned wagon, exasperated yet again. "Gods, all of you are so annoying!" She turns toward the wagon again. She pulls her leg back to give it a big kick again, but stops. "Rodolfo, I meant that I'm going to try this L-thing. I owe Rowena that much."

"You *are* in love with that automaton!" Rodolfo says. "You could have just said so."

"No! She's not even alive anymore. How can you be so smart and still so dimwitted? She wanted me to do this. Do you think I want to be this way? No one ever taught me this stuff. This is so scary for me. I'm not *supposed* to be scared. Okay? I'm going to try it with you! All right? Gods. I'm going to try the L-word with *you*! And that's all I'm going to say. End of story. Complete. Period. *Nada más*." She walks away from the wagon and spits on the ground, trying to clear the L-word from her mouth.

THE END

Hero! What do you mean *THE END*? It can't be the end!

H. Murray, argh! I don't want to talk about feelings anymore. I'm done. I did what Rowena wanted. The end! Nada más!

How do you even know Spanish?

H. What's Spanish?

Never mind. You can't just end it. What about Noo Yolk and Fant? We agreed!

H. Fine. We can go on. But I never want to talk about feelings again. Don't make me do it!

I haven't been making you do anything since, like, Chapter Twelve? Thirteen?

H. I don't even want anyone mentioning that I

talked about feelings. I just want to forget it all happened.

Wait, you want Rodolfo to forget you have feelings for him? You want him to forget he has feelings for you?

H. No, not like that. I don't know. Just . . . argh! I don't want to talk about it.

But readers want to read about feelings.

H. Ew, who are these people? What's *wrong* with them?

They're just readers. Looking for a love story. With a little "end of the world" dystopian flavor. Mix in a little horror and violence . . . Oh, wait, I see your point.

H. See? That's what I've been saying the whole time. I have to *live* in this world. And what if it doesn't work out?

Your world?

H. No! With Rodolfo! Things in the Lands never work out.

Look, Rodolfo actually loves you.

H. You sure? How can you be sure? He probably just wants to claim me.

Hello, I'm the Author here. I'm pretty sure. But you can't tell the readers I'm sure.

H. Isn't that cheating? Telling me you're sure?

Okay, look. Sometimes you need to bend the rules a little. We all do it. In fact, I'm going to just hop off the typewriter for a second and get a pint of ice cream.

H. What's ice cream?

It's a sweet treat. Milk and sugar and all that.

H. I hate your fantasy world. More sweet treats.

I know, I know. Tree bark and bugs and camel piss. I still can't believe I wrote all that. Hey, can you finally let Rodolfo out now? We kind of have to get on with the story before Fant shows up. They scare me.

H. Oh, good point. Sure. Go get your *sweet treat.*

And Hero took an abnormally long dramatic pause.

Chapter 28

Don't Let It End

Hero calls over to Toaster, "Hey, help me get this wagon up."

"What about the zombie?" Toaster asks nervously.

"She's not a zombie!" Rodolfo yells from inside the wagon. "She's a half-zombie, half-girl hybrid, emphasis on *girl*! She was only partly transformed and the zombies don't even want her. They left her here. She's only, like, five years old. I'm all she has. And she has a letter from her mother where she mentions *Mother*."

"Mother?" Hero asks. *My* Mother?

"Yes, it says *Mother*. Do you know anyone else named *Mother?* Just let us out."

"Why didn't you say that before, dimwit? Toaster, now!" Hero says as she turns around and leans over to pick up the wagon.

"Wait!" Rodolfo exclaims.

"Wait? Now you *don't* want out?" Hero asks.

"Why are the zombies not attacking you? We can hear them. That's why we're hiding in the wagon. We thought you were zombies before also. How do we know you're not zombies also?" Rodolfo asks.

"It's, like, way too late for that, nudnik," Mauricio says. "You just told her you loved her. You can't call a girl a zombie *after* you tell her you love her."

"Ignore him," Hero says to Rodolfo. "It's a long story, but we have a magic wand from Mother that keeps them away."

"Cool. What a coincidence," Rodolfo says. "But wouldn't that have meant Pesto wasn't a zombie this whole time? We could have avoided all that arguing."

"I'm sorry, brother, but we don't really know how the wand works. We couldn't be sure," Toaster argues, defending himself.

"Okay, I know, little brother," Rodolfo replies calmly. "It's okay. We're all just a little bit on the defensive. You can let us out now."

"Wow, we're just going to trust him?" Mauricio scoffs. "Well, I have a damned Brooklyn Bridge to sell you."

"A what?" Periwinkle asks.

"The Brooklyn Bridge. You know, the bridge to the city," Mauricio replies. The group just stares at him. "You don't know the fire-trucking Brooklyn Bridge?"

"Never heard of it," Hero answers for everyone. "Where are you from, anyway?"

"I'm from Brooklyn," Mauricio says proudly, but everyone stares at him and shrugs their shoulders, not understanding. "You shnooks never heard of it? Flatbush. That is, until I

found myself magically attached to a carriage in the desert out of nowhere. What, you guys aren't from Brooklyn either? I thought yooz were *all* from Brooklyn too."

"Never heard of it either," Toaster adds.

"*I'm* from the Kingdom of Morpovia, deep in the Enthralled Forest, past the Pixie Meadow, and kitty-corner to the Elven Hideout," Periwinkle answers. "I just thought we all were."

"Uh . . . not a chance," Hero says.

"I thought that was just one of those new ritzy neighborhoods," Mauricio replies. "You know, with the condos."

"Come on, Toaster!" Hero orders. She gets back to business trying to pick up the wagon.

Mauricio has his eyes closed and head turned in fright, but Periwinkle watches, curious.

Toaster bends over to pick up the wagon too but doesn't want to let go of the wand.

"Rodolfo, we're going to try and lift the wagon completely, but you may need to help too. On three," Hero says.

Hero counts to three, and they all lift the wagon, Rodolfo helping from the inside. With all their strength they are able to lift it on its side, and then Hero kicks it over. The large wagon lands with a crash.

Hero, Toaster, and the horses just stare at the little balled-up five-year-old half-zombie, half-girl hybrid with the beautiful fluorescent pastel wings lying on the ground. Next to her are a Koleman Kamping LED Lantern 9000XD, two uneaten turkey legs, two uneaten carrots, and one teddy bear—which looks peculiarly like Hero, complete with a black trench coat and morning star tied to its hand. One additional flying zombie-looking teddy bear dressed in pink is in the girl's arms.

"Wow, you weren't kidding," Hero says, breaking the ice. "She's, like, half-zombie."

Pesto whimpers.

Rodolfo kneels on the floor to embrace the child. "Pesto, it's all right. These are my friends. Can I pick you up?" Pesto nods, and Rodolfo picks her up in his arms. Again, she turns and burrows into his chest.

"It looks like you had a party in here," Hero adds. "What's with all the food?"

"Food?" Mauricio exclaims.

"Oh, right. I almost forgot," Hero says. "Hey, guys, your food is ready."

"Murray sent us turkey and carrots," Rodolfo explains.

"Turkey and carrots, just like we promised the horses? What are the chances? The probability must be infinitesimal," Toaster wonders.

The horses start to make their way where the wagon was overturned to eat the leftover food. They are quiet as they eat their well-deserved feast.

"I can't believe it," Hero says to Toaster and Rodolfo, out of earshot of the horses as they start munching. "You actually have turkey and carrots? We were totally just lying out our—"

"Didn't Murray tell you about the food?" Rodolfo asks, confused.

"Why would you think Murray told us about your little party?" Hero asks. "Or was it just a tea party for the dolls?"

"Hero," Rodolfo replies with an angry tone. "We were *dying* in there. I asked Murray for the food for Pesto, so she wouldn't die, and it just showed up. You're not the only one who can talk to the gods. It just goes to show you, if you show some reverence and respect for the gods, they will provide. And Pesto's a special girl who's been through a lot, so please stop insulting us. It was *not* a party. Why did you even rescue us if you were just going to be so mean?"

"I'm sorry," Hero says, Rodolfo's words a sharp reminder of everything she needs to work on. She bites her tongue and looks at the ground.

"What happened to your pretty friend there?" Toaster asks, knowing that Pesto can hear, and also trying to distract Hero and Rodolfo from another fight.

"Thanks, little brother," Rodolfo acknowledges, happy for someone to treat Pesto nicely. "She has a pretty incredible story involving zombies and Mother."

"Mother?" Hero asks, genuinely interested.

Rodolfo looks at her and uses the opportunity to tell his story. "Pesto and her mom were taken by the zombies. Her mom was fully transformed, but somehow the zombie sickness didn't take a full hold on Pesto. Her body fought it somehow, so she was still human on the inside, but on the outside, she was left as the beautiful and really special girl you see now." Rodolfo minds his words, knowing she's listening and gives her a squeeze.

"The zombies ignored her," he continues, "and kicked her out of their zombie society. So here was this five-year-old girl left to die in the middle of the desolate roads. What luck I crashed there! I was already under my overturned wagon after our battle with them, so I took her in. And guess what?" He turns to look at Pesto who is still in his arms, "Can I show them the note?"

Pesto nods.

Rodolfo hands over the note to Toaster, who scans it. He immediately hands it to Hero. "You have to read this," Toaster says.

Hero takes it. "You know Mother?" Hero asks Pesto.

She nods.

"You, like, met her? Seriously?"

Pesto nods again.

"Holy buckets! You're, like, five years old."

Pesto nods again.

Hero turns to Toaster. "Max was right! She's alive! She has to be!"

"Max?" Rodolfo asks before Toaster can respond.

"Never mind," Hero says. She turns back to Pesto. "What was she like?"

For the first time since they were rescued, Pesto opens her mouth. "Mother's nice. Mother helped Mum and me leave hospital."

"Hospital?" Hero and Toaster ask at the same time.

"You know it?" Rodolfo asks.

Hero ignores him. "Big white building in the middle of the desert? With automaton nurses?"

"Au . . . mot-ton? What?" Pesto asks.

"Oh gods, what did Murray call them?" Hero asks herself. "Um . . . robots?"

Hearing the word, Pesto shrieks. "Scary robots! Needles! Baths!"

Hearing Pesto respond to the word *robot* and her strange accent, Hero says, "Pesto, I'm going to ask you a question. Do you think you can answer it?" Pesto nods. "What year are you from?"

"It's 2005," Pesto says.

"2005?" Rodolfo asks. "It's 10786!"

"You silly," Pesto says to Rodolfo with a giggle.

"You never thought to ask her this?" Hero scoffs at Rodolfo.

"It didn't come up. I was only trying to save her life," Rodolfo replies snidely.

"You did well, brother," Toaster interjects.

"Yeah," Hero admits. Then she turns to Pesto again. "Where are you from?"

"I live in London, with me mum and dad," Pesto says, looking proud. Rodolfo and Toaster look at Hero, as she's the experienced traveler.

"I never heard of it," Hero replies to their looks.

"It's a queendom," Rodolfo says.

"Rodolfo," Hero replies. "She must be an ancient. From all those years ago. It must be a queendom from ancient times!"

"How's that possible?" Rodolfo asks.

"It just is. Believe me," Hero insists curtly because it would take too long to explain.

"We met some ancients, brother," Toaster adds. "In the same hospital."

Then Hero turns back to Pesto. "So, you were at the hospital with Mother?" she asks.

"Uh huh. Mother helped us escape in the telly after they killed Dad," Pesto says looking down. She wants to cry but is just holding it in to look strong.

"Toaster," Hero says. "I think maybe she got the vaccine and it protected her from the zombie sickness. Like Rowena said?"

"Yeah," Toaster answers. "With side effects, though. And she escaped the same way we did. But without Rowena's help because Mother somehow did it."

"She's amazing," Hero says. "Mona and Big were right."

"And there's more," Rodolfo says. "Maybe this is why Mother helped her escape? Pesto can read Murrayskindacoolish. She read all the relics to me in the wagon. I think I know Mother's secret. The knowledge of the ancients. It's in a place called—"

"Noo Yolk!" Hero and Rodolfo say at the same time. Hero is so excited she runs to give Rodolfo a big hug, along with Pesto, who is still in Rodolfo's arms.

"Don't leave me out!" Toaster says as he goes in for a hug too.

"Do you knuckleheads mean *New York*?" Mauricio interjects while eating his food. The hug ends abruptly.

Hero turns to him. "New Yawk?" she asks, repeating Mauricio's accent.

"New Yawk?" Toaster repeats, trying Hero's pronunciation.

"Yeah, yooz got it. That's where I'm from. I told you."

"You said *Brooklyn*," Toaster replies. "I distinctly remember it. A flat bush in Brooklyn."

"Yeah, New York," Mauricio says.

Rodolfo kneels again and looks into Pesto's eyes. "By chance do you mean *New Yawk*?" he asks.

"Yeah! That's what I've been saying! Noo Yolk!" Pesto says angrily, hands on her hips. "I was there!"

"I guess it's this New Yawk," Rodolfo mumbles.

"You know, she's actually pretty cute," Hero says under her breath as she playfully punches the little girl on the shoulder. Pesto giggles. "I like your wings," Hero tells the girl. "I wish my coat was that beautiful."

"Thanks," Pesto replies. "Trade?"

Hero looks uncomfortable, not wanting to give up her coat but also knowing that Pesto can't lose her zombie wings. *What kind of trade is that? Oh, hell.* Hero takes off her long black trench coat, revealing her tattered, sweat-stained white tank top, and wraps it around the small child. "Just for a little bit, Pesto."

Pesto beams a smile as large as the sun as she runs her hands over it. "Super."

"Just don't use the weapons," Hero warns.

Pesto immediately opens the coat and stares wide-eyed at all the weapons inside.

Rodolfo takes the opportunity of Pesto's apparent acceptance into the group to set her down, the bottom of Hero's coat now covering the ground.

"I can't believe it," Hero says to the group. "It shouldn't be possible, but Mother might still be alive. She's really out there somewhere!"

"Not necessarily, Hero," Toaster says. "You know the hospital traveled along space-time to alternative times and places. Mother could have left the hospital thousands of years from now or in the past. Or to another world. Maybe she left at a different time from Pesto and her mum?"

"Oh, right. But it's still possible," Hero says, trying to tamp down some of her enthusiasm.

"Now, what in the Lands was this hospital?" Rodolfo asks Hero.

"It's a long story," Hero says, not wanting to talk about it, or Rowena, anymore. And she sure as hell doesn't want anybody else to tell her Mother isn't still alive. The gods themselves mentioned she might be, and even if they do her bidding, she's the wizard behind her control and the automatic writing. *If Murray is the God of gods, and Barnaby is the god boss, what is Mother then? Whatever, I'm going to find her.*

"Hero, the Virus-o-Nomitor-Extracto-Supreme 7000XL!" Toaster finally remembers.

"Oh, right. The Extracto," Hero says. She pulls out the small handheld metal box with a needle on the end from her coat pocket. "Rodolfo, we have to stick this into you."

"What?" Rodolfo exclaims.

"Rodolfo," Hero whines, "it has something called a vacc . . . a sickness medicine in it that will protect you from the zombie sickness. It's from that evil hospital Fant made, and we think it's what kept Pesto from being taken by them."

"Wait, you want me to use evil Fant evil magic? *You?*" Rodolfo asks.

"Yes, believe me," Hero replies. "Someone really smart at the hospital made this device, and Rowena gave it to me. The guy was kind of an a—"

"Rowena saved us," Toaster cuts in. "Please, just take the vaccine."

"Okay, okay, sheesh," Rodolfo answers.

Hero takes some pleasure in jabbing him with the device.

"Ouch!" Rodolfo says reflexively.

Hero rolls her eyes at him as she puts the device back into her pocket. "Baby," she jeers.

"I thought you didn't like babies." Rodolfo laughs.

"How can I not? I'm surrounded by them now!" Hero snorts a laugh, as she waves her arms at her new gang.

"Hero, did you just make a joke?" Toaster asks, bewildered.

"Your laugh is kind of weird," Rodolfo adds. Hero stares daggers at him.

"Rodolfo," Toaster changes the subject from Hero's awkward laughing. "Does Pesto have any idea where New Yawk is?"

Rodolfo shakes his head. "While the relics talk about New Yawk, it looks like the only direction they say is, 'beyond the Lands, where the sea meets sands, go east, not west, you idiot in the vest.'"

"*Idiot in the vest?* It really says that?" Toaster asks.

"No one here is in a vest," Hero says. *Maybe Pesto isn't as great a reader as we think. I bet I can read better than her.*

"I'm just saying what it says. Right, Pesto?" Rodolfo asks.

"Yes, Rolfo," Pesto answers angrily. "I can read." She's standing tall and proud.

"She sounds like you, Hero," Toaster jokes.

"Ha," Hero replies, dryly. "So, does anyone know where 'beyond the Lands' is? Anyone know what 'east' or 'west' is?" she asks. "Do you, Pesto?"

"East and west are directions," Pesto answers proudly. Then she plops herself down on the ground and starts playing with her ballerina doll.

"Do you know which way is east?" Hero asks her, but Pesto just shrugs her shoulders.

"Dunno," Pesto says while playing. "Never eat soggy worms."

"Those are the best kind, kid!" Hero scoffs. "Meat and drink at the same time!"

"Don't *you* know which way east is?" Rodolfo asks Hero. "You're the one who survived the desolate roads all these years."

"Come on," Hero grumbles. "I navigated by landmarks and birds and types of bugs and stuff like that. I don't know east and west."

"So, it's a dead end?" Toaster asks. All the excitement saps from the group.

"Well," Rodolfo says, stopping to think. "Pesto can start reading these other relics now that we're out of that wagon."

So, Toaster sets up Pesto near some of the other relics on the ground, sits down next to her, and she starts reading.

"I can't believe it. I thought you would know what east was," Rodolfo says to Hero, as they watch the pair go through other books. "Maybe the horses do?"

"Seriously? Sure, let's try with those clearly genius horses." Hero turns to the horses, who are now lying down and napping after such a good snack. "Stupid horses!" she yells.

Periwinkle and Mauricio lift up their heads and look at Hero.

"Either of you know what 'east' is?" Hero asks.

"Feast? Another feast!" Mauricio exclaims. "You really are the best humans ever! Periwinkle, you hear that? Another feast!"

"She said 'east' not 'feast,'" Periwinkle says and puts her head back down on the ground.

"What's *east?*" Mauricio asks. Both horses are still lying down.

"I think it's a medical thing," Periwinkle says. "I once needed the kingdom's sorceress of herbs when I had that." The horses lay their heads down again, but Mauricio shimmies a little farther from Periwinkle.

"See, Rodolfo? They're useless," Hero says. "Gods, this is it, then. Unless Pesto can find anything else, we have one damn clue and can't do anything about it. What was the whole point?"

She walks over to Rodolfo, rests her head on his shoulder, and starts weeping.

H. Weeping? I'm weeping again? What's wrong with me? Are you controlling me again?

No, Hero, it's all you. But it's okay, Hero. Everyone weeps sometime in their life.

H. Not me. I don't want to be in control anymore. Take it away!

Hero isn't weeping anymore. And because she feels so close and comfortable with Rodolfo, she blows her nose on his sleeve, wiping snot all over him.

"Hero, I L-word your snot, too. Let it all out," Rodolfo says. "And you were doing that thing again. What does Mur—"

H. You jackass. I'm a little stuffed up from crying, but I wouldn't do that.

All right, I'm sorry.

"Hey, Toaster," Hero calls out, one last chance for hope. "Pesto got anything else?"

"No, sorry," Toaster informs her. "She says these other relics are just something called bowling scorecards."

H. Murray? You jackass. You give us a clue we can't do anything about!

I'm sorry, Hero. But I, or Mother maybe, wrote us into a corner. You people don't know what east is. I'm stuck.

H. Seriously? Why doesn't Pesto know? She's an ancient!

Hero, she's five years old. It wouldn't be true to character. My book would get laughed at.

H. Who cares? Just make her know it.

She doesn't know it.

H. Gods, why can't you just tell *me*, then? Or make up some relics.

You're assuming I even made up the east clue! I didn't! It was automatic writing. I knew Pesto knew the language and could read the relics, but I didn't know what the clue would be. The east thing was from the wizard.

H. You mean Mother!

Or Fant.

H. Why would Fant give us a clue to ancient powers?

Right, so it's Mother! But if she really is controlling me too, she would know it's cheating. I shouldn't tell you.

H. Yes, you should! Just tell me where east is! She would want—

But Mother knows that's cheat—

H. You should've thinked of this before you started a story scroll. And don't blame Mother. You're still the weaver of all things. Now I'm stuck here and never going to free Dystpopia.

But Mother is the one—

H. Mother is the one who wants us to find the ancients.

Yes, but she also gave you a clue she knows you wouldn't know. It's pretty clear—

H. You're the weaver. Tell me what east is.

But Mother—

H. Murray! Even if she doesn't want cheating, are you just going to listen to whatever Mother says, or be your own man?

She's pretty powerful. She's controlling me. Controlling you, even. Look, she didn't even want Max, and now he's gone. Why do you think that is? And how? Is it your fault or hers? It's probably hers—she's controlling everything. It's clear to me now. How is she doing this?

H. Murray! You live in heaven-world! You're gonna let some woman from the Lands in your own story scroll tell you what to do? You're gonna let her tell you Max is evil?

He's not! He's my friend!

H. Right! So go find Max, and then you both can tell us where east is! Isn't he your bestie? Your bestie will help you with your dream to have a beautiful baby.

Uh, that's not exactly how I would phrase—

H. Support, Murray. Max supported your dream!

I mean, yeah. Maybe. We've hung out some. We watched my old sci-fi. He has a complicated home life. We bonded a bit over that, too. You know, Felicia and all. He encouraged me, too. Believed in me, even after she left. You think we're besties?

H. Come on, Murray. Do you have any other friends?

Katrina?

H. *Human* friends, Murray.

Not anymore. Felicia was . . .

H. See? You *need* Max. Mother doesn't control us. Murray, you have to get him back. You don't need Mother, and you don't need Felicia. She didn't appreciate you. You need a true bestie like Max. Like I had Rowena.

You make it sound so . . . it's not like that.

H. Can't you use your fantasy cell-phone thing? It has that location services thing like the wand. You can find him!

He's probably still mad at me.

H. Because you chose me over him? But you're *besties*, Murray. He'll understand. Go use your location services, and get your fantasy-world bestie! Don't worry about Mother. We're on the same side, but we should also have control. Right? And once you find him and tell him you L-word him.

Uh, I think I know what you mean.

H. Then you can tell me where east is. Together you two can do incredible things, because someone supports your dream of a beautiful baby.

I guess I could find a way to make it plausible. You know, Hero, you're pretty smart.

H. I would be even smarter if you told me what east is! Hurry up!

Chapter 29

Dude, Who Stole My Girl?

During a restful nap on the ground for the entire group, safe in the assurance of Mother's magic wand, which kept the flying zombies at bay—the screeching sound acting like an expensive white, or zombie-gray, noise machine—the group started to hear a rumbling sound.

Mauricio and Periwinkle were the first to lift their heads and notice it. Then Hero did. Then Graham.

H. Holy buckets, Murray! What the hell is Graham doing here? And he's sleeping next to me! Ew! And what's east?

M. I'm baaaack! Murray needs me to help write the big finale.

H. Murray! I said he can help. Not write the entire ending!

But I'm out of ideas! He's thought of some cool things. We talked a lot. But he doesn't want you to know what east is yet.

H. What? That was my whole plan, you jackass!

"Hey, babe, you need to listen when I talk to you," Graham says, looking passionately into her eyes. "I decided—"

Slap!

Graham winces and recoils in pain.

"No one wants you here," Hero says as she backs away from Graham, the man who suddenly appeared lying on her left, with Rodolfo on her right. Toaster and Pesto are on Rodolfo's other side, and the horses are lying down near the food.

"Hey, girl," Graham says as he rubs his cheek, massaging the pain. "You're really not like my Grahammies at all. It's actually kind of exciting. A real challenge."

"Hero?" Rodolfo says, still rubbing sleep out of his eyes, as he leans over her. When he sees Graham, his eyes go wide, and he yells, "You're leaving me already?"

H. Fine, don't tell me where east is, but why'd you have to bring Graham back?

M. It's a classic love triangle! I can't believe Murray didn't already play it up some more.

H. Murray, stop this! I helped you! What was I thinking?

Look, I know how much you hate Graham, but Max said you'll need him soon.

H. Need him? Why in the Lands would I need *him*? I need to know what east is!

M. No, no, not yet my little Hero. And you'll need a medic because of what's going to happen next.

His idea, not mine. I'm sorry, Hero.

The low rumbling sound starts to grow louder.

"Hero," Rodolfo says. "You can't answer? Is that why you zoned out? You're just pretending to talk to Murray?"

"No, I *was* talking to Murray. And Max," Hero answers.

"Max?" Toaster interjects, with a shiver. "The Guardian of the Space-Time Control Room? He's back? Oh, that's bad."

"Space-Time Control Room?" Graham remarks. "That sounds like a cool show. I should talk to my agent. I can do sci-fi. Send me the deets. Oh, wait, you're all crusty dystopians. Can you chisel it on something? Or, better yet, just tell the town squire to tell that extremely competent Barnaby fellow that Graham wants a role." He stands up and flexes both his biceps. "You may have seen me in *Paramedics Emergency Medical Care: Bangor*. I always get the girl. Sometimes the guy."

"I know who you are, dimwit," Toaster says. "You're that wrestling barber."

"I like that name. That could be my wrestling name!" Graham says happily, flexing again. "Prepare to get chopped! Or trimmed? Do you like trimmed?"

"Hero, but I told you I loved you," Rodolfo protests. "And he sullied your honor!" He gets up to face Graham. Pesto wakes up and hugs Rodolfo's leg, looking for safety.

"Dude," Graham says. "You said the L-word? And had a kid while I was gone? It's been like three days! She's a crusty little thing." Graham squints at Pesto. "But it's not fair! I want to say the L-word and have a kid with you, Hero. I'm a commitment kind of guy, I swear. But my kid would look much better than—"

"Gods!" Hero yells. "Everyone just be quiet! Listen!" Then she closes her eyes for a few moments. She finally gets up and instantly prepares for action. Toaster gets up too when he sees Hero's concern.

"You gonna say anything? Or just leave us in this love triangle?" Graham asks. "I'll fight for you again if I have to."

"Yeah, you need to choose," Rodolfo cries. "Graham or me!"

Hero lets out a huge sigh. "Shut up, you dimwits and listen to the sounds. Out there!" They all listen. "Something is coming. It's getting louder. Max said we would need a barber. That's why he brought Graham back. Something *bad* is coming."

The sound is suddenly above them.

"Everyone get ready!" Hero orders and takes back her trench coat from Pesto. She hands out two daggers, one each to Rodolfo and Toaster, and readies her morning star.

"Hey, don't I get a weapon?" Graham asks. "I'm the star! Give *me* a morning star, wench!" He lowers his voice and asks, "Do I sound dystopian?"

"Wench?" Hero, incredulous, spits in Graham's face. She's challenging him, ready to fight him instead of what's coming.

"Uck." Graham wipes his face. "You know, *wench*, like in your dystopian world, right?" he offers defensively. "Isn't that a thing?"

"Go hide in the carriage with Pesto," Hero orders him.

M. Hey! Hero! I know Murray promised you control and everything—

H. Promised me? I took control. My mother gave it to me in a dream and a magical talisman she left for me because I'm destined!

M. So he says, but I'm the one on the typewriter now. I didn't believe Murray's automatic writing thing before, but I have to admit, it's happening to me too now. At least, I think it is. But stop it! Please! It's even hard to control the characters you're interacting with after you do stuff.

I know, right? It just keeps getting worse. Their reactions are getting written before you can control it again.

M. Yeah, and I don't want Graham stuck in the carriage. He has a professional wrestling background. He could help you fight, too. Why are you doing this to my scene?

H. You only said you needed a medic, not a fighter. Don't you remember?

M. At least I can still control the story and make it really bad for you.

H. Unless Mother stops you.

M. Heard from her lately, Hero? Do you really think she's going to step in? One little dream of her is going to help you? Even when I'm about to bring Fant down on you?

H. Fant? Argh! Do you know the evil you're playing with? Now I see why Mother doesn't like you. She was right!

M. Eh, she's just some old lady. She doesn't know everything. She can't control me. And she can't control them. Murray says so. But look what I'm about to do. I control them!

H. Max, it's really dangerous. Murray tried and lost control of Fant. These are our lives you're playing with! Didn't you see what happened with

the zorcs? Did Murray tell you about SkeLord's romantic bath? Doesn't that prove it's all real?

M. It doesn't prove anything!

H. You just agreed I was controlling the story.

M. It could just be Murray's psychosis, which is rubbing off on me. Or maybe he misunderstood or was just scared of them. But I'm willing to do what needs to be done for an awesome ending. This is kind of fun!

H. Holy buckets, Murray! Are you really going to let him do something bad to us for *fun*? What is he doing with Fant? Doesn't he know they have their own wizard who can control you? Or is Max working for Fant? Or is he the wizard? I shouldn't have told you to bring him back.

I'm sorry, Hero. But it's nothing like that. Calm down. Max said we have to do this in order to get the most exciting ending possible. That's all this is. I still want to sell this thing. I need to if I'm going to win her back—prove to her I'm worthy. And maybe he's right. Maybe I was too scared of Fant myself. She always said I was too scared. Maybe my breakdown is really a breakthrough?

H. I don't even know what that means. But you know how powerful they are. Why would you do this? You two are jackasses! Whatever. With or without Mother, I can still control what I do!

Graham complains, "But I want to stay out here with—"

"Now!" Hero yells impatiently.

"Are you sure she's safe with him?" Rodolfo asks Hero, thinking about Pesto, who looks scared. "Pesto is *my* responsibility, and he has no respect for women. Or zombie hybrid girls."

"Dude, I love all hybrids! I even have a plug-in one at home," Graham protests.

The group stares at Graham, trying to make sense of his words, but they cannot. So, Hero walks over to Rodolfo, puts a hand on his shoulder, and says, "He would never hurt Pesto, because he knows I would kill him slowly and painfully."

"I've gotta talk to my agent about love triangles where I don't get the girl," Graham says as he takes Pesto's hand and climbs into the carriage with her.

"Rodolfo, please don't worry about trigles," Hero says, after Graham leaves. She touches Rodolfo's sleeve. "I don't L-word Graham's huge muscles, er, I mean Graham. I want nothing to do with them, er, him."

Rodolfo looks at her a moment, trying to figure out what she's trying to say. "Of course you'd say that, because you're busy playing both of us against each other. You just want my saloon, and then you'll take my money and run off with Graham, leaving me with our ten starving children, one of whom takes expensive piano lessons, which maybe is actually worth it if I can get the fancy piano saloon running again. But still . . ."

H. Stop ruining Rodolfo!

M. Stop ruining my love trigle—I mean triangle!

H. Stop using Fant against me!

M. Stop being so stubborn!

H. Murray!

Hero, we haven't really been controlling your friends since the flying zombies.

M. Don't tell her!

She deserves to know, Max. But we're still controlling Pesto and the horses now.

M. Murray, I'm not sure you should take credit for the horses. That Mauricio—I know you said he's from Brooklyn, but you're doing both Italian and Yiddish. It's kind of weird.

Oh, is that wrong?

H. What are you jackasses even saying?

Never mind. Did you not realize Rodolfo was in control this whole time? I guess I should have told you.

M. Don't tell her! You're ruining the love triangle.

H. You mean he *really* L-words me? Like for real?

"Are you even listening to yourself, Rodolfo?" Hero shouts at him. Then, before Murray or Max can do anything, she walks over to him. He leans back defensively, but always quicker, she kisses him passionately. Well, it feels passionate to her, but to Rodolfo and the others, it simply looks and feels very awkward. Hero's eyes are open and pointing to the side, as if she's still looking for danger, and her body is tense like she's prepared for battle.

H. Hey! I've never done that before. Stop making fun of me!

"Oh, how beautiful!" Periwinkle gushes in delight. "Even if it looks like two brothers kissing on the lips. But you still owe me, Mauricio. Pay up."

"Seeing that was nauseating," Mauricio says, and spits a half-eaten carrot onto the ground. Periwinkle picks it up in her mouth. "I really thought my boy Graham would win."

"Yeah, Rodolfo! You won!" Toaster cheers. "See? She loves you!"

"Shut up, Toaster," Hero says, after finishing the kiss. Her face turns red from embarrassment, so she points a finger at Rodolfo and adds, "You too. I don't know how to do it. Never had to before."

Rodolfo is too busy smiling to say anything, but ekes out, "You did very well."

Unfortunately, ten bright-yellow racing motorcycles show up and surround the group in a half circle. In the middle of the half circle is a skeleton man made with Fant's evil magic and a black-and-red beret with a silver feather sticking up straight from the front of the hat. SkeLord.

Surrounding SkeLord are the Death Soldiers. Nine tall, burly, and unbathed men with long, unbathed hair. They each ready a long sword while still seated on their bikes.

"What the hell is that?" Graham screams from the carriage.

"Hero said quiet," Pesto scolds him. "You bloody daft, you nutter?"

"Language!" Graham replies. "You're going to ruin our age rating. Don't you know anything?"

"You git," Pesto adds.

M. Now that's how you do accents, Murray.

You're really good at this!

"Hey, those yellow horses are kind of cute," Periwinkle says. Both horses are now standing a few feet away from the humans. "Hey, horsies, come on over here, and let's make a rainbow."

"Shut up, Periwinkle," Mauricio says. "They're not horses! They're like Cow-uh-sakees or something. They're dangerous!"

"They wouldn't harm royalty," Periwinkle replies. "Especially one from the Kingdom of Morpovia, deep in the Enthralled Forest, past the Pixie Meadow, and kitty-corner to the Elven Hideout. In fact, I really think they should bow—"

"Silence!" SkeLord yells and then points a bony finger at one of the Death Soldiers. The Death Soldier takes out a throwing knife from his leather jacket and readies it. He is staring, and aiming at Periwinkle, who is now frozen in the shock that someone would harm royalty.

H. Murray! Stop this if you can! You can't kill Periwinkle. Holy buckets, you're going to let them kill a beautiful princess talking horse? You're a weak—

M. What, now you *like* the horses? You complained about them the whole time. Besides, I don't feel like writing horse characters. This is YA, not *Saddle Stories*, which, by the way, my baby sister and I actually really love.

I know. That's kind of why I added them.

M. Thanks, friend! You were always a good listener.

H. I will *not* let you kill my princess horse!

Hero runs over to Mauricio and hits the red button on his jetpack. Then she yells, "Mauricio! Attack! Save her!" She takes out the small, handheld device that drives the jetpacks from her trench coat pocket while putting back her morning star.

"I'm a horse, not a cannon!" Mauricio screams as the jetpack starts rumbling.

"What is that?" the Death Soldier who was ready to kill Periwinkle asks in his burly voice. It is slightly hard to hear what he is saying, because his long beard and mustache cover his mouth.

Unfortunately for Hero, the jetpack on Mauricio's back runs out of fuel, and the rumbling ceases before he leaves

the ground. She should have found a filling station as soon as they landed.

"Hernando, forgive me for my sins," Mauricio prays in relief.

Hero's shoulders slump as she feels deflated.

M. Hero! See? I'm not going to let you ruin the big action-packed ending! I can't control you guys, but I can control everything around you. And Fant.

H. But you can't! No one can control Fant anymore. You don't even believe your best friend? Unless you secretly work for them. Unless you *are* them.

Hero, he's not the Queen of Fant and he doesn't work for them. He works for Pizza Kingdom.

M. Not anymore. Unemployed again. And I never even heard of Fant before this story. I don't believe you guys anyway about how powerful they are. I'm controlling them fine, see? Murray was just scared or something.

"Get them!" SkeLord yells.

The other motorcycles start to rev their engines and come after Hero, Toaster, and Rodolfo, who stand ready to fight again. Periwinkle and Mauricio are now praying loudly to The Great Revered One. Graham and Pesto are in the carriage, hiding.

Hero throws the useless jetpack driving device to the ground and takes the morning star out of her coat. But her fingers touch something else in her pocket. *My talisman.* She holds it in one hand and uses her other hand to push in the air at some of the other motorcycle men. Five of the men go flying off their bikes and land unconscious.

That leaves five motorcycle men left—and SkeLord. *That was easy. I can just do that again.* She lifts her hand up again, ready to strike.

"You think I wouldn't be prepared this time?" SkeLord says, as one of his bony hands caresses his feather, and his other waves at the Death Soldiers on the ground. They instantly start rising again.

Oh crap.

M. Uh, I'm not doing that.

H. I told you, page! You can't control them!

You believe me now?

M. But I was doing just fine before.

H. They *let* you control them.

M. But why would they do that?

H. To find us, you jackass.

M. But you're in their flying-zombie country. They could find you, anyway.

H. The wand! They couldn't find us because of the wand.

It has to be.

H. And that's how they got Mother before with the dragons. The hospital took her wand, and then they sent dragons to kill her. Don't you see how evil they are now?

M. Uh, yeah. And using me was not cool or friendly.

Before the soldiers can rise fully, Hero charges—with Rodolfo and Toaster charging after seeing her—at the dazed Death Soldiers.

At least it's a fair fight now. Ten against three. While thinking all this, Hero takes out two Death Soldiers—one with a swing of her morning star and one with a simultaneous roundhouse kick to the face, whom she then stabs with a dagger while he's bent over in pain. Afterward, she throws the dagger at another unsuspecting Death Soldier who was just standing and watching the action. He falls over. *Three for me, none for you.*

"Wow, she's amazing," Rodolfo has time to say. He was able to down one Death Soldier, getting a jump on him with his dagger before the soldier rose from unconsciousness.

He actually got one. Now it's five soldiers and one skeleton man against the three of us.

Hero then notices Toaster having trouble. The Death Soldier that Toaster charged now has him by the neck, lifting him off the ground. Both Rodolfo and Hero take a step toward Toaster, but the Death Soldier sees them and puts a sword to Toaster's throat while bringing him back down to the ground. The Death Soldier warns, "Take another step, and your precious Toaster will get toasted."

H. Seriously, Max? *Toaster get Toasted?* Was that you?

M. I wish it was, that catchphrase is awesome. But they're still controlling me.

I have to admit, Fant is creating an exciting ending. And they're fantastic writers.

M. I agree, Murray. We can still totally sell this. Even if it's a sad ending.

H. Holy buckets!

"Toaster get toasted?" Hero scoffs. "Wow, you're stupid." She points a finger at him.

"Hey!" the Death Soldier exclaims. "Don't insult my character."

"Oh, I'm not insulting you. That was a good one," Hero replies sarcastically, which the soldier does not notice. He stands taller with pride. "In fact, I bet you're so good at this Death Soldiering thing that if you hurt him, we'll really need a medic." She says the word *medic* loudly. "Preferably one from *Bangor*."

"Medic?" the Death Soldier asks. "What is that? Is that like a wizard?" The soldier turns to SkeLord and asks, "She has a wizard."

"A medic wizard is no match for Fant!" SkeLord exclaims with fury.

M. Hero, I'm not sure they'll fall for that now. They may know my plan.

H. Oh, now you're scared of them too?

Max, can't you still control Graham?

M. Yes, for the most part. His initial reactions are harder to control, though. I'm finding that with Pesto and the horses, too. That's how Hero got him in the carriage in the first place. I think he's secretly scared of her.

H. Good!

"What part of *medic* don't you understand, Graham?" Hero yells, throwing her hands up in the air.

"My name's not Graham," the Death Soldier says. "It's Shlemovitz the Destroyer. Get ready to feel the *Shlem* in *Shlemovitz.*"

"God, Max! That's just so stupid!" Hero yells to the sky.

M. Wasn't me! But I agree, that catchphrase wasn't as good as the other one.

"I'm not Max, either. You just killed him," the soldier replies, pointing at one of the fallen soldiers.

Hero can hear Pesto complaining to Graham, "Are you daft? She needs you!"

"No way I'm going out there," Graham replies.

H. Max! It was your plan! Just make him go.

M. But I'm scared too! I'm attached to the guy! I like writing about his muscles.

Hero sighs in disbelief. Graham and Max are even more disappointing than she remembered. But Graham is also just as handsome. Perhaps she should forget Rodolfo and kiss Gra—

H. Gods, Max, you're still trying this? Even now?

M. Murray said we can sometimes sneak in a little—

H. Just stop!

M. It was worth a shot.

"Don't let her distract you, Shlemovitz," SkeLord finally speaks up. "Now, Marmalade, put down your weapons and come with us, and your precious Toaster won't get toasted."

"My name's Hero. I'm a hero," Hero says proudly.

"This whole time we've been tracking a little girl named Marmalade! Whatever," SkeLord says. "We were told to take you in for questioning."

Hero spits at him in anger at being called a little girl. "I'm not a little girl!"

SkeLord continues, "Marmalade—"

"Hero!" Hero yells.

"I don't care. The Queen of Fant herself ordered me to find you," SkeLord continues. "She said you were using unknown magic. This means you're important to her. Way more important than the dumb barmaid you purported to be. I wasn't told the whole story, and I don't really care.

"My orders were to find you and bring you back to Fant if I can. If not, I am to eliminate you all from existence. And I grow tired of you and your companions, especially the horses, and cannot see enjoying a ride back to Fant with *all* of you. You'll probably have to stop and pee a lot, like the little girl you are." Hero spits at him again. "And we probably don't even have the same tastes in music. What is your favorite song? Are there any minstrels you are truly fond of?"

H. Uh, Max? This seems really dumb and not like SkeLord at all. Is this you?

M. Just because it seems dumb, you think it's me?

H. Uh, yeah.

M. I don't think it's me. This really is Fant or SkeLord.

He was supposed to be fearsome. What happened to him?

M. The romantic bath?

H. Oh gods. If he's this dimwitted, we really do have a chance.

"Nothing?" SkeLord replies. "This is why you cretins will eventually lose to the power of Fant! You do not know the true power of music. But it is what it is. I will simply recite my top minstrel artists for comparison purposes."

As SkeLord goes on and on about his favorite minstrels, Hero sees Pesto climbing out of the wagon through the corner of her eye. *Oh my gods, this is too dangerous for a little girl.*

Pesto leaps off the carriage, and her fluorescent pastel wings carry her toward the Death Soldier named Shlemovitz, who is holding Toaster. Pesto lands on the Death Soldier's back.

"Aaah! Get her off!" Shlemovitz screams as he lets go of Toaster to flail his hands at his back and circle around in a dance with the half-zombie, half-girl hybrid.

"What?" SkeLord yells. "Get that zombie!"

H. Max, is that you? You would use a little girl like this?

M. It wasn't me. It was automatic, I swear.

It's not us, Hero.

H. I don't believe you!

The distraction is enough for Hero and the group to start fighting the Death Soldiers again. Toaster is able to stab the Death Soldier struggling with Pesto. The large man goes down.

Hero, almost out of daggers, takes out some throwing stars and starts throwing them at two of the Death Soldiers, striking their necks. They fall over, bleeding. That leaves one more, the one Rodolfo is having a hard time taking down. *If only he had an iron pot.*

Rodolfo lost his dagger and the soldier is currently sitting on top of him, pummeling Rodolfo into the ground.

"Rodolfo!" Toaster shrieks. "Hero! Help!"

But SkeLord picks up a bony hand and aims it at Hero. "No more Mr. Nice Skeleton!" Suddenly, a trail of bones magically leaves his hand and flies at Hero, wrapping around her entire body like chains. She's standing but unable to move her arms or legs.

If he could have done this the whole time, why wait?

SkeLord shoots chains of bones at Pesto, Toaster, Mauricio, and Periwinkle, wrapping them up. Pesto and Toaster are now like Hero, standing but unable to move.

"Rodolfo!" Pesto screams.

H. Max, now would be a good time to do something!

M. Do what? Fant is completely in control!

"Yarmuckle, kill the weird-looking teenage boy already," SkeLord barks at the Death Soldier currently sitting on top of Rodolfo. Yarmuckle unsheathes his long sword again.

"Wait!" Hero yells.

"Aw, man," Yarmuckle complains.

"What do you want, Marmalade?" SkeLord asks her, with the confidence of someone in complete control of a situation.

"Let them go and you can have me," Hero replies, not even correcting the name error. "I'm the one with the magic—"

"Hero, no!" Toaster cries out. Rodolfo would have yelled, but he's nearly unconscious.

"Yes, Toaster. I have to. We lost," Hero says. "I've never lost before, but I'd rather lose a fight than lose you all."

"Hero, you can't," Pesto speaks up.

"I'm sorry, Pesto," Hero replies. "But I can't let anything happen to you either. This is *my* fight. You shouldn't even be here."

"Silence!" SkeLord yells at them. He turns to Hero. "Come here, and I will let them all go. The queen did say they were useless without you."

"Kind of hurtful," Rodolfo ekes out.

"Okay," Hero says. "But I'm kind of tied up."

"Oh, right," SkeLord says to her. "Yarmuckle, that boy is probably dead by now. Come pick her up and strap her to one of the bikes."

Yarmuckle walks to Hero and picks her up like a piece of lumber.

H. Is this the ending you wanted, Murray? You
    wanted a sad ending for your sad life? You

should have stuck with manuals. I'll never save my kingdom now. You chose Max over me. I'll never find Mother. You should never have borned me!

Suddenly, a little fuzzy teddy bear that looks like a ballerina zombie, complete with fluorescent pastel wings and a glittery pink tutu, flies at Yarmuckle. On the little flying teddy bear's back is another teddy bear dressed as a warrior, with a black trench coat full of little teddy bear weapons. Warrior Bear jumps off Ballerina Bear holding a real but tiny morning star and lands right on Yarmuckle's face.

"Ah! Get off!" Yarmuckle screams.

Warrior Bear swings at Yarmuckle's eyes with the tiny but real morning star.

"What in the Lands? What manner of magic is this?" SkeLord cries.

Unfortunately, he is so distracted, he does not see Ballerina Bear still flying at Hero while holding one of Warrior Bear's swords.

Ballerina Bear quickly flies around Hero, slashing at various points in the chain of bones, to break Hero's bonds. The bones separate and fall to the ground. Ballerina Bear does a little pirouette at Hero. Hero doesn't know what to do in response to a flying zombie teddy bear that helped her, so she just nods her head in thanks and then charges at SkeLord, who was headed toward Yarmulke and his battle with Warrior Bear.

Hero slams into SkeLord, catching him by surprise, and the two go tumbling across the ground. Ballerina Bear flies to help Warrior Bear, and the two dispatch Yarmuckle, who now lies lifeless.

Hero, with her morning star, and SkeLord, with his sword, now circle each other. *How do I kill something that's already dead?*

Meanwhile, Warrior Bear and Ballerina Bear have flown, together again, to Toaster to free him of the bony bonds.

"What are you?" Toaster asks the bears as he's freed. Ballerina Bear gives a pirouette and Warrior Bear gives a nod of her head. Then they fly to Pesto to free her as well.

After being freed, Pesto points toward SkeLord and the two bears, Ballerina Bear with Warrior Bear on her back, fly toward the horses lying on the ground to free them too.

"Pesto, what's going on? Did they just listen to you?" Toaster asks Pesto.

But Pesto just says, "Go check on Rodolfo."

"Oh!" Toaster replies and runs to Rodolfo. He looks him over. "Pesto, my brother's not moving!"

"Graham! We need you now!" Pesto shouts at the carriage.

"Is it safe?" Graham calls back from the safety of the carriage. "Those bears might kill me, too."

The two flying teddy bears come back to land on Pesto, one on each of her shoulders.

"If you don't come out right now and help, I *will* sic my bears on you!" Pesto warns him. Clearly, Graham saw everything from the carriage, including the two killer teddy bears.

"Okay, okay. I'm coming out," Graham replies.

"Who the hell *is* this girl? She skeeves me out," Mauricio asks Periwinkle. Pesto snaps her head around to face the horses with a look of impending death. "No, no, I mean, uh, thanks. You rock, zombie girl."

"Thank you, milady," Periwinkle says to Pesto, lowering her front legs in a royal equine curtsey.

Meanwhile, Hero kicks SkeLord onto the ground with a strong right boot to the ribcage. But he keeps getting up. He has no muscles, no nervous system, and feels no pain. Unless she can break a bone, she could end up fighting him forever.

But, before SkeLord gets up, the two teddy bears, with Warrior Bear on Ballerina Bear's back, land on SkeLord's ribs. He swats at them like flies, but he keeps missing as the bears flitter about.

Warrior Bear jumps off Ballerina Bear slashes at SkeLord's joints with the tiniest, most adorable dagger one might ever see. Ballerina Bear also stabs at SkeLord's joints with a teddy-bear-sized sword.

Hero gets the idea from the two teddy bears and starts aiming directly for SkeLord's joints as well. Carving at the joints breaks the skeleton man apart, and he starts crumpling piece by piece. Then SkeLord is no more. He's nothing but a pile of bones.

Ballerina Bear does her pirouette at Hero, and Warrior Bear just nods stoically. They fly back together onto Pesto's shoulders.

What the hell just happened? Pesto and her toy bears just saved us all?

M. That's what I want to know, Hero! How did she do that? She was just some zombie girl.

Yeah, Hero. We're not writing her. It's all automatic writing. Who the hell is she?

H. What do you mean, Murray? You created her!

I know! But she doesn't even know about us and the writing and the talisman for control. How did she take control?

H. Don't know, don't care!

Hero looks over to check on Rodolfo, then sees Graham sitting on top of Rodolfo's body, trying to crack his ribs, and occasionally kissing him. She runs screaming at Graham. "Aaahhh!"

But to an actual smart ancient, and a cast member of *Paramedics Emergency Medical Care: Bangor*, Graham is just trying to perform life-saving cardiopulmonary resuscitation, known as CPR.

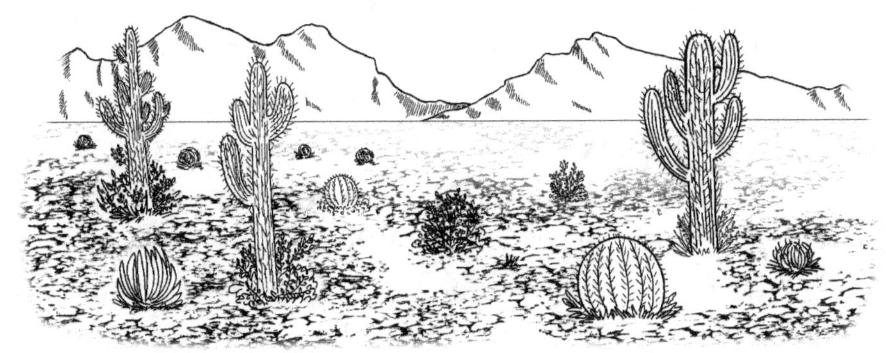

Chapter 30

The Revealing Magic of Pesto

Hero, in full speed, runs and jumps at Graham, knocking him off Rodolfo.

"You conniving, misogymnastic, womanizing . . ." Hero keeps hurling insults at Graham as she bashes in his face.

"What, you think Rodolfo is a woman?" Graham asks between punches.

"Hero! Hero!" Toaster cries, trying to pull her off. Pesto just giggles at Graham's pain.

"Fight! Fight!" Mauricio chants. "This is how weez settle things in Brooklyn. Come on, tough guy! You gonna let a girl hit ya like that?"

"Mauricio!" Periwinkle exclaims, aghast. "Are you really saying Graham should hit a lady?" She gives an angry whinny.

"Oh, er, um, Your Highness," Mauricio replies, embarrassed. "I, uh, is she really a *lady* though? Nothing like you."

Periwinkle gives another, more pleasing, whinny.

"Hero!" Toaster repeats. "He was helping! He's a healer, remember? Please! Let Graham help!"

"Toaster, he was trying to kill Rodolfo so he can get the girl," Hero explains and throws another fist into Graham's face.

"Hero, I was just trying to help. Honest!" Graham says through now-cracked teeth. "You don't know anything about modern medicine!"

"Honest to the gods!" Toaster pleads. "Let him help!"

Hero looks at Toaster and stops beating Graham's brains in. "Go help him then," she says matter-of-factly.

M. A little late, Hero!

H. It better not be, page!

"I was about to tell you, you know," Graham says. "He's *gone*, Hero. I can't do any more. I'm sorry, Toaster. But Rodolfo's a goner. Kicked the bucket."

Hero starts hitting Graham again. "Fix him!" A punch with her right hand. "Fix him!" A punch with her left hand. "Fix hiiiiim!" Another flurry of punches.

"Mommy!" Graham cries.

M. Hero!

This isn't helping, Hero!

Hero rolls off Graham, not because of his pleading, but because she's tired of hitting someone who is not even putting up a fight. Lying on her back, all she can hear is Toaster in the background yelling, "Rodolfo! Rodolfo! Please!"

"I'm sorry, Toaster," Pesto says.

While lying on the ground in agony, Hero turns her head to Pesto. She's kneeling over Toaster, with her arm around him.

"I lost." Hero sobs. "I couldn't save him no matter how hard I tried. I've never lost. I thinked we had won."

"I'm sorry, Hero" Graham says, surprisingly genuine. "I tried to save him. Even Murray wanted me to. If I had my medical equipment, maybe." He's kneeling on the ground and rubbing his bloody jaw in pain.

Hero gets on her knees and looks up at the sky. "Gods! Gods! You said I needed Graham. But he couldn't do anything. What I need is Rodolfo! Please! Murray! Please!" Hero is crying. "I love him!"

"Geez, get a room," Graham says, also genuinely.

I'm not sure that fits the mood.

M. Whatever, it was funny. And I'm getting bored of just automatic writing this thing.

Hero turns to Graham in almost uncontrollable anger—the most anger she's ever felt in her whole life. "You jackass!"

"Hero?" Pesto says in a high, adorable voice, while tapping Hero's shoulder. Hero sees the five-year-old standing next to her, her face eye level to Hero's, with two teddy bears on her shoulders—the same two murder bears that just saved everyone. The juxtaposition of it breaks Hero's concentration. While she wants to attack Graham, Hero also knows how important Pesto was to Rodolfo. She needs to help Pesto through this, just like she did with Toaster, and not waste time taking out a grudge on Graham.

"Uh, what, Pesto?" Hero says, still kneeling.

"I can help."

"Help me kill Graham and Max? I don't think that's a good—"

"No, silly," Pesto says with a giggle. *It's weird to see a little girl giggling in the middle of all this carnage.* "I can help Rodolfo. If you let me."

"Toaster?" Hero says, looking for some understanding from her own little brother. *He's the smart one.* "What is she talking about?"

"You silly," Pesto says. "I can *help* him."

Hero looks at Toaster, whose eyes are wide with hope. But Hero doesn't believe in hope any longer. "Pesto, he's gone." She takes Pesto's hands in hers. *Maybe she doesn't understand.*

"I know!" Pesto says with a stomp of her foot. "Listen to me! Why don't you listen? I can help!"

Hero throws her arms around Pesto, hoping to calm her. But to Pesto, this seems dismissive.

"You're not listening!" Pesto screams, squirming out of the intended hug.

Swirls of light erupt from Pesto's body, traveling around her like a blanket. "If you had only listened!" Pesto gives one last shout. She's engulfed in a golden-white light, as if she were a newly formed sun.

The rest of the group shields their eyes.

The newly formed half-sun, half-zombie, half-girl—

Max, that's one too many halves.

M. I'm not doing it, remember? Pesto's controlling herself. Like the battle. She doesn't know math? Or *maths*?

Oh, I got caught up in the story. It's very exciting.

M. Yeah, def.

H. Shut up, you jackasses!

—starts spinning like a top, getting faster.

Hero finally stands up, and Toaster runs to her side to take her hand. Graham runs back to the carriage for safety.

"Is she going to blow up?" Toaster asks. "Maybe she really was from Fant? Should we go to the carriage also?"

"It's beautiful," is all Hero replies.

Toaster gives her a strange look, as her reaction is very un-Hero-like, but he just stands there, holding her hand. Mauricio and Periwinkle also walk over to Hero and Toaster, watching the sun quietly.

Crack! A shot of lightning slams down from the sky onto the spinning sun-girl. The group reflexively jumps back and shield their eyes at the sound.

Then the light starts slowly dripping off the sun-girl down to the ground, as if she were a melting candle. The light that hits the ground melts into the dirty clay and disappears immediately.

The melting speeds up, and underneath the light, the group can make out a shape. It's a person. An adult. Blonde hair appears. It's long and wavy. A woman's shape appears. She's wearing a dress of the same golden-white light, which is the only part of the sun that doesn't melt away aside from an aura of light.

"Pesto?" Hero asks.

"After a fashion," the woman says. "Oh, Hero, you look so beautiful."

"I'm beautiful? Seriously?" Hero exclaims. "Are you out of your mind? We just did war with Fant's soldiers and some skeleton freak. I'm covered in blood."

"Yes, you're beautiful. I never thought I would lay eyes on you. You're amazing," the woman says.

"Who the hell are you?" Hero asks. "Because no one calls me *beautiful* and lives. So, if you're not going to help Rodolfo, you can get the fire truck out of here!" She starts taking out her morning star. *Maybe I made a mistake waiting for whatever this is to appear.*

Suddenly, in two flashes of light, the woman is holding a bar of soap in one hand and a washcloth in the other. "I'm going to wash that mouth out!" she cackles.

"Don't you touch my sister!" Toaster yells at her. "Wait, are you …?"

But the woman just smiles at Hero, whose mouth is agape.

"Mother?" Hero asks.

The bar of soap and washcloth disappear in another flash of light.

"Yes, dear. It's me."

M. No way!

What a story!

M. I knew she was still alive, but this is truly mass psychosis, Murray.

"Mother? How do I know it's really you?" Hero asks defiantly.

"I see you're wearing my trench coat," Mother says.

"Mother!" Hero says as she runs to the woman and throws her arms around her.

"Oh, baby," Mother says as she embraces Hero.

"Save Rodolfo! Please!" Hero begs, suddenly escaping the embrace.

"Yes, of course. Why do you think I had to reveal myself? My Rolfo," Mother says.

Rolfo?

Mother kneels down next to Rodolfo. "Everyone, stand back," she orders, and lifts her arms. Her long sleeves of light follow her arms. She immediately brings down her hands, and a lightning bolt comes from the sky and crashes down onto Rodolfo's body.

Those among the group who are not enchantresses look horrified.

"Some help, lady," Mauricio comments.

"Let her finish," Periwinkle admonishes him.

But then Rodolfo's body starts to shake. His eyes open, and there's the sound of a loud, deep breath.

"Hero! Toaster!" Rodolfo screams. He pulls his torso up so his body is in a sitting position and looks around for them. "What happened?"

"We won, brother," Toaster says as he runs over and kneels next to his brother.

"Rodolfo!" Hero runs over as well, but stands over him. She suddenly feels awkward showing affection in front of her mother.

"Where's Pesto? Is she safe?" Rodolfo asks. "Who is this lady? I think my eyes are still blurry." Rodolfo nods toward the new woman of light.

"Um, about that," Hero says.

Then Mother interjects, "Hi, Rolfo."

"Who the hell is this, Hero?" Rodolfo asks.

"It's me . . . Pesto," Mother says as she kneels and takes Rodolfo's hand.

"Hero?" Rodolfo asks her.

Hero and Toaster nod.

"We saw it with our own eyes, brother," Toaster says. "Pesto won the entire battle for us using the two teddy bears she had. They were flying all around kicking a—"

"Language, Toaster," Mother scolds him.

"Oh, right," Toaster replies sheepishly. "And then, in a flash of light, Pesto just turned into Mother."

"Yeah! What an episode in our lives!" the group hears from the carriage. "And she's, like, superhot!" It's Graham, wearing out his welcome. "Hey, Murray, maybe I can get the mother instead of the girl in this episode of our lives? I'm down with that!"

Uh, Max? We still want this to sell still, right? Even I think it's getting kind of . . . weird.

M. I told you, it's so boring just sitting here automatic writing. And Graham is such a fun character. He's the only one we're controlling still.

And the horses.

M. They're horses! And everyone just ignores them now. Just let me have some fun.

Mother exhales a large sigh, stands, and lifts a hand toward the sky in the direction of the carriage, then lowers it. Instantly, a fireball comes from the sky and smashes into the carriage, instantly engulfing it into flames.

"How did you ever put up with that guy?" Mother asks as the carriage, and Graham, disintegrate.

See what you did? I can't kill off a character from an entirely different show!

M. I'm not even sure you were allowed to include him in the first place. But it's not my fault. It's that damned Mother.

Hero said Mother didn't like you.

M. Well, I don't like her either. I hate mothers! *What happened to college? What are you doing with your life? You can't deliver pizzas the rest of your life. When are you going to get a real job? Oh, by the way, I need you to watch your baby sisters all day. Argh!*

Mother lifts her hand up, so the back of it faces the heavens. She looks in the same direction, and sticks up her middle finger.

Wow, she does not like you, Max.

The group doesn't notice, as it is still a bit stunned by Mother's violence, except for Hero, who excitedly leans into Mother in a wolf hug.

Rodolfo, getting past his momentary shock, asks, "So Mother was Pesto the whole time?"

"Not exactly, Rodolfo," Mother says. "Let me explain."

"Yeah, you died before I was borned. How are you here?" Hero asks.

"How much do you know about parallel universes?" Mother asks.

"You mean the host spittle?" Hero asks excitedly. "The one you told me to enter?"

"Yes, and I'm sorry about that," Mother says. "I sent you into a Fant stronghold. But I had my reasons. Were you able to save any of the patients?"

"Yes, Mona and Big Frederico," Hero replies proudly.

"Oh, how wonderful," Mother says, clapping her hands. "I sent you in there to save as many as you could, but those two were my favorites. I won quite a lot of glop from Big when we played something called cards. And did you recover my wand?"

Hero steps away from Mother and throws up her hands. "You sent us into that horrible place just to get your property?"

"Hero," Mother says, surprised. "I knew you could handle it. And it wasn't just for me. You saw how powerful that wand is."

"They killed Rowena! My friend! You sent me there to experience more misery. That's all you've ever done to me! You don't do that to your kid!"

Mother puts her arms on Hero's shoulders. Hero initially flinches, but then lets her.

"I'm sorry, Hero. But I knew you could handle it. You're a hero."

"Can you bring Rowena back, too? Do what you did to Rodolfo!"

"I'm sorry, Hero," Mother explains, her hands dropping to caress Hero's hands. "Rowena is in Fant's territory. They've become so powerful since I was there. I can no longer see what's going on there—not from the outside. That's why I had Murray sneak in your talisman. It helped you have powers on the inside because I can't see inside Fant."

"Why not?" Hero cries. "You control everything! You even control the gods!"

"She does?" Toaster and Rodolfo ask, in shock.

"Tell them, Mother!" Hero snaps her hands away from Mother's grasp. "You chose Murray. You controlled him. You're controlling the whole story!"

"Yes, and no, Hero," Mother says. "My magic is powerful. There has always been some magic in the Lands for as far as anyone can remember, just not in Dystpopia. Maybe because

I was free to develop on my own without any constraints, where I had the freedom of creativity. I was able to take it further than anyone—I developed the power to control even the gods. But solely for the good of Dystpopia! I could find us water, keep the warlords at bay, force the gods to improve our story, give me a daughter. You never knew Dystpopia back then. It was wonderful.

"And I could always hear the gods. I can hear them even now—a low hum of conversation that took me years of meditation and focus to isolate. But I've never been able to talk directly to them, like you can. That power is only yours, Hero. Something you must have been born with. Something about your stubborn willpower. Though I didn't really need to talk to the gods from here; I developed the ability to travel into their world."

"What?" all the humans and horses exclaim in sync.

Mother puts her hand out to Toaster and cocks her head in his direction. He understands and hands over her magic wand. She takes it, caresses it for a bit, and it starts glowing a golden yellow in her hand. She swirls it in the air to her side. A portal of white light opens up next her.

"What the hell is that?" Hero exclaims.

"It's like a window—like that thing we went through in the hospital," Toaster says. "The Space-Time Control Room."

M. Dude, she's been here?

I mean, it's all starting to make sense, in a nonsensical way.

M. She's a story character! She can't come *here*. There's no way.

Hero! Ask her what she did when she was here!

"You've been to heaven-world?" Hero asks, incredulously. "Then you can just crush Fant right now!"

Hero! Just ask her, please!

H. Shut up, Murray! I have more important things to do. You're not even in control anymore! You're a weaver of nothing! They should just call you the horse-weaverer.

"It doesn't work like that, Hero," Mother says. "Fant was too powerful back then, so I could only hold them at bay. But now, they have grown even more powerful. They're controlling the story now too, though it's not perfect. They can't control the gods.

"Much like your powers, they can build a hospital where they study and improve their magic, but if Murray finds it, he can manipulate around it. Nor has Fant figured out how to enter heaven-world, *yet*, but they're working on it.

"What I'm trying to say is, even the gods can't beat Fant now. We need to beat them from inside the story, for good, for real, and soon. There is no time to waste. We need the ancients."

We can still control some things, Hero! Like inside the hospital. I'll make her answer. Let me take a stab at it, Max.

M. Of course, friend.

With all the emotion coursing through their veins, the only way to express it and release the pressure is through song.

"I'm just a princess," Periwinkle starts to sing, with the most beautiful voice. "And I've never been in distress." Periwinkle walks up to Rodolfo and points her nose in his face. "So, I need your warm caress—"

"Hey!" Hero exclaims. But Periwinkle is still singing a love song to Rodolfo.

"On the hooves of looove!" Periwinkle belts out.

"Hero," Mother adds. "I hate musicals. And these two buffoons won't stop."

"We could eat the horses," Hero replies thoughtfully.

"I meant Murray and Max," Mother corrects her. "I think I'd better answer their questions."

Finally!

The group quiets down, awaiting Mother's explanation.

Mother looks up at the sky. "Heya, honey-dumpling. I'm home."

Felicia?

M. Uh.

"You're Felicia?" Hero stares at Mother with wide eyes.

"Temporarily. But long enough," Mother explains, yet again, with no concrete answer. Never a simple yes or a no. "I needed Murray to quit those stupid technical manuals. I needed *him* to weave this story. I couldn't leave it to anybody

else. But he never would have done it until he lost everything. That's just who he is, and precisely why I chose him. So loyal, so true. His heart could only take care of the people around him. There's not a selfish molecule in his body."

M. That's true, Murray. You know you helped me through some bad sh—

"Language!" Mother yells at the sky. She looks at Hero again. "I never liked that guy."

"He's not so bad. As much as I hate him, he's good for Murray," Hero says, surprising herself.

M. Wow, thanks, Hero. You're still annoying, though.

H. If I wasn't annoying you, I wouldn't be happy.

"If you say so," Mother says with a shrug. "Anyway, but I needed Felicia to build him up ..."

You're the one. You told me I should write YA instead of technical manuals. You said I'm a great writer!

"Chew him up ..."

You also told me that I'm wasting my life. All my friends are more successful, and you never wanted to be married to a stunning failure. You couldn't spend the rest of your life in a fifth-floor walk-up with a loser.

I'm an embarrassment to you, and your entire family laughs at me, and you because of me.

"And spit him out."

You left me in the middle of night with only Katrina to love me. You left before I even found the courage to chase my dream.

"I was going to take the cat, too, but you know the Lands. We hate cats," Mother explains. "Once I left him at rock bottom, I stayed in heaven-world a few more months to make sure the divorce went through. And to make sure he started weaving the story. Then I left Felicia's body."

"Left her body?" Hero asks.

"Like Pesto? Where is she?" Rodolfo asks, worried.

"With my magic, I can transfer parts of my consciousness into bodies. The transfer slowly undoes itself over time. And the host sees and understands everything that is going on. During this, I can assume other forms, like my former body, temporarily. But it's always temporary, never permanent.

"I'm sorry for taking over Felicia's life, but I had to save our kingdom. Did she ever come back, Murray?" Mother looks up at the sky.

No! I never heard from her again.

"I didn't quite catch that," Mother says to Hero.

"Murray says no," Hero informs her.

"Ah, I always got the sense she was happy I actually chose to piss instead of getting off the pot, as they say in heaven-world," Mother says.

"Language!" Toaster snaps.

"Hey, I'm the Enchantress of Dystpopia, I can say whatever I want. And I've already died twice, and about to die a third time," Mother replies dismissively.

"You're dying?" Hero runs and grabs her in a real human hug, only the third intentionally initiated hug of her entire life as far as she can remember—except for that one surprisingly friendly sand-wolf on that desperately cold night where they both thought they might die.

"Yes, I'm dying," Mother says plainly.

"Will Pesto die?" Rodolfo asks, shocked and concerned.

"No, Rodolfo," Mother says. "She will come back most certainly, and permanently. I will be the one who is gone."

"But why? You just got here! And where is east?" Hero rants.

"One thing at a time, dear," Mother says. "I'll spare you the details, as none of you are enchantresses, sorceresses, or have something called a PhD in theoretical astrophysics. But if I had more time, and any remaining magic, I would enroll Toaster in a nice program."

"Huh?" Toaster asks. "Enroll me? You want me to be an enchantress?"

"No, Toaster." Mother laughs. "In a school in heaven-world. For astrophysics. Rodolfo tells me how smart you are. I can see it for myself. I'm not surprised, having met your parents."

"Dr. Mathers said I was smart, too," Toaster replies, embarrassed.

"Who?" Mother asks.

"Some annoying smart guy at Fant's hospital," Hero answers.

"Never heard of him. Regardless," Mother continues, "everything was fine in Dystpopia for thousands of years. But one day Fant just showed up. It didn't just show up: it showed up with its own thousands of years of history—our king suddenly changed from Reginald the Devout to Reginald III—and power that matched mine. Technology *and* magic. Maybe because of my own magic, I was the only one who knew that it shouldn't be that way. It never was before. But at the same time, we were suddenly at war with Fant too, and had been for a hundred years.

"Even before Fant, we had always heard of ancients with immeasurable powers, even greater than anything in the Lands. What better way finally to best Fant. So, I went in search of the ancients' secrets, stumbling on to Fant's hospital. I met Pesto's family there. My goal was to save them all. Her family had already told me about the ancients of New York."

"East! Tell us!" Hero urges.

"I'm sorry, Hero. Pesto doesn't know. When I probe her mind, I just keep getting back something about worms. She's just a kid. And Felicia's knowledge left me when I left her. Scientific knowledge does not cross the barrier. I don't know why. But *you* can speak to them."

"Murray and Max know," Hero whines. "They won't tell us."

And you think I'll tell Mother now that I know she was the one who left me?

"I didn't. Felicia did," Mother says to the sky. "He's coming in nice and strong right now. He must be angry." She gives a genuine smile.

She was acting through you! You chewed me up and spit me out! Your words!

"True," Mother says. "Regardless, I think it's time you tell us, Murray."

No! Not after what you did to me!

M. Yeah, you can't do that to us! We're gods!

H. Murray! Max! Get off it. We have the power to control the gods. So just tell us and let us defeat Fant. You're the one who weaved them!

But that's the thing, Hero. I didn't! Don't you remember? I didn't remember ever creating that part of the story. You told me I did, but I don't think I did. I assumed I had just thrown it all out. My story was going to be a warm-hearted musical.

M. Yeah, with babies!

H. Holy buckets, it's not a musical! And no more babies! Why do you even like babies so much, Max?

M. I like my baby sisters. Sometimes I think
   they're a burden, but they made me learn
   essential things like responsibility and—

"Enough!" Mother shouts at the sky. "If you won't tell them, I have just enough magic left for this before my consciousness succumbs to its injuries and departs this story for good." Mother takes her wand and starts swirling it in the air. Another portal starts to open, glowing with golden-white light.

M. Uh, Murray, what is she doing? Is she coming
   back here to spit you out again?

I don't know!

"Mother, no!" Hero cries.

Mother stops swirling the portal, and it's half formed, a floating half circle in the air.

"I'm sorry, Hero," she says. "I wish we had more time together. But my wounds from the hospital were always too great for this much magic. I could only survive in Pesto's body. I may have failed you, but I did it for Dystpopia, to give you a better life. Maybe I—"

"No, Mother, you can't go," Hero says. "We're survivors."

"We're more than that, Hero," Mother says. "Something you may have learned on this quest. We're entrusted with Dystpopia, and we need to do what we can to keep it going. Our wonderful Dystpopia. We're protectors, Hero. Like Rodolfo and Toaster protecting Town—"

"That's its name!" Rodolfo exclaims.

"I believe you're right, brother," Toaster says with a giggle. "This whole time, it was on the tip of my tongue."

"Town! It seems so simple now. Why couldn't I remember it?" Rodolfo asks himself.

"Oh, that was me also," Mother replies. "After the hospital, with Fant on my tracks, we, I mean, *I* cast a Tip of the Tongue spell to hide its name—make it harder for Fant to catch me . . . us. I hid there for some time.

"But what I was saying, Hero, is like Rodolfo and Toaster, we also need those we love. I thought I did the right thing leaving you to find the ancients. My job was to protect Dystpopia. So, I set off on my own, not looking back.

"But Pesto's family, Mona, Big, they taught me love is your greatest source of strength. Hero, you could not have gotten this far without realizing that. And I should have learned it long ago. It's why I left you a talisman and a dream—to make up for it. But you learned the lesson on your own. And you found a wonderful *man*. I'm so proud of you."

Hero turns red and looks down at the ground. Rodolfo had started inching closer to Hero to display some affection, but wisely stopped when he saw Hero's embarrassment. "But Mother," she asks. "How was I borned after you died if you left me?"

"And how did you become Pesto?" Rodolfo asks.

"And if you were Pesto, why did you have to hide in Town?" Toaster asks.

"If you love us, do you have any more food?" Mauricio finally speaks up.

"We don't have time for all these answers," Mother says. "Safe to say, unless you had that PhD—"

"In apple-fizzies?" Hero asks, slowly. Toaster giggles and Hero shoots him a nasty look.

"Yes. Do any of you understand the multiverse?" Mother asks. The group just stares at her blankly. Toaster shakes his head. "I did say I've died twice already."

M. Dude, I've seen this movie before. She's totally coming back.

Yeah. Honestly, it's a bit telegraphed. It's like, why even have other characters if she can do everything herself?

M. Maybe we'll let it all play out and then fix it all in editing. Or maybe Mother is really the villain! I bet that's what she's doing with the portals.

Revising hasn't worked before, but you're right, maybe at the end it will. Then we can finally change it to *Bangoor.* Oh, and we can change her name then too! Remind me.

M. Will do, friend.

Mother sticks her middle finger up at the sky again.

"Is that a prayer to the gods?" Toaster asks then repeats it.

"In a way," Mother replies, with a laugh. "But now it's time to let me finish. Goodbye, Hero. Goodbye, all. Please take care of my daughter. She's a protector, but it doesn't mean she doesn't need protecting sometimes also. Please tell Murray that, too. That's what he's good at, anyway." Mother then completes the entire circle of yellow, golden light.

M. Uh, Murray? Is that what I think it is? How the hell is it here in your apartment?

Is she coming back here? I don't want to see her! Wait, how's my hair?

Chapter 31

Intermission *Tres*

M. Dude, who cares about your hair? This lady is crazy! She's probably going to kill us.

Kill a god? I think not.

M. We're not really gods. We're just two low-income dudes in your studio apartment.

Oh, good point. Get behind the . . .

M. There's nothing to get behind! It's a *studio apartment.*

The bathroom! Grab the typewriter!

M. This is heavy! Why do we need it?

Someone still has to weave, er, write. She doesn't like it when—

434

M. Never mind that, Murray! The bathroom door just blew right off. The portal is coming for us. Quick, get in! Grab that shampoo bottle. Herbals Essences, dude?

Forget it, I don't think she's coming here. Don't you feel that? I think we're—

Chapter 32

Now You're Dumped

The forty-five-year-old out-of-shape writer and the in-a-rut twenty-one-year-old pizza delivery boy (and part-time mom) are expelled out of the portal onto the hard clay ground. The typewriter lands with a *thud* next to them.

Murray and Max land on their backsides. Murray is rubbing his thinning hair and looking around. Max is shielding his eyes from the blinding sun, a much different visual landscape than the dark, fifth-floor walk-up apartment's bathroom.

They see a motley crew of humans and two horses on the clay ground, not moving. There is also a white figure of floating light in the form of a woman staring at them.

The woman of light—Mother—moves to envelop both Murray and her in a shield around only them. The figure of light then morphs slowly into a five-foot Jersey girl: big brown hair, excessive makeup, and tight black leggings along with a sultry retro Deft Leppard T-shirt ripped at the shoulders. "Write, Murray, write!" She points a wand at him.

"Felicia?" he asks.

"Yea, Murray. It's kinda good to see ya. We had *some* good times, don't ya think?" Felicia asks him in her New Jersey accent.

"You're really Mother, aren't you?" Murray asks.

"Oh, you're a smartie. You need to keep writing the story, honey-dumpling," Felicia replies with a giggle.

"Oh God," Murray says. "Am I really here?" He looks at the clay ground below him, under his backside. "That's really them, isn't it?" Still sitting, he points somewhere outside the wall of light surrounding them—where he saw all of them. *Them!*

"Yeah, Murray," Felicia replies. "You're in the Lands. Reminds me of when I dragged you to see the fam in Joyzee, right?"

"Uh, not really," Murray says. "But regardless, why do this?"

"Becawz," Felicia replies, "it's essential Hero finds the ancients' powah. And you wasn't gonna let her. You wouldn't even tell her where east is? Your own daughtah?"

"That's cheating!" Murray exclaims, finding an ounce of confidence. "It's *my* book!"

"No, honey-dumpling," Felicia says. "It was never your book. It's their book, their lives. And you wanna be all high and mighty up in heaven-world?" She points up at the sky. "Well, let's see all your morals when you're stuck down here."

"Yeah, we'll see." He groans, not wanting to give up but knowing he's up against a power even higher than heaven-world. Well, his real world. He rubs his temples in frustration. "But even so, it's going to be hard to carry a heavy typewriter throughout the Lands. You know, running from sand-wolves and flying zombies and all."

"What am I, a Best Buyz?" Felicia scoffs. "You always said you wanted to be a real writah, on your clunky old thing."

"It felt good," Murray replies defensively.

"Oh, Murray," Felicia says. "I wish you would one day find someone who actually loves you. Someone stuck in your old ways too. You were never ambitious enough for me. Weez was working at cross purposes. You know that, right?"

He nods, even though he still doesn't really believe it.

"But for now, you have a job to do. And, just to prove I'm not as cruel as you thinks I am, what would make it easier for you?"

Murray looks over at the black and silver clunky typewriter. "Uh, for traveling the Lands, I guess, uh, maybe a tablet? With, uh, some awesome autocorrect?"

"Oh, look at you so modern," Felicia says with a squeak. "Is that all?"

"Oh, and if I'm going to be automatic writing anyway, since it seems everyone is now controlling themselves—"

"Sorry about that. My fault. The talisman was just a bit too strong." Felicia squeezes her index and middle finger together. "It really was meant only for Hero. And the horsies—"

"Oh God, what about the horses?"

"Never mind. You'll see."

"Look, can it just auto-write everything other people are doing so I only have to write my parts? If I'm really here, I need to focus."

"Of course, I want you to focus on protecting Hero. Granted," Felicia says, pointing the wand at the typewriter which turns into a large-screen modern tablet, the screen already lit. Murray scuttles over to it and picks it up. "The tablet will auto-write everything until you want to affect the story. Then you just start typing. You better help them, Murray. And yourself. I don't really know what will happen to yooz gods if"—she slices a finger across her throat. "Ya get what I'm sayin'?"

Murray nods. "One question," he asks, a finger in the air. He just can't let this go. A flashback of Toaster at the checkpoint runs through his mind. Hopefully, Felicia doesn't slice and dice him. Instead, she nods. "I thought technology couldn't transfer the barrier. But the typewriter and now a modern tablet? Why not just make a compass?"

"Oh, poor Murray. My poor, poor Murray. See? You're still stuck in your old ways." Felicia shakes her head. "This is a new world. Open your eyes, Murray. It's magic, not technology." She flicks her wand and golden sparks fly off the end of it.

"But the compass?"

"What's a compass?" Felicia asks genuinely.

"Little thing, about this big."

"Reminds me of something—"

"It tells you directions!" Murray exclaims, interrupting her.

"How can I make a magic compass if I don't even know where east is?" Felicia asks derisively. "Do *you* know how one works?"

"Look, I'm not even sure where east is here," Murray replies. "Like you say, it's a different world."

"But you have an idea."

"I think I do."

"And you won't tell me?"

"No."

"So then, no compass. Are you ready?"

He just stares at her. How can one be ready for *this?*

"What's going to happen to you?" Murray asks.

"I'm actually a little jealous of you, Murball."

"Stop calling me that! I told you."

"You're no fun. It was funny. Seeing you all balled up on the couch, crying all the time."

"Because of you!"

"That's true. Oh well." Felicia sighs. "You're actually lucky. You get to live out the rest of the story. I'm at the end of mine. You gonna miss me?" She blows him a kiss.

"Not a chance," Murray replies, purposefully rude, yet insincere. He still misses Felicia. A lot. Well, *a* Felicia. He's not even sure which one.

"We created a great kid together, don't ya think?" she asks in an unexpected moment of shared experience and mutual respect.

"I don't even know that I had a part in it anymore," Murray replies. "This was all you, or Fant, or—"

"You always sell yourself short, honey-dumpling," Felicia remarks. "It's your biggest downfall, ya know? The story was always out there. But we needed you. *She* needed you."

"I'm not sure I understand."

The figure of Felicia disappears in a blinding flash, along with the shield of white light. With no more explanations coming, Murray scuttles over to the tablet, picks it up, and the magic item starts automatic writing as he exclaims, "Holy buckets!"

"That's my line," Hero says, taking out her morning star and aiming it at the two newcomers.

"Hero, no!" Max cries. "It's us!" He points at himself. "Max." He points at the older man. "Murray." They're both still on their backsides.

"Holy buckets!" Hero says.

"I know!" Murray agrees. "You have no idea." His head is glued to the new tablet, and the sight of the godly device shuts up the dystopians. His entire manuscript, even the conversation with Felicia, including her insults, is on the screen. From his seat on the ground, he scrolls it up and down to make sure it's there, seeing his name in the manuscript as he's doing it. Murray scrolls up. Murray scrolls down. "This is totally freaky." He stares at the screen, dumbfounded. "Freaky." Murray might wet his pants. "Not true!" he yells at the tablet.

In his head, he hears Felicia's soul-crushing giggle and a soft, "Miss me, Murball!"

And then he knows deep inside that she's gone for good. A part of him feels dumped all over again—still pining over Felicia, even after all the truths that just assaulted him.

"Is that what I think it is?" Max asks.

"Yup. A fancy new tablet," Murray replies, amazed that the story is typing itself, yet despondent at the words.

"What's that logo? F? I don't recognize that brand," Max remarks as he leans closer.

Murray sighs. "It's Felicia's," he replies sadly. "Mother did that to taunt me. She wants me to keep writing the story."

"From in here?" Max asks, bewildered.

"You jackasses are really Murray and Max?" Hero asks, wide-eyed.

Rodolfo, Toaster, Mauricio, and Periwinkle suddenly all kneel to the ground in the face of real gods. A giggling Pesto is back to herself, but the appearance of the two gods distracted the group from her retransformation (or un-transformation). She's holding just one teddy bear now, against her chest, and without any extra garments.

Pesto wonders if it's still a murder bear, but it's not worth mentioning aloud at a time like this. So, she whispers quietly in the teddy's ear, "Are you a murder bear?" The bear does not respond, and Pesto nods slightly. What she, and the larger group, did not see is the bear's eye wink.

"No! No! Get up everyone. It's just two jackasses!" Hero orders.

"But Hero, these are real gods," Rodolfo says. "It's Murray, who helped even me. It's just polite." He remains kneeling.

"Murray? Murray?" Max waves to get Murray's attention. "Are you still writing the story? You aren't typing anything."

"She set it up with an auto-write if we're not the ones controlling it," Murray informs him. "I only have to type the new things."

"No fair," Max complains. "I was having fun writing it. Well, until Fant and Mother took over, and we got sucked in."

"They're daft," Pesto says, pointing at the two men. "Not gods." She walks over to them and pokes Murray in the leg.

"Hey, kid!" Murray reprimands her. "I wrote you into the story, and I can write you out!" He wields the tablet in front of her, clearly stressed.

"Murray, she's just a kid," Max reprimands him. But then Max takes a close look. "Oh God, what's wrong with her? I know it said that in the manuscript, but when you see it up close, she's all—"

"Shut up," Rodolfo scolds Max, and Pesto runs to him, looking for comfort. "Pesto is right. You can't be a god and be that rude. Get up, everyone."

Toaster and the horses get up. Max and Murray follow the mere mortals.

"Yeah, I knew they weren't gods," Mauricio says. "I was just kneeling so the humans wouldn't feel like schmucks."

"Oh, Mauricio, you're so smart," Periwinkle replies, and whinnies in his direction while shuffling closer to him.

"Hey, at least you've got your wit still," Max lauds Murray. "Talking horses at a time like this. You're a true professional."

"Oh God, that wasn't me." Murray wields his tablet around again. "Felicia warned me. The horses have control now, too." His forehead is in his hand.

"It's okay, friend," Max replies. "You don't need that burden. Look around. We're really here, in this dystopian nightmare. That Mother lady actually pulled us in. Man, it's hot here. Like twenty thousand degrees. This is one hellhole of a story."

"You're the ones who made it so hot!" Hero shouts at them.

"I thought you liked the story," Murray replies to Max, too focused on the negative feedback to respond to Hero.

"I liked the brief escape from my crappy life, but I didn't actually want to be somewhere even crappier," Max replies. "My shirt's already soaked through. How is she wearing a leather jacket through all this? How?" Max points at Hero. "And do you even see a Starbux?" He waves his hand at the bleak horizon.

"I don't want to be stuck with you two jackasses either," Hero scolds them.

"Yeah, you git," Pesto adds, kicking Max in the shin.

"Ow!" Max cries, bending down to rub his shin. "See, this is what I mean, Murray. It was fun but you've got dystopians, a Brit that's a zombie, a horse that's either Italian or Yiddish, or both—which is much more ridiculous when you're actually inside. And Fant likes astrophysics, and the dystopians can do magic? It doesn't really make a lot of sense."

"Look, let's all just calm down," Murray says, holding his hands palms-out, not wanting to hear more complaints about his story.

"I agree," Hero says. "As bad as it is that my own mother left you two jackasses with us, I first need to check on someone I actually like." Hero kneels on the ground in front of Pesto. "How are you feeling, Pesto? Do you have any idea what just happened?"

"Mother used me to talk. I like her. She's funny," Pesto says with a giggle.

"She wasn't married to her," Murray chides.

"Holy buckets, Murray!" Hero shouts. "It's not always about you."

"The fact that we were magically pulled into a story I was writing?" Murray asks frantically. "I'd say it's *totally* about me."

"I'd say you were going crazy, Murray, if I weren't here too," Max adds.

"Ugh," Hero scoffs. "Quiet!" Her hand is conspicuously inside her jacket pocket.

"And now, we're gonna get killed by your very own story character," Max mumbles.

"I'm glad you're okay, Pesto," Hero says and gives Pesto a kiss on her half-zombie forehead before standing again.

"Hey, you give her a kiss, no problem," Rodolfo protests. "But I get almost thrown out of a carriage and have to be near-death for you to even—"

"He is a bit whiny, right?" Max asks Murray, who just nods in reply, being too stressed to think straight.

After reading his tablet, Murray groans. "I'm not too stressed." His voice sounds stressed. "Ugh."

Hero walks up to Rodolfo and plants a kiss on his lips, mainly to shut him up about Pesto's kiss, and distract him from the older men's insults. Yet again, it looks and feels awkward to the entire group, like Hero is still primed for battle. She realizes everyone is staring at her. "What's wrong?"

"I can offer you lessons, my dear," Periwinkle says.

"What?" Hero shouts to the whole group. "I don't know how to do it, okay, everyone?"

Pesto grabs her hand, teddy in her other, distracting her.

"Uh," Murray interjects. "I hate to break this up. But there's an issue."

"Yeah, the fact that you're here." Hero laughs, with a snort.

"You know," Murray says, "that's no way to talk to me."

"I can talk however I want," Hero replies, taking a battle stance. Rodolfo stands proudly next to her. Toaster and the two talking horses join them.

"Not that we're against the gods or anything, but I feel like it's safer over here," Mauricio says. "You know, with the scary girl."

"Show some respect. I'm like your father!" Murray exclaims.

"Yeah, you didn't see how much he worried about you," Max adds.

"Some father. Look at you," Hero scoffs. "Are all gods in heaven-world that out of shape?"

"Hey," Max interjects. "I keep in good shape. I ride a bike for all my deliveries." Hero grunts back, but doesn't disagree. "And technically Murray was even married to your mother, so you should definitely show him some respect because then you're also respecting Mother."

"Argh, fine!" Hero relents. "What would you like to tell us about your issues, *Father*?"

"Not *my* issues," Murray replies. "*An* issue. What do we do now? Why would Mother bring us here?"

"I don't know!" Hero exclaims. "That was the first time I ever met her. You were married to her for months. You tell me."

"I have an idea," Toaster interjects.

"I can't believe you named him *Toaster*." Max laughs. "He doesn't really look like one though. He's not really that boxy." Max puts his hands perpendicular, like he's measuring out a box or vogueing.

"Maybe one of the upright ones?" Murray replies, instinctively. "You know, the ones that pop up the toast."

"Hey!" Toaster growls. "Hero, I think it's because they wouldn't tell us which way east is. Do you remember? You told her how they were keeping it secret?"

"Yeah!" Hero agrees. She takes out a sword. She aims the morning star at Murray and the sword at Max. "Tell us which way east is."

"But, Hero," Murray says, "that would be cheating. I told Mother that. I didn't come all the way here just for a bad story. She must have thought we can help some other way?"

"Yeah, Murray. We can still sell this thing," Max adds, which makes Murray feel a little more confident. "Hopefully that tablet has Wi-Fi."

"Maybe the book will be even better now?" Murray theorizes. "You know, it'll be that much more realistic? Especially if we don't cheat."

"Still?" Hero grunts as she thrusts the morning star and sword closer to the two former gods. "You're still just trying to sell a *book*? After everything?"

"You wouldn't hurt your own father," Murray says confidently.

And then, they hear the loudest growl they have ever heard. Hero knows instantly: the dragons are coming.

"Maybe not," Hero agrees and points her sword up at the sky, behind her. "But they will!"

Chapter 33

How to Blame Your Dragon

"The sun rises in the east. I think!" Murray yells over the growling, giving up his morals at the first sign of danger.

"What do you mean, you *think*?" Hero asks.

"I mean, I assume your world is like ours. Physics could—"

"Murray! It's the only thing to go on," Max interrupts him, also justifying the means to avoid an untimely end. "Hero, where does the sun rise?"

"What do you mean where?" Hero asks, bewildered. "It's always different."

"Always different?" Murray exclaims.

"Yes!" Hero rages. The other dystopians nod.

"Dude," Max says with a laugh. "You really wrote a crazy story."

"Do you have any other bright ideas?" Hero asks.

"Hero!" Toaster blurts out. "There is another bright light in the sky. At night. Would that help at all?"

"There is?" Murray asks. He turns to Max. "A star?"

"Where does it show up, Toaster boy?" Max asks.

"The name's *Toaster*," he corrects the elder god. "And there." He points to the sky.

"If we assume that's the North Star?" Max asks.

"Then we go that way!" Murray points toward the horizon. "Wow, that boy is smart." Luckily, east appears to be in the opposite direction of the growls.

"I guess it's good you didn't tell them where east was before." Max laughs.

"Whatever. It doesn't even matter," Hero announces. "We're never going to outrun a dragon, especially one from Fant. Maybe we could outrun one of the friendlier ones from the Alliance of Humor the Great. Those dragons usually just want to talk."

"The horses!" Max offers.

"*Those* horses?" Hero scoffs. "Good luck."

"Hero," Rodolfo cuts in. "Isn't there anything we can do?"

"No," Hero says. "It's over."

"Don't you dare say it's over again, Hero," Toaster thunders at her. "For a survivor, you're always whining it's over. It's *not* over! We'll think of something. We now know where east is!"

Hero looks at the precocious Toaster curiously, actually willing to speak back to her. *He's growing.* "The teacher becomes the master." Toaster smiles at her.

"I have an idea," Murray says.

"*You* have an idea? This I gotta see," Hero laughs.

"The motorbikes!" Murray says louder, ignoring her derisive laughter.

"Huh?" Rodolfo replies.

"The vintage motorbikes," Murray insists. "The Cow-uh-sakees!" Mauricio cries. "The yellow things the Death Soldiers were riding."

"Yes! Those!" Murray confirms.

The roar grows closer.

"They're over there," Hero says, pointing at the ground in the distance where the initial battle took place.

The group runs over to them. Murray and Max pick them up off the ground and sit on them. "It's like a horse," Murray says.

"It's more like a bike," Max says.

"Would you like to explain them?" Murray says.

"Have you ever ridden one?" Max asks.

"No. And you have?" Murray asks.

"Yes!" Max exclaims. "Well, a moped. For a while."

"Holy buckets, hurry up!" Hero chastises the grown men.

"Everyone hop on and turn the key all the way to the right, like so," Max explains. "Now, hit this starter key on the right!" The bikes' ignitions start growling too.

"These are like the jetpacks!" Toaster exclaims.

"Yes, in a way," Max replies. "Now hold the left handle, and twist the right handle while releasing the left handle." Max's bike starts moving.

"That's awesome!" Hero exclaims. She gets her bike going also. "But we need them to get faster."

"Just apply more gas with your right hand," Max says. "When I wrote them, in my head I made them automatics, so no hard manual shifting."

But Hero's bike is already moving quickly, headed east. "Yeah!" she cheers.

"Wait up!" Rodolfo says. His bike is also headed east now, with Pesto holding on to his back, teddy clutched in her hands as well.

"Yeah!" Pesto cheers, mimicking Hero.

All six humans are now on motorcycles, headed east. The horses are galloping to keep up, with useless jetpacks still on their backs. But, because everyone except for Max is new at this, the motorcycles actually aren't going too fast for the horses.

A dragon is overhead now.

"Holy hell!" Murray exclaims. "This is, like, real!"

"I've been telling you!" Hero shouts at him, exasperated. "It's my life, and you thinked it was fun!"

"It's not fun! What do we do?" Murray cries.

"Murray," Toaster says. "You still have some control. You can weave!"

The dragon, keeping up with them, breathes fire at them, hitting the talking horses in their rears.

"My ass is on fire again!" Mauricio cries.

"Mine too!" Periwinkle shrieks. "This is way hotter than before! Mauricio, does my ass look hot?"

"Holy buckets, their jetpacks are on fire!" Hero yells, after looking back at the horses. The remnants of fuel in the machines combust from the dragon's breath.

"Murray!" Toaster says. "Untie the jetpacks! Projectiles, Murray!"

"Oh! You really are so smart!" Murray's eyes widen, and he turns to the tablet in his hand, which is hard to do while driving a vintage Cow-uh-sakee. He starts typing furiously on his tablet. *Do I have to type that I'm typing every time I'm typing?* Murray types furiously on his tablet. It appears he automatically types that line whenever he actually starts typing on the tablet. *Weird. This world makes no sense!*

As he's typing, the straps to the jetpacks give out, and the jetpacks take flight. The force of the combusting fuel forces the jetpacks up and into the dragon hovering closely overhead. The dragon, in fear, lifts higher and away from the group.

"Did you do that?" Hero asks Murray.

"Yes, I did!" Murray says. "It was Toaster's idea! But I wrote it, and it happened. You know, typing everything all while riding a motorcycle is very hard."

"Holy buckets, stop complaining!" Hero yells at him. "Do something else to the dragon!"

"Like what?" he asks.

"I don't know!" Hero yells.

"But that's all I had. I have writer's block!" Murray cries. "It typically comes on during stress. Like being chased by a dragon!"

Suddenly, Max's motorcycle slows down to be near Murray. "I have an idea. Something Hero said."

"See? I'm not a dimwit!" Hero roars, but is dismayed when she can't hear the idea over the motorcycle revving.

"Oh, that's good," Murray says. "You really are a great writing partner. I think you found your natural talent, Max."

"You think?"

"Yeah, I guess I always knew when we would watch—"

"Hurry, you jackasses!" Hero yells.

"Oh, right," Murray says. He starts typing furiously on the tablet. Suddenly, four other dragons appear alongside Fant's dragon.

"Murray!" Hero erupts. "That's worse! You guys are the worst weavers in fire-trucking weaving history!"

"No, no," Murray says. "Just wait."

"Hey, you from Fant?" the new dragon along the Fant dragon's right side says.

"Uh, yeah," the Fant dragon replies.

"They can talk too?" Hero exclaims.

"I didn't even know." Murray giggles. "It was Max's idea. We're not controlling the Fant dragon, though, so it might not work. Be ready for anything."

"What's it like, Fant? We've never been outside the Alliance of Humor the Great. You ever hear of it?" a second dragon asks the Fant dragon, who is suddenly slowing down a bit, trying to fly and talk at the same time.

"It's, uh, miserable. In a good way. Lots of pain and agony," the Fant dragon replies.

"Ya don't say," a third dragon replies.

"Hey, want a stick of gum?" the fourth dragon from the Alliance of Humor the Great asks.

"Gum?" Fant's dragon asks, slowing down even more.

The motorcycles are well ahead now, but the group can still hear the loud dragon voices.

"Yeah, you chew it, like so," the fourth dragon says and blows an enormous bubble.

"Hell yeah," Fant's dragon says, and the fourth dragon uses its small paw to pop a piece of bubble gum into the Fant dragon's mouth.

The Fant dragon is now at a crawling speed, trying to fly, talk, and chew bubble gum all at the same time.

"You want to hear a joke?" the first Alliance dragon asks.

"What's a joke?" Fant's dragon replies.

"What's a joke!" the first dragon exclaims. "Oh, don't worry, you'll love this one. What did the warlord say to the flying zombie?"

Hero, Rodolfo, Pesto, Toaster, Murray, Max, Mauricio, and Periwinkle are so far ahead now, they never hear the punch line.

Chapter 34

Way Too Much Screen Time

The group stops somewhere in the middle of nowhere, far from the dragons and any sound of roars, or roaring laughter. They're all standing near the motorbikes, trying to stretch their legs. There doesn't look to be anything dangerous in the vicinity, finally.

"Wow," Hero says aloud. "You all really came through back there. I didn't even have to do a thing." The group is now far away from Dystpopia, Fant, Town, and the Lands. Hero's nerves are tense, not knowing what dangers lie ahead, but she knows she has a group she can rely on. Even those damned gods with admittedly good ideas.

"It's like Mother said," Toaster replies from his motorcycle. "We have to protect you also."

"You all did; you really did," Hero says. "I'm glad you're weaving again, Murray."

"Great, we're all awesome," Mauricio says. "Can we finally get back to New York? I've had explosives tied to me, been tied up with bones—"

"Don't forget the flying zombies," Periwinkle adds.

"Yeah, flying zombies attacked us," Mauricio continues.

"They attacked *us*," Hero reminds him. "They didn't care about you horses."

"What, so yooz think you're better than us? Is that it?" Mauricio asks.

"Mauricio, just wait until the upris—"

"*Madone!* I told you not to talk about it!" Mauricio interrupts Periwinkle. "Guys, she didn't mean what you think she meant. She meant uprising loaves of bread at my favorite Brooklyn bakery. How would you like to nosh on some of the finest blackout cake?"

"Is that a type of magical cake?" Toaster asks.

"Yes, indeed," Mauricio answers. "*Very* magical."

"Then, yes! Let's go nosh in New Yawk!" Toaster cheers.

"Noo Yolk!" Pesto joins in.

"Murray," Max says, "are we where I think we are?"

"Arizona?" Murray asks.

"Yeah, like from the movies," Max replies. "Arizona."

"No, we're not," Hero corrects them. "Ari and Xona's Bathhouse was back in the Lands. I never actually used it, though."

"Oh, thank the gods." Rodolfo exhales.

"And what if I had?" Hero snaps at him. "I'm not your property."

"It's just . . . I've heard things," Rodolfo says.

"You either L-word me or you don't, Rodolfo," Hero warns him.

"Yeah, Rolfo!" Pesto adds, giving him a squeeze.

"Okay, okay, you're right," Rodolfo says. "I L-word you. But then *I* can go to all the bathhouses I want?"

"Absolutely not, you jackass!" Hero scolds him.

"See?" Rodolfo seethes. "You're insufferable."

"And you wouldn't have her any other way, brother," Toaster says.

"Yeah, what he said," Hero says. "But he doesn't have me! It's a parnutship."

"Partnership?" Murray asks.

"Yeah, that's what I said," Hero agrees, pointing at Murray while still staring at Rodolfo.

"Ah, young love." Max laughs. "Reminds me of high school. Except for the bathhouses. Well, there was that one party—"

"Regardless," Murray interrupts. "If your world is remotely like ours, which I can't guarantee, seeing as how your sun is like, bonkers, but if it is, we're like two thousand miles from New York City. We can't make it by bike like this."

"Train?" Max asks.

"It would also take too long. And I didn't think to bring a map," Murray says. "Fant knows we're out here. I can't believe I just said that."

"You're the idiot who created Fant," Max replies.

"We've been over this," Murray says defensively. "I don't even remember creating Fant. Mother said they just appeared."

"So how do we get to New Yawk, and quick?" Hero asks.

"Yes, it's probable they sent more than one dragon to search for us," Toaster hypothesizes.

"I suppose we can try a portal, like Mother?" Murray asks.

"You think you can weave a portal like Mother?" Hero scoffs. "You're nowhere near as powerful as her."

"Look, Hero," Murray insists. "It's our only shot to get there quickly."

Murray starts typing furiously on his tablet. *Portal.* Then he starts furiously waving the tablet around in the air, as if it were a wand. Nothing happens.

"It's not like when Mother did it," Toaster says. "Nothing's happening."

"Are you waving hard enough?" Max asks. "What did you type?"

"Portal, Max!" Murray shouts. "I typed *portal.* And, yes, I'm waving like a lunatic! It's not working!"

"Yeah, you look like a chimpanzee fighting over a banana." Max laughs.

"Where?" Hero cries, whipping out her morning star and a short sword. She hands a dagger each to Rodolfo and Toaster.

"Uh?" Max asks.

"The spidpanzee! It's five feet tall, Max. It has to be somewhere. Where the hell did you see it?" Hero asks.

"Spidpanzee?" Max asks.

"The man-eating beasts with the eight legs that can fly and shoot webs." Hero mimics a spidpanzee ejecting webs from her belly. "Where did you see it?" She keeps looking around.

"This is bad," Toaster says.

"I've got you, brother," Rodolfo replies. They both have daggers pointed outward.

"Uh, I meant *chimpanzee*. Chimp—as in a five-foot furry, friendly monkey that likes bananas. The only danger would be theft and laughter."

Hero, Rodolfo, and Toaster relax, and she takes the daggers back. "Be more careful next time," Hero warns Max.

"Look, we're just not used to this world," Max replies.

"Yeah, I'm under a lot of stress," Murray adds. "Weaving your damned story and trying to survive at the same time from flying man-eating spiders."

"Just stop!" Hero orders, and Murray finally stops waving the tablet. "If we have to, we'll just ride these motorcycles for . . . what's a mile?"

"A long time," Max answers.

"Gods!" Hero yells at the sky. "I don't even know who I'm yelling at anymore. And that makes me madder!"

"Would this help?" Pesto speaks up, and hands Mother's wand to Rodolfo.

"Where'd you get this?" he asks her.

"In my pocket," Pesto says, pointing to her dress.

"She left it with Pesto," Hero says with a laugh and slaps her forehead. "But then, how did the dragons find us?"

"They probably sent a lot out to search for us all over the Lands," Toaster theorizes. "That's why only one dragon found us."

"Try it," Rodolfo says as he hands the wand to Hero.

Hero takes it, but the wand doesn't do anything. "I'm not magical. Never have been."

"But you can talk to the gods?" Rodolfo asks.

"Well, that's not even magic," Hero replies. "That's just determination."

"So, where's your determination now?" Rodolfo persists.

Hero just grumbles at him but gives the wand another weak wave, to no effect.

"You gotta wave it, girl," Max says. "Don't you know anything about magic?"

"Holy buckets, you jackass. I live in a world of magic!" Hero shouts, stomping in Max's direction. "You don't!"

"Yeah, but I saw *Harry Popper.* On Broadway! Did you? They danced in it," Max asks.

Hero sticks a finger in Max's face. "Your heaven-world sorcerers are no match—"

"Wizard!" Max says, not giving in. "Although he's kind of fallen out of—"

Before Max can finish, as if to defend the magical superiority of the Lands, including Fant, Hero starts waving the wand in the air harder and quicker. While she would never admit it to herself, she is also dancing.

Murray giggles.

Hero stops. "What are you giggling at?" Her eyes are daggers of fire.

"Oh, nothing," Murray lies. "Please, continue."

"No, you think I look stupid," Hero challenges him.

"I don't, Hero," Murray replies. "I think you look like someone who would do anything to save Dystpopia. And her friends."

Hero nods, then starts dancing, and waving again. This time, Murray stifles his laughter.

The wand begins glowing a golden yellow with a trail of golden light following after it.

"It's working!" Rodolfo cheers.

"What do I do now?" Hero asks, frantic.

"Think about New York City while you do it!" Murray orders her.

"I don't know anything about New Yawk City!" Hero cries.

Murray rubs his hair and exclaims, "Think—"

"Traffic!" Mauricio says.

"Travis?" Hero asks.

"Bagels!" Mauricio adds.

"Birds?" Hero asks.

"Ugh," Max says.

"Think of a library! Full of books!" Murray finally finishes what he wanted to say.

"And hot dogs!" Max adds.

"Trash bins full of food!" Mauricio offers.

"That sounds wonderful, Mauricio," Periwinkle says.

"Stick with me, girl," Mauricio replies, giving a soft whinny. "I'll show ya the best parts of New York."

"I think he's next with the L-word," Max jokes.

"Uh," Mauricio stammers awkwardly.

And then Hero's portal is finally ready. It's not a perfect circle like Mother's. It's an oddly shaped egg.

"Uh," Rodolfo repeats Mauricio's stutter. "Is that safe to go through?"

"Shut up, you jackasses. It's a portal," Hero explains. She's standing at it, smiling.

"It looks like a duck," Max says.

"Duck?" Hero asks, crouching.

"Dude, I meant a bird." Max laughs with a finger pointed at her.

"Max," Hero whines. "Why are we always fighting? Can't we just get along for once? How about a hug?"

"Did the magic affect her brain, brother?" Toaster asks.

"Perhaps," Rodolfo agrees. "Or it's that canker."

"Holy buckets, it's not a canker!" Hero exclaims. "It's just that we need to show our love for each other. Right, Max? I don't give a lot of hugs."

"Uh, sure? I don't mind a hug," Max replies.

"You know, she's mine," Rodolfo adds.

"Dude, she's not my thing," Max adds. "So, Hero, how do you want to do this?"

"Come here, Max, my friend," Hero says with her arms out. Max closes in with his arms out. As he gets closer, Hero's arms appear as if they're going to close around Max. In a flash, she does a roundhouse kick into his chest, causing him to fly into the portal. "It's not a duck, jackass!"

"Hero!" Murray cries. "That's my best friend!"

"She did it again." Toaster giggles.

"She did that before?" Rodolfo asks, a bit horrified.

"The tablet says he's still alive," Murray informs the group.

"Aw, hell." Hero genuinely laughs with a snort.

"You laugh funny," Pesto says with a giggle.

"Murray!" the group hears from the portal. "I'm all right! It's okay over here. You have to come see this! It's a huge building of light! And I think I see the George!"

"Ugh, Jersey," Mauricio and Murray say at the same time.

"Jinx!" Mauricio exclaims quickly.

"We don't have time for this," Murray replies, throwing his hands up in frustration, making sure to keep hold of the tablet.

"You heard the man! Everyone into the duck!" Hero orders.

Chapter 35

About Eight Thousand Years' Worth of Overdue Library Fees

The remaining travelers—Hero, Rodolfo, Toaster, Pesto, Murray, Mauricio, and Periwinkle—materialize in front of a sight even more shocking than Fant's pristine, white hospital building.

They are standing on a field of grass. It's a hill that slopes down into a site that is clearly magic. At the bottom of the slight hill is a circle of glimmering light, seemingly reaching up into the heavens, and inside of the circle is a large stone building—the kind only seen in Town's ancient books. Only Pesto knows this, since she is the only one of the group who knows the ancient language of Murrayskindacoolish, but the building's sign says Boston Public Library.

"Periwinkle! Look!" Mauricio cheers. "Grass! This must be Central Park!" Mauricio immediately starts eating. "Ah, this is the life."

"Mauricio, you always take me to the nicest places." The two horses munch on the grass.

"Murray, what the hell is this *grass*, and is it dangerous?" Hero asks, in a defensive posture, hands ready to grab weapons from her coat.

"Grass?" Murray asks, confused.

"You really can't take her anywhere." Max laughs.

"Dangerous?" Mauricio asks, with a mouthful. "I think you mean *delicious*."

"It's not a man-eating plant?" Hero asks. "Then how did it become so powerful to control such a wide area of land?"

"Calm down, Hero," Murray says, putting his hands out, palms down. "It's not harmful."

Hero relaxes, but eyes him and the grass suspiciously.

"So, is this the right place, Hero? Do you think this is what Mother was looking for?" Toaster asks.

"Murray? Max? Is this your city?"

"Um," Murray starts, "Mauricio is right. It kind of looks like Central Park. But I lived here like eight thousand years ago."

"And the writing on that building makes no sense," Max adds. "Murray, I thought Murrayskindacoolish was basically English. But it looks so different."

"It's probably a derivative," Murray explains. "But it's been eight thousand years, Max. It wouldn't have been realistic to just use English."

"Realistic?" Max exclaims. "You have zorcs and dragons!"

"Pesto?" Hero asks the little five-year-old half-zombie, half-girl hybrid.

"It says, *Baaahston Public Library*," Pesto answers. "I don't remember it from me holiday."

"Boston!" Murray and Max exclaim.

"I thought it looked like New York," Max adds. "Maybe the Boston Common took over the city in the intervening eight thousand years?"

"What is Bawston?" Hero asks. "Isn't that the town Graham mentioned? With the crabs? And also man-eating grass?" Hero instantly has two daggers out.

"Crab legs?" Mauricio chimes in. "This is turning into an awesome trip."

"Hero," Murray says. "Calm down."

She puts her daggers away but notes, "I still think the crabgrass is dangerous."

"Look," Murray replies. "Yes, Graham mentioned it, but the crab thing was just a wrestling, er, fighting move. Boston is just another town in heaven-world, or the ancient world, which is based off of heaven-world eight thousand years in my future, even though I'm currently standing right here. Oh, man, this is complicated. But however you want to pronounce it, it's *kind of* like New York."

"But way more awesome," Max notes.

"I can't believe you just said that," Murray scolds Max, giving his friend a look of extreme disbelief.

"What?" Max replies with disbelief also. "I've had so much fun in Boston. I always wanted to move here, er, there, but I couldn't because of my family. They depend on me; I couldn't leave them. Go Sox!"

"It's like I don't even know you," Murray scoffs.

"I agree with Murray," Hero says. "It can't be awesome if Graham liked it."

"Team," Toaster starts. "Can I call you all that?" They each nod in their own respective ways. "If it's kind of like New York, can't we just go in? It's still a library."

"My brother is right," Rodolfo adds. "We didn't come all the way here for nothing."

"Yeah, he's wicked smaaaht," Max jokes.

"What did you call him?" Rodolfo snaps at Max.

"Wicked smaaaht," Max replies.

"Take that back!" Rodolfo exclaims.

"Yeah, he's the most good person I know!" Hero seethes.

"No, no," Max replies. "Stop being so whiny. In Boston, *wicked* means *good*."

"Murray?" Hero asks.

"He's right, Hero," Murray says. "It's just a saying, regardless."

"It sounds ominous," Rodolfo says. "A town that thinks wicked is good. The ancient world is just as bad as ours. Maybe we did come all this way for nothing."

"They have a library, though," Toaster replies. "They can't be all bad."

"True, brother," Rodolfo agrees.

"But the clue said *Noo Yolk*, not *Baaahston*," Hero says, taking Pesto's pronunciations. "It's the wrong place."

"Hero," Murray says. "It's still a huge library with tons of books and artifacts."

"They have artifcats in there?" Hero asks.

"Yeah," Max answers.

"But Mother was looking for Noo Yolk," Hero insists.

"Hero, we can't always just do what Mother wanted," Murray says, walking next to her. "Isn't that what Rowena said, too?"

"They're both gone," Hero replies softly.

"But we're not," Rodolfo adds, walking to her other side. Hero whips her head to look at him. "I'm truly sorry for your loss. If anyone knows what it's like, it's Toaster and me."

Hero looks softer but still upset.

"Hero," Max tries, walking next to Murray. "We're all sorry. We know you've had a rough life, and you just met your mother for the first time, and she was taken from you so quickly. But speaking as someone who's let his mom control his whole life too, even in heaven-world, sometimes we have to be the ones in control. Sometimes we need to grab the reins."

"Not after the upris—"

"Shh! Geez!" Mauricio reprimands Periwinkle. The horses go back to munching grass.

"I want to see Baaahston," Pesto says, taking Rodolfo's hand. "With Rolfo."

The group looks at her.

"Then we will, Pesto," Hero agrees. Pesto finds a spot between Hero's and Rodolfo's legs, holding each of their hands.

"Uh, just to be clear, you don't need us, right?" Mauricio asks. "I mean, it's literally like fifty feet ahead, and there are no crab legs if I'm hearing yooz correctly. We can just stay here and eat this luscious grass, right? This Boston has nice grass."

"Yes, yes," Hero says. "You guys earned it." The horses quickly go back to munching away on the fresh grass.

"I told you to stick with me, Periwinkle," Mauricio says. "That I'd take you to see Boston's finest grass."

"Oh, Mauricio, you were right," Periwinkle says with a giggle, then nuzzles her nose into Maurico's snout.

"So, we actually did it? We found an ancient library?" Toaster asks.

"It's definitely ancient," Murray replies. "Boston is even older than New York."

"Older? We did it! Baaahston!" Hero exclaims, as she throws one arm each around Rodolfo and Toaster, bringing them, and Pesto, in for a hug. "We actually won!"

"You did it, Hero," Rodolfo says. "We could never have done it without you. We're now one step closer to saving Dystpopia and Town. What a beautiful name. Town."

"So is *Baaahston*. And I couldn't have done it without *you*, Rodolfo," Hero says. "You always challenge me and make me better." She kisses him on the cheek.

"We make quite a parnutship," he replies.

"We do," she agrees.

"Well, what are we waiting for? Let's go," Toaster says.

"But the building is protected by some sort of barrier," Rodolfo says.

"Come on, Rodolfo," Max says. "Stop whining. With Mother's wand working, no barrier can stop us. Right?"

"Oh gods," Toaster replies. "I happened to learn on this quest that if you're not scared, you're dead."

"Bratwurst is right," Hero says, showing Toaster a knowing smile.

"Thanks, hoagie," he replies, with a wide grin.

"Stay on guard, everyone," Hero continues. "But whatever it is, we will survive. Not because of some wand, but because we have each other. Isn't that right, Father?" She turns to Murray.

"Yes, Hero," Murray replies with a smile and walks to stand in front of her. He moves to embrace her, but she shrugs him off.

"Too much," she says.

"Oh, sorry," Murray replies, looking down, faced with rejection yet again. Then Hero playfully hits him on the shoulder, adding a non-awkward, unforced smile, which elicits an also non-awkward, unforced smile from the forty-five-year-old down-on-his-luck author, who is finally the hero in his own story.

So, leaving the happy horses, Hero, Rodolfo, Toaster, Pesto, Murray and Max start walking toward the Boston Public Library, finishing the first part of Hero's quest to find the knowledge of the ancients and defeat the Queendom of Fant.

And while they did not end up at the library they intended, inside that building is the knowledge they seek—knowledge that can save Dystpopia and Town. Or destroy it.

H. Wait, what?

The End

About the Author

David Horn lives east of the Kingdom of Dystpopia with his family. He is the author of the young adult novels *Becoming Trixie: It's a Dog's Life*, *Admins: Simulation's End*, and the *Eudora Space Kid* and *Tairy Fails* early reader chapter book series.